Bestselling Author of the
MacKinnon's Rangers Novels

# Ride the Fire

INCLUDES
NEW
MATERIAL

BERKLEY
SENSATION

**$7.99 U.S.**
$8.99 CAN

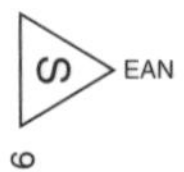

"Riveting, exciting . . . Pamela Clare delivers what readers want." —Connie Mason, *New York Times* bestselling author

"A taut, sensual adventure . . . Sexy, sensitive, and resourceful frontiersman Nicholas Kenleigh, Clare's larger-than-life hero, will seduce readers as he wins the heart of young widow Elspeth Stewart." —*Publishers Weekly*

"This book has everything—great sexual tension, an action-packed story, high stakes, compelling characters, beautiful writing, and a historical authenticity that you can almost touch, it's so vivid . . . A truly magnificent story! Pamela Clare, take a bow!" —*Romance Novel TV*

"Suited for those who like their history with grit and their romance with emotional power—with an added lesson about how love heals all wounds." —*RT Book Reviews*

"One of the best historical romances I've read! . . . Words cannot express how magnificent it is. The passion with which Ms. Clare writes is overwhelming, humbling, incredible. *Ride the Fire* is a brilliant masterpiece to be savored like a fine wine." —*Fresh Fiction*

"Pamela Clare . . . creates heroes, heroines, and villains with the ease of a master [and] draws the readers irresistibly into the story, making them part of the pain, the fear . . . and the passion." —Leigh Greenwood, *USA Today* bestselling author

*continued . . .*

Praise for the MacKinnon's Rangers Novels

## SURRENDER

"Be forewarned that this is not a book you'll put down lightly. Once you start, you'll be hard pressed to do anything else but travel along on this journey filled with action, danger, fantastically vivid historical events, and written in almost liquid prose: nonstop and ever-flowing words that blend together in a lifelike portrayal of colonial times and the people that stood up to almost unimaginable hardships, written only as Pamela Clare can write them. *Surrender* is a must-have . . . I can't recommend this book highly enough."

—*Romance Reader at Heart*

"Trust me, you do not want to miss this exciting and *hot* start to what promises to be a fabulous new series. I have loved all of Pamela Clare's novels from the first one and this is one that I hated to see end." —*Night Owl Reviews*

"A compelling story that I found difficult to set aside. I was totally submerged in the characters and the story through the very end." —*Once Upon a Romance*

## UNTAMED

"Captivating . . . Clare's detailed attention to the history of alliances forged and battles fought near Fort Ticonderoga adds authenticity, and the characters evolve and change with a realism that readers will love."

—*Publishers Weekly* (starred review)

"Sizzling sensuality, touching emotions, and great historical detail make this a sure winner . . . Magnificent . . . You need only to read the first page to know that you are beginning another historical romantic masterpiece by Pamela Clare, a master storyteller who always delights readers . . . *Untamed* will leave you breathless and cheering with its attention to historical detail, characters you can almost reach out and touch, a story line that's deeply riveting, and a love story that will melt your heart . . . You must always keep a Pamela Clare book on your keeper shelf. She is not just a read, she is a reread." —*Fresh Fiction*

"Riveting. Clare cleverly combines history and fiction to bring us a tale full of drama and sensuality, with well-drawn characters and continuous action." —*RT Book Reviews*

"Surrounded by the lush backdrop of the historical wild frontier, *Untamed* is the extraordinary story of how Morgan and Amalie find a once-in-a-lifetime love. The pages are filled with danger, excitement, and suspense. Compelling characters, a seemingly impossible conflict, and one of the most magnificent men I've ever read about make *Untamed* unforgettable . . . Every moment they share is incredibly sensual and erotic . . . *Untamed* is the ultimate angst-filled romance . . . *Untamed* is perfect." —*Joyfully Reviewed*

"A powerful story about two people who discover love despite war and betrayal . . . I felt truly invested in the characters in *Untamed* and found the time period captivating. Morgan has now taken the lead as my favorite hero of the year." —*All About Romance*

*Berkley Sensation books by Pamela Clare*

RIDE THE FIRE

*The I-Team series*

EXTREME EXPOSURE
HARD EVIDENCE
UNLAWFUL CONTACT
NAKED EDGE
BREAKING POINT

*The MacKinnon's Rangers series*

SURRENDER
UNTAMED
DEFIANT

# Ride The Fire

Pamela Clare

**THE BERKLEY PUBLISHING GROUP**
**Published by the Penguin Group**
**Penguin Group (USA) Inc.**
**375 Hudson Street, New York, New York 10014, USA**
Penguin Group (Canada), 90 Eglinton Avenue East, Suite 700, Toronto, Ontario M4P 2Y3, Canada (a division of Pearson Penguin Canada Inc.) • Penguin Books Ltd., 80 Strand, London WC2R 0RL, England • Penguin Ireland, 25 St. Stephen's Green, Dublin 2, Ireland (a division of Penguin Books Ltd.) • Penguin Group (Australia), 707 Collins Street, Melbourne, Victoria 3008, Australia (a division of Pearson Australia Group Pty. Ltd.) • Penguin Books India Pvt. Ltd., 11 Community Centre, Panchsheel Park, New Delhi—110 017, India • Penguin Group (NZ), 67 Apollo Drive, Rosedale, Auckland 0632, New Zealand (a division of Pearson New Zealand Ltd.) • Penguin Books (South Africa), Rosebank Office Park, 181 Jan Smuts Avenue, Parktown North 2193, South Africa • Penguin China, B7 Jiaming Center, 27 East Third Ring Road North, Chaoyang District, Beijing 100020, China

Penguin Books Ltd., Registered Offices: 80 Strand, London WC2R 0RL, England



RIDE THE FIRE

A Berkley Sensation Book / published by arrangement with the author

PUBLISHING HISTORY
Berkley Sensation mass-market edition / February 2013


Cover art by Gregg Gulbronson.
Cover design by George Long.
Map illustration copyright © Susan France.
Interior text design by Laura K. Corless.



ISBN: 978-0-425-25730-2

BERKLEY SENSATION®
Berkley Sensation Books are published by The Berkley Publishing Group,
a division of Penguin Group (USA) Inc.,
375 Hudson Street, New York, New York 10014.
BERKLEY SENSATION® is a registered trademark of Penguin Group (USA) Inc.
The "B" design is a trademark of Penguin Group (USA) Inc.

PRINTED IN THE UNITED STATES OF AMERICA

10 9 8 7 6 5 4 3 2

*This book is dedicated to all victims of sexual assault.*
*May you find the courage, love, and healing*
*you need to live a full life happily ever after.*

# Acknowledgments

With special thanks to Douglas McGregor, educator at the Fort Pitt Museum in Pittsburgh, for his generous help. He rocks. Anything I've managed to get right about the siege at Fort Pitt is due to his time and effort.

Special thanks also to Susan France for her wonderful illustration of Fort Pitt.

Additional thanks to Natasha Kern, my agent, for her unflagging faith, and to Cindy Hwang, my editor, for bringing this story, one of my readers' favorites, back to life again.

Personal thanks to Kristie Jenner, who single-handedly raised awareness about Nicholas and Bethie as only Kristie can. I told her she deserved a bronze plaque in the reissued version, but I can't give her a bronze plaque, so a shout-out will have to suffice.

Hugs and thanks to my sister and best friend, Michelle, for always being there.

And as always, thanks and much love to my family and my sons, Alec and Benjamin. You are everything. I could not do this without you.

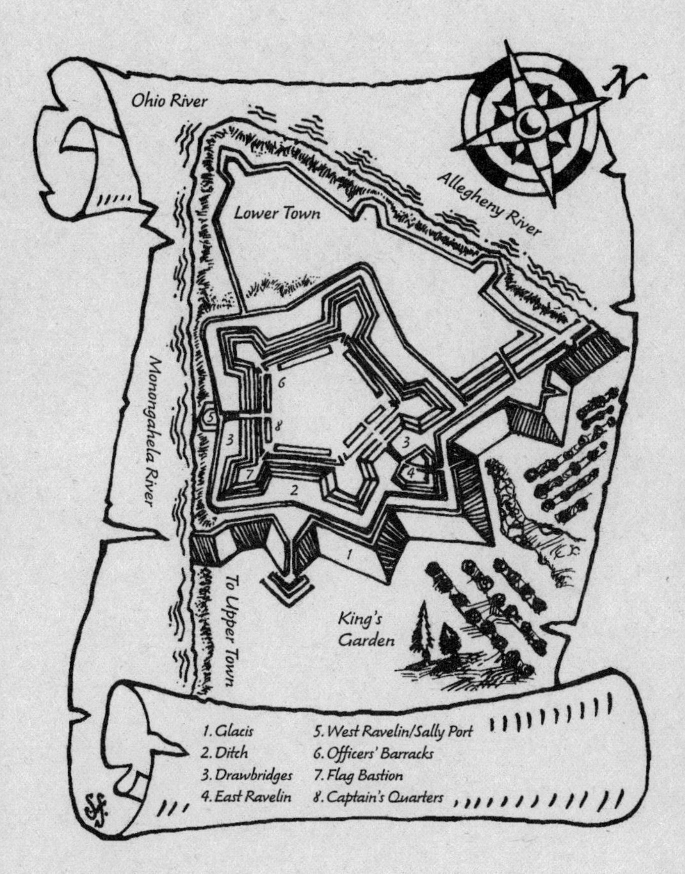
N
Ohio River
Allegheny River
Lower Town
Monongahela River
To Upper Town
King's Garden
1. Glacis
2. Ditch
3. Drawbridges
4. East Ravelin
5. West Ravelin/Sally Port
6. Officers' Barracks
7. Flag Bastion
8. Captain's Quarters

# Prologue

July 15, 1757
The Ohio Wilderness

"They're going to burn us, aren't they?"

Nicholas Kenleigh ignored the panic in Josiah's voice and Eben's frightened whimpering, strained in vain to free himself from the tight leather cords that held him to the tall wooden stake. His hands, bound fast above his head, had long since lost any feeling.

There would be no escape.

"I don't want to die!" Eben sobbed, his freckled face wet with tears.

Nicholas took a deep breath, sought for words to comfort the two younger men, found none. He had taken them under his wing shortly after he'd joined Washington's forces, tried to teach them to track and to shoot well.

None of that mattered now.

"I have no wish to die either." *Especially not like this.* "But if death is all that is left to us, then we must face it with courage."

His words sounded meaningless, even to his own ears, but seemed to calm them. Josiah was nineteen, Eben only seventeen. They reminded him of his younger brothers—Alec, William, and Matthew. They didn't deserve this.

No one deserved this.

Nicholas had known from the moment they were taken captive what the Wyandot would do to them. He'd warned Josiah and Eben, but they had not listened. Instead, they'd allowed themselves to be deceived by feasts, promises of adoption, and the pleasures of sex with comely, young Wyandot women. But those promises were false, food and sex merely part of the ritual of sacrifice.

Nicholas supposed that caring for the physical needs of their prisoners and bringing them pleasure took away some of the guilt the Wyandot must feel at torturing people to death—if, indeed, they felt guilt. But he had seen the deception for what it was, had eaten his food in silence, turned the woman away. Dark-eyed and pretty she had been, but he would not risk getting her with child and leaving a piece of himself behind to grow up here. Nor would he betray Penelope, his fiancée.

Fidelity when death was imminent might seem strange to most men, but Nicholas had been raised to keep his word and to put loyalty to family and friends above all else. He would try to die the way he had lived.

Washington's force had been encamped near the Ohio when the Wyandot had attacked under cover of night. Nicholas had been discussing the next day's march with George over a bottle of Madeira when they'd been interrupted by the sounds of war cries, shouts, and gunfire. He'd fought his way across the camp toward Josiah's and Eben's tents and spied them in the distance, wild with bloodlust, pursuing a group of fleeing Wyandot into the forest.

He'd charged after them, shouted for them to stop, warned them it was a trap. But it was too late. They had been ambushed and overcome before his words reached them. And though Nicholas had managed to kill several warriors in an attempt to free them, there were simply too many. One blow to the temple with a war club, and Nicholas had found himself a prisoner, too. Now they would die together.

His mind flashed on his mother, and he felt a moment of deep anguish. His death would be hardest on her. She had opposed his decision to join Washington and serve as a tracker, had begged him to stay at home, take up his role as heir of the Kenleigh shipbuilding empire, and produce an heir himself.

But at twenty-six, Nicholas had felt certain there was still plenty of time for such things. Besides, Washington was a good friend and a fellow Virginian—and his need was dire. The outcome of this war would make or break British authority on this continent.

Jamie—Nicholas's elder by four years and his uncle—had served with Washington during his march north in 1754 and had fought beside George in the blood and mud of Fort Necessity. But Jamie now had a wife—lovely Bríghid—and two small sons. He would not leave them. Nicholas had reasoned he could do the job just as well as Jamie, as they had been taught together by Takotah, the old Tuscarora healer who had made her home with his family since long before he'd been born. It had seemed right that he fill Jamie's shoes.

And now?

Now he would need every ounce of strength, every bit of courage he possessed. He was not immune to fear.

Eleven fires had been lit in fire pits running down the center of the enormous longhouse. Old women busied themselves building up the fires, adding wood until the lodge was uncomfortably warm in the already stifling July heat.

As the fires crackled, Eben again began to weep, Josiah to curse the Wyandot.

"W-will it be quick?"

Nicholas had heard stories, accounts of the French priests who'd first encountered the Wyandot a hundred years before. He prayed the priests had lied. "I don't know."

"Bloody savages!" Josiah spat on the dirt floor. "It's good they like fire, because they're goin' to burn in hell!"

Wyandot villagers began to drift through the low entrance—men, women, children. Soon the longhouse was packed from end to end. The Wyandot stared at their prisoners with solemn eyes, and Nicholas could sense an undercurrent of expectation.

Last to enter was the Wyandot war chief, Atsan, who had dressed in ceremonial garb, a great bearskin cape draped over his bare, aged shoulders, a single eagle feather in his scalp lock. He held up his hand to silence the murmurs and whispers of his people, began to speak in Wyandot.

His words floated just beyond Nicholas's comprehension, strangely familiar and yet utterly foreign. He did not speak

Wyandot, but it sounded somewhat like Tuscarora, which he knew well. Several times he thought he understood a word or phrase—Big Knives, fight, river—but the words were spoken so quickly that Nicholas couldn't quite catch them.

And then Nicholas recognized one: *"See-tah."*

*Fire.*

A few feet away Eben wept like a frightened child. Josiah trembled but glared at the Wyandot with youthful bravado.

*How vulnerable and alone men are at the hour of their deaths.*

The thought, detached from emotion, flickered through Nicholas's mind, left dark regret in its wake. Why hadn't he been able to get to them faster? Why hadn't he been able to stop this? Why hadn't he found a means to escape?

He closed his eyes, sent up what might have been a prayer. *Let it be fast. Let us be strong. Do not let them suffer!*

Even as the last thought faded, several women stepped forward from the crowd and walked toward the captives. Nicholas felt cool fingers brush against his skin as his shirt and breeches were cut from his body, leaving him entirely naked. A glance showed him Josiah and Eben had likewise been stripped. Both were red in the face, and Nicholas realized they felt shame at being unclothed before strangers.

As Atsan's last words drifted into silence, the women who'd undressed them moved to the fires and began to stir the flames.

Something twisted in Nicholas's gut. He tried to force down his fear.

A young woman appeared at his side, the same young woman he'd rejected the day before. She looked up at him, her brown eyes dark with an emotion that might have been anger—or lust. In her hand was a knife.

Nicholas just caught a glimpse of the blade before she slid the tip into the skin of his belly. His muscles tensed in surprise at the razor-sharp pain.

To his left, Eben shrieked.

Nicholas watched in odd detachment as the woman deftly carved a small pocket from his flesh and wondered for a moment if she intended to skin him. Hot blood poured down his belly, past his exposed groin to his bare thighs.

She looked up, met his gaze, a faint smile on her lips. Then she stepped aside to make room for an old woman, who carried a small glowing ember from the fire on a flint blade. Nicholas realized what they were going to do a moment before they did it, and took a deep breath.

*I will not cry out. I must not cry out.*

The crone slipped the tip of her blade into the cut, pried the pocket of flesh open, and dropped the ember inside.

A sizzling sound. Searing pain. The smell of burning flesh—his own flesh.

It hurt far beyond anything he had imagined.

He heard screams. Were they his screams?

No. It was Josiah and Eben.

A hiss of breath was all that escaped him. His gaze met the young woman's and held it.

*They will not break me.*

The women worked efficiently. Swiftly they cut him again and again, carved deep gashes in his belly, chest, and back, tucked live embers inside each.

Pain consumed him—blistering, searing pain. His entire body seemed to burn. Sweat poured down his face, stung his eyes. He fought to control his breathing, to keep his thoughts focused, but felt himself growing dizzy, disoriented, almost delirious, as if his mind were seeking escape from the unbearable torment that had become his body.

*They will not break me.*

Several feet away, Josiah jerked and writhed like a tortured puppet on a string, screaming in agony. Eben had fainted and hung limply in his bonds. Women worked to revive him, splashed water on his face and chest. It was not compassion, Nicholas knew, but a desire to prolong the boy's suffering.

Rage. It cut through Nicholas's pain, through his muddled thoughts, burned like a brand in his gut. He searched the crowd for Atsan, found the old man watching him, met his gaze. Drawing on his knowledge of Tuscarora and doing his best to imitate Wyandot inflection, Nicholas spoke, his voice rough with pain and hatred.

*"E-hye-ha-honz, o-negh-e-ke-wishe-noo."*

*I am dying, but I will conquer my enemy.*

Whether Atsan understood him, Nicholas could not tell.

The old man did not react. And Nicholas wondered for a moment whether, in his pain, he had imagined speaking or whether his words had been meaningless babble.

Another cut, another ember.

Breath rushed from his lungs. Every muscle in his body screamed in protest. He closed his eyes, bit his tongue, fought desperately not to cry out. Dear God, how much more of this could he take?

Lyda stepped back from the prisoner, her hands slick with his blood, and tried not to show her surprise at his words. Though the man spoke with difficulty—in what sounded more like the speech of their enemies, the Tuscarora, than their own language—his meaning was clear.

He would die, but he would not give in to pain.

Something fluttered in her belly.

Here was a warrior.

He was a beautiful man—taller than most men in her village with hair almost as black as a raven's wing. His face was proud and strong, its male strength softened by long, dark lashes. And his body . . . She let her gaze travel the length of him, seeing beneath the blood and burns, from his powerful shoulders to his broad chest, slim hips, and muscular thighs. His breast was sprinkled with an intriguing mat of crisp, dark hair that tapered in a line between the ridges of his belly to his sex. She let her eyes rest there for a moment and felt renewed outrage at his rejection of her. Had he not turned her away, she would now know what it was like to have such a man pleasure her.

She had noticed him the moment the warriors had brought him and the other Big Knife prisoners into the village. The men claimed he had slain at least nine Wyandot warriors before one of them managed to strike him on the head with his club, leaving a gash on his left temple. Still, it had taken four men to subdue him and bind his wrists.

Lyda had known from the moment she saw him that she wanted him. When he looked her up and down and then turned her away as if she were worthless, the humiliation had been almost unbearable. She was considered a great beauty by the people of her nation. More than that, she was a woman of power, a holy woman, granddaughter to holy women dating back to the beginning of her people and a daughter of Atsan, the great war chief. No man had ever turned her away. Until yesterday.

She had rejoiced then to know he would be sacrificed in flames and had vowed to play a role in his torment. But now?

Her grandmother slipped another ember beneath his skin. His body jerked, every muscle taut as he strained against the cords that held him. Breath hissed from between his clenched teeth. His brows grew furrowed with obvious agony. Sweat drenched his black hair, ran in rivulets down his face.

But he did not cry out.

Lyda knew what she wanted. She'd had lots of men in her twenty-three years, had taken a few into her mother's lodge as husbands. Though she had grown tired of them all rather quickly and set them aside, she had rejoiced in the pain of birth and rush of waters that had brought her three daughters into the world. But with a man such as this—a man who looked at her with hatred in his strange blue eyes, who was bold enough to reject her, and who endured suffering with the strength of the bravest Wyandot warrior—think of the children she might bear! They would be proud, handsome, and strong, and their courage would bring her honor.

She would have his seed.

Of course, it wouldn't be easy. Her father had already committed him to fire and death. And after witnessing his courage, the warriors would be eager to eat his flesh, particularly his heart, so that they might take in his strength. They would not wish to spare him.

But, of course, her father had never been able to deny her anything.

# Chapter 1

March 3, 1763
Fort Detroit, Northwestern Wilderness

Nicholas leaned back in the wooden tub, closed his eyes, let the hot water soak the chill from his bones. It had been months since he'd had a hot bath. It was a luxury he availed himself of only when he came into one of the forts to trade—three or four times a year at most. The rest of the time he bathed in icy rivers and lakes when he could. Survival took precedence over cleanliness in the wild.

The lingering scent of the woman's perfume—a cheap imitation of roses—mingled with the smell of lye soap as Nicholas allowed his mind to drift. From beyond the door came the rumble of men's voices, the thud of horse's hooves, and the tread of boots on wooden walkways. Fort Detroit was crowded these days—too crowded for Nicholas's tastes—and abuzz with rumors that some of the northwestern tribes were banding together for an organized attack against settlers and the English forts that protected them.

The rumors were true, of course. Nicholas had run into a small band of Shawnee not a month ago and had been warned by one of their warriors, a man Nicholas had traded with in the past, that Englishmen were no longer welcome west of the mountains—with very few exceptions.

The war with France had just ended, and already the frontier was about to collapse into new violence and redoubled bloodshed. Whether they were Indian or white, it seemed to be the nature of men to kill. Nicholas ought to know. He had more blood on his hands than most.

Footsteps approached the door.

He reached for his pistol, which sat primed and ready on the wooden floor beside the tub, wrapped his fingers around its polished handle. It was a reflex born of six years in the wilderness. He was no more aware of this action than he was of breathing.

The footsteps passed.

His grip relaxed, and he began to doze in the steamy water.

Doze only. He never slept, not deeply. He didn't want to dream.

The water was still warm when the sound of quick, light footfalls roused him.

She was back.

The door to the tiny room opened, bringing a rush of cold air and the rustle of skirts.

Nicholas opened his eyes, watched as she approached him. She was young, not yet twenty, he guessed, and pretty. Her dark hair and skin revealed her mixed ancestry—probably the daughter of a French trapper and his temporary Indian wife.

"Is monsieur finished with his bath?"

"Aye." Now it was time for pleasure of another sort.

Without ceremony, he stood, dried himself with the linen towel, walked over to the small bed. She had removed her gown and lay passively on her back in her chemise, a tattered bit of cloth that might once have been white. She parted her thighs, bared her small breasts, drew one rosy-brown nipple to a taut peak, smiled. It was a smile that didn't quite reach her eyes. Then her gaze came to rest on his scars. Her smile faded.

She had, of course, seen his scars when she'd helped him bathe. Then she had averted her gaze. Now she simply stared, clearly repulsed. "Was it terrible, monsieur?"

Nicholas ignored her question, allowed himself to feel only the pulsing need of his erection. How long had it been since he'd been inside a woman? Six months?

He stood at the foot of the bed, grasped her hips, pulled her toward him. Then he lifted her legs, rested her slender calves on his shoulders, filled her with one slow thrust.

It felt good, so good. And he found himself rushing headlong toward completion.

It was over in a few minutes, his seed spilled in a pool of pearly white on her belly. Nicholas lay staring at the timbered ceiling while she washed all trace of him away in the cooling bathwater. Neither of them spoke.

A vague dissatisfied feeling gnawed at his gut. When had he become the sort of man who would take pleasure with a pretty woman, even a whore, without so much as knowing her name?

Normally, he tried to forget the past. But now he wondered when he'd last made love to a woman, when he'd last devoted himself to giving a woman pleasure heedless of his own? His mind stretched back through the emptiness of the past six years, back through the nightmare that was Lyda to Penelope.

Sweet Penelope. Fickle Penelope.

He tried to conjure up an image of her face, failed. They'd been engaged to marry when he'd ridden away to war with Washington, but when she'd learned he had been taken by the Wyandot and was believed dead, she'd waited all of two months before marrying someone else. When he had finally escaped and made the long journey home to Virginia, he had arrived to find her quickening with her husband's child.

"What was I supposed to do, Nicholas? Was I to wait for you? For how long? We all believed you dead!"

And, indeed, he *was* dead.

He had tried to go on as if nothing had changed, to return to his old life. His parents, overjoyed at his unforeseen return, had done all in their power to help him. But nothing had been able to silence the screams that haunted his nightmares or restore the spirit that Lyda had so expertly wrenched from his body. Hatred for the Wyandot had consumed him, but no more than hatred for himself.

And when he'd awoken from one of his nightmares to find his hands fast around his little sister Elizabeth's throat—poor Elizabeth, only sixteen, had heard him cry out and come to comfort him—he'd known he was no longer fit to live among those he loved. He had packed a few belongings—a bedroll, his pistols, his rifle, a hunting knife, a change of clothes, powder and shot—and had saddled his horse and prepared to ride away, hoping the wilderness would finish what the Wyandot had not.

But his mother had awakened, and standing outside the stables in her nightgown, she had begged him to stay, tears streaming down her face. "Please, Nicholas, don't go! You've just returned! Give us a chance to help you, son!"

Her words, the desperate tone of her voice, had almost been enough to stop him. He did not wish to cause her further pain. But then he had remembered Elizabeth's frightened face, his hands wrapped tightly around her throat. He might have killed her.

He had climbed into the saddle, steeled himself against his mother's tears. "I regret to inform you, madam, that your son is dead."

Then he had urged his horse to canter and ridden west, away from home, away from war, away from memories. He'd ridden over mountains, across rivers, through forest and grassland to the great mountains in the far west that no other Englishman had seen—but never fast enough or far enough to escape himself.

He had not yet found death, but in the vastness of the wilderness and the rhythm of the seasons, he'd found some measure of . . . if not peace, then forgetfulness.

*"Excusez-moi, monsieur."*

The young prostitute. She wanted her fee.

*"Pardonnez-moi, mademoiselle. Il est temps de régler notre compte, n'est-ce pas?" It's time for us to settle up, is it not?*

He rose from the bed, still naked, and strode to the corner where his peltries lay in a bundle. Quickly he worked the knots and unrolled the bundle, his hands moving deftly over the soft furs, searching.

*"Vous parlez très bien français." You speak French well.*

He glanced up at the surprised tone in her voice, on the brink of saying that he had studied French at Oxford and had traveled extensively in France. But he was struck again by her youth and her beauty, felt a momentary stab of guilt at his thoughtless use of her young body. The words died on his lips.

He released the marten pelt he had been about to give her, pulled free the white wolf instead. Much larger, much more rare, its value far surpassed that of the marten pelt. He stood, handed it to her.

She gaped at it, then at him, her brown eyes wide. *"M-merci, monsieur!"*

Nicholas felt an absurd momentary impulse to apologize or explain himself. There'd been a time in his life when he would have asked her what had happened to make her sell her body, when he might even have tried to help her find a better life. But those days had long since passed. The truth was he no longer cared. *"De rien." It was nothing.*

And as she hurried out of the room, wolf pelt clutched to her breast, that's what Nicholas felt.

Nothing.

Elspeth Stewart woke with a start, heart racing.

*The geese!*

She rose as quickly as she could, grabbed the rifle, which sat next to the bed, primed and ready.

If it was the same vixen that had harried them yesterday, she would shoot, and this time she wouldn't miss.

And if it were Indians or renegade soldiers?

Her mouth went dry.

Quickly, quietly she crossed the wooden floor of the cabin that was her home, lifted the heavy bar from the door and slowly opened it, dread like ice in her veins. Outside it was still dark, the first light of dawn only a hint in the eastern sky. She peered past the door toward the poultry pens and saw a small honey-colored fox dart into the underbrush.

In a warm rush of relief, Elspeth stepped quickly onto the porch, raised the rifle, cocked it, fired. A yelp, followed by silence, told her she had hit her mark.

She stepped back inside long enough to put down the rifle, put on her cloak, and slip into her boots—she had taken to sleeping fully clothed since Andrew's death, but that didn't include boots—before going outside to see what damage had been done.

The vixen lay dead in the bushes. Its teats were swollen

with milk, and Elspeth felt an unexpected pang of empathy for the dead animal. It had only been trying to eat so that it could feed its new litter of kits.

She pressed a hand protectively to her rounded belly. In a few weeks, a month at most, she would be doing the same. Which is why she needed to protect the geese and chickens, she thought, brushing aside her sentimental response.

She squatted down, picked the vixen up by its tail, and carried it away. She didn't want the smell to attract bears or wolves.

When she returned, the geese were still honking and flapping angrily about, but there were no bloody wings, no broken feathers that she could see. Andrew's fence had held.

"Quit your flaffin'!" she scolded. She wasn't truly angry with them. Geese were better than dogs when it came to alerting their masters to danger. Her life—and that of her unborn baby—might well depend on them one day.

As it was so close to dawn and she'd be getting up soon anyway, Elspeth decided to start her morning chores. She fed the geese and chickens, gathered the few eggs that had been laid, and set off to the cowshed for the morning milking. By the time the animals had been fed and Rona and Rosa, her two mares, had been led out into the paddock, the sun had risen behind a heavy blanket of clouds.

She drew water from the well and carried it inside to heat for washing and for her morning porridge. She had just stepped through the door, when she saw the fire had died down to embers and needed wood. But there was no firewood stacked in the corner. And then she remembered.

She hadn't had time to split more wood for the fire yesterday and had been so tired after supper that she had fallen asleep at the table, leaving the chore undone.

Her stomach growled.

"Well, Bethie, you cannae be expectin' the wood to chop itself." She lifted the heavy water bucket onto the table, took the ax from its resting place beside the fire, went back out into the chilly morning.

The woodpile stood on the west side of the house, and it was dwindling. She hadn't worked out how she was going to fell trees by herself; that was a problem for another day. She awkwardly lifted a large piece of wood onto an old stump, hoisted the ax, and swung. The ax cut halfway through the wood, stuck. She pried it loose, swung again. The wood flew into two pieces.

In the two months since Andrew's passing, she had gotten better at chopping firewood. She no longer missed and sometimes even managed to split the wood with one blow as Andrew had done. Still, it was an exhausting chore, one she did not enjoy.

How long could she last out here alone? The question leapt, unbidden and unwelcome, to her mind. It was followed by another.

Where could she go?

She lifted another piece of wood onto the stump, stepped back, swung, and soon found herself in a rhythm.

Perhaps after the baby was born she could go to Fort Pitt or one of the other forts and find work there. At least she and the baby would be safe from Indians and wild animals. But would there be other women? Would they be safe from the soldiers?

Perhaps she could journey to Harrisburg or even to Philadelphia. But that meant traveling for weeks alone through wild country, across the mountains, over rivers, and through farmsteads. The very idea of swimming across rivers with her baby or sleeping in a bedroll in the open without the protection of four sturdy walls terrified her.

One thing was certain: she could not go home.

Nor could she stay here forever. She'd managed well enough so far, but what would she do when it came time to plant crops? Could she manage the plow? And what of the harvest? Could she care for her baby, harvest the crops, slaughter the hogs, make cider, and salt the meat all at the same time? Her days had been full and long when Andrew had yet lived. How could she manage to do both his chores and hers with a newborn?

And what would she do when her time came?

She'd never given birth before, had never seen a baby born. And though she'd helped cows to calve, she knew having babies was different for women. Would she know what to do? Would both she and her baby survive the travail?

And then there was the threat of Indians and others who

prowled the frontier. Few families had escaped unscathed during this war. Men, women, and children had been butchered like cattle—shot or burned alive and scalped by Indians fighting for the French. A family only a few miles to the north had been attacked at midday while working in their fields. The oldest sons had been killed and scalped, the daughters and younger boys kidnapped. The oldest daughter had been found several miles away a few days later. She'd been tied to a tree, her body consumed first by fire, then by wild animals.

Of course, Indians weren't the only two-legged danger. Criminals flocked to the frontier, eager to escape the gallows. Deserters, too, hid in the forests, both French and English. Everyone knew of the family near Paxton that had welcomed two travelers to sleep before their hearth one evening, only to be murdered in their beds.

Andrew had done his best to protect her from these dangers. But he had died just after Christmas of a lingering fever. Although Bethie had tried everything she knew to save him—every poultice, every herb, every draught—he was not a young man and had died one night in his sleep while she sat beside him and held his hand. Already in her seventh month, she had barely managed to dig a shallow grave for him in the frozen earth.

She hadn't had a peaceful night's sleep since, waking to every sound with her heart in her throat.

There was one other possibility, of course, one she almost refused to consider. She could try to find another husband. After the baby was born, she could ride to the nearest settlement, visit the church or meetinghouse, and tell the minister that she was widowed and needed to find a husband. But would any man want both her and her child? And if she *did* find a husband, would she regret it?

Her mother, widowed when Bethie's father was killed by a falling log, had found Malcolm Sorley in much the same way. A big man with a dour temperament and fists like hams, he'd moved with his bully of a son, Richard, into the cabin that had once been a happy home and had done his best to beat the fear of God into his new wife and stepdaughter. Bethie had done her best to avoid the rages of her new father, but Malcolm Sorley had left his share of welts and bruises on her. Then he had turned her mother against her.

Richard had done far worse.

And while a husband brought protection, marriage brought duties that pleased her not at all. She had no desire to lie beneath a man, to feel him touch her, to feel him inside her. If she could devise it, she would be content to live as a widow for the rest of her life.

And so Bethie arrived at the same stalemate she always came to whenever she allowed herself to think of the days ahead. There was no place for her to go and no way she could safely stay.

Coming to the frontier had been Andrew's idea, not hers. And though he had been kind to her and had taken her from a living hell, she found herself feeling angry with him for abandoning her and her baby to this life of fear and doubt.

She rested the ax on the ground, out of breath, her arms and lower back aching, glad to find a good stack of wood piled beside her. It was enough to last her the rest of the day and the night, but she would need to chop more this afternoon if she didn't want to be in the same fix tomorrow morning.

She rubbed a soothing hand over her belly, felt her baby kick within her. Then she squatted down and picked up as many pieces as she could carry. She stepped around to the front of the cabin, her arms full, and froze, a scream trapped in her throat.

*A man on horseback.*

# Chapter 2

He sat on a great chestnut stallion only a few feet away from the cabin's door, stared down at her through cold eyes, pistol in hand.

The firewood fell from her arms, forgotten. She glanced wildly about for the rifle, realized that she had left it inside the cabin. A fatal mistake?

She forced herself to meet his gaze, tried to hide her fear, the frantic thrum of her heartbeat a deafening roar.

Where had he come from? Why hadn't she heard him? And the geese—why had they made no sound?

He was an Indian. He must be to have crept up on her so quietly. Dressed in animal hides, with long black hair and sun-browned skin, he certainly looked like an Indian. But his eyes were icy and blue as a mountain lake, and most of his face was covered with a thick, black beard.

Heart pounding a sickening rhythm in her chest, she swallowed, pressed her hands protectively to her belly. "M-my husband will be back soon."

"Your husband?" His accent was distinctly English and cultured, his voice deep. He smiled, a mocking sort of smile. "Is he the poor fellow buried out back? Aye, I've already met him."

The man started to dismount.

"Nay!" Close to panic, Bethie wasn't sure where her words came from. "Stay on your horse, and ride away from here! I am no' wantin' for means to protect myself!"

He climbed slowly from the saddle, his gaze dropping from her face to her swollen belly, a look of what could only be amusement in his eyes. "I'll keep that in mind."

It was then she saw the blood. His hands were stained with it.

Her heart beat like a hammer against her breast, and for one wrenching moment, she knew he was going to kill her. Or worse.

If only she had the rifle! If only she could get inside the cabin, bar the door. But he stood between her and refuge. She took several steps backward, was about to run into the darkness of the forest, when he sagged against his horse.

Blood. It had soaked through the leather of his leggings on the right side, darkened the back of his right leg all the way to his moccasin. Was it *his* blood? Aye, it must be. He had tied a cloth around his upper thigh to staunch the flow.

He was injured, weak, perhaps nigh to collapsing. Some part of her realized this, saw it as the chance she needed.

She ran, a desperate dash toward the cabin door, toward safety, toward life. She had only a few steps to go when arms strong as steel shot out, imprisoned her.

"Oh, no, you don't!"

"Nay!" She screamed, kicked, hit, fought to free herself through a rising sense of terror.

"Ouch! Damn it, woman!"

The click of a pistol cocking. The cold press of its barrel against her temple.

She froze, a terrified whimper in her throat.

His breath was hot on her cheek. "I have no desire to harm you or the child you carry, but you *will* help me, whether you wish to or not! Do you understand?"

She nodded, her mind numb with fright.

Pistol still in hand, he forced her to hold the stallion's reins while he unsaddled it and carried its burdens inside the cabin. Then he watched as she led the animal to a stall in the barn, settled it with hay and fresh water from the well. And although she had hoped he might fall unconscious, he showed no further sign of pain or weakness apart from a bad limp.

"Get inside, and boil water."

She crossed the distance from the barn to the cabin, her stomach knotted with fear, the heat of his gaze boring into her back. Then she saw the firewood scattered on the ground. She stopped, turned to him, half afraid to speak lest she provoke his ire. She had no doubt this man was capable of killing. "I—I'll need the wood."

Blue eyes, hard and cold as slate, met hers. He nodded—one stiff jerk of his head.

She eased her way down, began to fill her arms.

Nicholas watched the woman pick up firewood. She had no idea how close she had come to escaping him moments ago on her doorstep. Dizzy from blood loss, he had found it surprisingly difficult to subdue her, had been forced to wield the threat of his pistol. He could not risk getting close enough for her to knock it from his grasp. He was fast fading, and without the weapon he would not long be able to bend her to his will. He had no doubt that if given the choice, she would leave him out here to die, even kill him herself.

He didn't blame her. There was only one rule on the frontier—survival. A woman without male protection could not be too careful, particularly a young and pretty one. And even heavy with child, she was a beauty.

How old was she? Nicholas guessed eighteen. Her cheeks were pink from exertion, her skin flawless and kissed by the sun. A thick braid of sun-streaked honey-blond hair hung down her back to her waist. Her curves, enhanced by her pregnancy, were soft, womanly, and easily apparent despite the plainness of her gray woolen gown. And although she was great with child, she'd felt small in his arms. Her head just touched his shoulder.

He looked on as she struggled to stand. Though she was obviously very near her time, she was surprisingly graceful and was soon back on her feet and walking toward the cabin, arms full, her braid swaying against the gray wool of her cloak with each step.

Nicholas followed, but even this small effort left him breathless. His heart hammered in his chest, fought to pump blood no longer in his body. The Frenchman's blade had gone deep, and though it had failed to sever his tendons and drop him to the ground as the bastard had no doubt hoped, it had clearly cut into a major blood vessel.

He'd left Fort Detroit early in the morning almost a week ago, having earned more than enough from his pelts to replenish his supplies. He'd traveled south for most of four days before he got the feeling he was being followed. The signs were subtle—the twitching of Zeus's ears, the cry of a raven startled from its perch somewhere behind him, a prickling on the back of his neck. He'd urged Zeus to a faster pace, kept up his guard, hadn't stopped to rest or eat until well past nightfall.

They'd attacked just after midnight. The first had sprung at him out of the darkness and might have succeeded in killing him had Nicholas not been awake and waiting. And while he'd grappled with the first, the second had leapt from hiding to deal a surprise deathblow. Nicholas had quickly dispatched the first attacker, but the second managed to slash his thigh before Nicholas had buried his knife in the man's belly. He'd recognized them both from the fort—French trappers who weren't ready to relinquish the Ohio Valley to the English.

Nicholas had realized immediately he was badly hurt. He'd have treated the wound himself had he been able to see it and reach it with ease. Instead, he'd tied a tourniquet around his leg and had reluctantly ridden through the night hoping to cross some farmstead where aid might be available.

As he'd grown weaker, he'd all but resigned himself to death. He was already dead inside. What did it matter if his body died, too? Wasn't that what he'd secretly been searching for all these years? But just before dawn, he'd heard a gunshot to the east and had followed it until he'd heard the sound of someone chopping wood. He hadn't expected it to be a woman, much less a woman alone.

He hadn't asked a soul for help in more than six years. It galled him to have to do so now. He followed the woman inside. "Build up the fire."

The cabin was small with a puncheon floor that looked as if it had been newly washed. The only light came from a small window covered with greased parchment. A rough-hewn table sat in the center of the room, a hand-carved bedstead against the far right wall. In the far left corner on the other side of the fireplace sat a cupboard and before it a loom, a spinning wheel, and a rocking chair. Dried onions, herbs, and flowers hung from the rafters, a feminine touch that for one startling moment reminded him of the cookhouse on his plantation. A rifle leaned against the wall beside the door.

Nicholas checked the rifle to make certain it was not primed and loaded. Next he removed his bearskin coat and his jacket, tossed them over one of the wooden chairs.

Black spots danced before his eyes. He pulled out another chair, sat, watched as she stirred the fire to life and poured water into the kettle to boil. "You'll need thread and a strong needle."

She started at the sound of his voice. She was terrified of him, he knew. He could taste her fear, smell it, see it in the way she moved.

Smart woman.

Of course, he hadn't meant to frighten her, not until she'd left him no choice. Had his need not been so dire, he would have tried to win her cooperation in some more civilized fashion. Then again, if his need had not been dire, he wouldn't be here.

"If I wanted to kill you, you'd be dead already."

He heard her gasp, saw her eyes widen in alarm, realized his words had done nothing to calm her. But then it had been a long time since he'd tried to comfort a woman.

He tried again. "I'm not going to hurt you."

She set needle and thread on the table and began to ladle hot water into an earthenware bowl, watching him through wide and frightened eyes. "P-please. Y-you'll need to . . . to remove your leggings and lie down on your belly if I'm to stitch you."

She had a faint accent—sweet and melodic. Scottish?

But what she'd suggested was easier said than done. To remove his leggings, he would need to remove the tourniquet. If he removed the tourniquet, the blood would flow freely again. He would surely lose consciousness, perhaps even die. But she wouldn't be able to treat him if he kept his leggings on.

There was only one solution. He pulled out his hunting knife, began to cut through the supple leather.

Bethie watched as he sliced the leather from his right leg with smooth, strong motions, noticed things she hadn't noticed before. A thin white scar ran down his left temple to his cheekbone, made him seem even more dangerous. But his face was ashen—what she could see of it above his beard—and his lips were pallid, bloodless.

Clearly, he had come close to dying. He might die still.

When his leg was cut free, he tossed the blood-soaked leather by the door. Pistol still in hand, he stood, a bit unsteady at first. Then he took up his bearskin coat, strode to the bed, spread the skin on the homespun coverlet. In one fluid motion, he stretched out over the skin and lay down on his belly. He was trying to keep from getting blood on the coverlet, she realized—an oddly considerate thing to do.

The sight of him lying on her bed was more than a little disturbing. His dark hair spilled over his broad shoulders, fanned across the undyed linen of his shirt to his narrow hips. He was so much bigger than Andrew—leaner, more muscular, taller. His feet hung off the foot of the bed, and he seemed to fill it, just as his presence dominated the tiny cabin.

Then she saw his wound. Gaping and raw, it was at least six inches long, parting the skin of his upper thigh, digging deep into the muscle. If it festered, he would lose his entire leg, perhaps even die.

She must have gasped.

"That bad?"

"I'll need to wash the blood away first." She added a bit of cold water to the hot, tested the temperature with her fingers. Then she pulled a chair over to the bed, set the bowl of water on it, together with the needle, thread, and several clean strips of linen.

Careful to keep her distance, she sat beside him and tried to gather her thoughts, which had leapt in all directions like frightened deer at the first sight of him. He would not harm her now, she reasoned. Not yet. His hurt was grievous, and he needed her help. But what would he do when he recovered his strength?

As Bethie knew only too well, there were many ways a man could hurt a woman. And this man was dangerous. Every instinct she had told her that. Hadn't he already threatened her with his pistol and used his strength against her?

She must not give him another chance to harm her. She must find a way to take his weapons from him, to render him helpless, to gain the upper hand. Christian charity might demand that she help him, but that didn't mean she had to leave herself defenseless against him.

She dipped a linen cloth into the water, squeezed it out, began gingerly to wipe the blood from his leg. It was unsettling to touch the stranger in such an intimate way, to feel his skin, the rasp of his dark body hair, the strength of his muscles beneath her hands. She tried to take her mind off what she was doing, gathered her courage to ask him the question she'd wanted to ask since she'd seen he was wounded. "If you dinnae mind my askin', how did this happen?"

"I was attacked by two French trappers. I killed them, but not before one of them tried to hamstring me."

The way he spoke of killing, as if it were nothing, sent a chill down her spine.

He seemed to read her mind. "They tried to murder me as I slept."

Bethie said nothing, afraid her voice would reveal her fear and doubt. Instead, she bent over his injury to examine it. Blood still oozed from deep within despite the tourniquet, pooling red in the gaping wound. She parted the flesh with her fingers, felt her stomach lurch. He was cut almost to the bone.

She could not stitch this.

She stood, took deep breaths to calm her stomach, washed his blood from her hands. "I—I'm sorry. But I'm goin' to have to . . . to cauterize it."

He turned his head, looked back at her over his shoulder, held out his hunting knife. "Then do it. Use my knife."

She hesitated for a moment, stunned by his seeming indifference to the prospect of so much pain, then took up the knife. She walked to the hearth, thrust the knife blade into the hottest part of the fire, waited for it to heat.

Worries chased one another through her mind. She didn't want to do this. She'd never done it before, and she was afraid—

afraid of doing it wrong, afraid he would thrash about and hurt her, afraid he would blame her for his suffering.

She turned to look at the strange man in her bed. He appeared to be sleeping, his face turned toward her, long dark lashes softening his otherwise starkly masculine features. She did not trust him, knew he was dangerous. But she did not want to hurt him.

Then, an idea half formed in her mind, she crossed the room to the cupboard, took out her bag of medicines and the jug of whiskey Andrew kept for cold nights. Careful to turn her back to him, she poured a stout draft of whiskey into a tin cup, added several drops of herbal tincture, sure the alcohol would mask the taste.

His voice broke the silence. "What's your name?"

"Bethie." Startled, she answered quickly, without thinking, then corrected herself. "Elspeth Stewart."

"Check the blade, Mistress Stewart. Surely it's hot by now."

She turned toward him, cup in hand, walked to the bed, and offered it to him. "You'll be needin' this."

He lifted his head, his brows knitted in puzzlement, looked into the cup, and grinned darkly. "Corn whiskey? You'd best save that to clean the wound."

"But it will help to dull your pain."

He shook his head. "A cup of whiskey cannot help me. Besides, 'tis only pain."

*Only pain?*

She gaped at him. What kind of life had he led that certain agony meant nothing to him? "Fine. Suffer if you like, but I cannae hold you down. What promise do I have that you willna thrash about or kick me?"

He laughed at her. "I give you my word I will hold perfectly still."

"But your sufferin' will be terrible! Should I no' at least bind you to the—"

"No!" There was an edge of genuine anger in his voice now. "I've given you my word. Now let's get this over with."

Sick to her stomach and trembling, Bethie set the whiskey aside and retrieved the knife. Wrapping her apron around the hot, wooden handle, she carried it to the bed.

The blade glowed red.

Dreading what she must do, she stood next to his injured leg and tried to figure out how best to apply the heat.

"Do it!" The man reached above his head, grasped the carved rungs of the headboard, his large hands making fists around the wood.

She took a deep breath, pressed the red-hot steel into the wound.

The hiss and reek of burning flesh.

His body stiffened, and his knuckles turned white, but he did not cry out. Nor did he thrash or try to pull his leg away.

The hissing faded.

Bethie pulled the blade free, stepped back from the bed, drew air deep into her lungs, afraid she might faint or be sick. Stray thoughts flitted through her mind like wild birds. Had it worked? Was he still bleeding? Would his leg fester? How had he managed to hold still through such torment?

Gradually, her breathing slowed, and the dizziness and nausea passed. Gathering her wits, she carried the bucket and what was left of the fresh water to the bed.

She sat beside him, expecting him to be unconscious, but he was not. Beads of sweat glistened on his forehead, and his face was even paler than before, if that were possible. But his eyes, though glazed with pain, were open, and he watched her.

"I—I'm sorry! I didna want to hurt you." She dipped the cloth into the bucket, pressed the cold, wet cloth to his brow and cheeks.

"Has the bleeding . . . stopped?" His voice was tight, ragged, betraying his pain.

Almost afraid to look, Bethie bent over the wound. What had been a raw, bleeding gash was now burned, blistered flesh. But there was only one way to know for certain. She took up a knife and, after a moment's hesitation, cut away the tourniquet. "Aye, the bleedin' has stopped."

"Pour the whiskey in."

"Are you cert—"

"Aye. Do it!"

She hurried to the cupboard, withdrew the jug once more, then returned to the bed. With a jerk, she pulled the cork free, then poured fiery liquid into the wound, and set the jug aside.

Not so much as a sound escaped his lips.

She took a fresh strip of linen, sat beside him, blotted the excess.

"A pouch of ointments . . . in my saddlebags. The big pocket. Fetch it." He sounded weaker.

"Aye, in a moment. Should you not first have somethin' to strengthen you? You've lost a lot of blood." She reached for the tin cup with the whiskey mixture, lifted his head, held it to his lips. "Swallow."

To her great relief, this time he drank.

The sight of her eyes—lovely eyes almost the color of violets—would be the last thing Nicholas remembered.

# Chapter 3

*Nicholas was on fire. Every inch of his chest, belly, and back seemed to burn, pain ripping even into his sleep. The ropes chafed his wrists and ankles, imprisoned him, made his right leg ache.*

*Lyda was again cleaning his wounds, rubbing ointment into his burns, her fingers like glass shards against his tortured skin. He would have killed her, would have broken her neck had he been able to free himself.*

*But she knew that, and so she kept him bound.*

*How long had he lain here, drifting in and out of consciousness, half mad with pain and fever? Hours? Days? Weeks? And why was he still alive? Why had they spared him?*

*Screams.*

*Josiah and Eben! The Wyandot were burning them, tormenting them. But they were already long dead, weren't they? Why then could he still hear them?*

*"Nicholas! For God's sake, help us!"*

Nicholas awoke with a jerk, caught between the nightmare and wakefulness, his heart pounding, his body covered with sweat. He struggled to open his eyes, found himself lying on his stomach in someone's bed, his head on a pillow. His right leg throbbed, burned. His head ached. His throat was parched as sand, and a strange aftertaste lingered in his mouth.

From nearby came the swish of skirts, the sound of a log settling in a fire, the scent of something cooking.

*Where was he?*

Through a fog he tried to remember. He'd been attacked. The Frenchmen from the fort. He'd lost a lot of blood, had ridden in search of help. The cabin. The woman.

Bethie was her name. Elspeth Stewart.

She'd helped him, cleaned his wound, cauterized it—not altogether willingly.

Nicholas lifted his head, started to roll onto his side to take in his surroundings, found he could not.

His wrists and ankles were bound to the bedposts.

Blood rushed to his head, a dark surge of rage, of dread.

"You're awake." Her voice came from behind him. "You must be thirsty."

"You little bitch!" He pulled on the ropes, his fury and dread rising when they held fast. "Release me! Now!"

"I—I cannae do that—no' yet. I've made broth. It will help you regain—"

"Damn your broth, woman! Untie me!" He jerked on the ropes again, outraged and alarmed to find himself rendered powerless. Sharp pain cut through his right thigh.

"Stop your strugglin'! You'll split your wound open and make it bleed again."

Infuriated, Nicholas growled, a sound more animal than human, even to his own ears. He jerked violently on the ropes, but it was futile. He was still weak from blood loss, and the effort left him breathless, made his pulse hammer in his ears.

*Damn her!*

He closed his eyes, fought to subdue the slick current of panic that slid up from his belly, caught in his throat.

*She is not Lyda. This is not the Wyandot village.*

His heartbeat slowed. The panic subsided, left white-hot rage in its wake.

"Why did you do this? I told you I meant you no harm!" He craned his neck, saw that she stood before the fire, ladling liquid into a tin cup, a brown knitted shawl around her shoulders.

"Is that no' what the wolf always says to the lamb?" She carried the cup to the bed, sat. "Drink. It will help to replenish your blood. Careful. 'Tis hot."

Tantalized by the smell of the broth and suddenly aching with thirst, Nicholas bit back the curse that sat on his tongue. He drank.

Bethie held the cup to his lips, watched as he swallowed the broth, her heart still racing. For one terrible moment, she'd feared the ropes would break or come loose. She'd known he would be angry with her, but she hadn't expected him to try to rip the bed apart.

Truth be told, she feared him despite the ropes. Although he'd given up for the moment, she could feel the fury coiled inside him. She could see it in the rippling tension of his body, in his clenched fists, in the unforgiving glare in his eyes. He made her think of a caged cougar—spitting angry and untamed. He was not used to being bested.

The arrogant brute! Did he imagine she would grant him warm hospitality after the way he'd treated her? It served him right to be bound and helpless!

As if a man of his strength were ever truly helpless.

Her gaze traveled the length of him as it had done many times while he'd slept, and she found her eyes focused of their own will on the rounded muscles of his buttocks where the butter-soft leather clung so tightly.

Mortified, she jerked her gaze away, felt heat rise in her cheeks. Her stepfather had always said she was possessed of a sinful nature.

"More." His boorish command interrupted her thoughts. He glowered at her through eyes of slate.

"Aye." She stood, hurried to the fireplace, ladled more broth into the cup, uncomfortably aware that he was watching her.

"How long do you intend to keep me a prisoner?" His voice was rough, full of repressed rage.

She walked back to the bed, sat, feigned a calm she did not feel. "'Tis your own fault you lie bound. You cannae be expectin' to be treated as a guest when you behaved like a felon. Drink."

He pulled his head away, his gaze hard upon her, held up the ropes that bound his wrists. "This isn't necessary."

"You threatened me, held your pistol to my head, forced me to do your will, and admitted to killin' two men. Do you truly expect me to trust you?"

He frowned, his dark brows pensive. "I didn't mean to frighten you."

"As I recollect, you seemed quite bent on frightenin' me."

"I didn't have time for social graces. My need was dire."

"So is mine!" She stood in a surge of temper, met his gaze. "I cannae risk you regainin' your strength and then, when you no longer need my help, hurtin' me or my baby or takin' what is ours and leavin' us in the cold to starve! I dinnae even know your name!"

For a moment he said nothing. "Kenleigh. Nicholas Kenleigh."

She repeated his name aloud.

"Now that we've exchanged pleasantries, Mistress Stewart, you *will* release me."

"Nay, Master Kenleigh. I willna—no' just yet." She lifted her chin. "You'll stay as you are till I'm certain you pose no threat to me and my baby."

He gave a snort. "And how will you determine that?"

"Drink." She held the cup once more to his lips. "Perhaps I shall have you swear an oath, a bindin' oath."

He drained the cup, looked up at her. "And if I am a murdering liar, a man with no honor, the sort of man who would harm a woman ripe with child, how would this oath prevent me from doing whatever I want the moment you cut me free?"

Bethie stood, walked back to the fireplace to refill the cup once more, the truth in his words dashing her sense of safety to pieces. "Are you sayin' I should never set you free, Master Kenleigh?"

"No, Mistress Stewart. I'm saying that unless you plan to keep me a prisoner forever and care for me as if I were a babe untrained in the use of a chamber pot, sooner or later you have no choice but to trust me."

She walked back to the bed, felt her step falter. In truth, she hadn't thought about how or when she would release him when she'd bound him to the bed. Nor had she considered what keeping him bound would mean. She'd been thinking only of a way to restrain him and deprive him of his weapons, and she had accomplished that.

*A babe untrained in the use of a chamber pot?* Good heavens!

She reached the bed, sat, held the cup once more to his lips. "Very well. I shall cut you free. But you shall first swear to me by all you hold sacred that you willna do anythin' to harm me or my baby or to deprive us of our hearth and home."

He swallowed, licked broth from his lips. Then a queer look came over his face. He stared at the tin cup, then gaped at her. "You drugged me!"

*How did he know?* "I—I gave you medicine to ease your pain—and make you sleep."

He laughed, a harsh sound. "You drugged me so that you could bind me and take my weapons."

He stated it so plainly that Bethie could find no words to soften the truth of what she'd done. She rested a hand protectively on her belly, felt her baby shift within her. "Y-you left me no choice."

Nicholas saw the defiant tilt of her chin, noticed the pink that crept into her cheeks. He noticed, too, the way her hand softly caressed the swollen curve of her abdomen as if to calm the small life inside her.

*What would I have done in her place?*

He dismissed the question—and the irritating impulse to defend his previous actions toward her. There was only one rule in the wild—survival. He'd only done what he'd felt he had to do to stay alive.

*And so had she.*

"Very well, Mistress Stewart. I swear that I will not harm you or your child or try to take from you that which is yours." His next words surprised him. "And for the short time I shelter under your roof, I swear to protect you from any man who would."

What in the hell had inspired him to say that? She was not his problem. Clearly, whatever potion she'd given him had addled his mind.

For a moment she stood as still as a statue, her gaze seeming to measure him in light of the words he had just spoken. "Very well, Master Kenleigh."

She took up his hunting knife, which had lain on the table, then disappeared out of his range of vision. He felt her fingers pulling on the rope that bound his left ankle, felt the cold blade of his knife slide between the rope and his skin. A few tugs later, his left ankle was free.

In a matter of moments, only the bonds around his left wrist remained. He rolled onto his back, watched her as she rounded the bed with agonizing slowness. He could feel her doubt, her trepidation. She watched him as if he were a wild animal that might attack at any moment, her violet eyes wide.

"I promised not to harm you. I am a man of my word."

The cool touch of a blade. A few sharp tugs.

His wrist was free.

Quickly, she backed away from the bed, out of his reach, his knife still in her grasp.

Nicholas pushed himself up onto his elbows. Outside the parchment window, all was dark. Nighttime already?

Slowly he sat, let his legs fall over the edge of the bed, touched his feet to the wooden floor. The muscles in his right thigh screamed in angry protest. Dark spots danced before his eyes. The cabin swam.

Nicholas drew air into his lungs, felt the labored beating of his heart. He cursed his weakness, knew he had come terribly close to dying. It would take days, perhaps even weeks, for him to regain the blood he had lost and, with it, his strength.

"You see, Mistress Stewart? I'm in . . . no shape to harm . . . anyone."

And then, as if to prove his point, he slumped to the floor in a dead faint.

Bethie knelt beside him, touched his forehead, let out a long sigh of relief to find it still cool. He stirred in his sleep, his brow furrowed as if in response to her touch. Asleep like this, his long lashes dark upon his pale cheeks, his brow relaxed, he seemed harmless, not at all the kind of beast who'd hold a pistol to a woman's head.

He lay on the floor much as he had fallen. She could not lift him, or even drag him, without risking harm to her baby. She tucked a pillow beneath his head and draped his heavy bear-skin coat over him to keep him warm, but there was little more she could do for him.

Slowly she stood, one hand held against her lower back, the other stifling a yawn. She had already stoked the fire, paid one last visit to the privy house, and drawn in the door string. There was nothing left to do but go to sleep.

But how could she sleep with this huge Englishman, this rough and wild stranger, in the same room?

"He cannae hurt you, Bethie, you silly lass. He cannae even—"

Her words were interrupted by another yawn. 'Twas surely near midnight. She needed to sleep.

She picked up his pistol from the table where she had left it after she'd primed and loaded it, carried it with her around his prostrate form to the other side of the bedstead. Then she drew down the covers, crawled into their warmth.

The baby kicked restlessly as she settled onto her pillow. "Quiet now, little one. You wouldna want to keep me awake, would you?"

But despite her exhaustion, sleep would not come, and the baby was not to blame. Each time she began to drift off, something woke her. Several times she abruptly found herself sitting up, pistol in hand and pointed into the darkness. Once it was a log settling on the fire. Then it was the howl of a wolf in the distance. And then the stranger shifted in his sleep, bumped one of the chairs.

Twice, Bethie arose, checked him for fever, made certain the door string was pulled in, added wood to the fire. And when she had to use the chamber pot, as she seemed to have to do constantly these days, she found she could not—not with him in the cabin. Quietly, she crept outside and saw to her needs under a cold canopy of stars, surrounded by furtive noises and the impenetrable darkness of the forest.

With unbearable slowness, the hours drifted by. The fire

burned down to embers. The silence of the night, filled with dark possibility, deepened around her.

The first thing Nicholas noticed when he awoke, besides the relentless pain in his right thigh, was the underside of a pinewood table. It took him a moment to remember where he was and why. But how had he come to be on the floor?

He remembered Mistress Stewart cutting his bonds. He remembered trying to sit. And then?

Had the little wench drugged him again?

No. He had passed out.

He cursed under his breath, felt his tongue stick to the dry roof of his mouth. He needed water. A water skin full of it.

It was then he noticed the pillow. She had placed a pillow beneath his head and had covered him with his bearskin coat while he slept. The thoughtfulness of her gesture left him feeling annoyed. He didn't need her compassion.

Slowly he sat, waited to catch his breath, his heart drumming.

Although the sun had risen, she was still asleep. Even in the dim light, he could see dark circles beneath her eyes, and he knew she'd slept poorly out of fear of him. If his gut hadn't told him this, the pistol she clutched tightly in her hand—his pistol—certainly would have.

She looked helpless, very young and utterly innocent. Her smoky lashes rested on her creamy cheeks. Her long braid had come unbound, leaving her hair to tangle in thick, honey-colored coils against her pillow. She had slept fully clothed, as if to be ready for anything at any moment. Her blankets were twisted in disarray around her thighs, proof she'd had a restless night.

It wasn't his damned fault if she was still afraid of him. He'd given her his word. What more could he do?

He fought to ignore the pricking of his conscience, was about to drag his gaze from her when he noticed something that stopped him. Beneath the plain gray cloth of her gown where it stretched across her rounded belly, he could actually *see* her baby move. At first he thought he'd imagined it. But as he watched, it happened again—an abrupt movement, almost like a twitch, beneath her gown.

Without thinking, he pressed his hand against the surprising hardness of her abdomen. And there it was—a light pressure against his palm, faint at first, then stronger, as if the child could feel his touch and was pushing back. His throat grew tight with unexpected emotion.

*A baby. His baby.*

Conceived in hatred, it had died before birth. He had killed it, as surely as he'd driven its mother to her death.

Nicholas fought to push the unwelcome memories from his mind, tried to force them back behind the carefully forged steel wall that separated him from his past.

The gentle pressure against his palm increased, undeniable, persistent, as if in tender mockery of his attempts to forget. It held him in thrall.

A gasp. A flurry of blankets and gray skirts.

And Nicholas found himself staring down the barrel of his own pistol.

# Chapter 4

"Dinnae touch me! Get away from me!" Eyes wide with alarm, she sprang from the opposite side of the bed, backed away from him as if he were a copperhead.

But her aim did not waver.

Nicholas didn't know what angered him more—his own inexplicable behavior moments earlier or the fact that he was about to be killed with his own damned pistol. Had he not been so weak, he could easily have taken it from her. But in this state, he'd probably only succeed in getting himself shot.

He mumbled something he intended to be an apology, tried to get to his feet. Sharp pain shot through his right thigh, and he came close to sinking back to the floor. But he needed air. He needed to be alone, away from her, away from whatever had just happened.

He grasped the edge of the table for balance, ignored the strained pounding of his heart, willed his bandaged leg to bear his weight despite the pain. Slowly, deliberately, he turned his back on her. Then he limped to the door, threw it open, and walked out into the bracing chill of morning.

Bethie watched him walk outside, lowered the pistol when the door shut behind him. Only then did she realize she'd been holding her breath.

Trembling, she sat on the bed, exhaled.

She'd been in a dreamless sleep when she'd opened her eyes to find him touching her belly. At first, she'd been too sleepy to be afraid. As if in a dream, she had watched him. The look on his face had been one of wonder or grief—or both. She had smiled to see him so lost in her baby's tiny movements—until, with a jolt, she'd come fully awake, remembered who he was.

How dare he touch her in her sleep! How dare he touch her with such familiarity! He was lucky she hadn't pulled the trigger!

She pressed her palms to the hard curve of her abdomen where the warmth of his touch lingered. Strange that she didn't feel the revulsion and fear a man's hands usually aroused in her. Perhaps her mind was still fogged with sleep.

She glanced toward the window, realized with a start that it was already well past sunrise. How could she have slept so long when there was work to be done?

"Bethie! For shame!" For a moment her voice seemed to take on her mother's unforgiving tones.

She rose, hurried around the bed, set the pistol down on the table with a wary glance toward the closed door.

Where had he gone? She hoped he'd get on his horse, ride far away, and never return. His very presence unnerved her. She didn't want him anywhere near her when the baby came.

What was he doing out there? He'd catch his death for sure walking about in this chill barefoot, in half a pair of breeches with no coat or cloak.

Why did she care? She cared because she'd be forced to tend him if he fell sick, and already she'd had more than her fill of him.

Quickly, she combed her fingers through her tangled hair, worked it into a braid. Satisfied her hair would stay out of her face, she built up the fire, took her shawl from its peg, wrapped it around her shoulders. Then she picked up his pistol, slipped it into her apron pocket.

While he'd slept, she'd hidden his other weapons—a rifle, another pistol, a bayonet, and the two hunting knives—under the loose floorboard to the right of the fireplace. They were fine weapons, the pistols graced with intricate inlaid handles, surely far beyond the means of a simple trapper. She'd kept one pistol for her own protection. Easier to wield than Andrew's rifle, it would be just as deadly if Master Kenleigh's promise proved worthless. The bayonet told her he was a soldier, perhaps a deserter who had wearied of war and fled west.

Slowly, cautiously, Bethie opened the door.

She half expected to find him sprawled unconscious on the ground or lying in wait near the door. Instead, he stood by the well, drinking deeply from the tin dipper. He did not turn to her, did not acknowledge her.

She hurried past him to the poultry pens, tried to act as if his presence didn't bother her. When she came back out from the chicken coop, the morning's eggs in her apron, he was nowhere to be seen. She found him when she went to milk old Dorcas, her favorite cow.

He stood in the barn, tending his horse. He spoke reassuringly to the animal, brushed its chestnut flanks with sure strokes.

Bethie faltered on the threshold, uneasy at the idea of being in a dark, confined space near him. But there was nothing to be done about it. Drawing reassurance from the weight of the pistol in her apron pocket, she went about her work, doing her best to ignore him.

She had just settled on the milking stool when he spoke.

"Return my weapons, and I'll sleep here in the barn." His voice was deep and soft as velvet.

'Twas surely just such a voice Satan had used when he'd enticed Eve. And his suggestion *was* tempting. She'd sleep so much better with him out of the cabin. Or would she? Once he had his weapons, there was nothing to stop him from using them against her again. "I'll return them when you ride away."

For a moment there was no sound but the hiss of milk against tin.

"Some would say that to deprive a man of his firearms is a grave and dangerous offense." This time his voice carried an edge of warning.

A shiver of fear raced along her spine. She knew she was playing with fire. Her fingers grew awkward, earned an angry swish of Dorcas's tail. "And some would say a woman who doesna protect herself against strange men on the frontier is daft and deservin' of whatever befalls her."

He chuckled, a warm sound so contrary to his rough and callous character that it surprised her. "Let no man daresay you're daft, Mistress Stewart."

Bethie stood, untied Dorcas so the cow could wander back to her new calf, which lay nearby curled up in the straw, watching its mother with soft, brown eyes. Then she lifted the pail of fresh milk by its handle and let herself out of the stall.

He was still brushing his stallion's chestnut coat, his back to her.

"If you've the strength to feed and water the horses and loose them in the paddock, you can give your stallion a portion of my oats and hay. I'll have porridge ready by the time you're done."

She had his weapons, and she wasn't going to give them back.

If she'd been a man, Nicholas would have settled the issue with his fists. On the frontier, the only law all men acknowledged was the right of each man to arm himself. Any man stupid enough to trifle with another man's firearms could expect to wind up as fodder for wolves and ravens.

But she wasn't a man. She was a young woman heavy with child—alone and desperately vulnerable. And she was doing her best to stay alive.

She should not be here. What a fool her husband had been to drag her out here, to put her in harm's way and then leave her defenseless! She should be in the care of her family in some safe little town back east with older women to fuss over her, not left to fend for herself in a land without pity.

He released the second of her two gray mares into the paddock with a slap on the rump, turned back for Zeus, fighting dizziness.

It would not be hard to take the pistol from her by force. He could easily overpower her without hurting her, take it back, end this whole damned game. Once he had it, she would almost certainly tell him where she'd hidden the rest of his belongings.

But she would probably view any such action as a breach

of his vow. And that bothered him. He had not yet slipped so far as to break his word to anyone.

*Damn it to hell!*

Did she not realize that he would be better able to defend both of them if he were armed? Did she truly believe she could keep him at bay with one stupid pistol? If he were the kind of man she feared he was, she would have already suffered whatever fate he had chosen for her.

Zeus was restless, no doubt attracted to the mares, though neither appeared to be in season. The stallion stamped, snorted, dropped his phallus, his sleek body rippling with tension. He was unfamiliar with confined spaces, unused to the company of mares, though clearly eager for it.

Nicholas led the stallion from its stall, knew it would not be long before Zeus covered both mares and mingled his more noble Arabian bloodlines with theirs. "Behave yourself, boy. Mistress Stewart probably wouldn't approve of what you've got in mind."

By the time he had fed and watered the three horses, what little strength he'd had was gone. He walked slowly back to the cabin, cursing his weakness with each painful step. Only once in his life had he been so weak.

No, then it had been far worse.

As soon as he opened the cabin door, the rich smell of fried pork made his mouth water and his stomach growl. How long had it been since he'd had a meal?

She placed a wooden bowl on the table beside a spoon and a wooden tray of fried pork. "It's no' much, but I thought it might help to build up your blood."

Revived by a sudden onslaught of appetite, he sat, dug into the porridge, which was in truth but ordinary cornmeal mush. It was hot, almost too hot, but he was ravenous. Never had such simple fare seemed so delicious.

He was aware of her gaze upon him as he ate. She watched him guardedly, stood well beyond his reach, as if she expected him to lunge for her at any moment. After what he'd done earlier today, he could not blame her. What had he been thinking? What had induced him to touch her?

He emptied his bowl and ate several slices of pork before

fatigue again began to overwhelm him. He swallowed his last gulp of tea, fought to stand. Then some part of him remembered his long-forsaken table manners. "Thank you for breakfast, Mistress Stewart."

He had just enough strength to spread his bedroll on the floor in the far corner before exhaustion claimed him.

Bethie stopped to catch her breath, rubbed the ache in her back. The sky was clear blue, and the air held the first whispered promise of spring. In the forest, the beeches and maples had begun to bud. Soon cardinals, bluebirds, and mockingbirds would return to nest in their branches and the forest floor would burst into flower. The long, cold winter was almost past.

She looked down at the small pile of chopped firewood. She would need much more than this to see her through the night. She lifted another piece of wood onto the tree stump and swung the ax, let her mind wander.

A stew of rabbit and winter vegetables cooked over the fire, the work of preparing dinner largely behind her. Master Kenleigh had caught the rabbit in one of his snares this morning, had dressed it, and surprised her with it, handing it to her without a word.

Almost two weeks had passed since he'd arrived near death on her doorstep. He was getting stronger each day and would soon leave—and the sooner the better. Though he had not touched her again, his gaze followed her everywhere. She could feel his eyes upon her when she drew water from the well, cooked dinner, sat at her spinning wheel.

Bethie did not like to be noticed by men. Nothing good ever came of it.

And although the two of them had reached a truce, it was an uneasy truce. They barely spoke a word to each other, yet she knew he wanted his weapons back, and he knew she was not going to return them until he departed. To his credit, he had not tried to take them from her, though she suspected he wanted very much to do just that. She had not really expected him to keep his promise.

He ought to be grateful. She had tended him, fed him,

shared her medicines with him. What's more, she continued to allow him to shelter under her roof. She might just as easily have forced him to sleep with his horse or demanded that he pack up his goods and gear and depart. Though he was still weak and sitting on horseback was painful for him, he'd not die from it.

Why hadn't she forced him to ride on? Had the sight of him dismounting tight-lipped and in obvious pain after his short ride yesterday aroused sympathy in her heart? Or could it be that, although she did not entirely trust him, she felt a wee bit safer with him beneath her roof? Because he had kept his word thus far, did some part of her hope that he'd keep the second half of his promise—to protect her—as well?

Perhaps. But she didn't want to think about that.

He was getting stronger, but it was clear his health was not yet fully restored. His face was still pale, and his strength seemed to fade much faster than she would have expected for a man of his size and apparent vigor. He slept a lengthy portion of each afternoon, taking to his bedroll when it seemed he could no longer stay on his feet.

And so their days had taken on a rhythm. Each day, he greased and repaired his traps, tended the horses, worked on a new pair of leather leggings, and slept, while she saw to the other animals, prepared meals, spun wool, chopped wood. And each night, he slept in the far corner on the floor, while she slept in her clothes, his pistol in her hand.

Bethie lifted the ax, was about to swing again, when a sharp pain spread across her lower belly. She gasped, lowered the ax, pressed her free hand against the pain. Quickly, the twinge lessened, began to pass.

'Twas not yet her labor, at least she didn't think so. She'd had pains like these before, though they were becoming more frequent now. Her mother, who had borne nine children of which only Bethie had survived, had never shared with her the mysteries of birth, except to say it was a woman's duty and God's curse upon all women for the sins of Eve. And so Bethie did not know what to expect beyond great pain.

"You shouldn't be doing that." His deep voice startled her.

Without bothering to glance his way, she snapped at him. "I dinnae fear hard work, Master Kenleigh."

She'd started to lift the ax again, when his large hand closed over hers on the wooden handle.

"Let me."

The heat of his touch scorched her. She let go, stepped back, overwhelmed to be so near him. But when she looked up at his face, her breath left her.

He had shaved away his thick beard to reveal a face that was far bonnier than she could have imagined, with a strong chin, full lips, and cheekbones that now seemed sculpted and high. His scar looked more prominent, a thin line of white that ran the length of his left temple and cheekbone. His blue eyes seemed larger, more penetrating.

His hair hung damp and unbound to his waist, dark as a raven's wing. He wore his new leggings and a fresh shirt of linsey-woolsey dyed a deep indigo blue. The ties at his throat were undone, exposing a sliver of tanned flesh and a scattering of soft, dark hair. At his side in its sheath hung a knife—one she had not discovered among his possessions.

She'd been afraid of him before, but now she was positively terrified. That was the only way to explain this strange and rapid beating of her heart.

Then it dawned on her. She felt her apron pocket. The pistol was still there.

"Aye, I could have taken it from you, but I did not." He lifted a large piece of wood to the stump, lifted the ax, swung. The force of his blow split the wood cleanly in half, sent the pieces flying. "But an ax makes a deadly weapon, as well."

He lifted another piece of wood onto the stump, raised the ax. Then, in a blink, he turned toward her, hurled the ax end over end like a tomahawk.

Bethie gasped, heard it whistle past her, missing her by inches.

Nicholas saw the blood leave her face, saw her sway on her feet. Cursing under his breath, he crossed the distance between them, slipped an arm around her waist, pulled her against him to steady her. "I did not do this to frighten you, Mistress Stewart, but to make a point. If I had wanted to kill you, I could easily have done so at any time—with the ax, the hayfork, the poker in your fireplace, this knife, or my bare hands. It's time you trusted me and gave up this foolishness."

She looked up at him through terrified violet eyes, her breast rising with each rapid breath. Then color flooded her cheeks, and she seemed to find her tongue. "L-let go of me!"

He released her, stepped toward the cabin, jerked the ax free from the log in which it was embedded. He had not intended to deal so forcefully with her, but the moccasin prints he'd discovered at the river, where he'd gone to bathe, had changed his mind. He needed his weapons back—for both their sakes. "You're lucky it was I who came upon you and not one of the Delaware warriors who just passed by a mile north of here. They had arrows, spears, and rifles—more than a match for a woman with one pistol."

She whirled toward him, both hands on her swollen belly. "You're lyin'! You're tryin' to scare me!"

He smiled at her predictable reaction. "Why don't you come with me? I'll prove it. It's a war party. They're traveling fast and light northward, but it's a good bet they know you're here. I tracked them a short distance, far enough to be reasonably certain they won't double back tonight."

He watched her eyes give play to her emotions—fear, suspicion, fury.

She slipped a hand into her pocket, withdrew the pistol, aimed it at him. "Lead the way."

Nicholas kept the ax as he led her a short distance through lengthening shadows to the riverbank. Mindful of her condition, he asked her twice if she wanted to rest, but to her credit she shook her head and kept moving, pistol still in hand.

When he could hear the gurgling of water ahead, he motioned for her to stop and wait. Silently, he moved through the trees, his senses alert for any sound or movement. He checked for new tracks, watching the riverbank beyond for anyone who might be lying in wait. Then he motioned her forward.

Though he could tell she was afraid, she quietly moved toward him.

He knelt, pointed to the overlapping tracks in the soft mud of the riverbank. "About a dozen warriors," he whispered. "No women or children. A war party."

She looked at the prints, looked at the moccasins on his feet. "How do I know you didna make those?"

Frustrated, he placed his right foot next to one of the footprints, placed his weight upon it. His footprint was much larger than the rest. "Do you believe me now?"

She shivered, pulled her gray cloak tight around her.

He took her by the elbow, led her back to the cover of the trees. "We need to get back before nightfall."

She nodded, then turned toward him, held the pistol out to him. But fear and doubt lingered in her eyes. "If you betray me . . ."

He took the weapon from her, checked the impulse to touch her cheek. "I gave you my word."

Without speaking, they hurried back through the darkening forest toward the cabin. He stopped her before they reached the clearing in which it stood, made certain no one was hiding in the cabin or lurking in the barn.

"Get inside. I want you indoors in case I'm wrong and they come back this way." He was surprised to hear himself speak such words. Since when had she become his problem?

"Master Kenleigh." She smoothed her hands on her apron.

"Aye."

"You'll be sleepin' in the barn from now on." In a whirl of gray wool skirts, she turned and walked—or rather waddled—inside.

Nicholas grinned despite himself, amused. Then he looked down at the pistol, checked it, blew out a surprised burst of air.

The damned thing was primed and loaded.

# Chapter 5

Bethie awoke the next morning to the sound of splitting wood, startled to have slept so soundly. She couldn't think of a time since the onset of Andrew's sickness when she had truly slept. With a band of Delaware on the prowl, she ought to have been awake all night.

Instead, she'd slept deeply—and dreamt of her real father. She'd seen his smiling face, had watched his callused hands as he made a doll of cornhusks for her, had heard his warm voice as he laid the doll in her arms.

*That's my good lass.*

In her dream, she'd felt happy and surrounded by the warmth of his love. It was as if all the troubles of life had been lifted from her shoulders, all her fears soothed, her needs quenched. Now only a bittersweet ache remained.

Outside, an ax cleaved wood.

She stretched, yawned, wondered how much of her good night's sleep was due to the presence of a certain armed and handsome Englishman in her barn—and not in her cabin. Having him out of the cabin had restored her sense of privacy for certain. But hadn't she also felt a wee bit safer knowing he was still nearby?

She sat up, shook her head. That made no sense. He had

frightened her out of her wits yesterday. Aye, he had. And in more ways than one.

When he'd hurled that ax, he'd moved so quickly she hadn't even had time to react. She'd expected to look down and find its blade buried in her breast. But he hadn't been aiming at her. If he had, she'd have been dead before she could scream.

Then, when the shock of it had turned her knees to water, he'd quickly wrapped a strong arm around her, kept her on her feet. The heat of his touch—and the way it made her feel—was as unnerving as any band of roving Indians.

To think they had passed so close to her home . . . She shuddered.

Master Kenleigh had said he had been trying to make a point, and she'd believed at first that he sought merely to control her through fear. Then he'd led her through the forest to the riverbank, and she'd seen the truth for herself. He hadn't been lying, at least not about that.

It was clear to her that he had spent much time living among Indians, had perhaps even been raised by them. She had never seen anyone move like that before—quiet and deadly as a cougar on the prowl. The sight of it had made her shiver, and she'd known she'd been right about him in at least one respect—he was dangerous.

She arose, feeling better rested than she had in weeks, dressed hurriedly in the chilly cabin, placed more wood upon the fire. She opened the door and was on her way to fetch water for washing and porridge, when she found a bucket, already filled with fresh water, waiting outside the door.

Surprised by his thoughtfulness, she picked it up, brought it inside, and shut the door behind her, making certain to leave the door string out. Then she poured water into the kettle to boil, using the rest to wash her face and hands. She was in the midst of brushing her hair when he entered, still limping slightly, arms full of firewood.

"Good morning, Mistress Stewart. I hope you slept well."

She looked up, met his gaze, felt her pulse trip under the penetrating power of those blue eyes. She'd forgotten how bonny he was without his beard, could scarce find her own tongue. "Good morning, Master Kenleigh." She started to ask him how he'd slept, but felt a bit awkward given that she had banished him to the cold of straw and barn. "Thank you for the water."

He dropped the firewood one piece at a time onto the sizable pile already next to the fireplace. "You're welcome."

Strange it was to talk with him this way, as if he were a friend or acquaintance. Too flustered to braid her hair in his presence, she simply used the thong to tie it back. "I'm afraid I overslept again. I'll soon have breakfast ready."

He nodded, strode outside again. Beyond him, she could see that the horses already roamed the paddock.

While he carried in the rest of the firewood, she measured cornmeal into boiling water, cut salted pork into thick strips, set them on the fire in an iron skillet to fry. Then she hurried to the well for more water for tea.

By the time he'd carried the last load of firewood inside and had fed the rest of the livestock, she had breakfast on the table.

They ate in an awkward silence at first.

Then he spoke. "How long have you been out here, Mistress Stewart?"

"Almost four years. Andrew traded a team of horses and a wagon for the claim to the land and the cabin shortly before we were wed. And you, Master Kenleigh?"

He didn't answer her. "The people who started this farm returned east to escape the war. Yet you and your husband chose that time to build a life here. Why?"

Bethie sipped her tea, willing herself to meet his steady gaze. "Andrew came over from Ulster with my father when they were young lads. It had always been his dream to have a farm of his own. He worked off his indenture, tried farmin' back east, but he kept movin' west, startin' over. He said the frontier was the only place a man could truly breathe free."

"Is that where you were born—Ulster?"

"Nay. I was born on my father's farm near Paxton, but my parents came from Ulster." She did not like to talk about her family.

He finished his breakfast, leaned back in his chair, one arm draped lazily over the back of the chair beside him. "Lots of settlers in this part of the country have been killed in this war."

"Aye. I knew a woman who . . ." She looked into her teacup. "I was so . . ."

"Afraid?" He finished her sentence, his voice soft, almost soothing.

She closed her eyes, remembered nights of sleepless terror. "Aye. But Andrew wouldna leave. He said no Frenchman or red Indian would drive him from his land."

"He's dead. Why do you stay?"

Shocked by his brusque words, the cold tone of his voice, she could only stare at him.

*Because I have no place to go.* She thought it, but she did not say it. Any answer she might give would come too close to her secret shame, too close to the truth. And she would not speak of that with anyone.

Shaken, she stood, walked to the hearth, picked up the milk pail. "Poor Dorcas. I nearly forgot her. She'll be aching with milk by now."

And with that, she turned and fled to the safety of the barn.

Nicholas brushed the mare's dusty gray coat, certain the animal hadn't received a proper grooming or a bath in months. She was filthy and shaggy, and wax had built up between her teats, proof she hadn't been bred in some time, perhaps ever. Not that he blamed Mistress Stewart. She had more than enough to contend with, and as pregnant as she was, she could not be expected to run a farm on her own. He blamed the old fool who'd been her husband.

Mistress Stewart. Bethie.

He'd wanted to ask her what plans she had for the birth of her child, but he had hurt her today, had roused her grief. He'd seen the color leave her face the moment he'd spoken. He'd seen the pain in her eyes. Her husband, the man whose child she carried, was not yet three months in the grave.

"He's dead," Nicholas had said with all the sensitivity of a rock. Perhaps he'd spent too many years talking to his horse.

But, damn it, she should not be out here! She should be on her parents' farm near Paxton, where the women of her family could fuss and fret over her, where her father could send for the midwife and see to it that his daughter was brought safely to bed when the hour came.

He supposed she hadn't made the journey home because she was too far along by the time her husband had died. She would have had to forsake her livestock and all her belongings to travel a long distance on horseback, pregnant and alone, across icy rivers and through the mountains in the cold and dark of winter. Taken together, he could see why a woman wouldn't find that appealing. No doubt she'd felt safer remaining here than trying to make her way back home.

It was far too late now to attempt any such journey. From the look of her, the baby would be born within the month. That meant the baby would be born here. There was no help for it now.

Nicholas dipped the currycomb into the bucket of soapy water and began to scrub grime from the mare's coat.

Perhaps there was a wife on a nearby farmstead who would be willing to aid her, someone he could fetch for her. Or perhaps Mistress Stewart had some plan of her own.

Nicholas was suddenly irritated to find himself so caught up in her plight. This wasn't his baby. He hadn't put her husband in the grave. She wasn't his wife. He had promised to protect her only so long as he sheltered beneath her roof, and he was strong enough now to pack his things, saddle Zeus, and ride west along the Ohio River as he'd planned.

So why didn't he leave?

*Because I'd never forgive myself if I left her out here, helpless and alone.*

But what could he do to help her? As a man who'd once bred prized horses, he knew a great deal about helping mares to foal, but next to nothing about childbirth. He was the oldest and could remember when his mother had been brought to bed with the youngest of his siblings. He'd been six when William, the second of his younger brothers, had been born. He'd heard his mother's moans, had feared she was dying. He'd managed to elude the servants set to watch him long enough to creep upstairs and open the door to his parents' chamber. There, he'd caught just a glimpse of his mother, clad in her shift, leaning back against his father's chest, her hands clasped tightly around his. Her eyes had been closed, her face wet with sweat and twisted with pain. Then his intrusion was discovered. After his nurse had led him away, she'd promptly given him a sound swat on the behind.

His father had spoken a little of birth to him, describing the wonder of watching as Nicholas and his siblings were born. And Jamie, his uncle and perhaps closest friend, had confided in him of the helplessness and wrenching guilt he'd felt holding his wife, Bríghid, as she had labored to bring their two sons into the world.

Surely Jamie and Bríghid would have more children by now. Six years was a long time, and they had been deeply in love.

Nicholas had been a man and newly returned from Oxford when his mother had given birth to little Emma Rose. As he'd sat below with a glass of brandy in hand, he'd found himself enraged that his father had not exercised better restraint and had thus forced his mother to endure this anguish again. He'd told his father so, only to receive a tongue-lashing from his mother the next day.

*Emma Rose.*

His stomach knotted at the thought of his littlest sister. When he'd ridden away she'd been only three. She'd be nine by now—a spoiled little princess with their mother's red-gold curls and their father's deep blue eyes. Strange to realize that in all these years he'd not thought of her.

An unexpected shard of pain sliced through his gut, made it hard to breathe.

Nicholas fought to squelch the sudden rush of emotion. He dipped a bit of old wool into the bucket and began gently to wash the valley between the mare's empty teats. She tried to pull away from him, raised one hoof off the ground as if to kick.

He stroked her flank, spoke softly. "Steady, girl."

What was wrong with him? First the nightmares. Then memories of Lyda and his baby. Now his family.

He needed to return to the wild, where the emptiness and the wide-open spaces would drive aught else from his mind. He needed to gaze upon the dark waters of the great river to the west, listen to the friendly chatter of beavers busy with their dams, sleep under an endless heaven bright with stars. He needed to ride away. But first he would find a farmwife to help Mistress Stewart and see her safely settled out of harm's way.

Bethie's water broke just after she'd gone to bed. On the brink of sleep, she felt a trickle of liquid between her thighs, feared for a moment she had wet herself. She sat up, only to have the trickle become a torrent as warm water spilled from inside her. And she knew.

Her time had come.

She rose, changed into a dry gown, put birthing linens on the bed, added wood to the fire, set water on to boil for tea. Then she took out the fresh linens she'd set aside for the baby, a knife to cut the cord, and a length of yarn to bind it. Beyond that, she did not know what to do. Although her womb had begun to tighten, the pangs were far apart and caused her little pain. She drank her tea, rocked in her rocking chair, tried in vain to ignore the fears that had assailed her these past months.

Would she know what to do? How badly would it hurt? What if something went wrong? Would the baby be born alive? Was this the end? Would she die tonight and the child with her?

There were many worries, but no answers.

Then, believing it was best to sleep while she could, she crawled back into bed and closed her eyes. But her fears would not leave her, and she slept but little.

Finally, sometime in the dead of night, she gave up trying to sleep and began to alternate pacing the floor with rocking in her chair. Her pangs began to grow stronger and more frequent. Each started as a tightening across her lower belly that spread to her back. But still the pain was bearable.

Her fears began to lessen. She could do this. She could bring her baby into the world alone. She could survive.

*"Nicholas, you bastard! What did you say to them? Help me! Oh, God, help me!"*

*Josiah's desperate screams mingled with Eben's, as Wyandot warriors used flaming torches to shove the young men, who'd been cut free of their ropes, into the fire pits. The women had smeared them with pitch to ensure that they burned. The two tried to escape, staggered from the flames, only to be pushed in again.*

*Tied to the post, Nicholas fought to free himself, fought to stay conscious. Why weren't they burning him? Why were the women bathing his wounds, rubbing salve on his burns?*

*"Let them go!" He'd glared at Atsan, shouted his words in Tuscarora, in French, in English. "Take me, but let them go free! Take me!"*

*"Oh, God, it hurts! Kill me! Nicholas!"*

Nicholas lurched from sleep, found himself sitting up in the barn, drenched in sweat, heart pounding in his chest. He threw off his blanket of skins, staggered from the barn, sucked cool, sweet air into his lungs. Until he'd come here, he'd thought he had left the nightmares behind him. He'd thought he was free from them, free from the guilt, the bitter remorse.

Perhaps he would never be free.

A glow on the eastern horizon heralded the approach of dawn. Hoping to wash the aftertaste of horror from his mouth, he strode toward the well, but stopped in his tracks.

Through the parchment window he could see the glow of candles. Odd that she was already awake. Since he'd moved into the barn, she'd almost always slept until the sun was up.

And then he heard it, a soft moan, almost like the sound of a woman lost in the pleasures of sex. But this was no moan of pleasure.

She was having the baby.

He walked to the door and, when the moan had ceased, knocked softly. "Mistress Stewart? Is there aught you need? Is there any farm nearby where I might find a woman able to help you?"

Her voice was muffled by the closed door, but Nicholas could still hear her fear. "Nay. No one. Please! Leave me in peace!"

He tried to do as she asked. He fed the horses, the chickens, the geese, the cattle, the hogs. He spread fresh straw for the horses and the milk cow. He fidgeted with his traps.

But he could not keep his eyes off the cabin. Nor could he

prevent himself from hearing her moans, which had grown louder and more frequent.

If there was one thing he understood, it was pain.

But she was not his wife nor his lover nor even kin. She was little more than a stranger, a woman whose path he'd chanced to cross at an unlucky time. Why should her anguish distress him so deeply?

Had he become so hard-hearted that he could even ask himself that question?

A sobbing wail.

He swore under his breath, threw the trap he held aside, stomped to the door. He could not sit idly by and do nothing. "Mistress Stewart, if you don't open this door, I'll break it down!"

# Chapter 6

Then it occurred to Nicholas that perhaps she was in trouble or too weak to reach the door. He stepped back and was about to kick the door in, when a better idea came to him. He slipped his knife from its sheath, strode to the window, and cut away the parchment.

She lay on her side on the bed clad only in her shift, eyes closed, whimpering as another pain came over her.

He quickly hoisted himself over the sill, went to her side.

She opened her eyes, glared at him. "Nay!" But the word became a wail as her pain reached its peak, and she closed her eyes again.

Now that he was beside her, he was not certain how to help her. If she were a broodmare, he would know how to make her most comfortable, how to check her progress, what to do in case of trouble. But she was a woman, and he was at a loss. He tried to remembcr anything his father might have told him, tried to remember what he had seen.

Bereft of any better idea, he turned toward the hearth, found the bucket half full with water, carried it to the bedside, sat beside her. Then, taking up a strip of linen, he dipped it in the water, pressed the cool cloth against her furrowed brow.

As the pain subsided, Bethie felt the blessed coolness of the cloth against her cheeks. She hadn't the strength to shout at him. "You shouldna . . . be here."

"Are you thirsty?"

"Aye."

In a moment she felt the tin cup touch her lips. He lifted her head, and she drank.

Then she felt it begin to build again. Though she would not have thought it possible, the pain was still getting worse. She heard herself whimper.

"Take my hand, mistress." He placed her hand in his much larger one.

She held it fast as pain and fear assailed her. Why was it taking so long? Was something wrong? Was the baby still alive?

Slowly, too slowly, the pain passed.

"You should be sitting up." His voice was deep, soothing, as he again bathed her brow.

She was too tired to answer him, began to doze.

The scrape of a chair on wood made her eyes open. Master Kenleigh stood, removed his boots. As the next pain began to take her, he slipped his arms beneath her, lifted her into a sitting position, slid into the bed behind her.

"Wh-what—" The pain cut her off, turned her words into a moan.

"Easy, Bethie. Let me help you. Rest against me."

She would have fought him, would have pulled away. He shouldn't be near her like this. She didn't want him in her bed. She didn't want him touching her. But he was insistent, and the pain was so bad.

No longer in control of anything, she sank against his chest, felt him take both of her hands in his. She bit her lip, tried not to cry out. How much longer?

His breath was warm on her temple. "Breathe deeply. Don't fight it. This one will soon end."

Before long, Bethie had lost all track of time. Relentlessly, the pangs came one upon the next, giving her little time to rest, shaking her apart. She was aware only of how badly she hurt and of Nicholas—the reassuring sound of his voice, the strength of him behind her, the mercies he showed her as he held her hand, pressed cool cloths on her cheeks, or gave her sips of water.

Nicholas looked down at the face of the woman who dozed against his chest. She looked so young, her sweet face lined with suffering, her hair damp with sweat. Not for the first time he found himself cursing her husband. The man was lucky he was already dead. Otherwise, Nicholas would have been sorely tempted to kill him with his bare hands. As it was, he might still dig up the bastard's grave just to kick his worthless bones.

It was past midday already, and if her pains had started when she'd gone to bed last night, as she'd said, that meant about sixteen long hours had gone by. If she'd been a mare, she'd have been in deep trouble and he would have intervened hours ago. He would have reached inside her to make certain the foal was positioned correctly to allow birth, then he'd have tied a rope around its hooves to help pull it from its dam's body. But she wasn't a mare, and even if she allowed him to check her, he wasn't entirely sure what was normal for human babies. And what exactly would he do about it if something were wrong? Babies didn't have hooves, and a woman's body was far more delicate than that of a broodmare.

She shifted in his arms, began to whimper. Her head rolled from side to side on his chest. "Nay! Please! I cannae take this!"

Nicholas pressed his lips to her ear, tried to speak with a certainty he did not feel. "Yes, you can, Bethie. You'll get through it. Don't fight it. Just let it roll over you. Breathe. That's the way. It will pass."

Her body trembled. She squeezed his hands, and her moan became a desperate cry.

After what seemed an eternity, she relaxed and began to doze again.

Nicholas tried to remind himself that women endured this all the time. He told himself this was only natural. Still, her suffering tore at him. He wished he could somehow take the pain upon himself or speed her release from anguish.

"If I die, promise me you'll bury me and say a prayer for me and my baby."

Her voice—and her words—startled him. He'd thought her asleep.

"You're not going to die." He smoothed a strand of damp hair from her cheek, hoped with all his heart he was right.

"Promise me. Dinnae leave me for the animals."

The image her words conjured turned his stomach, and he spoke more harshly than he'd intended. "I'm not a barbarian, mistress."

"Promise me?" She sounded weak, exhausted.

For the first time Nicholas truly began to fear she might not survive. "Aye. I promise."

"Stay with me. I'm so afraid!"

He ran a finger down her cheek, wondered at this strange tenderness he felt for her, a woman he barely knew. "I'm not going anywhere."

At his words, she seemed to relax, her body melding limply into his.

And for the first time in six years, Nicholas prayed.

Lost in a fog of pain, Nicholas her only succor, Bethie felt a dark eternity had passed, when in the midst of another pang something felt different. She found herself suddenly bearing down, compelled to push with all her might. Though it still hurt horribly, there was more pressure than extreme pain. "Ooooh!"

"Bethie?" Nicholas's deep voice sounded softly in her ear.

She fought to catch her breath. "I think it's coming."

"Are you sure?"

"Aye. I can feel it. What should I do?"

For a moment he said nothing. "Do whatever your body tells you to do, love."

And so she gave in to her body's demands. Knees bent, she pushed again, felt her baby move down through her body. Again and again she pushed, until pain began to spread between her thighs like fire. "Oh, God, it hurts!"

"Reach down, Bethie. Can you feel your baby?"

At his urging, she reached between her thighs, felt a small portion of the hard curve that could only be her baby's head. Despite her pain, she couldn't help but smile. "Aye, I can feel it." But then her fingers touched something else. She knew little about birth, but she knew enough for her heart to fill with fear. "The cord!"

In an instant Nicholas had slipped out from behind her, laid her gently back on the bed. His face was lined with worry.

"Wh-what are you going to do?"

She got her answer when he sat on the bed just below her bent legs and started to lift her gown.

"Nay!" She tried to slap his hand away.

He caught her wrist, held it. "Listen to me, Bethie. I'm sorry if this violates your sense of modesty, but I must move the cord if your baby is to have any hope of being born alive. I'll do my damned best not to hurt you."

She closed her eyes, felt him lift her gown, and she fought the desire, so instinctual, to kick at him or run.

"Let your thighs fall open, Bethie."

Tears sprang into her eyes, but they were not tears of pain.

"Whatever you do, you must not push. Do you understand? The cord is caught above your baby's head. If you push, you'll cut off your baby's blood supply for certain, and you might well break the cord. Then you'll both be lost."

She felt another pang begin to build. She tried to do as he asked, but the urge was overwhelming. She arched her back, panted, tried not to bear down. She felt his fingers slip inside her, and she screamed.

"Now, Bethie. Push, and push hard."

She tried to forget that he was sitting between her legs, gave herself over to her body's commands, pushing with all her might. She pushed again and again, until the fire between her thighs was unbearable. The pain consumed her. She was being split in two, ripped apart. She could not do this! A scream tore itself from her throat.

And then the pain abruptly lessened.

"The head is out, Bethie. You're almost there."

With the next pang, she pushed, and in a final surge of fire and water, felt her baby slide free. Out of breath, relieved, exhausted, she lay back on the pillow, awaiting the child's first cry.

But no cry came.

She opened her eyes, dread in her heart, watched as Nicholas, his face grave, held and massaged her little baby. It was blue, limp. Tears blurred her vision, rolled down her cheeks.

Then abruptly the baby's arms jerked as if in surprise, and it gave a tiny wail. In an instant its skin turned a bright shade of pink.

Nicholas looked up, and his gaze met hers. The tenderness in his eyes, so unexpected, stole her breath.

He smiled. "It's a girl."

Nicholas rose from his bedroll, stole silently across the floor, quietly added wood to the fire. He knew Bethie was exhausted after her long ordeal and he didn't want to wake her or the baby. When he was satisfied with the blaze, he turned back toward his skins in the corner.

He was surprised to find his feet carrying him toward the bed instead. He stopped beside it, gazed down at the baby, still in awe. She lay next to her sleeping mother, swaddled in linen, a tiny miracle.

To his surprise, her eyes were open, and she seemed to examine the world around her with keen interest. But then, as if on cue, she began to fuss—a little squeak more than a cry. Moved by some irresistible impulse, he reached down, lifted the baby gently into his arms. Perhaps he could rock her back to sleep, win Bethie another hour or two of rest.

He strode silently to the rocking chair, settled himself, stared down at the bundle in his arms. She was so tiny—her pouty lips, her toes, her fingernails all perfect, but unbelievably small. Her little head was covered with hair so golden and so fine that it was almost invisible. She had her mother's features.

Bethie had named her Isabelle.

Isabelle turned her head toward him, her little mouth open like a baby bird, and he knew she was seeking her mother's breast. He loosened the swaddling and, as he'd once seen Jamie do, guided her tiny thumb into her mouth. She sucked greedily, and her eyes drifted shut.

Nicholas felt an overwhelming swell of protectiveness, and he thought he understood something of what his father and Jamie must have felt. Bethie's suffering had been agonizing to witness. And yet this—the tiny creature he held in his arms—had been the result. And although he was not the baby's father, he was proud to have played at least some role in her birth. The cord had been looped over her head and wrapped once around her little neck. She had come close to suffocating before she'd taken her first breath.

Those seconds when she'd lain in his hands, blue and seemingly lifeless, he had found it hard to breathe. He'd done what he would have done with a foal—cleared her throat, wiped her face, rubbed her skin. But then she had drawn that first weak gulp of air and seemed to come to life in his arms. And he'd known Bethie's anguish had not been in vain. His relief had been overwhelming.

Did saving one life atone for causing the loss of another? He hoped that perhaps in some small measure it might. He had not meant for his baby to die.

As he watched Isabelle suck her thumb, Nicholas was surprised to find himself feeling some sense of regret that he would not be around to watch her grow. He cursed his foolishness. He had long ago given up all hope of a life with a wife and children. He'd already spent far more time in this cabin than he had planned.

But even as he mocked himself, he knew he would not feel truly free to ride west again until Bethie and her baby were somewhere safe, perhaps with her family back in Paxton. The last thing he wanted to do was to ride east; the very idea left him feeling trapped, smothered, agitated. And he tried one last time to tell himself that the two of them were not his problem. But gazing upon the newborn baby's sweet face, watching Bethie sleep, he knew he could not abandon them.

Then Isabelle's thumb escaped her, and she began to cry.

"Is she hungry?" Bethie's sleepy voice interrupted his thoughts. She lay on her side facing him, concern in her eyes.

"I was hoping to lull her back to sleep so that you could rest."

She gave him a weak smile, tried to sit.

"Let me help you up." He rose, walked to the bed, tucked little Isabelle into the fold of one arm, held out the other.

"I can do it." She pushed herself up, winced.

She'd be sore for a long time, Nicholas knew. That part of a woman's body was very tender, exquisitely sensitive. He'd seen what Isabelle's birth had done to Bethie.

And men thought *they* were brave.

Nicholas slipped a pillow behind Bethie's back as she undid the front of her gown. Then he placed her baby daughter in her arms.

Bethie bared a creamy breast, tickled Isabelle's cheek with a rosy nipple, gasped when the baby latched on and began to suckle.

A torrent of tangled emotions surged up from Nicholas's gut, so intense and raw that he wasn't even sure what he was feeling. Sexual attraction? He must be an animal to think of sex knowing how much Bethie had just suffered. Regret that he would be leaving them soon? 'Twas best for them. He was no longer a gentleman and could only bring them grief. The desire to be a husband and father? The kind of life he led was unfit for women and children. Envy that he wasn't Isabelle's father? Clearly, he was out of his damned mind.

He felt sweat bead on his forehead, felt his heart pound. He turned his back, walked away, and, needing something to do, took up the poker and jabbed angrily at the fire.

"Nicholas?" Her voice was sweet, like music.

"Aye."

"Thank you."

He said nothing.

"If no' for you, I dinnae think I'd have made it. You were my anchor. You saved Isabelle. You saved us both."

He fought to subdue the maelstrom inside him, forced himself to speak. "I'm glad I was able to help."

"How did you know what to do?"

He hadn't spoken of his past to anyone, not for six long years. He hesitated, feeling that he stood upon some kind of perilous edge. "I . . . used to breed horses. The same thing sometimes happens with foals. It can be fatal."

"You must think me weak and cowardly. I—I couldna help cryin' out."

There was shame in her voice.

He turned to face her. "No, Bethie. You were very brave."

She started to say something else, but he could take no more.

"I'll be outside if you need me." With that, he turned and strode out into the darkness.

# Chapter 7

Bethie stirred shavings of lye soap into the steaming cauldron, careful to keep the hems of her skirts away from the fire. The sun was shining brightly today, not a cloud in the April sky, and with the warm spring breeze the laundry would dry in no time.

In the month since little Belle's birth, laundry had become an almost daily chore. There were Belle's many diaper cloths. There were also the linen cloths Bethie used to staunch her flow. There were bed linens stained with blood and milk and Bethie's shifts, which, too, were stained.

Nicholas had cleaned and rehung the heavy iron cauldron, which was suspended over a fire pit dug midway between the cabin and barn. Now Bethie was able to boil a large amount of laundry at once. There was only so much she could do over the hearth fire, and it took time away from cooking.

She reached down, picked up the pile of bloodstained linens, dropped them in the cauldron, glad Nicholas was off in the forest setting his traps and not here to see them. She felt somehow uncomfortable that he should see something so private. And yet hadn't he seen everything?

Aye, he had. He had even put his fingers inside her.

Heat rushed into Bethie's face, and her stomach turned.

She fought the nausea, fought the clammy sense of dread that threatened to close over her. Nicholas was nothing like her stepbrother. He was nothing like Richard Sorley. He'd done what he'd done for her sake and that of her baby, not to slake his own lust.

She stirred the contents of the cauldron, forced her mind along different paths.

Nicholas was unlike any man she had known. He was a big man and strong, like her stepfather, but, although he smiled but rarely and was not a man of many words, he did not use his strength in fits of violence. Though he was more thoughtful than Andrew, he was also stronger and more virile, a man for whom hard work offered no challenge. And though he was but a trapper, he spoke in surprisingly cultured tones.

How unexpected that he, a rough stranger from the wild, had been her lifeline during her travail, his encouraging words and the soothing tone of his voice her only comfort. For so gruff and cold a man, he'd been surprisingly gentle and caring, and she remembered him calling her "love" more than once.

"Bethie, love," he'd said.

She knew he hadn't meant it, that he'd simply been trying to console her in her desperation. But the sound of those words on his lips filled her memory.

In the days following the birth he'd become withdrawn again, distant and pensive. That didn't mean he'd been rude to her. Far from it. He'd taken over the man's chores about the farm, chopping and hauling wood, seeing to the bigger animals, repairing the leaky barn roof. He'd fixed the window he had ruined and built a shutter inside the cabin to prevent anyone else from doing what he had done. He'd even brought down a yearling buck, the first venison Bethie had tasted in many months.

She was grateful for all of this, but other things he'd done had touched her even more. The day after the birth, he'd cleaned the old wooden washtub, carried it into the cabin, filled it with hot water so that she could soak her pain away. How had he known that sitting and using the chamber pot were excruciating for her or that hot water would help her feel better? Now bathing was a pleasure she enjoyed almost every evening.

When her milk had come in and her breasts had grown hard and painful, he'd given her heated cloths to press against them though she'd not complained. And when her nipples had become chapped and sore from nursing, he'd shared a special ointment with her, one that magically relieved the pain and quickly healed them.

He had shown her every kindness a woman could hope for from a husband, and yet he was not her husband. Nor was he Belle's father, though clearly he was besotted with the baby. He had taken an old wooden chest, strengthened it, built legs for it, turning it into a little cradle, which he'd lined with soft rabbit fur. And just last night he'd presented Bethie with two pairs of moccasins that he'd made from the salvaged leather of his ruined breeches—one lined with gray rabbit fur that fit her and another pair so tiny that the sight of them had made her laugh. They, too, were lined with soft fur, and though they were the smallest pair of shoes Bethie had ever seen, they were still too large for her newborn daughter.

"Room to grow," he'd said, before turning and heading silently back outside.

Still, Nicholas was a man, and she could not deny the sense of danger, the darkness that seemed to surround him like a shadow, despite his kindness. At times, she felt him watching her, felt his gaze upon her. And once in a while he would brush against her by accident, or his hand would touch hers by mistake, leaving her unsettled. She didn't exactly fear him, and she knew he would not deliberately hurt her. But she didn't feel at ease around him, either.

Bethie set her stirring stick aside, smoothed her skirts, walked back toward the cabin to check on Belle, the soft feel of fur against her feet. She'd never had moccasins before. Her stepfather would have considered them sinful, as they came from the heathen Indian. And Andrew had no skill to make such things. For most of her life, her shoes had been nothing more than smooth blocks of wood with a leather shell nailed on top. Moccasins were much warmer, much more agreeable to her feet.

Inside the cabin, Bethie found Belle peacefully asleep in her cradle, her wee fists pressed to her chubby cheeks. Bethie's heart swelled with love. Though she had known she would feel affection for her child, she hadn't expected to love her so fiercely that it stole her breath and made her heart ache. From her tiny eyelashes to her wee toes, Belle was perfect. And she was Bethie's to love and to care for, someone who needed Bethie and would grow to love her in return.

It was strange to think that Isabelle was also Andrew's baby. Belle's skin was fairest cream, her hair soft gold, while Andrew's complexion had been ruddy, his hair sandy brown. With a shock, Bethie found herself struggling to remember his face.

Silently, she chided herself, ashamed. Andrew had been a kind husband. He had rescued her from a life of misery and shame. He had forgiven her unspeakable taint. He had never hurt her or raised his voice at her. And only rarely had he taken his pleasure with her.

"I must have sons, Bethie, lass," he would say by way of apology. Then he would reach for her in the dark, lift her gown, climb upon her, finish silently and quickly.

Bethie had not enjoyed it, but then she couldn't imagine any woman did. Hadn't her mother said as much? "'Tis a Christian wife's duty, though it often seems a curse," she'd said on the day Bethie had left to become Andrew's wife. And so Bethie had never complained, had never refused him. It was his due as her husband, and her feelings about it mattered little.

Bethie said a silent prayer for Andrew's soul, added more wood to the fire. Then she picked up a large wooden bowl, checked on Belle one last time, and started toward the river. She needed more moss to line the baby's diaper cloths. If she was lucky, she might even find milkweed pods from last fall. Once the seeds were removed, the silk would make an even softer lining than moss.

It was truly a lovely day. Birds filled the sky, and the forest was rich with their tuneful chatter. Violets and bluebells bloomed beneath her feet, and a green mist of newborn leaves hovered on the branches of the trees. As she walked along the path to the river, Bethie found herself wondering when she'd last felt this carefree or happy.

Only one thing marred her joy—the knowledge that Nicholas would soon be leaving.

As disturbing as he might be, she was all but certain he would not go back on his word. He would not harm her or Belle. And he would protect them from any man who tried to do so. As long as he was with her, she'd be as safe as any woman could be in this untamed land.

But she could tell he felt restless. He seemed distracted, overwrought, as if many matters weighed on his mind. She realized she knew nothing about him—where he'd come from, whether he'd truly lived with the Indians, whether he had a wife and children waiting for him somewhere. She tried to forgive herself if in moments of fear she hoped there was no one waiting for him, wished he had no other life to return to, for she could only stay here as long as he remained.

Yet his mind seemed to stray far from here. She could see it in the way his gaze always sought the dark wall of the forest, in the tense lines of his face and the impatience that seemed to boil beneath his skin. Now that he was again hale and hearty, there was no reason for him to stay. And that meant the uncertain future Bethie had been trying so hard to avoid was drawing closer.

Nicholas let cold river water run over his naked body, welcomed its invigorating chill. He was beginning to feel strong again. Though he hadn't recovered his full strength, he was no longer out of breath or dizzy. His injured leg was healing, as well, thanks to the salve Takotah had taught him to make long ago. And although it still hurt to walk or sit a horse, he was certain the wound would eventually heal completely.

He waded back to the riverbank, startled a breeding pair of mallards from the shelter of new reeds, reached for the leather pouch he'd dropped there. He dug to the bottom, withdrew soap and a sharpened knife. He spread the soap on his face, scraped the knife over his skin with quick strokes, felt the day's growth of whiskers give way.

It was strange to shave regularly now when he had forsaken the habit for almost six years. He didn't want to think about what had motivated him to start again—or admit that Bethie's reaction when she'd first seen him clean-shaven had affected him. His shaving was a whim, nothing more.

He rinsed his face, took up the soap again, began to wash his body.

The river was running high and fast this year. Heavy snows had fallen in the mountains this past winter, and he expected that by the middle of next month, the river would overflow its banks. He'd have to wait to take Bethie back east until the middle of June. They had several rivers and creeks to cross to reach Paxton, and he wouldn't risk losing her or the baby to the raging waters of the freshet.

Of course, he hated to wait that long. Spring had brought new life, but by summertime the Ohio wilderness would again be rank with death. He didn't want Bethie and Belle anywhere near here when the Indians attacked. Even Paxton was too far west for his tastes. He'd rather see her settled in Philadelphia, which enjoyed the protection of an entire British garrison. But she belonged with her family, so he would take her to Paxton.

Still, the delay gave her time to heal. Already much of her strength had returned, though she tired easily due to night feedings and she hadn't yet stopped bleeding.

He hadn't discussed his plan with her yet, but he was certain she'd be grateful for his help in returning home. He knew she was afraid to be here, knew it hadn't been her idea to come here in the first place. He remembered the look of terror on her face when she'd turned, her arms full of firewood, and discovered him outside her cabin that first morning. It was only a matter of time before that scenario played itself out again, only next time the man on the horse would be someone else.

Aye, she'd be grateful to be safely at home again.

God's blood, but he couldn't quit thinking of her. He'd believed her lovely before, but now she was positively breathtaking. Her waistline was pleasingly slender again, her hips rounded, her breasts full with milk. And she glowed with love for little Belle, happiness shining on her sweet face like a sunrise.

Unnerved by his reaction to her, he'd been doing his best to keep his distance. Fortunately, she seemed to want to stay as far away from him as possible. Skittish, easily startled, she pulled away from him any time he accidentally touched her, as if even the brush of his hand against hers unsettled her. How she could still fear him he knew not, but he'd begun to suspect her husband was the kind of man who hurt women. It gave Nicholas yet another reason to despise him.

Still, Nicholas supposed her fearfulness was for the best. If he were left to follow his own impulses, she'd soon have another babe in her belly. More than once, he'd found himself wanting to kiss the plush curve of her lips, to run his fingers through the long silk of her golden hair, to cup the soft weight of her breasts in his hands, savor their rosy tips, taste their milky nectar. But he tried to slam the door on such thoughts the instant they arose. To give in to such fantasies would only make his need for her worse. Already his body was growing persistent, demanding. He felt like a boy of seventeen again, his cock hard more often than not.

And if there were moments late at night when he watched Bethie nurse her baby in the light of the hearth and wished for all the world both mother and child were his? 'Twas only proof that he had not been himself of late.

Bethie was no whore who earned her living off of men's lust. And lust was all Nicholas could ever truly give her. As soon as he could safely see Bethie and her baby girl to her family's farm, he'd take his leave of them and return to the only life he was fit to live.

Bethie worked her way down the riverbank, keeping a safe distance from the swirling waters as she peeled soft moss from the earth and placed it in her bowl. She walked quietly, warily, remembering the war party that had passed this way only weeks ago. But the air was so sweet and the singing of the birds so lovely that she could not linger on dark thoughts.

On impulse she began to pick the wild violets that grew beneath the trees. They would make a pretty bouquet for the table. Or perhaps she would tie them at the head of Belle's cradle. She followed the violets around a bend in the river, picking them in clusters of purple, white, and yellow, when a movement caught her eye.

Heart in her throat, she froze.

*Nicholas.*

He stood with his back to her in the river just around the bend, water up to the middle of his thighs.

And he was completely naked.

She meant to avert her eyes, to turn away, to flee before he saw her. But she could scarce breathe, much less move. She had never seen a fully naked man before. Oh, aye, she'd cared for Andrew in his illness and after death. But he had not looked anything like . . . this.

Nicholas's body was all muscle, lean and hard. His thighs were heavy and corded, his bum twin mounds of smooth muscle that tightened and released as he moved his weight from one leg to the other. Dark, wet hair clung to his skin, hung down his powerful back all the way to his narrow hips. The muscles of his arms and shoulders bulged and stretched as he washed himself. His skin, bronzed from the sun, was slick and wet.

'Twas like stumbling upon some heathen river god.

Bethie stood as if under a spell, her mind beyond fear or reason. And although some part of her knew what she was doing was wrong and sinful, she could not make herself turn away. Never would she have imagined that she could find a man beautiful. Yet beautiful he was.

Time was measured in heartbeats as she stood, watched.

And then it happened. She could not say when, but suddenly she became aware that he was looking straight at her.

Blue eyes.

Even at this distance, they pierced her.

She felt naked. And although she knew she should turn away, apologize, leave him in peace, she continued to stare. Against her will, her gaze dropped from his bonny face to his broad chest, with its sprinkling of dark hair and wine-dark nipples tight from the chilly water. Then, as if by some deviltry, her gaze was drawn down along a trail of hair to his rippled belly and then, farther still, to his sex.

Bethie felt her womb clench.

Bereft of thought, of breath, she stared at what she had never seen in the light before. To her eyes, he seemed huge, his shaft thick and heavy, his stones full and nestled in dark curls.

Heat and heaviness seemed to spread through her belly, a

new sensation and more than a little frightening. She meant to look away, tried to look away, but his raw maleness enticed her, called to her.

And some unknown part of her answered.

Her gaze moved up his body again—and she saw them.

Countless scars.

Ridges and rings of pinched, puckered skin, they dotted his belly and chest, reached around his side. They looked like burns long-healed. And spread in a pattern as they were, they could not be the result of an accident.

Someone had done this to him. Someone had hurt him terribly.

The horror of it broke the spell.

She gasped. Shame flooded her, and she lifted her gaze to meet his impenetrable stare.

"I'm sorry! Forgi'e me!"

She took two steps backward, then turned and ran back to the cabin.

Nicholas shut the barn door, leaned against it, looked up at the clear night sky. A thousand points of silver light spread across the black velvet heavens. But their beauty held no comfort for him tonight.

He ought to have expected it. Women were repulsed by his scars. He knew that. Even the most baseborn whore stared at his body with loathing. He had learned long ago not to care.

Why, then, had Bethie's reaction cut him to the quick?

Because he'd seen desire in her eyes, and like a fool he had dared to hope.

He hadn't heard her approach—itself an oddity. He'd turned to find her staring at him as if she'd never seen a naked man before, a look of feminine need blatant upon her face. Only the chilly water had kept him from becoming hard as granite.

Her gaze had traveled over every inch of him in seemingly innocent appraisal, her eyes growing wide at the sight of his penis. He might have preferred that her first sight of him come elsewhere, out of the icy stream, which tended to humble and wither a man. Still, he'd seen appreciation on her face.

It had been so long since a woman had gazed upon him with anything other than revulsion. Raw hunger for her had surged through his veins, and for a moment he'd considered going to her, ripping away her gown, and pleasuring her right there on the damp moss. He'd known he could not take her in the normal way, as she was still healing. But there were many ways to please a woman, many ways he could find release with her. And he'd been willing to use them all. Hell, he'd have been happy to forgo his own orgasm for the sheer pleasure of watching her face as she climaxed.

But even as he'd been about to take a step toward her, the passion had fled her face and was replaced by a look of horror. And she had turned away from him and run.

She had avoided him all day and into the afternoon, unable to look him in the eye. She'd barely spoken as they'd eaten their evening meal, had seemed nervous, uneasy, her cheeks stained with color. Perhaps she was simply embarrassed to have come upon him when he was unclothed. Or perhaps the record of violence, carved into his flesh, frightened and sickened her.

Why did it matter? As soon as he delivered her to her family, he'd bid her farewell and ride into the west. He'd never see her or Belle again. What she thought of him would not matter then, so it should not matter now.

That was what he told himself, but that was not how he felt. And he cursed himself again for his irrational thoughts. His desire for her was clouding his mind. It was time he began making serious plans for taking Bethie back to her family, not only for her sake and that of her baby, but for his own, as well.

And if she didn't want to leave?

Unthinkable. No woman would choose to stay out here.

He strode to the cabin, resolved to put other thoughts behind him and begin discussing plans with her tonight. But when he opened the door, he found her lying sound asleep on her bed, little Belle asleep beside her.

He lifted the covers over them, added wood to the fire, pulled in the door string. Planning would have to wait for morning.

# Chapter 8

Bethie tried to keep the shock from her face, put down her spoon, and buried her hands in her apron to hide their sudden trembling.

Nicholas continued to speak. "We dare not tarry. If we leave by the beginning of June, we should be able to reach Paxton by the first week of July."

Her heart beat so fiercely she could scarce hear his final words. Her mind was fixed on one thought only: He wanted to take her to Paxton. He wanted to take her back to Malcolm Sorley, back to Richard, back to the mother who hated her, back to the hell that had once been her life.

*I will no' go! I cannae go!*

Even as the panic cut off her breath, shards of hope, like shafts of sunshine, broke through her sundered thoughts.

Four long years had gone by, years of war and deprivation. She couldn't be sure her family still lived on the farm. Perhaps they had fled farther east to avoid the slaughter.

For that matter, she couldn't be certain Malcolm and Richard were still alive. And even if they were, there was every chance that Richard, who was a good ten years older than she, had married and gone off to farm his own land. That would still leave Malcolm to contend with, but he no longer ruled her. Bethie was now a grown woman and a widow, not a defenseless young girl.

Besides, she didn't have to go all the way to Paxton. She could ask Nicholas to leave her at one of the forts or settlements along the way. He held no power over her. He could not force her to go to Paxton. And yet she knew she ought to be grateful. He was offering her his help in escaping the frontier—no small favor.

"Bethie?" The sound of his voice pulled her from her thoughts. He sat across from her, gazed at her with those piercing blue eyes, his dark brows furrowed.

Unable to bear his scrutiny, she stood, her breakfast uneaten, and busied herself mindlessly at the hearth, her back to him. She tried to keep her voice cheerful, free of the sickness that gnawed at her stomach. "Isabelle is too little to travel, nor can I yet make the journey. And you can scarce sit a horse such a long way with your leg still healin'."

She heard the scrape of his chair on the wooden floor, knew he stood right behind her. "Another month is more than enough time. We cannot remain longer than is necessary. I've told you why."

Aye, he'd told her the Indians had banded together in hopes of driving settlers back over the mountains. 'Twas every settler's greatest fear. "Y-you said they wouldna attack yet, that they are gathering to the north."

"Aye, but they will come. They will not leave this valley in peace. 'Tis their hunting grounds, the land of their grandfathers, and they want it back. You must seek safety with your family."

Bethie choked back a panic-stricken laugh, felt tears fill her eyes. She wanted to scream, to shout at him, to tell him there was no safety anywhere near Malcolm Sorley or his accursed son, but she could say nothing without revealing her shame.

"Bethie?" The tone of his voice told her he could see her distress. "What is it?"

"What is what?" Dismayed that he was able to perceive so much, she snapped at him. "I dinnae know what you're bletherin' about, Master Kenleigh."

"I think you do."

She sought for excuses, kept her back to him, blinked her tears away. "'Tis such a long journey, and . . . it pains me to think of leavin' the home I shared with Andrew."

'Twas a lie, of course, but she had to say something.

"You loved him?"

The question took her by surprise. She hesitated. Loved Andrew? Certainly, she'd come to feel affection for him and gratitude. He had rescued her from hell, shown her kindness, and he hadn't hurt her in any way. "H-he was my husband."

"I'm sorry." Nicholas didn't sound particularly sorry.

But when she at last turned to face him, she saw an emotion in his eyes that might have been concern. He lifted a hand, cupped her cheek, his gaze locked with hers. His touch was warm, a gentle caress, and for the space of a heartbeat the storm inside her stilled. Then her mind flashed on the image of him standing naked in the river, so breathtakingly male, and her gaze dropped first to his lips, then farther still to the wedge of dark hair revealed by the loose ties of his shirt.

And suddenly it was too much—her family, Indians, Nicholas. She took an instinctive step backward. She needed to get away from him until she was herself again. With a quick glance to make certain Isabelle was safe in her cradle, Bethie picked up the water pail, and almost ran to the door. "I'll be needin' water for dishes."

She'd just stepped outside when something hit her hard from behind, threw her onto her stomach on the ground, knocked the air from her lungs. A hard body held her down, and she both felt and heard the cloth of her skirts being ripped from her.

Lacking breath to scream, she kicked, fought, tried in vain to roll away.

This could not be happening! She would not let it happen! Not again!

"Damn it, Bethie! Stop!"

The panic she had suppressed moments earlier surged through her with renewed strength, and she was blind to all else. Air at last filled her aching lungs, and she screamed. "Stop!"

But his strength was unyielding. Strong arms forced her roughly onto her back, and the weight of his body held her fast.

Then suddenly he released her.

She crawled quickly away, sobbing for breath, then turned and stared in horror at the man she had almost come to trust.

And then she saw.

Beside him on the ground lay a large piece of cloth, gray woolen cloth from her skirts. It was scorched black and smoldering. The front of his shirt was also scorched. The sharp smell of burnt wool hung in the air between them.

Her gaze rose until it met his.

"Your skirts . . . on fire." His chest rose and fell as he caught his breath. "Are you hurt?"

She couldn't hear his question, began to tremble uncontrollably.

Alarmed by her silence, Nicholas crawled to her, lifted what was left of her torn and scorched skirts, ran his hands over her slender legs, searched them for burns. Her skin was soft and creamy white, unscathed by the flames. And he realized as she stared at him in shocked silence that it was not the knowledge that her skirts had been on fire that made her tremble.

"Bethie." He pulled her against his chest, held her, his relief that she was safe grappling with concern for her obvious suffering. He knew it was a measure of how shaken she was that she did not try to pull away from him. Even so, he was grateful she allowed his touch. She felt soft and precious in his arms.

When he'd realized the back of her skirts was afire, he'd felt a jolt of genuine fear such as he hadn't known in years. For one horrible moment a vision had flashed into his mind's eye: Bethie on fire, her body horribly burned, her violet eyes lifeless. On raw instinct, he'd leapt after her, cast her to the ground, thrown his body on the flames to squelch them.

She'd clearly thought he was trying to hurt her.

No, she'd thought he was trying to *rape* her.

He could think of only one reason a woman would react with such intense fear, lashing out in a desperate panic. Someone had violated her before. Someone—some man—had hurt her in the worst way a man could hurt a woman. And even as the revolting thought came to him, he knew in his gut he was right.

So many things suddenly made sense to him—her skittishness, her excessive modesty during Isabelle's birth, her decision to sleep fully clothed, to drug him and tie him to the bed. She so greatly feared a man's touch that she had all but stepped into the hearth fire to avoid him, for God's sake!

Nicholas found himself itching to bury his knife in the whoreson who had placed such fear in her. Had it perhaps been her husband? Nicholas didn't believe for one moment she had loved the man despite what she'd said earlier. She hadn't called her husband's name once as she'd labored to bring forth his child, hadn't mentioned him as she'd held little Isabelle in her arms for the first time. In truth, for a woman recently widowed, she seemed remarkably unburdened by grief. Perhaps her husband had been the sort of brute who took the notion of wifely duty too seriously and had forced Bethie to submit to his lust. If so, she was well rid of him.

Or perhaps it had been marauding Indians. Aye, perhaps that was it. Nicholas had seen her reaction when he'd told her that Obwandiyag of the Ottawa, known to her as Pontiac, was gathering all of the tribes in the region to his side for a renewed war on settlers. The color had drained from her face. Her breathing had become erratic, shallow, and her hands had begun to shake, just as she trembled now.

Nicholas ignored the voice that warned him to keep his distance, held her closer, overcome by a rush of tenderness for her. He fought to keep the anger that seethed inside him from his voice. "I frightened you. I'm sorry. I didn't have time to explain. In a moment you'd have been engulfed by flames."

"I—I'm sorry. I didna mean . . . I didna know . . . I thought . . ." She shivered.

"I know."

"Th-thank you, Nicholas. If you hadna—"

"Shhh, love. It's over."

He heard her gasp, felt her hands tug on his shirt.

She pulled away from him, looked up at him, her eyes wide. "You've been burned!"

He could feel the sting, but it was little worse than the pain of sunburn. "'Tis nothing, Bethie, truly."

But she was already on her feet and tugging on him to follow her toward the well. "Come. We'll put cold water on it."

Nicholas stood, followed, mostly because he liked the feel of her small hand in his.

"Take off your shirt." She released his hand, began to draw water from the well.

He hesitated for a moment, aware that he would be baring his scars to her again, then did as she asked, strangely pleased by the worry on her face.

Bethie grabbed the ruined shirt from his hands, dipped it in the full bucket, squeezed it out, her gaze dropping to his reddened chest. Regret coursed through her. When had she last done something so stupid? Even the littlest girl knew better than to drag her hems too close to the hearth. "Oh, this is my fault! If I hadna been so careless—"

"It's not bad. Don't blame—"

She pressed the sodden cloth against the hard wall of his reddened chest and belly, heard his quick intake of breath, felt his muscles jerk in response. "Oh, I'm sorry! I dinnae mean to hurt you!"

His chuckle surprised her, and she looked up to see not a look of pain on his face, but a smile, his white teeth a sharp contrast to his dark hair and skin. "You didn't. It was the shock of cold water, nothing more."

She bit her lip and, unable to bear the penetrating warmth of his gaze, looked at the backs of her own hands, suddenly aware how close to him she stood. Heat, like that of a fever, radiated off his body and through the wet cloth, seeming to seep into her. Beneath her left hand, she could feel the ridges and valleys of his abdomen, the slow rhythm of his breathing, beneath her right, the firm planes of his chest and the steady beating of his heart.

But she could feel something else, as well—the puckered crests of countless scars. Some were round and looked like burns, pinched circles of colorless flesh. Those she had seen from a distance yesterday. Others appeared to be cut marks, thin lines of faded silver against his sun-browned skin. Not only did they cover his chest, but also his sides, disappearing behind the muscled strength of his arms. She didn't have to look to know she'd find them on his back, as well.

Without thinking, she reached with her right hand, gently

ran her fingers over one of the burn marks, her heart filled with compassion for him. "Such cruelty! Who did this to you?"

Silence stretched between them, interrupted only by the chorus of countless songbirds.

"The Wyandot." His voice was rough, strained. "I was taken captive years ago."

She looked up, saw the bleakness in his eyes, and his words of weeks ago came back to her.

*'Tis only pain.*

At last she understood. He hadn't feared the heated blade because he'd already survived much worse. The Indians had tormented him with fire, had forced him to endure untold pain.

*And yet he willingly threw himself on my burnin' skirts to save me.*

She felt tears prick her eyes, wanted to speak, to offer him some comfort, to thank him, but at that moment, Isabelle began to cry. "Belle."

"Aye. Go to her."

But just before she turned, she caught in his eyes a glimpse of anguish so deep that it nearly broke her heart.

Nicholas stacked another load of firewood in his arms, struggled to make sense of his own feelings, tried to understand what had happened this morning.

He hadn't spoken of the Wyandot to anyone since he'd left home, had barely spoken of them to his family. He had tried to put those ceaseless hours of unbearable agony—and the even worse horror that had followed—behind him, hoping through his own silence to somehow silence his memories. He had ignored curious glances, overlooked surprised gasps, pretended not to hear even the most pointed questions. Until today.

Why was Bethie different? Why had the gentle brush of her fingers over his chest drawn the air from his lungs? Why had her soft words loosed his tongue?

He had expected to see disgust or pity in her eyes, as he thought he'd seen the day before when she'd watched him at the river. Instead he'd seen compassion and the bright sheen of tears. It had disarmed him, opened a gaping fissure inside him, and for a moment the darkness within him had seemed nigh to escaping. He'd wanted to push her away, but had found he could not.

'Twas the first time in six long years a woman had touched him of her own choosing and not for the pelts he could give her. And it had scorched him to his core.

Aye, he cared about Bethie. He couldn't deny that. Nor could he deny that his desire for her was growing. But she had her own shadows. Someone had abused her, had taught her that a man's caress was hateful, a thing to be feared, not savored. And what a shame it was. A woman as beautiful and sweet as Bethie was made for pleasure.

Suddenly Nicholas found himself wishing he could be the man who healed that deep hurt and initiated her into the delights of sex. How he longed to be the one to awaken her desire, to drive her hunger to a fever pitch, to make her cry out in delight. How he ached to sheathe himself inside her and feel her melt around him as one climax after the next claimed her. The thought of it sent blood rushing to his cock, made him harder than the firewood in his arms. And even as the idea came to him, even as a part of him rejected it wholly, he began to wonder how he might accomplish this.

Could he, who trusted no one, win her trust? Could he, with his scarred body, heal the wounds hidden within hers? Could he as a man heal the pain caused by another man?

He knew there was passion inside her, knew she felt some attraction to him. He'd seen it on her face yesterday as she'd watched him bathe. He'd seen it this morning in the way her eyes had grown dark and her breath had quickened as she'd held the wet shirt against his chest. Even the sight of his scars had not banished the look of feminine need on her face this time. But how could he show her that it was safe to touch him, to want him, to give herself to him when such feelings clearly made her afraid?

As he might gentle a timid mare, he would have to approach her with kind words and soft caresses that would not provoke her fear. He would have to control himself, to rein in his desire, so as not to frighten her with the force of his own need. He would have to win her trust and arouse her slowly.

He would have to wait until her hunger was such that she overcame her fear, came to him, begged him to please her.

And then, when she lay sleepy and sated in his arms, what would he do? Call it a fair trade? Turn Zeus's reins to the west and ride away? Leave her to whichever man claimed her next?

Bethie deserved better than that. She deserved the love of a husband, a man to protect her and watch over her and Belle and the other children she would bear. And Nicholas knew he could not be that man. He did not deserve to be that man. Sooner or later, the darkness inside him would drive him back into the wild, back to the vast emptiness where he could forget.

'Twas far better never to touch her than to risk hurting her.

Yet even as he acknowledged this, he knew that unless she stopped him, he *would* touch her. He would run his fingers through the sun-drenched silk of her hair. He would kiss her lips, savor their fullness with his tongue. He would feel the velvet of her nipples grow hard beneath his palms. He would part her thighs, taste her sweetness, bury himself in her liquid heat, feel her muscles clench in climax as they milked him to orgasm.

Such thoughts did nothing to quiet his erection, which strained against the leather of his breeches until he felt he might burst. Unable to do a damned thing about it, he strode to the cabin, his arms full, and nudged the door open with his boot.

Bethie sat in the rocking chair, humming a quiet lullaby to the baby at her breast. She did not look up, but gazed down at her daughter, a look of dreamy happiness on her sweet face.

He walked to the hearth, stacked the firewood as quietly as possible, closed the door, drew in the string. Since the night Isabelle was born, he'd taken to sleeping in the cabin again, and Bethie had not asked him to leave. If he'd possessed any sense, he would already have moved his bedroll back into the barn, where the sight and scent of her would not taunt him. Clearly, he was an idiot. Without glancing in her direction again, he strode to his bedroll in the corner and lay down to try to sleep.

But his body was tense with unspent energy, taut with lust, and sleep would not come. Cursing silently, he reached into one of his bags, dug around until his fingers closed over hard leather. Then he withdrew the book he'd purchased on a whim last time he'd been in Philadelphia, the latest satire by that French fellow Voltaire. But though the words danced on the page before his eyes, in his mind he could see only Bethie.

Bethie laid Isabelle in her cradle, pulled the soft furs up to her little chin, gazed longingly at her own bed. If she was lucky, Belle would awaken only once tonight and she could get some sleep.

She began to fasten the front of her gown, but stopped. With the arrival of spring, sleeping in her clothes had become uncomfortably warm. When Andrew was alive, she'd slept in her shift. But she hadn't dared to do so since. First, she'd been alone and afraid to be caught unprepared by some danger. Then Nicholas had come out of the forest, and she'd been afraid to do anything that might draw his attention.

But hadn't he proved himself to be trustworthy? Hadn't he slept in the cabin for more than a month now without once trying to creep into her bed? Besides, there was no reason for him to see her. She could disrobe now while he was asleep, then wait under her covers until he had risen in the morning. She would be so much more comfortable without the bulk of her gown, and it would be easier to nurse Isabelle.

Her mind made up, Bethie unbuttoned her gown—she'd had to switch to her old gown of homespun because the fire had ruined her newer gray gown—and draped it over one of the chairs. Clad only in her shift, she turned to check the fire, found it already banked. Next, she went to check the door, found the string pulled in. Fresh water sat in a bucket on the table, ready for her should she grow thirsty in the night from nursing. It seemed Nicholas had taken care of everything before he'd gone to sleep.

Stifling a yawn, she turned back toward her bed, gasped.

Clad only in breeches, Nicholas lay on his side on his bedroll, propped up on one elbow, his blue eyes looking straight at her.

# Chapter 9

"I—I thought you were asleep." Bethie instinctively crossed her arms to shield her breasts, feeling suddenly naked in her shift.

He said nothing, but continued to watch her, the skin of his bare chest golden in the firelight.

Then she saw the book in his hands. For a moment she did not quite comprehend, and then she gaped at him, astonished. "You can read!"

The corners of his lips turned up in a slight smile. "Aye."

Forgetting her state of undress, she asked the first thing that came to mind. "How did you learn?"

He seemed to hesitate. "My parents wished me to have an education."

It was the first time she could recall him speaking about his family. She knew so little about him—only that he lived in the wild as a trapper, had been captured and tormented by Indians, and had probably once fought against them. Yet there was clearly so much more to Nicholas than he revealed. His manner of speech, so refined for a soldier and trapper, told her that if nothing else. And now she knew he could read.

Curious, she wanted to know more. "Where did you grow up?"

Slowly, he sat up, his gaze fixed on her, book still in hand, the muscles of his abdomen and chest shifting as he moved. With his long, dark hair spilling over one shoulder almost to the floor, he looked every bit the Indian, apart from his blue eyes.

Bethie took one step backward, forgot her question, alarmed as much by the strange fluttery feeling in her belly as by the heat in his eyes.

"Would you like me to teach you?"

"Teach me?"

"To read."

Learn to read? 'Twas something she'd never dreamt of doing. Neither of her parents had been able to read, and though her father had often spoken of sending his daughter to the nearby minister's home for teaching, her mother had needed her help about the farm and had refused to spare her. Malcolm could read and had insisted that Richard learn his letters so that he could read the Bible, but he'd kept Bethie at home because she was a girl.

Was Nicholas, almost a stranger to her, truly offering her this gift? "My stepfather says readin' is a skill wasted on women."

The flash of anger in Nicholas's eyes was unmistakable. "Your stepfather is a bloody idiot."

She gasped to hear Malcolm Sorley spoken of with such casual contempt. No one had dared speak ill of him—until now. Why did the words frighten her? Did she expect him to storm through the door to punish her? Malcolm was nowhere near here.

She released the breath she hadn't realized she'd been holding. "You would teach me? Truly?"

"'Tis no more than the kindness you've shown me, helping me when I was injured, tending my horse, sharing your hearth and home." His voice was velvet, as dark and deep as midnight.

She felt heat rise into her cheeks. "You repaid that debt many times over the night Isabelle was born."

"There are no debts between us, Bethie, no ledger to tally ere we leave this valley. You have shown me kindness, and I would but do the same. I'll teach you to read, and one day you can teach Isabelle."

She glanced at Isabelle, who slept soundly in her cradle, imagined one day sharing such knowledge with her daughter.

*A skill wasted on women.*

The thrill of rebellion stirred her blood. She met Nicholas's gaze. "Aye, Nicholas. I'd be most grateful."

Bethie dipped the quill, which Nicholas had fashioned from a goose feather, into the clay pot of red dye she'd made of madder root, and tried to form the letters that spelled her name. *E-L-S-P-E-T-H.*

The watery dye sank quickly into the parchment of birch bark Nicholas had prepared for her, but left enough of a crimson stain for him to read what she'd written. She looked up at him, hoping to see in his eyes that she'd done it right.

He sat on her left, his hands busy cleaning his pistol. He glanced down at the parchment, met her gaze, smiled. "Perfect. Now try your surname again."

His smile seemed more dazzling to her than the warm May sunshine that streamed through the open cabin door, and she felt her breath catch and her own smile brighten.

For two weeks now she'd been studying her letters with Nicholas's help whenever she found a few spare moments—during the midday meal, after supper, just before going to sleep at night. He'd taught her the alphabet, then shown her how different letters came together to make sounds. Though the rules always seemed to change, she was learning. Watching the letters, before just strange shapes, transform into words before her eyes felt like magic. Never had she done anything so exciting.

She had to admit, if she were to be wholly honest, that it was not learning to read alone that brought her happiness, but the time she spent with Nicholas, as well. The way he spoke to her as if her thoughts mattered to him, the way he endured her many mistakes with good humor, the way he encouraged her with praise—no man had ever treated her like this.

Being near Nicholas made her feel alive in a way she had never felt before. Oh, aye, he was bonny, but he was also strong, almost frighteningly manly. One look from him was enough to make her feel as if her blood had turned to sun-warmed honey. His smiles, which seemed to come more often these days, made it hard for her to think. Even the way he moved, with the confidence and grace of a predator, affected her. She found herself searching him out with her eyes, looking for reasons to cross his path, worrying about the meals she made for him, even fretting over her hair.

Could it be that she was coming to fancy him?

She dashed the thought away, started to dip her quill again, glanced down at Belle, who had fallen asleep while nursing. She set the quill aside, used her little finger to free her nipple from Belle's mouth. "Come, little one."

Nicholas watched covertly as Bethie settled little Isabelle for a nap and walked back to the table to finish her lesson.

Blood rushed to his groin.

She'd forgotten to fasten the front of her gown, leaving the silken cleft of her breasts open to his view. It had been difficult enough to sit so close beside her as she nursed her baby, her breasts bared, her nipples puckered like sweet raspberries ripe for the picking. He'd been forced to keep his hands busy cleaning his pistols to prevent himself from touching her.

Touching her? Hell, he wanted to do a lot more than touch her. He wanted to tear off that old gown of hers, to feast on the sight of her body. He wanted to taste her skin, to lick and suck her tenderest flesh until she screamed his name. He wanted to bury himself inside her tight heat, to take her on her bed, on a pile of soft furs, on the sandy riverbank.

His cock hardened to steel, throbbed heavily against the leather of his breeches, and he found it damned near impossible to drag his gaze away from her exposed flesh to the other steel in his grasp. When had he last wanted a woman like this?

Had he felt this way for Penelope? No, he hadn't, and that was odd, considering that he had respected her wish to remain a virgin until after their wedding and had forsaken other lovers to court her. He ought to have been as randy as a bull around her, and yet it had been easy to restrain himself.

Certainly, months of solitude in the wilderness had often left him longing for the pleasures of a woman's body. But on those occasions when he had sought out female company, one woman had been as good as the next.

Now he wanted only Bethie.

He'd told himself repeatedly that his obsessive need for her was nothing more than the result of having lived away from women for so long and then having been thrust into close contact with one. He'd told himself that when he left her with her family and disappeared into the wild once more, his life would return to normal. He'd even told himself that he would forget her with time.

He hoped to Satan he was telling himself the truth.

Being near her was making his life hell. It wasn't just his extreme hunger for her that tormented him, but the way she seemed to unleash memories and feelings he'd thought far behind him. How she did this he knew not. He only knew that he had not been himself since the first moment he'd looked into her guileless violet eyes.

Still, offering to teach her to read had proved to be an inspiration. He truly enjoyed watching her learn, took pride in her quick mind, found satisfaction in teaching her something that had the power to change her life. At the same time the interaction was helping her to trust him, whether he was worthy of her trust or not. He could feel her fear of him slipping away day by day. Though she likely did not realize it, she now tolerated his casual touch—a hand on her slender shoulder, an accidental brush of his fingers against hers, the unintended press of his thigh beneath the table—without shrinking from him as she had done before.

But like a young mare gentling to the touch of her groom's hand, she was still far from ready to be ridden. If he moved too quickly, he would awaken her dormant fears, and she would pull away from him. Still, he knew she felt some attraction to him, whether she recognized it as such or not. He had not been in the wilderness so long that he did not know the scent of a woman's desire. Nor was he blind to signs of it—the way her pupils dilated when she saw him working without his shirt, the flush in her cheeks when she stood near him, the catch in her breath when his skin met hers.

But he could take her only so far. If he pushed her in any way or took advantage of her inexperience to manipulate her, he would be no better than the bastard who had hurt her. He might be able to wake her desire, but only she could claim it.

Nicholas heard the nub of her quill tap against the little

clay pot, felt his gaze drawn to her once more. Her brows were furrowed in concentration as she wrote: *S, T, E, W, A . . .*

She dipped the quill again, bit her lower lip, hesitated. Her gaze lifted from the parchment, met his, her eyes full of doubt. "'R'?"

He found himself wanting to kiss that lower lip, to run his tongue over the spot where her teeth had troubled it. "Aye."

"I cannae remember how to start it."

He stood, laid his pistol on the table, barrel facing the door, walked around behind her. Then he bent down, reached around her, took her small hand in his, began to guide her. "Like this."

Barely aware of what his fingers were writing, he let his gaze fall to the slender column of her throat, where her pulse beat a frantic rhythm beneath the satin of her skin, then drop lower to the bared swells of her breasts, which rose and fell with each rapid breath she took. She smelled of honeysuckle and sunshine. He didn't have to taste her skin to know it would be sweet.

He was certain she felt the heat between them as surely as he did, and his erection grew by another painful inch. Yet he knew he must not kiss her, not so soon, not like this.

But his lips would not be denied.

Against his will, they brushed her cheek as he spoke. "See? It's easy."

He felt a tremor run through her, heard her breath catch, saw her lips part and her lashes drift to her cheeks as her eyes closed. The quill fell from her grasp, forgotten.

"Aye. Easy." Her voice was a breathy whisper.

And even as he savored her response, even as his lips sought her throat for a second taste of sweetness, he cursed himself for playing at seduction with a vulnerable woman, a woman who deserved more than he could give her, a woman who'd already been cruelly used. Was not this scheme of his to heal her past hurt just another way of using her? Was his head so clouded by lust that he could not admit, even to himself, that he was doing this as much for his own pleasure as for hers? Were the few nights of bliss and the emotional release he could give her justification for the pain he would inevitably cause?

He knew the answer, and yet he could not stop himself. It had been so long since any woman had desired his touch, so long since he'd watched a woman melt from his kisses. The taste of her need, the scent of it, drove him to the brink. God's teeth, he wanted her!

Bethie felt the heat of him behind her. Her skin blazed white-hot where his lips had touched her. Unsure what she was doing, unable to think, she leaned back until her head rested against him. He felt so solid, so strong, while she felt weak and shaky.

Good heavens, what was happening to her?

The large hand that had held and guided hers slowly slid up her arm, caressed her through the thin wool of her old gown, leaving a hot trail of awareness as if her flesh had just been wakened to life.

Then he stood, pulled away from her, and she would later not be able to say whether he had truly moaned in frustration or whether she had imagined it.

When he spoke, his voice sounded strained. "I need to check my traps."

"Aye."

He'd taken a few steps toward the door before he stopped, spoke over his shoulder. "Your gown—you forgot to fasten it."

Bethie slipped into the warm bath, felt the day's strain melt away. Sprigs of fresh lavender floated in the water, the first from the spring garden, their sweet scent released by the hot water to tickle her nose and soothe her mind. She took up the soap and began to wash the day away.

Everything that could have gone wrong this evening had gone wrong.

Isabelle had been fussy and had wanted only to be held. Bethie had been so distracted trying to nurse a crying baby that she'd let the venison stew she'd been cooking burn and stick to the bottom of the stew pot. In her haste and frustration, she'd become careless and knocked the madder-root dye to the floor, where it had spread in a pool of crimson, leaving a bright red stain on the honey-colored wood, before sinking through a crack between the floorboards. She had just salvaged what she could of their dinner and cleaned up the mess, when Nicholas had come in from the day's chores to find her cross and flushed, trying to dish stew while bouncing a squalling baby in her arms.

He had stepped through the door, closed it, his sharp eyes seeming to take in everything at once. A faint smile had tugged at the corners of his mouth. "Shall I take her?"

He hadn't waited for an answer, but had scooped Isabelle from Bethie's arms and begun to walk the length of the cabin, crooning softly and holding the baby upright against his chest.

As if this were what she had been waiting for all along, Belle had immediately quit crying and begun to suck her thumb.

Bethie might have voiced her frustration had not the sight of Nicholas doting on her wee daughter stolen her breath. She had marveled that a man as raw as he could be so tender with a babe not his own. What had he done to enthrall them both, mother and child alike?

Somehow she'd gotten dinner on the table—venison stew, corn cakes, field greens, fresh buttermilk. She'd been able to eat despite the distraction of his presence across the table from her. But then he'd brought up the subject of leaving again, of taking her back to her family.

She had tried to ignore him, tried to change the subject, but he had persisted, watching her all the time with that piercing gaze of his.

"The river is still running high and fast, but within a week, perhaps two, it will have dropped enough to ensure safe passage. We'll stop at the nearest trading post and trade for a wagon so you need not suffer horseback the entire journey. 'Tis a long way to Paxton."

She had tried to find a way to refuse that would not arouse his suspicion or reveal her secret. "I—I'm no' ready to leave here yet. My husband—"

"Would want his wife and daughter to be safe." His blue eyes had seemed to measure her, as if he were probing for the cause of her reluctance.

Did he know she had a secret or was she just imagining it?

"And if I wish to stay longer?"

"Then you lack all sense, madam. You cannot truly wish to

remain here when you know full well that you risk death—and worse—for both yourself and Isabelle. Is not the brutality of this war written in me?"

He'd stood so abruptly his chair had toppled backward. Then he'd turned his back to her and left the cabin without a word.

Bethie had felt like crying, though she hadn't known exactly why.

"Nicholas Kenleigh. Nicholas Kenleigh." She whispered his name as if somehow the secret to her feelings for him were held within it. She spelled it in her mind—or tried to.

Why did the very sight of him make her feel this knot of longing in her belly? Why did she feel as if her blood were singing when he smiled at her? And the way she felt when he touched her, like snow melting into a tremulous trickle of water—

Was this desire?

Even as she asked the question, panic welled up in her heart at the answer.

*"You've the heart of a harlot, Bethie Stewart."*

Could it be that Malcolm Sorley had been right about her all along?

She could not desire Nicholas! Why would she desire him? She was not an innocent virgin, but a widow who had borne a child. She knew all there was to know about what went on between men and women, and she had no need for it. Not only did it not please her, but she'd found it painful.

She sank into the water, rinsed soap from her hair, tried to rinse him from her thoughts. She had just stepped from the tub and reached for the linen towel, when the door suddenly opened and Nicholas stepped inside.

# Chapter 10

She gasped, clutched the towel to her breasts.

He stood still, frozen in the open doorway. His gaze blatantly traveled the length of her body. "My apologies, Bethie. I thought you were finished. The string was out."

"I—I must have forgotten to pull it in."

The door string was their signal. If the string was in, he couldn't enter because she was in her bath. If the string was out, she was finished and he could come back inside. But she had forgotten, and now he was here, and she was naked, covered only by her hair and the small, threadbare towel.

She assumed he would leave her to dress, so she was surprised when he stepped inside and closed the door behind him. "Wh-what—"

Nicholas turned toward his bedroll in the corner, tried to act as if nothing earthshaking had just happened, and began to sort mindlessly through his gear. "Take your time, Bethie. You've nothing to fear from me."

He knew she stood rooted to the spot, almost smiled when she finally resigned herself to his presence and began to dress—hastily, from the sound of it.

He had used up the daylight scouting the riverbank and the forest around the cabin for signs of other men, white or Indian, then settled the livestock for the night. He'd been watching storm clouds gather to the north of the setting sun, his mind on the evening reading lesson, when he realized the string was already out. He'd opened the door, expecting to find Bethie sitting before the fire brushing out her long tresses as she usually did after her bath.

Now the sight of her was burned into his memory—wet hair clinging to her body, water running in rivulets down her satin skin, the swell of her breasts, the curve of her hips, the wet thatch of golden curls at the juncture of her thighs. The floor had seemed to drop out from under his feet, the air to vanish from his lungs. His cock had risen to stiff attention like a young recruit ready for battle.

He rooted among his traps and tools with no purpose, determined to show no sign that seeing her naked and dripping wet had any effect on him.

"I'm dressed."

Nicholas glanced her way. His mouth went dry.

She stood facing the fire clad only in her shift, combing the tangles from her hair. Clearly she had no idea that the firelight rendered her shift all but transparent, displaying the luscious curves beneath in tantalizing detail.

He struggled to compose himself, picked up his book, stood and faced her. "I used to brush my mother's hair at night. Sit and read, and let me take care of the snarls."

In truth, his father had held the brush, but Nicholas had often watched, as charmed by his mother's long, red-gold curls as his father had been, though not in the same way. But this was different. He did not feel a boy's innocent fascination with Bethie's long locks, but a man's knowing hunger.

Bethie looked up at him, tried to read the emotion behind his eyes, hesitated. No one had combed her hair since she was six and had learned to braid it herself. She supposed there could be no harm in this beyond the pinch she would feel when he pulled too sharply on her tangles. Then, just to be safe, she took up her shawl and wrapped it around her shoulders, hiding herself beneath a layer of wool, despite the warmth of the evening.

He pulled out a chair for her. "Sit."

She sat, traded the wooden comb for his book. He had

marked the page with a small strip of leather. She opened it, careful not to tear the page, and searched for the place where they'd left off the night before.

He sat behind her, gathered the heavy weight of her hair into his hands, lifted it over the back of her chair.

She began to read. "Candide, thus . . . driv-en out of this . . . ter-res . . ." She paused.

"Terrestrial."

"What does that mean—'terrestrial'?" She shivered as he ran the comb slowly through her wet hair.

"'Terrestrial' means 'of the Earth,' the opposite of 'heavenly.'"

What he was doing with his hands was heavenly. He worked gently to part the tangles at her sensitive nape, his fingers brushing her skin, making her scalp tighten, tingle.

"Candide, thus dr-driven out of this terrestrial . . . paradise?"

"Aye, paradise. Good." His voice was husky, deep, as he combed her hair with slow, steady strokes.

"Candide, thus driven out of this terrestrial paradise . . . rambled a long time without knowing where he went." Where was she going? What path were her feet treading tonight? She could never have imagined that having another person comb her hair could be so pleasurable. Always when her mother had done this, it had hurt, the sting sometimes enough to bring tears to her eyes.

"Good. Keep going."

"Sometimes he . . . raised . . . his eyes all be-dewed . . . with tears toward heaven, and sometimes he cast a mel . . . mel-an . . ." She felt her attention slip from the pages as his fingers slid through her tresses.

"Melancholy." His breath caressed her cheek as he leaned forward to glance at the page, and she caught his scent—leather, forest, man.

He'd been this close to her this afternoon. And he'd kissed her, his lips scorching her.

". . . melancholy look toward the . . . mag . . . ni . . . fi . . ." She wanted him to kiss her again, willed him to kiss her again, desperate to feel his lips on her skin.

"Magnificent."

But she had forgotten the book, forgotten everything except the feel of his fingers as they massaged her temples. Strong fingers, they moved in slow, deliberate circles, then delved deeply into her hair to caress her scalp.

A frisson of pure pleasure skittered along her spine.

She let the weight of her head fall back into his hands as they moved to caress her nape. A voice in her mind reminded her that she shouldn't be enjoying this. She shouldn't want this. She shouldn't want him. But she did.

Then his lips pressed a featherlight kiss against the sensitive skin beneath her ear, and she heard herself whimper.

Aware of her every breath, Nicholas felt her tremble, heard the small sound that escaped her throat. Was it desire? Or fear?

He looked for the answer on her face. Her eyes were closed, her lips parted, and even as he tasted her skin again, she tilted her head away from him, baring her throat to his kisses.

*Desire.*

Good. He didn't want to stop kissing her just now, didn't want to stop tasting her. He trailed kisses along her throat, felt the frantic rhythm of her pulse against his lips.

She whimpered but did not pull away from him.

Emboldened, he leaned farther forward, touched his lips to the corner of her mouth.

He heard her quick intake of breath, felt his stomach tighten, his erection already full and heavy.

She turned her head toward him, her lips pliant, a dreamy sigh caught in her throat.

It was all the encouragement he needed. He cupped her cheek, turned his head from side to side, brushed her lips ever so lightly with his. Then he claimed her mouth in a slow kiss.

It was a tender kiss, but the power of it was nearly his undoing. He felt another tremor pass through her, felt his body answer with a craving so potent it bordered on violence.

Her eyes flew open, their pupils dark with a woman's longing. Her hands were clenched together in her lap so tightly that her fingers were white. Even so, it did not still her trembling. "W-we shouldna be doin' this."

He pulled her hands into his, began to stroke their backs lazily with his thumbs. "Why not?"

She did not answer, but dropped her gaze to the floor, the conflict within her written on her face.

"Do my kisses frighten you, Bethie, love?"

Her answer was a whisper. "A little."

"Why?"

Bethie fought to clear her muddled mind, sought the right words. "B-because I know what you would do next."

His thumbs traced maddening circles against the sensitive skin of her wrists. "Tell me. What would I do next?"

She forced herself to meet his gaze, saw that his eyes had darkened to the color of midnight. "Y-you know."

"No, I don't."

"You would be overcome by . . ." She looked away again, felt the heat of embarrassment in her cheeks.

"Overcome by what, Bethie?"

She had to fight to speak the next word. "Lust."

"And that frightens you?"

She looked into his eyes again, fought to recover her resolve. "I am no' a silly girl, Nicholas, but a woman who has been a wife. I know all there is to know about . . . about *that.* There is no pleasure in it for a woman, only pain."

He looked at her through eyes that held only tenderness. "If you believe that women don't also enjoy sex, Bethie, then you have much to learn."

Her face flamed with anger and embarrassment at his words, but something deep inside her belly clenched. "You only say this to persuade me."

He ran a finger down her cheek, traced the line of her lower lip with his thumb. "Did I hurt you, Bethie?"

She shivered. "N-nay."

"Did you feel pleasure when I kissed you?"

She hesitated, squeezed her eyes shut, wished she did not have to answer him. What would he think of her if she admitted that she didn't want him to stop, that she wanted him to keep kissing her?

*You've the heart of a harlot, Bethie Stewart.*

"Answer me, Bethie. Did you feel pleasure?"

Eyes still closed, she spoke the truth, her voice barely a whisper. "Aye."

"Have you ever enjoyed kissing a man before?"

Her blush grew hotter. "Nay. But it is no' a fair question. I have never been kissed before, no' like that."

"A husband intent on pleasuring his wife would kiss her like that every day." He kissed her lips again, softly, slowly. "And every night." Again he kissed her.

Bethie's mind was a riot of emotion. Her lips tingled, ached. Her body shivered uncontrollably, flooded with unfamiliar sensations. "Nicholas!"

His name was a plea, a prayer. Could he be telling her the truth? Was there more to the joining of men and women than she understood? Was this longing his touch aroused in her part of that?

"I want to kiss you, Bethie. One kiss to show you that I'm right. One kiss to prove that I can bring you pleasure."

She opened her eyes, saw the look of sensual hunger on his face, knew he was holding himself back. "And if I hate it?"

"If you hate it, I'll never kiss you again. But if you enjoy it, then we shall end each reading lesson with a kiss."

"And you promise not to . . ."

"Whatever else I may be, I am not the sort of man who would force himself on a woman, love. I will do nothing that you do not ask me to do." The sincerity and intensity of his gaze stole what remained of her breath.

*Nothing that you do not ask me to do.*

The words hung in the air between them. Outside a robin sang a sweet farewell to the sun, but Bethie barely heard it. She was lost in Nicholas—his gaze, his scent, the lingering taste of him on her lips, the enthralling sound of his voice, the power of his words.

*Nothing that you do not ask me to do.*

She swallowed her fear. "Aye, Nicholas. Show me."

He growled low in his throat, slid one hand beneath her hair to cradle her head, drew her close with the other. Then his mouth gently captured hers.

Heat licked through her, flared deep in her belly, as his lips teased, stroked, caressed hers. She felt weak, reckless, almost faint with need. "*Nicholas.*"

He caught her whisper with his mouth, traced the line of her lips with his tongue, until her lips parted in anticipation of she knew not what.

He groaned, took the kiss deeper, his tongue seeking hers, tasting her, stroking the inside of her cheeks, his fingers tracing her spine through the thin cloth of her shift.

Awash in new sensations, she melted into the hard wall of his chest, found herself kissing him back, her tongue meeting his, tasting him in return.

Nicholas knew he should stop. But she was so warm and willing in his arms, and she tasted so good—like wild honey and woman. He wanted more of her, needed more of her. But what he wanted he could not take. For her sake.

Slowly, he released her, sat back, stroked her cheek with the back of his fingers.

Breathless and trembling, she looked up at him through eyes filled with yearning. Her lips were wet, swollen, maddeningly ripe. Her hands still rested on his shoulders.

He was terribly close to pulling her into his arms again when he remembered to ask the question. "Tell me, Bethie. Did my kiss bring you pleasure?"

She closed her eyes for a moment, as if struggling with the answer, then met his gaze. "Aye."

Nicholas kicked the malfunctioning trap across the forest floor, let out a stream of profanity that would have shocked even another trapper.

He wanted to hit something, anything.

What in the hell had he been thinking when he offered to give Bethie a kiss each night? For five agonizing days he'd been living with the consequences of that decision—sleepless nights, restlessness, frustration. His balls were on the brink of exploding, and his cock was in a near-constant state of arousal. And his dreams . . .

Dear God, his dreams had him spilling in the night like a boy of sixteen!

It wasn't that Bethie was a slow learner or unwilling to kiss. It was her natural talent and eagerness that was killing him. Each night he held her soft, pliant body in his arms, kissed her with every bit of passion and skill he possessed, and she returned his passion measure for measure.

Nor was it that his kisses had no effect on her. She came

alive in his arms, her body melting against his, her lips soft, her tongue eager to spar. She arched against him, moaned, clung to him in feminine surrender. Last night, she had scattered bites across his throat, nipped his lips, even bitten down gently on his tongue. It had taken every ounce of his resolve not to lift her shift, part her thighs, and impale her right there before the fire.

The trouble was that she never asked for anything more.

"I will do nothing that you do not ask me to do," he'd said.

Would she be content with kissing forever? Did she not long to follow her passion, to see where it led? Was she trying to drive him mad?

With another curse, he stomped over to the place where his trap had landed, pulled it from a tangle of underbrush, examined it. One of the joints was bent. It wasn't bad, just enough to ensure that the trap didn't spring fully shut. He carried it back to the spot where Zeus grazed in contentment, draped it across his saddle, took out another.

It was easy for the stallion to be content. He had a small harem of two mares to keep him satisfied and had already planted foals inside both of them. Bethie had taken it in stride, said she had expected as much.

"Lucky bastard." Nicholas stomped back to the riverbank, where he had chosen to place his trap.

Surely Bethie's husband was to blame for this. He had taught her to fear men. He had abused her. He had taken her sweet body to bed, had spread her legs, and hurt her. It was a good thing the son of a bitch was already dead. For God's sake, the man hadn't even kissed her!

Nicholas picked up a rock, brought it down hard on the stake that held his trap in place, forcing the stake deep into the mud.

And then it dawned on him. If her husband hadn't kissed her, perhaps there were other things he hadn't done. As hard as it was to imagine, perhaps he had simply lifted her shift, spread her thighs, and rammed himself into her. Perhaps she had no idea what pleasures could follow kissing—all the touching, tasting, licking, and . . .

A spray of crows scattered across the sky a half mile to the north, their raucous cries echoing through the forest. Then all was silent.

*Bethie!*

Nicholas pulled his hunting knife from its sheath and ran.

Bethie knelt in the dirt, freed the row of marjoram from the weeds that threatened to engulf it. Nicholas had told her not to bother planting a kitchen garden this summer, to save her seeds for planting elsewhere. But that didn't mean she had to neglect her herbs. The wet winter meant the plants were especially healthy and robust this year. 'Twas a shame she would soon leave them behind. But she didn't want to think about that.

Isabelle cooed cheerfully from her basket in the nearby shade. She was growing so fast. She had already begun to sleep through the night once in a while.

That was more than Bethie could say for herself. She hadn't slept well since the first night Nicholas had kissed her. Instead, she had lain awake until late into the night, listening to his breathing, wanting . . . Wanting what?

If only she knew.

Every time he kissed her was better than the last. Never had she imagined that the simple touching of lips, the swirl of a tongue could leave her feeling so desperate, so needy. Each taste of him made her hungry for more, until she felt she could never be satisfied.

*Nicholas. Nicholas.*

Her mind seemed always to be filled with thoughts of—

A hand fisted brutally in her hair, jerked her painfully to her feet. She would have screamed had a hand not closed over her mouth.

Out from behind her strode two Indians. Both wore a mix of Indian and white man's garb—leather leggings and breechcloths with homespun shirts. Their heads were bald apart from scalp locks.

One walked inside the cabin, knife drawn, rifle in hand.

The other strode toward the shade, toward little Isabelle.

# Chapter 11

The slick taste of terror filled Bethie's mouth.

*Belle! Dear God, not Belle!*

Silenced by the man's big hand, her scream died before it could leave her throat. She watched in horror as Isabelle was lifted none too gently out of her basket, her gown lifted, her diaper cloth probed to see what sex she was.

Infuriated and desperate to save her daughter, Bethie began to fight. She twisted, kicked, scratched her attacker. Her elbow connected with his belly, and she heard him grunt. But he was much stronger than she, and she could not break free.

But then his hand slipped from her mouth, and she screamed.

A cry for help. A warning.

*Where is Nicholas?*

Something exploded against the back of her skull.

Shattering pain. Flashes of white.

She felt herself swirl to the edges of consciousness, felt her body go limp.

Nicholas watched from behind the barn, bit back a growl of fury as the warrior struck Bethie a second time. He crept closer, watched for a moment.

One misstep on his part and both Bethie and Belle would die.

There were two of them. Two to one—good odds. Then the man who held Bethie's limp body turned toward his companion and Nicholas got a clear look at his face.

*Mattootuk.*

Something twisted in Nicholas's gut.

The rules of the game had just changed.

"Mattootuk wishes to die today. That is why he mistreats my woman and child." Nicholas spoke in Wyandot, then stepped out from behind the barn, his pistol fully cocked and pointed at Mattootuk's head.

Mattootuk's eyes grew wide and he gaped at Nicholas as one who has seen a ghost, his face suddenly ashen. Then he released Bethie.

Nicholas kept all trace of emotion from his face as Bethie fell unconscious to the ground. Then movement at the door of the cabin caught his eye as a third warrior emerged from the cabin, rifle in hand.

Nicholas wasted no time. He fired, hitting the warrior squarely in the chest. The man fell dead.

Frightened by the gunfire, Isabelle began to cry. The young warrior who had handled her so roughly gently lowered her back into the basket, his wide gaze fixed on Nicholas.

Nicholas pulled his second pistol from his waistband, cocked it. "Tell me why I shouldn't kill both of you where you stand?"

Mattootuk smiled, apparently recovered from his shock. "*Ha-en-ye-ha,* brother, it is good to see you."

Bethie's head ached as she struggled to wake up from her nightmare. She had dreamt three Indians had come out of the forest, had attacked her and Isabelle while Nicholas had been off checking his traps. She'd tried to free herself, had been struck on the head. And then . . .

Then she had heard Nicholas's voice, but he hadn't spoken words she recognized. There'd been a gunshot, and Belle had begun to cry.

It had been a terrifying dream.

From outside came the sound of voices, men's voices. She

could not understand what they said. Their words were strange, guttural. Somewhere nearby, Isabelle fussed.

A bolt of alarm surged through her.

She fought to open her eyes, heard herself moan. "Isabelle!"

"Easy, Bethie. Drink this. Isabelle is fine, though I think she's getting hungry."

'Twas Nicholas.

She felt his hand slip behind her head to lift her, felt the tin cup against her lips. She took a sip, pulled away.

"I know it's bitter, but it will take away some of your pain without making you sleepy. Come, love. Drink."

She did as he asked, opened her eyes to see his face hovering inches above hers, his eyes filled with concern. "I-it wasn't a dream?"

"No, Bethie, it wasn't a dream. There are two Wyandot warriors sitting outside roasting a goose over the fire pit. I'm afraid we have uninvited guests."

"Two? But there were—"

"I killed the third." He said it without emotion.

"I dinnae want them here!"

"Nor do I, but it is far safer to have them here where I can keep my eye on them than to drive them off only to have them return to attack in stealth."

"I'm afraid."

"They will not touch you again. I've told them you're my wife and Isabelle is my daughter. Do nothing to make them think otherwise."

"But—"

"It is more complicated than I can explain, Bethie. Just trust me." He glanced toward Belle's cradle. "Are you up to feeding the baby?"

Bethie's breasts ached, heavy with milk. She nodded, tried to sit, gasped as pain seemed to shatter her skull.

"Easy, love. Just lie on your side, like you do at night."

She rolled onto her side and began to unbutton her gown, wondering vaguely how he knew that she nursed Isabelle on her side at night.

Nicholas lifted Belle, who was now wailing, from her cradle, and laid her by Bethie's bared breast.

Bethie guided her nipple to Isabelle's little mouth, felt her baby latch on and begin to suck hungrily. Her breasts tingled as her milk began to flow. She felt drowsiness overtake her again.

Nicholas's lips were warm on her cheek. "Just rest, Bethie. I'll watch over both of you."

By the time Belle had finished nursing, Bethie was fully awake. The potion Nicholas had given her had taken away most of her headache.

She checked Belle's diaper cloth, found it soaking wet. Carefully, she rose, took up a clean, dry cloth, and changed her daughter, who gazed about with bright blue eyes, as if nothing terrible had happened.

And nothing terrible *had* happened. Thanks to Nicholas.

Bethie had no doubt that both she and Belle would be lying dead outside the cabin now if not for him.

She felt suddenly sick to her stomach, and trembling, lifted Belle into her arms.

Nicholas tore off another bite of roast goose, chewed, oblivious to the taste of the succulent meat. His thoughts were focused on the two Wyandot men who sat across the fire from him. They ate with abandon, having already consumed all of Bethie's corn cakes and the potatoes she'd boiled.

It was all part of the game. Mattootuk wanted to show Nicholas that he wasn't afraid, wanted to put Nicholas at ease. It would make it easier for Mattootuk and Youreh, his companion, to carry out whatever scheme they had in mind.

Mattootuk might call him brother, but Nicholas was not fooled. The Wyandot warrior hated him, had hated him from the moment Lyda had claimed him. Mattootuk wanted nothing more than to see him dead.

Mattootuk drew out his knife, cut off another sliver of meat, held it to his mouth with greasy fingers, spoke in Wyandot. "The years have been good to you. A wife. A daughter. The years have not been so good for the Wyandot."

Nicholas cut another strip of meat for himself, aware that

Bethie watched from the shadowed doorway with Belle in her arms. He answered in Wyandot. "The Wyandot should not have made war on the Big Knives. They are now neighbors to the Wyandot and will not be driven away. It would be better to make peace."

Mattootuk smiled, bared his teeth. "We shall see, brother. All of the People now make league together. We follow Obwandiyag, whose cousin you killed today. If we join together, who can stop us?"

Nicholas chewed, pretended to mull over the question, swallowed. "Today I stopped you."

For a moment Mattootuk's face twisted into a scowl. Youreh, who'd been but a boy when Nicholas was taken prisoner, gaped in astonishment at Nicholas's insult.

Then Mattootuk laughed and nodded at Nicholas, but hatred gleamed in his brown eyes. "Let no one say you are not a man of courage. Did we not witness your bravery in the face of fire and torment? How I wanted to partake of your heart! It would have been sweeter meat than this old goose."

Now it was Nicholas's turn to laugh. "Ah, Mattootuk, but I have no heart."

The warrior glanced over at Bethie, his gaze raking her in appraisal.

She withdrew deeper into the shadows.

"I've seen how you look at your woman. You protect her like a sow bear protects her cubs. You have a heart, brother, and she has the keeping of it."

Nicholas fought to keep his reaction from his face. Was Mattootuk implying that he was in love with Bethie? "She is my wife. It is my duty to protect her and our child."

A look of triumph came into Mattootuk's eyes. "Just as Lyda was your wife."

Nicholas had known the moment the words left his mouth what Mattootuk would say. He had walked into a trap. "I did not wish her death."

"You did not wish the child's death. For Lyda you cared nothing." Mattootuk's face was a scowl, his gaze daggers of ice.

All pretenses had fallen. No more games.

Nicholas preferred it this way. He smiled. "If you wish to

challenge me, Mattootuk, do it. I would gladly kill you with my bare hands."

Bethie could not understand what was being said, but she could tell Nicholas knew these men, or at least the older one. She could also tell that words had brought them to the edge of bloodshed. The glint in Nicholas's eyes, as cold and sharp as the tip of a blade, told her that.

The forest seemed to wait.

Then the older Indian laughed, said something that made the younger one smile, and the tension was dispelled. Except in Nicholas's eyes.

"She good wife?" The older man spoke in broken English pointing at Bethie and startling her. "Strong, brave wife?"

"Aye." Nicholas's gaze touched her for the briefest moment. "Bethie, go back inside. Shut the door."

Something was happening here she didn't understand. She was about to do as Nicholas had asked when the older Indian spoke in English again.

"You tell her? You tell her you kill your wife, my sister?"

Bethie stopped still, met the older Indian's gaze and saw there a dark, seething hatred.

"He kill my sister and her baby—his baby."

Stunned, Bethie sought for the truth in Nicholas's eyes.

What she saw there froze her blood.

It couldn't be true. It couldn't.

*He kill my sister and her baby—his baby.*

Bethie treadled her spinning wheel, watched the wool slip from between her fingers without really seeing it, her mind in turmoil, her nerves on edge.

The men were still outdoors, though the sun had set. They were still talking, their voices a deep murmur beyond the closed door. Every time one of them raised his voice or laughed, she jumped. She was terrified they would kill Nicholas and then come for her and Belle.

*Nicholas. Nicholas.*

She hadn't known he'd once had an Indian wife, hadn't known he'd fathered a child.

He'd told her he'd been held captive by Indians, not that he had married into the tribe. That was something different, wasn't it?

She felt the faint stirrings of jealousy, brushed them off.

Had he lied to her? Did he have reason to cover up his wife's existence and, with it, her death? Or was there more to the story?

She prayed it was the latter.

Apart from that first day, when he'd ridden out of the forest on the brink of death, he'd been good to both her and Isabelle. He'd seen her through her travail with a gentleness that almost stopped her heart whenever she looked back upon it. He had saved Isabelle's life. He'd saved her from being burned. He'd put meat on the table, taken care of the heavy chores. He'd done so many thoughtful things Bethie had lost count. He couldn't possibly be a cold-blooded killer, the sort of man who used his strength to prey upon the weak.

Why, then, had the look in his eyes told her that he was?

Belle began to fuss again. She couldn't possibly be hungry already, could she? Perhaps she was on edge, just like her mother.

Bethie set her spinning aside, lifted her daughter from the cradle.

The door to the cabin swung open, and she nearly jumped out of her skin.

She clutched Belle to her breast, turned to see Nicholas step inside, the two Indian men behind him.

"Are you and the baby ready for bed?" Nicholas said something to the two Indians in their own language, pulled his gear out of the corner, and motioned to the space where he usually slept.

Bethie watched in stunned surprise as the two Indians unrolled furs and laid them on the floor. "Wh-what—"

Nicholas carried his gear across the cabin and dropped it on the floor behind her spinning wheel, lowered his voice. "It would be an affront to their notions of hospitality to make them sleep outdoors or in the barn. You've no choice but to go along wi—"

"Them? Sleep inside? With us?" She tried to keep her

voice at a whisper, but she was so upset her words came out as a squeak. "Next time you want to have your *relatives* visit—"

He took her shoulders. "Aye, with us."

She looked at his gear behind the spinning wheel. There was hardly room for a child to sleep back there, let alone a man of Nicholas's size. Worse, if he were all the way across the room, it would mean she would be closest to the Indians. And then she understood.

She gasped, stared up at him. "And you will sleep—"

He bent close, as if to kiss her cheek. "In your bed. Beside you. As your husband, remember?"

She stared up at him, shook her head. "But Nicholas—"

He took her jaw firmly in his fingers, tilted her face until she had no choice but to look him in the eyes. "If you wish to survive this night, you will do exactly what I tell you to do, Bethie."

"And who am I to fear most—you or your former brother-by-marriage?"

His gaze hardened. "Get into bed, Bethie. And keep Belle with you."

Bethie quickly changed Isabelle's diaper cloth, then washed her hands and face.

The two Indian men sat on their furs near the foot of the bed, spoke softly to each other. The older one watched her every move. Then his gaze collided with hers, and he spoke in English, pointing to Nicholas. "He take Wyandot women, many in one day, every day, where all can watch him. Not with you, I think. We not watch him take you."

Bethie gasped at the vileness of these words. Nicholas had lain with Indian women openly as others watched? Many each day? It could not be true! But if it weren't true, why didn't Nicholas say something?

Holding Belle close, her skin crawling, she turned down the covers of her bed, climbed in, wishing she could grow wings and fly away.

She lay on her side facing the fireplace, watched as Nicholas pulled in the door string, shed his shirt, yawned.

How could he possibly be sleepy with two armed Indians inside the cabin? How could he behave so calmly when one of them clearly hated him? Had he forgotten he had killed a man today on the doorstep of this very cabin?

With one last glance about the cabin, Nicholas blew out the lamp.

Apart from the glow of the fire, the cabin fell into darkness.

Bethie began to pray, but her prayer scattered into fragments when she felt the mattress sag beneath his weight as he crawled over her to the other side of the bed.

The ropes creaked as if in protest of his intrusion.

"Excuse me, love." His voice was inches from her ear as he lay down beside her.

His scent was all around her.

And then he reached out and pulled her against him. She felt the hilt of his hunting knife and the outline of his two pistols inside the waistband of his breeches. How had he sneaked them into bed without her seeing?

His lips touched her cheek. He whispered. "Turn toward me. Put Belle between us."

Unable to hide her trembling, she did as he asked, found herself staring into his eyes. She mouthed the question that was burning within her. "Is it true?"

He stroked her cheek with his thumb. "I would never hurt you, Bethie, or your baby. I gave my word."

It wasn't an answer. She asked again. "Is it true?"

"Is what true? That I killed my wife and baby? Or that I tupped women in the open where everyone could watch, including my Wyandot wife?"

She said nothing, waited for his answer.

"Aye, Bethie. It's true." A look of anguish filled his eyes, then he closed them. "Go to sleep."

Nicholas watched Bethie sleep, listened to the deep, slow breathing of their unwanted guests. He'd bet his life that neither Mattootuk nor Youreh was truly sleeping, despite the occasional snore. They were feigning sleep, just as he was. They were waiting until they felt certain he was asleep before making their move.

It wasn't hard to stay awake. Regret was a knife in his gut, cutting him, shredding him. Today his past had caught up with him, and the price was almost more than he could bear.

He would never forget the look in Bethie's eyes—the shock, the fear, the revulsion, as if he'd broken a promise, betrayed her, shattered her world. She now thought him the worst sort of murderer, not to mention an adulterer. And wasn't he?

He had brought about Lyda's death, and that of the child she carried, as surely as if he'd pointed a gun at her head and fired. But he was not an adulterer. He had never agreed to marry Lyda, never agreed to live under her roof, never agreed to plant a child inside her. And when she'd left him no choice, he had merely bested her at her own game. With terrible consequences.

But would Bethie understand?

Nicholas didn't think so. She was afraid of men, had trouble trusting them. This wouldn't be the sort of thing she would ignore or forget.

Perhaps Lyda had gained her revenge after all, obtained at the hands of her brother.

Why should Nicholas care? As soon as he had delivered Bethie safely to her family, he would leave her behind, head back into the wilderness, forget her.

No. No matter how far west he traveled, he would never forget her.

God, she was beautiful, so young and innocent. He wanted to touch her, to run his fingers over the curve of her cheek, the swell of her lips. He wanted to kiss her again, to watch her come alive with passion in his arms, to feel her heart pound in her breast just because he had touched her.

And Belle—so small, so helpless. She lay asleep between them, hands clenched into tiny fists. She resembled her mother in every detail.

He would gladly give his life for either of them.

Something jerked Nicholas out of his thoughts.

Silence.

The deep, slow breathing had stopped.

Someone was moving in the darkness.

# Chapter 12

Nicholas kept his breathing slow and steady, closed his hands tighter around the handles of his pistols, listened.

The snake-glide of leather across the wooden floor. The creak of a beaded moccasin. The slow intake of breath.

Every muscle in his body tensed. He had only time to think how much this would frighten Bethie and Isabelle before instinct took over.

In one motion, he rolled onto his back, fired both pistols into the darkness.

Twin flashes of gunpowder.

A woman's scream. A baby's cry.

The thud of a body hitting the floor.

Mattootuk howled in rage and pain, stumbled across the cabin.

"Don't move!" Nicholas shouted the command at Bethie, leapt over her, tried to catch Mattootuk before he reached the door.

But in the darkness he stumbled over Youreh's body, and in the split second it took him to regain his footing, Mattootuk had fled into the night.

Jerked from sleep by gunfire, Bethie held her baby daughter

close, squeezed her eyes shut against the violence that seemed to be happening on all sides at once.

Then, as abruptly as it had begun, it was over.

Stillness.

Dreading what she might find, Bethie turned her head to glance back over her shoulder.

Nicholas stood, his back against the open door, his face and bare chest outlined in starlight. His hands were busy reloading a pistol, but his gaze was focused on the darkness beyond.

She sat up, felt her body begin to shake.

In her arms, Belle cried inconsolably.

Bethie pressed her lips to her daughter's cheek, felt Belle's wet baby tears, thought she might cry, too. Her voice quavered. "It's over, little one. Shhh, now."

"I'm sorry, Bethie." Nicholas turned away from the forest, slipped his pistols back into the waistband of his breeches. "I wish there had been some other way."

She tried to speak, could not.

"Stay in bed. I'll take care of this."

For a moment she wondered what he meant. Then he bent down, picked up something heavy from the floor, dragged it outside.

A body.

Her stomach turned. She fought not to gag, squeezed her eyes shut, clutched Belle to her breast.

A dead body.

*Nicholas had killed a man in her home.*

And she was grateful. He had saved her life—and Belle's—once more.

She chided herself for her weakness, struggled to quell her nausea and slow her breathing. Nicholas had faced this danger head-on. What was wrong with her that she trembled so?

By the time he returned, she had laid a hiccuping Isabelle in her cradle, lit several candles, and stood looking down at the pool of blood on the puncheon floor.

She met his gaze, forced her mouth to form words. "Sand. Sand should soak it up, polish out the stain."

"Bethie." He said her name, nothing more. Then he pulled her close, rained kisses on her hair, her brow, her cheeks.

Her trembling began anew. Tears rolled, hot and salty, down her cheeks. She let his arms enfold her, clung to him with every ounce of her strength. "Nicholas! Oh, Nicholas!"

"You've nothing more to fear tonight, Bethie. I'll bury Youreh along with his gear in the morning. Mattootuk fled into the forest. He's injured, but I don't know how gravely. He won't return tonight."

Her stomach churned. "I—I think I'm going to be . . . sick!"

She dashed past Nicholas, ran through the open doorway, sank to her knees on the ground. She felt Nicholas gather her hair, felt his reassuring hand on her shoulder as she lost her supper.

Bethie heard a baby fussing. It fussed a bit, then it began to cry in earnest.

She rolled over, tried to keep sleeping.

Her eyes flew open. *Isabelle!*

Bethie tossed back the covers, stepped from the bed, leapt back when she remembered what stained the floor near her feet. Then, careful not to step near the dark patch on the floorboards, she hurried to Belle's cradle.

"I'm sorry, sweet. You must be hungry." She lifted her daughter into her arms, sat in the rocking chair, bared a milk-sore breast.

Isabelle began to nurse greedily.

The shutters were latched over the parchment window, keeping the cabin dark. But daylight showed through the crack beneath the door. It was late—well past sunrise.

Bethie tried to clear her mind. She felt so groggy. But then none of them had gotten much rest last night.

It was strange to think that only a few hours ago, Nicholas had killed a man in this very room. Gunshots, her own screams, shouting—it seemed like a bad dream now. But the bloodstain on her floor proved it had been only too real.

She hadn't meant to get sick, felt embarrassed by her own spinelessness. She had grown up on the frontier, had grown up with tales of violence and brutality. So why had the sight of a dead man, a pool of blood, the sound of fighting terrified her?

It was one thing to hear such tales, quite another to find herself in one.

Nicholas had stayed with her until she'd been strong enough to stand. While she had rocked Isabelle back to sleep, he had soaked up most of the blood with one of the Indians' blankets and carried their belongings outside with plans to bury them after sunrise. Then he'd carried his own gear outside.

"Pull in the door string, Bethie. Try to get some sleep."

"Where are you goin'?"

He'd met her gaze for one moment, his blue eyes bleak. "If he returns, he'll expect me to be inside with you. I'll keep watch out here."

But she'd known there was more to it than that.

Things between them had changed. In the immediate aftermath of the attack, it had been easy to forget what Nicholas had admitted to doing. But when the dust had settled, the truth stood between them like a wall.

Bethie switched Belle to her other breast, tried to dispel the chill that had settled around her heart. She ought to have known that Nicholas was hiding some terrible secret. Hadn't she sensed it in his silence, the way he never spoke about himself? Hadn't she felt it in his anger? Hadn't she seen it in the shadows that haunted his eyes? Aye, a part of her had known since the beginning. But she had allowed herself to ignore it.

And now?

She thought of how caring he'd been toward Isabelle, the kindnesses he had shown them both, the barely restrained passion of his kisses, his patience as he taught her to read. How could such a man have intentionally killed a woman and a child, his own child?

She would never know unless she asked him, gave him a chance to explain.

With a sudden sense of urgency, Bethie finished feeding Isabelle, changed the baby's diaper cloth. Then she washed her hands and face, dressed for the day, and braided her hair. She picked up the bucket and was about to open the cabin door when a terrible possibility occurred to her.

What if during the night Nicholas had ridden away? What if he'd left her?

She grabbed her water bucket, lifted the bar from the door, threw it open, took one step into the morning sunlight.

"Stay inside, Bethie."

She whirled toward the sound of his voice, relief warm in her veins. He stood in the shadows, leaning against the corner of the cabin, his arms crossed over his bare chest. Both pistols were still tucked in the waistband of his breeches, the knife in its sheath.

He glanced at the water bucket in her hand, strode toward her. He hadn't shaven, the day's growth of beard dark on his face. The half-moon shadows beneath his eyes were proof he hadn't yet slept, either. He reached for the bucket. "I'll take that. I want you and Belle behind closed doors today."

She looked up at him, confused. "But you said he was injured, that he had fled."

He met her gaze for a moment. Then he looked at the dark wall of forest beyond the barn, his lips a grim line. "I can feel him out there. He must be more seriously injured than I realized. Otherwise, he would have either attacked us already or moved on."

"If he's injured, then I've naught to fear." She reached for the bucket.

"Even a dying man can throw a knife or fire an arrow from the shadows. I won't give him that chance. Go back inside, Bethie, and stay there."

Nicholas brought water, firewood, and fresh eggs and did the morning milking while Bethie prepared a quick breakfast. Neither spoke as they worked. Bethie half expected to see the Indian man's shadow in her doorway at any moment.

She had just poured tea into Nicholas's cup when she noticed the strip of old cloth he'd tied around his left forearm. "You've been injured!"

"It's nothing, Bethie."

"I'll be the one decidin' that." She set the teapot aside, took his muscular arm in her hands, began to unbind the wound.

"It's little more than a nick."

Beneath the cloth was not a nick, but a deep cut. He had already washed it and spread his special ointment on it. There was little more she could do. She looked up, saw an amused grin on his face that left her both cross and a wee bit breathless.

"Will I live?"

"If it festers, who can say?" She let his arm fall to the table with a thud and, ignoring his chuckle, walked to the cupboard, took out a strip of clean linen and her little crock of violet-leaf salve. "The least I can do is bind it in a clean cloth."

Aware his gaze was upon her, she worked quickly, trying to ignore the way that touching him made her heart beat faster and her blood grow warm. Still, she was painfully aware of even the smallest details beneath her fingers—the rasp of dark hair against smooth, sun-browned skin, the outline of veins, the firmness of his muscles.

"He meant to plunge his blade into my chest. Bad luck for him I chose that moment to turn and fire." He said it lightly, as if he were talking about a game of cards and not a life-and-death struggle.

"His knife did this?" She secured the bandage with a little knot, looked into his eyes. "I dinnae know how to thank you, Nicholas. You saved us."

Nicholas wanted to pull her close, to kiss her, to lift any shadow of lingering fear from her heart, but he held himself back. "I promised to protect you."

She looked away, covered the little crock of salve with a scrap of cowhide. "So you were just keepin' your promise?"

What would she have him say? That he cared for her more deeply than he would have thought possible? That he would sooner tear his own heart out and stomp it into the dirt than see either her or little Isabelle harmed? That he had never experienced such fear as when he'd seen her and Belle in the hands of Wyandot men?

It might be true, but he could not tell her this—for her sake. What a damned fool he'd been! How could he have imagined even for a moment that he could help her forget her past when he would never escape his own? He'd come so close, so dangerously close, to seducing her. But Mattootuk had shown up in time to remind him, to stop him.

He braced himself for the pain he knew he would cause her. "Aye, keeping my promise. What else would it be?"

And there it was—shards of hurt in her violet eyes. She swallowed, bit her lower lip. "You told me you were taken prisoner, no' that you had lived among the Indians with your Indian wife."

"I *was* their prisoner." Because he hated himself for hurting her, the words came out harsh and angry. "Think no more on it. You'll be rid of me soon enough, and then what I told you or failed to tell you will no longer matter."

He willed himself to stand, willed himself to walk away from her, leaving that stricken look on her face.

He had a dead man to bury.

Nicholas pulled the stiffened corpse into the shallow grave he'd dug within sight of the cabin, crouched beside it, gazed at the young man's face. Youreh had been a boy of twelve or thirteen summers when Nicholas had been held captive. Nicholas had never spoken with him, had never shared a hunt or a meal with him. Still, Nicholas remembered him.

At the onset of manhood that summer, Youreh had been called upon by the warriors to show his bravery the night Josiah and Eben had been tortured to death. More than once it was he who had pressed the lit torches to their skin.

*Nicholas, for God's sake, help us!*

Nicholas stood abruptly, dropped Youreh's gear in the grave, along with the things Mattootuk had left behind, shoveled dirt on top of it all. Then he cursed Mattootuk and Youreh to everlasting hell.

Bethie served Nicholas a second helping of stew, picked the biggest chunks of venison from the pot for him. "After this, you should get some sleep."

He shook his head. "I want to scout for tracks once more, make certain he hasn't been stalking the cabin."

She swallowed her objections, sat, picked at her dinner.

He'd barely spoken a word to her all day, and when he had, his words had been cold or gruff and angry. She wanted to believe it was just the strain of having gone all night and all day with no sleep and precious little food. But she knew it was more than that.

She had learned more than he wanted her to know about his life, and he was pulling back.

She supposed she should be grateful. 'Twas far better to learn the truth now than later. Had things continued as they were going, she might have found herself smitten with him. She might have become willing to overlook any fault to taste more of his kisses. She might even have hoped to marry him.

*You'll be rid of me soon enough, and then what I told you or failed to tell you will no longer matter.*

Oh, but it did matter! 'Twas one thing to learn he had dark secrets in his past. It was quite something else to think he had deceived her, kept something so important from her.

And yet, what did he owe her? Why should he tell her? They were little more than strangers to each other, two people whose paths happened to cross in a vast wilderness. Besides, didn't she have secrets? Had she not knowingly kept from him a truth as dark and terrible as the one he had kept from her?

Aye, she had. She had accepted his protection, enjoyed his many acts of kindness, received his kisses—and kept from him the shameful truth. Would he have kissed her so sweetly had he know of her taint?

She watched as he ate his last spoonful of stew, noticed the lines of fatigue on his face.

He pushed back his chair, stood. "Pull in the string once I'm out. I'll see you in the morning."

"It's still daylight, Nicholas. Will you no' get some sleep before you go back out? You cannae go forever without it. If he really is still out there, it would be better to face him well rested."

But Nicholas was already gone.

On a hilltop to the northwest of the cabin, Mattootuk fell to his knees. So much of his spirit was now gone that it was all but impossible to stand. But he had a task to complete before he was willing to die. So he struggled to his feet again, took several more staggering steps, spilled a thin trail of black powder on the forest floor.

The Sa-ray-u-migh's bullet had gone deep into his shoulder, made it hard for him to breathe, made blood well up in his throat. But neither the Big Knife nor his woman nor their daughter would escape his vengeance. Already the wind was shifting. Soon it would blow steadily from the northwest. Then Mattootuk would light the powder and watch.

He laughed, ignored the spray of blood and spittle that issued from his mouth.

Fire.

It consumed. It cleansed. It purified. The Big Knife had been pulled from its embrace once, thanks to Lyda's lust, but he would not be so lucky again. The powder would ignite, and the flames, pushed by the wind, would race headlong toward the cabin, reaching it so quickly that the Big Knife and all that was his would perish in a matter of moments, a delayed sacrifice to the gods, a gift to a sister long dead.

*I am dying, but I will conquer my enemy.*

His powder gone, Mattootuk spat the Big Knife's words from long ago back at him. Then he sank to the ground, watched the sun slip below the horizon, felt the wind—and waited.

# Chapter 13

*The leather cords bit painfully into Nicholas's wrists. No matter how he twisted or turned, he could not free himself. There would be no escape.*

*From nearby came the sound of weeping.*

*Eben and Josiah.*

*"I dinnae want to die!"*

*His stomach lurched at the sound of her voice.*

*Bethie!*

*She stood, tied to a stake beside him, still pregnant and stripped to her shift.*

*Mattootuk stood near the fire pit, laughed at Nicholas, a knife in his hand. Then he strode toward Bethie.*

*And Nicholas knew. They weren't going to kill him. It was going to be like last time. They were going to kill Bethie and force him to watch.*

*"Take me! Let her go! Take me, Mattootuk! It's me you want!"*

*Mattootuk laughed.*

*Then Nicholas felt a knife pierce his skin. He looked down, saw Lyda, his blood hot on her hands.*

*She said one word. "Fire."*

Nicholas bolted awake, jerked his knife from its sheath.

The cabin stood before him, dark and quiet. A breeze whispered through the new leaves on the beech trees, raised goose bumps on his sweat-drenched skin. Except for the swaying branches, nothing moved in the darkness.

But something wasn't right.

He trained his senses on the forest around him, got slowly to his feet.

The distant screech of birds frightened from their night perches.

The faint smell of smoke.

Nicholas ran out from the shadows that had concealed him to the north side of the cabin.

The northern sky glowed orange. A wall of flames as high as the forest and perhaps a mile wide raced toward the cabin. It was a good half mile away, but it was moving fast, driven by the wind.

*Mattootuk!* The bastard must be on the brink of death to attack them like this.

They had only minutes—if it wasn't too late already.

Nicholas dashed for the stables, shouted as loudly as he could. "Bethie, wake up! Fire!"

Roused either by his shouts or because they sensed the fire, the geese began to shriek.

He kicked their pen open as he passed, leaving them to scatter in a flurry of feathers. But he knew it would not save them.

Inside the cabin, Bethie sat up, heart pounding.

The geese!

*Nicholas!*

She leapt to her feet, grabbed the rifle, ran to the barred door, listened, expecting to hear the sound of fighting.

A horse's frightened whinny. The cries of birds. The lowing of cattle.

A fist pounded on the door, startled a shriek from her throat.

"Bethie, get up! Fire!"

She threw open the door, smelled smoke, found Nicholas standing on her doorstep, his horse saddled, the reins in his hands. Behind him Dorcas and her calf ran in panicked circles.

"Get Isabelle! Now! Hurry!"

"But I'm no' dress—"

"There's no time for that! Come!"

She tossed the rifle to him, ran to Isabelle's cradle, snatched her baby up, ran back to the open door. She had just managed to grab her shawl from its hook, when Nicholas scooped her up, swung her out the door, lifted her onto his stallion's back.

The animal pranced and whinnied, but Nicholas kept a firm grip on its bridle.

"There isn't time to adjust the stirrups, so hold on tight! Keep one hand in his mane, and hold on to Belle with all your strength. Bend low over his back!"

"But the animals—"

In her arms, Belle began to wail.

"There isn't time! Ride south! Stop for nothing! Go!" He released his hold, slapped the horse hard on the rump.

Bethie screamed, clutched Belle to her breast, as the stallion surged forward, a thousand pounds of muscle and sinew exploding into motion beneath her.

And then, in a moment so full of horror that it seemed to last forever, she saw.

The night sky glowing orange. A stampede of flames. The tiny cabin in its path.

Tongues of fire drifted through the air, settled on the cabin's roof.

"Nicholas!" She shouted for him over the roar of the blaze, caught only a glimpse of him as he ran back toward the stable before the stallion plunged headlong into the forest away from the inferno.

*Nicholas!*

Had he made it? Had he gotten away? Was he riding one of the mares?

Already she could feel the fire's heat.

Smoke caught in her throat, stung her eyes.

Gripped by terror, she fisted her hand in the stallion's coarse mane, clenched its flank with her thighs, bent over Isabelle, squeezed her eyes shut, prayed.

*Nicholas!*

The jarring thud of hooves against loam. The scrape of

branches against bare skin. The gust of breath from the stallion's nostrils as it plunged through the trees. The roar of the fire.

Bethie lifted her head, forced her stinging eyes open.

The forest in front of them glowed as if in the light of an unnatural dawn. Deer fled before the stallion's churning hooves, their dun hides glowing red. Streamers of flame flew from treetop to treetop overhead, dropped to the ground around them like burning raindrops.

The fire was overtaking them. And if it was overtaking them . . .

A sob caught in her throat.

*Nicholas!*

The heat grew almost unbearable, and she held Belle closer, determined to shield her baby from the blistering wind.

She felt the stallion pick up its pace, saw the flare of its nostrils as it fought for breath.

Then above the roar and crash of the fire she heard screams—the high-pitched screams of women, of children. They came from all around her, piteous, keening cries.

She lifted her head, looked to her left, to her right, saw only flames.

A shiver ran down her spine.

The screams were not coming from women and children, but from the *trees*.

A flaming branch fell from above, landed a few feet in front of the stallion.

The animal swerved.

A tree to the right exploded into flames. Bits of burning wood whistled through the air. One hit her on the cheek, its bite sharp and searing.

She might have screamed, but the smoke was so thick and the air so hot that she could not draw breath without choking.

A cougar dashed out from the underbrush, almost beneath the stallion's hooves.

Zeus shied, swerved, stumbled, and Bethie feared for one terrible moment that the stallion would fall, pitching them into the blaze. But Zeus knew the forest and quickly regained his footing.

The fire was ahead of them now, falling in graceful streams

from the forest canopy, rising up from the ground in great sheets.

The heat was excruciating, and Bethie began to feel dizzy.

But then the smoke began to clear, the fire to thin.

Had they outrun it?

Suddenly before them stretched what seemed to be a gaping chasm, its darkness lit by small glowing fires.

*We are going to die.*

The stallion was crazed with fear, and Bethie knew it would not stop. But she did not want it to stop. She would rather that she and Belle meet their deaths quickly at the bottom of a precipice than suffer the torment of flames.

Her last thought as the stallion's muscles tensed for the leap was of Nicholas.

Then the stallion stretched out its legs and leapt out above the brink.

They fell.

Bethie screamed, held Belle closer.

But then . . .

*Water!*

It was not a cliff, but the dark waters of a wide river. The Ohio.

Icy cold, it rose above Bethie's head as stallion and rider plunged as one into the current.

Bethie felt herself float from the stallion's back, kicked with all her strength, desperate to get Isabelle's head above water.

She broke the surface, sucked sweet, cool air into her lungs, lifted her baby above water.

Belle coughed, gave a weak cry that soon became a wail.

She was alive.

But she wouldn't be for long if Bethie couldn't make it to the other side. The current was strong and swept her along, and although she was a good swimmer, she knew the Ohio River was perilous, with falls and hidden rocks that mangled both boats and bodies. She knew she needed to reach the other side if she wanted to survive.

Embers from the fire above fell around her, hissed as they hit the water.

She peered through the darkness for the stallion, heard it snort a short distance downstream, spotted it in the fire's eerie glow. It was almost ten feet away from her and swimming hard for the other side. If only she could grab hold of its mane.

She reached for it, sank beneath the surface.

Belle coughed and cried harder.

Bethie took her baby under her left arm, rolled onto her back, reached with her right arm, kicking through the water with all of her strength.

Strands of coarse hair.

The stallion's tail.

She grabbed hold, pulled until she was near enough to reach the saddle. Exhausted, she sagged against the powerful animal, gasping for breath as it carried them to safety.

Behind them, the fire was an impassable wall of flame that seemed to stretch the length of the riverbank.

It was sometime after dawn when Bethie awoke, nudged from sleep by the velvet of Zeus's inquisitive muzzle.

The big stallion stood protectively over her, still burdened with the saddle she hadn't had the strength to remove last night. Zeus nickered, nudged her again.

Exhausted, every muscle aching, she sat up, patted the stallion's forehead, reached for Belle, who had begun to fuss, still wrapped snugly in the shawl. Though the shawl had been singed in places and was as damp as everything else, it was the only shelter Bethie could offer her baby.

"Come, little one." Bethie's voice was rough from smoke, which still wafted through the air from across the river.

She leaned against a rock, began to nurse.

And in the light of day, the terrible truth finally hit her.

Nicholas was dead.

There was no way he could have been behind her and survived. She squeezed her eyes shut against the images that rose up unbidden in her imagination. Nicholas racing behind her on one of her mares. The fire closing in on them, overtaking them, claiming them. Unbearable heat. Choking smoke. An agonizing, terrible end.

He had chosen to save her and Isabelle, to give them the swiftest horse, to send them on their way before him, and now he was gone, burned to death.

Tears filled her eyes, blurred her vision, ran hot down her cheeks.

She could not bear to think of his suffering, could not bear the grief that filled her at the thought that he, who had once been tortured by fire, should have died in flames. No one deserved to die that way.

*Nicholas!*

Even through her tears she could see the immensity of the destruction. The forest on the other side of the river was gone, reduced to blackened trunks, smoldering logs, and scorched earth. Smoke hovered above the charred landscape, now in great columns, now in spiraling tendrils that drifted on the breeze like unquiet spirits.

All of it was gone. The cabin. The barn. The chickens in their coop. Dorcas and her wee calf. Her loom and spinning wheel. Isabelle's cradle. The moccasins Nicholas had made for them. Her quill. The book.

"Nicholas!" She whispered his name, felt her heart shatter.

He had done so much for her and for Isabelle. He had treated her with a kindness no man had ever shown her, save perhaps her real father. He had awakened something inside her—feelings she didn't understand. And his kisses . . .

But now he was dead.

As the sun poured its golden rays across the landscape from the east, she wept.

Some hours later, Bethie stood on a rock, rubbed the horse's chestnut coat with a makeshift currycomb of dried reeds, while it nibbled at the soft green grass. She had lifted the heavy saddle and blanket from the stallion's back and hung them over a tree branch to dry. She didn't want the wet wool or leather to chafe and cause sores on the big animal's back or belly. They had many miles to cover, and the stallion would have to carry them nearly every foot of the way.

Their survival depended upon him.

It was nearing midday, and panic had begun to build in her belly. She kept her gaze off the dark wall of forest beyond, but still the weight of the wilderness pressed in on her. She was utterly alone. No food. No shelter. No weapons. No clothing. Even if she'd had all those things, she'd have faced a struggle to survive. Good heavens, how would she be able to keep both herself and Belle alive without them?

And yet she had no choice but to try.

Fighting despair, she found a small outcropping of rocks and set up a little camp on the leeward side. She knew she should move on. She needed to find food and shelter. Although there was grass and water aplenty here for the stallion, it was too early for wild berries, and she had no means to kill or capture game and no way to cook it. Until she found a trading post or a family that would take her in, there would be little more than wild greens and roots for her to eat, barely enough to keep up her milk for Isabelle. Besides, the nights were still cold, the forest alive with wild animals and even wilder men. Alone in the forest wearing little more than her skin, she was naked and defenseless.

But where could she go? She had no clear idea where she was. Oh, aye, she knew she was on the opposite bank of the Ohio River, but the Ohio was long and winding. That the stallion had covered so much ground so quickly still astonished her. The mares could never have run so swiftly.

Nicholas must have known that. He must have chosen—

Nay! She could not do this. Nicholas had died giving her and her baby a chance at life. And so she must pull herself together. She must survive.

She swallowed her tears, forced her grief-weary mind to think. She supposed she should follow the river until she came to Fort Pitt, but how long would that take? Weeks? A month?

She could not expect help. In this country, there were few women, and the men would be more inclined to take advantage of her plight than to help her. Those who weren't the sort to rape or kill her outright would likely expect something in return for aiding her.

And when she reached Fort Pitt . . .

Surely the officers would not let their men prey upon a woman with a baby, a widow, no matter how she was dressed.

She jumped down off the rock, walked over to check on Isabelle, found her sound asleep in the shawl, which Bethie had hung between two branches to make a sort of hanging cradle. Then she reached for the saddle blanket to see whether sunlight and fresh air had dried it; she found it still damp.

Her gaze drifted to the opposite shore for what must have been the thousandth time.

He was not there. He would never be there.

She forced herself to look away, fought to keep her mind on the task at hand, off the regret and sorrow she knew would overwhelm her if she let them.

Water. Food. Shelter. A way to protect herself.

She needed some kind of weapon. She picked up a few stones, placed them beside the tree that sheltered Belle. Then an idea came to her.

She sought among the piles of driftwood, gathered a handful of sturdy sticks, took up a sharp stone, began to hone one of the sticks to a point. It would not be the same as a blade of steel, to be sure, but it might be enough to save her life and Isabelle's.

She had just completed her first improvised dagger, when Zeus whickered. Ears up, the stallion stomped impatiently, whinnied.

From nearby came an answering whinny. Then another.

Her heart slamming in her breast, Bethie jumped to her feet, sharpened stick in one hand, a rock in the other. Whoever they were, they knew she was here. The stallion had given her away. She fought the urge to run and hide, forced herself to stand on watery legs and face them. She wouldn't let them hurt her baby.

The moment stretched into eternity. She heard the roar of her pulse in her ears. The distant cry of a hawk. The dull thud of horses galloping over sand and stone.

*Nicholas!*

From around the bend he appeared, riding bareback on one of the mares, the other following obediently behind bearing his gear. Clad only in his leggings, soot smeared across his chest, his dark hair blowing in the breeze behind him, he was the most welcome sight she had ever seen.

Dizzy with relief, she gaped at him, unable to believe her eyes.

*He is alive.*

She dropped her makeshift weapons and ran to him. “Nicholas!”

He slid off the mare’s back, crushed her to him, pressed his lips against her hair. He smelled of smoke and forest and sunshine. “Bethie, love! Thank God, you’re safe! Where’s Belle? Is she—”

“She’s fine. She’s asleep over—”

But before she could finish, his fingers had fisted in her hair, and he captured her mouth with his. This was not like the restrained kisses he’d given her in the cabin. This kiss was scorching, desperate, almost savage—a kiss of release, a kiss of death defeated, a kiss of life renewed.

Her heart soaring, she welcomed the sweet invasion of his tongue, arched against him, frantic to feel him, to be closer to him.

Then he cupped her bottom, pulled her hard against him, and she felt the heat of his arousal against her belly. An answering heat flared inside her.

She whimpered, whispered his name.

And then, without warning, the crest of her emotions broke. Tears pricked her eyes, and she began to tremble, as the terror and the grief of the past three days crashed in on her.

He wiped the tears from her cheeks. “Are those tears for me?”

She sniffed, nodded, rested her hand against the reassuring rhythm of his heartbeat. “I thought you . . . Oh, God, I thought . . .”

His gaze drifted to the burn on her cheek, and he touched it lightly with his fingers.

“I’m fine, love. A few scratches and bruises. But let me take care of that burn.”

She brushed the back of her hand over the wound, turning her face away from him. “It’s no’ bad.”

He ran his thumb across the curve of her lower lip, mimicked her brogue and the words she’d spoken to him only yesterday. “I’ll be the one decidin’ that. Go sit in the shade, or the sun will burn that pretty pale skin of yours.”

She watched as he quickly tended the mares, unable to take her eyes off him for fear this was only a dream and she would wake to find herself alone in her grief. From the lines on his face, she could tell he was exhausted. He must have ridden all night to find her, pushing both himself and the mares to their limit.

*But he was alive.*

Once the mares were settled and his saddlebags safely stowed, he sat beside her.

"Let me wash your burn. Then I'll put some of my salve on it." He dipped a cloth in the cool water, squeezed it, gently cleaned her cheek. "It's not bad. It ought to heal well. Flying cinders?"

She nodded, met his gaze. "I thought you were dead."

He dabbed salve gently onto the small burn mark. "I planned to follow you, but in the time it took to fetch my saddlebags, I'd been cut off. I was forced farther to the west and took shelter in a lake until the fire passed. Then I followed a creek until it came to the Ohio."

"If you had been behind me, you'd have been killed. The fire caught up with us." She shuddered at the memory. "The trees—they seemed to scream."

He set aside the salve, pulled her against his chest, held her. "It's over now. We're alive, and that's what matters."

She allowed herself to sink against him, savored the feel of him, his scent, his strength. Suddenly she was so very tired. "What are we goin' to do now?"

He stroked her hair, pressed his lips to her temple. "First, we're going to get some sleep. Oh, don't worry. The horses will warn us if anyone approaches. Then I'm going to find us a nice, fat rabbit for dinner. Tomorrow morning we make for Fort Pitt and from there on to Paxton."

# Chapter 14

Bethie reined in her mare, weary with pain and fatigue. She adjusted Isabelle's weight in the sling she had made from her shawl, tried to keep her mind off the ache in her shoulders and the chafed, raw skin of her inner thighs. Nicholas had given her his last remaining shirt to protect her skin from insects and the burning rays of the sun, but he had no spare breeches to protect her bare legs nor shoes or moccasins for her feet.

Ahead of her, Nicholas dismounted, knelt down, studied the ground for tracks, his brow furrowed in concentration, his dark hair tied back with a thong. The wilderness was his world, she realized. Here he seemed at ease. He saw things she didn't see, heard things she couldn't hear, exuded confidence when she felt only hesitation, fear. He showed no signs of the exhaustion that plagued her, but leapt agilely up onto the stallion's back, urged it forward.

She gritted her teeth, bit back a groan as Rosa followed, the animal's stride causing Bethie's unprotected thighs to rub against the leather of Nicholas's saddle. He had adjusted it to fit the mares, given it to Bethie to use, sure it would make the journey safer for her and the baby. But she had little experience riding and had never sat astride. If the insides of her thighs were not blistered and bloody, they certainly felt that way.

Hadn't Nicholas warned her it would be hard? Aye, he had. And so much of the responsibility of this journey rested on his shoulders. It was he who protected them, found them food, searched for the safest paths. She wouldn't add to his burdens by complaining.

Fortunately, both mares had accepted Zeus's dominance and followed docilely wherever the stallion led, so Bethie had no worries when it came to controlling her mount. Nicholas hadn't even bothered to tie Rona to Bethie's saddle, but had let her wander free, sure that she would stay close behind them.

They'd been riding since shortly after dawn, following the river as it wound its way slowly to the northeast then dropped sharply to the southeast. Nicholas had kept them hidden in the cover of the forest, beneath a canopy of beech, maple, and oak. Bethie could not see the sun, but she knew it must be near sunset. Surely that meant they would stop soon.

In the sling, Belle began to whimper. Though the sling freed Bethie's hands for riding and made it easy for her to nurse without stopping, it didn't prevent them from having to dismount whenever the moss lining in Belle's diaper cloth needed to be changed.

Bethie held her daughter close, whispered. "Shhh, sweet. We cannae stop just yet."

But Belle would not be comforted. She began to kick and cry.

Bethie opened her shift, brought her nipple to Belle's mouth, but the baby turned her face away and cried harder.

Nicholas stopped, looking back over his shoulder.

Fearing his rebuke—he had warned her that a baby's cries, so out of place in the wild, would attract predators, especially the human kind—Bethie tried to explain. "She's wet."

He nodded, his brow bent in a slight frown. "If you can quiet her for just awhile longer, there's good shelter ahead."

"I'll try." Bethie lifted Belle out of the sling, held her upright against her shoulder, patted her back. "Shhh, Belle. Just awhile longer now."

The change of position seemed to help. Belle began to suck

on her hand and gazed at the shadows of the forest. But the terrain became increasingly hilly, forcing Bethie to hang on more tightly with her tortured thighs, until she had to bite her lip to keep from moaning. Then the slope pitched sharply downhill, and Bethie heard the sound of running water.

In one fluid move, Nicholas dismounted and withdrew his knife from its sheath. "Wait here." Gaze on the ground, he moved forward in silence, swiftly disappeared down the hill.

Bethie's pulse raced. Had he heard something? She dared not ask. She strained to listen, heard nothing but water and the twitter of birds.

Belle began to squirm, and Bethie knew she was about to begin fussing again. She jiggled her baby, kissed her cheek, did her best to distract her.

"Shhh, little one. Shhh."

Then, just as suddenly as he had vanished, he was back. "We'll make camp here for the night." He mounted the stallion again and led Bethie downhill to an outcropping of rocks, one of which seemed to have toppled against the other, forming a kind of arch. They stood just above a rushing creek.

"We'll have to dismount and tie the horses here. It's not high enough for them to pass through." He leapt lightly to the ground and reached for Rosa's bridle.

Now that they had finally stopped and she had the chance to get out of the saddle, Bethie found she hadn't the strength to move. Where her legs didn't hurt, they felt as dead and heavy as rotted logs. She tried to shift, to lift her right leg back and over the horse's rump, and could not stop the moan that passed her lips.

She didn't realize Nicholas was beside her until he lifted her from the saddle.

"Hold on to Belle." His voice was soft, reassuring. "Can you stand?"

"Aye."

He placed her on her feet, his hands on her shoulders to steady her.

But twelve hours in the saddle had left her weaker than she'd imagined. Her legs buckled, and she sagged against him.

Nicholas bit back a curse. He'd known this would be tough on her. He hadn't realized quite how tough. It had been a lifetime since his first days in the saddle, so long that he couldn't even remember ever being saddle sore. Clearly, he'd pushed her too hard.

He scooped Bethie into his arms, ducked under the arch, carried her to the other side, set her down on a cushion of dried moss. This wasn't the safest place in the world to pass the night, but it was reasonably secure and offered them both protection from the elements and a defensible position should anyone come across them in the night. To the north, the rocks created a natural barrier, passable only through the easily defended arch. The creek itself, though shallow, offered some protection to the east. A sheer wall of stone almost forty feet high guarded them to the south and west. At its base, water had created a small alcove deep enough for a few people to spend the night out of the rain and out of sight from above.

"Just rest. I'll tend to the horses."

Nicholas ducked back through the arch, found the horses at the water's edge slaking their thirst. He quickly stripped the saddle from Rosa's back, rubbed her down with the curry-comb from his saddlebags. Then he gave Zeus and Rona a good rubdown, as well, and staked the three within distance of both grass and water.

"Keep an eye on things, old boy." He gave Zeus a hearty pat on his withers. The stallion, so protective of his mares, would alert him should man or animal approach.

Nicholas picked up his saddle and saddlebags and ducked back through the arch. There he found both Bethie and Isabelle sound asleep. Bethie had solved the problem of the wet diaper cloth by simply removing it and draping it over a rock to dry. Thanks to the forest fire, they had only the one. Isabelle lay naked as the night she'd been born on her mother's breast, covered only by the thin woolen shawl.

Nicholas wasted no time. First, he laid out a soft bed of furs in the alcove. Then he lit a small fire, built a tripod of sturdy sticks over it, took out his cook pot, put water on to boil. Last, he slipped off his moccasins and strode down to the water's edge, knife in hand.

By the time Bethie awoke, he had a cup of tea waiting for her and three spotted bass sizzling over the fire.

"That smells good." She tried to sit, gasped, bit her lip.

"Easy, Bethie." He picked up the tea, carried it to her. "I'll have supper soon. Drink this. It's made from willow bark. It will help take away some of your soreness. Be careful. It's still hot."

She laid Isabelle down gently on the bed of furs, took the cup from him, sniffed its contents, and wrinkled her nose.

"It's bitter, but it really does work. Trust me." He watched as she took a sip, smiled at the face she made. "Drink it."

While she struggled with the tea, Nicholas tossed wild onion onto the fish, flipped them once more, and pulled the corn cakes from the ashes. There was no butter, as she was accustomed to, but this would help her rebuild her strength and keep up her milk for Isabelle. He put half of the fish onto his tin plate, together with a couple of corn cakes and a fork, carried it to her, then sat to eat his from the pan with a spoon.

"Thank you." She took one small bite, moaned, took another larger bite, then ate with a dainty abandon that would have shocked the women of Virginia's stuffy drawing rooms. "This is tasty."

Nicholas chuckled. "Don't sound so surprised. I've had to survive on my own cooking for a long time now. I've learned a thing or two along the way."

She lowered her fork, licked her lips in an unconscious gesture that made Nicholas's blood heat by several degrees, then looked at him through guileless eyes. "Why do you live out here alone? Do you no' have family?"

Nicholas felt his good humor vanish. But it was an innocent question. "Aye, I have family—parents, brothers, sisters—in Virginia. I left home at the outset of the war and never went back."

Bethie watched the smile vanish from his face and knew she'd asked the wrong question. She finished her meal in silence. She watched as he cleaned up, set more water on to boil.

"It will be dark soon. You should try taking a quick bath in the creek. The cold water will make you feel better."

"But—"

"I won't watch." He reached into his saddlebags. "You can use my soap."

Soap in hand, she struggled to her feet, gritted her teeth against her aching muscles, and walked stiffly to the water's edge. She turned to face him. "Do I have your word you willna watch?"

"Aye, Mistress Stewart. I'll keep my eyes instead on your charming daughter."

She watched as he gently laid her shawl over Isabelle. Then she wandered a short distance downstream, out of his direct sight and slipped off his shirt and her shift, dropping them on the sandy bank. She tested the water with her toes, yanked her foot back. It was ice cold.

Not wishing to be a coward, she stepped slowly into the rushing water until it reached her thighs. Then she ducked beneath the surface and began hastily to wash herself with his soap. Although the water was colder than any she'd ever bathed in before, she felt some of her pain begin to slip away. By the time her bones ached from the chill, she was clean from head to toe and feeling much refreshed.

Nicholas watched, his promise broken to bits, as Bethie walked carefully over wet stones back to the bank, squeezing water from her long hair. Water ran in rivulets down her satiny skin, over her full breasts, over the soft curve of her belly, through the nest of blond curls that covered her sex, down her shapely thighs. Her rosy nipples were drawn tight against the chill, and her skin glowed pink.

His cock sprang to life, stretched the buckskin of his breeches. His testicles ached for release. He found himself wanting to pick her up, carry her to this bed of furs, pleasure her with his hands and mouth and cock until she trembled with need and begged him to take her over the edge. Then she lifted her leg to take a step . . . and he saw the deep, purple bruises on the insides of her thighs.

"Hell!" Caught between irritation and the frustration of pent-up desire, he rummaged roughly through his saddlebags until he found his little crock of salve. By the time she returned, he had managed to gain some control of himself. "Feel any better?"

She smiled, her face as sweet as sunlight, and sat beside him on the moss. "Aye.

He handed her the salve. "Spread this on the skin between your legs. And next time you're in that much pain, let me know. You won't last out here if you don't take care of yourself."

She gaped at him, eyes wide. Then a rosy blush suffused her cheeks, and she looked away. "You watched."

There was no way to deny it, so he didn't bother. "Only a little. Now put that on your thighs and the burn on your cheek. When you're finished, I'll get the tangles out of your hair."

She glared at him, then turned her back to him.

He tried not to think about the fact that she wore no drawers and now sat with her legs parted, so that she could spread ointment on her inner thighs. Instead, he focused on her hair, long golden strands, as soft as silk. Without a comb, he had only his fingers to separate the snarls. He waited until she finished, then took up her hair, starting at the ends and working his way up. "Too bad it's dark. Otherwise, we might have practiced your reading a bit tonight."

"You saved the book?" She sounded pleased.

"It was tucked away in my bags when the fire hit and so was spared. Did you think it lost?"

Bethie tried to answer, but he was doing something wonderful to her nape with his fingers, and the only sound that came from her mouth was a sort of purr.

"Does that feel good, Bethie?" His voice was deep, carried the husky tones she now recognized as desire.

"Oh, aye." She felt it, too—a strange heat, an awareness, a longing. "Kiss me, Nicholas!"

He groaned, a primal, male sound. Then he pulled her into his arms, laid her gently down on the furs, stretched out beside her. For an instant he gazed deep into her eyes, a look of barely restrained emotion on his face. Then his mouth claimed hers in a fierce kiss.

If Bethie thought she knew how good it was to be kissed by him, she soon realized she was blissfully mistaken. In front of the hearth in the cabin, his mouth had teased her, tempted her, but now it possessed her, consumed her.

She parted her lips, surrendered to the velvet invasion of his tongue, the terror and exhaustion of the past two days yielding to the hard press of his body against hers. Lost in the taste of him, the feel of him, lost in his scent, she found in herself a fervor to match his. She returned his kiss, arched against him, wanting . . .

Wanting what?

She whimpered, a sound of frustration, then whispered his name. "Nicholas!"

"What do you want, Bethie? Tell me." His mouth found the sensitive skin beneath her ear, nipped, licked, sucked.

Something deep in her belly clenched. Damp heat gathered inside her, spread between her thighs. She felt heavy, hot, on fire. "More!"

"Is this what you want?" He traced her lips with his tongue, thrust intimately into her mouth. Her lips were swollen and aching beneath his. Then he broke the kiss. Gazing knowingly into her eyes, he traced a lazy line on her collarbone with his thumb. "Tell me, Bethie."

"I—I dinnae know what I want!" She panted, breathless and desperate.

His hand stroked her wet hair as his lips brushed her cheek. "Do you trust me?"

Did she trust him? After all he'd done to help her and Belle? After he'd nearly died to save them? After he'd watched her bathe in the creek when he'd promised not to? "Aye. Mostly."

He chuckled softly, then nipped her throat, ran his tongue over the whorl of her ear. "Have I ever hurt you?"

She shivered. "N-nay." The word came out as a moan.

"Then let me bring you pleasure. Let me touch you. Only tell me to stop, and I will." He nibbled her earlobe, drew it into the heat of his mouth.

*Let me touch you.*

Dark memories pricked at the back of her mind—memories of groping hands, of pain, of humiliation. But there were other memories as well, memories of tenderness, of kisses so potent they stole her breath, made her pulse quicken, made her blood burn.

He was not Richard. He was not Andrew.

He was Nicholas.

Could it be different? Could a woman enjoy lying beside a man? Could she enjoy his hands upon her?

She wanted to know. She needed to know.

She met his gaze, felt herself begin to tremble, anticipation and apprehension twined together in her belly. "Aye, Nicholas. Please!"

# Chapter 15

Her whispered words unleashed a maelstrom inside Nicholas. He wanted to release the fire inside her, to bury himself in her silken heat, to devour her. He wanted to claim her, make her forget she'd ever been touched by another man.

But he could feel the conflict within her. The ardor of her body's response told him she wanted him, but the wariness in her eyes proved she was still afraid.

He brushed his lips over hers, kissed the corners of her mouth, forced himself to rein in his own need, to go slowly. "You are beautiful, Bethie. Do you know that?"

He didn't give her time to answer, but took her lips in a deep, languid kiss, using his tongue to make her forget fear, forget doubt, forget everything but his touch.

She moaned into his mouth—not in fear, but desire.

He took her breath into his lungs, pressed the kiss deeper, rested his palm over her heart. It beat like the wings of a frightened bird. "You've nothing to fear, Bethie. Tell me what you want, whatever you want. It's yours."

She whispered his name, arched against his touch, her body telling him what she seemingly could not.

He brushed the valley between her breasts with the back of

his knuckles once, twice, three times, felt her heartbeat quicken even more. Then he slid his hand beneath the thin, damp fabric of her shift, caressed the soft underside of her breast, his palm brushing lightly over her nipple on the way.

She gasped, one quick intake of breath, arched again, her nipples already drawn into tight, blushing buds.

"So soft." He continued to caress the naked silk of her breast, to mold its delicious fullness in his palm.

She had begun to tremble, to writhe in his arms, one hand fisted in the soft furs, the other pressed against his chest.

He flicked his thumb over her taut, rosy peak once, then again.

She gasped, moaned.

"You like that, too. What about this?" He leaned over, took her nipple into his mouth, suckled her. He would teach her to ask for her pleasure, to demand it, to savor it.

Bethie heard herself cry out, felt a shaft of searing heat shoot from her breast to her belly, then turn to dew between her thighs. It felt so good, and before she realized it, she had twined her fingers through his hair, pressed him closer.

"I've waited so long to taste you, Bethie." His voice had a ragged edge to it, and she felt his hand open her shift, bare her aching breasts to the cool night air. Then he cupped one breast in his callused palm, drew lazy circles over its tight peak with his thumb, descended on her again, his mouth closing over her other nipple this time.

Never had she felt anything like this. Sensation overwhelmed her. The rasp of his tongue. The sweet tug of his lips. The deep vibration of his mouth as he moaned.

"Nicholas!" What was happening to her? What had he done to her to make her feel so hot, so reckless? What was that wet, throbbing emptiness between her thighs?

"Mmm, warm and sweet." He flicked his tongue against the sensitive underside of her breast, then drew her nipple back into his mouth, sucked it, grazed it gently with his teeth.

"Oh, aye!"

He caught her pleasured cry with his mouth, ravished her with his lips and tongue.

The throb between her thighs became an ache.

As if he knew what she was feeling, he slid a hand down the heated skin of her belly, began to move it in slow circles over her womb.

She felt her hips lift off the furs, seeking, seeking . . . Oh, she did not know what!

Then he slid his hand down over her woman's mound, cupped her most intimate flesh.

A lightning shard of panic. A wave of nausea.

"Nay!" She pressed her legs tightly together, tried to push his hand away. "Please, stop!"

Nicholas felt her body stiffen. But he felt something else as well. Even through the cloth of her shift, he could tell she was wet. Her body wanted him, was more than ready for him.

But her mind was not. Her eyes were squeezed shut, her face turned away from him.

"It's all right, Bethie." He fought the raging of his blood, ignored the animal drive inside him that urged him to take her despite his promise, withdrew his hand. Then he pulled her into his arms, stroked her hair. "Tell me what you fear, love. Tell me who hurt you." *So I can kill the bastard—if he's not already dead.*

For a moment she said nothing, but trembled in his arms. "Th-there is nothing to tell."

Because she seemed so fragile, because he did not want to upset her further, he let the lie pass. He pressed his lips to her hair. "Sleep. We've a long journey ahead of us."

Soon her trembling stopped, and her breathing deepened.

But Nicholas lay awake for a long time, burning.

Bethie awoke just before dawn to a chorus of birdsong—and the scent of frying fish.

"I've made more willow-bark tea." Nicholas rose from his seat by the fire, walked toward her carrying a cup. His wet hair told her he'd bathed in the stream while she'd slept. "Drink."

Despite the thoughtful gesture, his furrowed brow, the grim line of his mouth, the tension in his jaw told her he was in a dark temper.

Was he angry because she had refused him?

She sat up, winced. Her bum was tender. Her inner thighs

felt as if they'd been stripped of skin. Even her neck and shoulders ached, no doubt from holding Isabelle all day.

She took the cup from his hand, unable to meet his gaze, her shame from last night still fresh in her mind. "Thank you."

*Tell me who hurt you, Bethie.*

How did he know?

Beside her, beneath the bear skin Nicholas had laid over them sometime during the night, Isabelle had begun to stir.

By the time the baby was awake and ready to nurse, Bethie had drunk her tea, eaten her breakfast, washed her dishes in the stream. She picked up her baby and settled down for a feeding.

Nicholas smothered the fire with sand, began to scatter the ashes. "We need to travel far and fast today, make it difficult for anyone who finds signs of our presence here to catch up with us."

She glanced down at Isabelle, worried. "I have only the one diaper cloth. Once it's wet, she's sure to start wailin'."

Nicholas nodded, then began to dig through his pile of furs. As Bethie finished feeding Belle, he pulled out a couple of small rabbit skins, cut away bits and pieces until two small hourglass-shaped furs remained. "Try this."

While Nicholas packed his saddlebags and rolled their bed of furs into a bundle, Bethie laid Isabelle on the trimmed rabbit fur and folded it around her like a diaper. The corners were thin and supple enough that Bethie was able to tie them to keep the fur in place.

Isabelle kicked and cooed, as if in approval, her chubby cheeks pink, her eyes bright.

"Line it with moss. I think the fur will absorb some of the moisture."

Bethie tucked the dried moss in place. "We'll still need to stop to change her."

But he had already ducked beneath the arch, saddle and saddlebags in hand.

Bethie quickly fashioned her shawl into a sling again and tucked Isabelle safely inside it. Then she followed him through.

Without a word, he draped the heavy saddlebags across the stallion's back and saddled Rona. Then he turned to lift

Bethie into the saddle. "I know this won't be comfortable, Bethie, but we need to cover as much ground as we can. Tell me if it becomes too painful."

Strong hands gripped her around her waist, lifted her onto the mare's back.

Bethie bit back a cry as she settled into the saddle and her raw thighs came to rest against the leather. The pain was already excruciating.

They rode at a quicker pace than they had the previous day, following the course of the river but holding to the shadow of the trees. Nicholas again took the lead, riding bareback on the stallion, dismounting every so often to search the ground for tracks, his mood pensive. Bethie rode behind him, Belle resting in the sling draped over her shoulders. Rosa followed them as Rona had done the day before, drawn down the trail by her loyalty to her tiny herd.

Bethie tried not to complain. She could tell Nicholas felt there was reason for haste, and she trusted his instincts to keep her alive. She didn't want to slow them down. But it was not yet midmorning when the pain was so bad that she was close to tears. "Stop! Please!"

He looked back over his shoulder, reined the stallion to a stop. He dismounted with one easy leap and strode over to her. "We'll walk for a while."

Strong arms lifted her from the saddle, placed her on her feet.

And so they walked in silence. Nicholas led the horses, while Bethie carried Isabelle and tried not to step on thorns or sharp rocks with her bare feet.

It was late in the afternoon when Nicholas stopped abruptly, motioning for her to do the same. He crouched close to the ground, examined the forest floor, then stood and pulled his pistols from the waistband of his breeches.

Bethie's heart began to hammer.

"Stay here. I'm going to scout ahead." He handed her one pistol and took his rifle from his saddlebags. "I assume you know how to use this."

"Aye."

"Good. If anything steps out of the forest that isn't me, shoot it, and don't miss. Do you understand?"

She nodded. "Nicholas, what—"

He pressed a hand to her lips. "And keep Belle quiet."

Then he was gone.

For a moment Bethie stood staring into the forest gloom where he'd disappeared, her pulse racing. Then she chided herself for her lack of courage. "Think, Bethie! You willna be of any use to him or Belle if you cower at the first sign of trouble."

She tied off the stallion's reins, then looked for a place where she and Belle could hide.

Knife and pistol drawn, Nicholas followed the tracks away from the river. He guessed there were about a dozen of them—another war party. Judging from their moccasin prints, which were placed far apart, they were moving fast. Strange that they had done so little to conceal their tracks. That meant they felt confident—sure of what lay both before and behind them.

He picked up his own pace and soon smelled smoke. He knew what he would find before he got there.

In the midst of a clearing stood the burned-out remains of a cabin. Smoke still rose from the charred ruins, a grisly pennant against the blue sky. Apart from a few chickens that strutted and pecked in the mud, nothing moved.

The bodies were scattered in the grass outside the cabin—a red-haired man, a dark-haired woman, two small dark-haired children. They had been slaughtered with war clubs and knives, their lives lost, all their worldly goods and everything they had worked for reduced to ash.

Fury, like a sickness, churned in his stomach.

So much killing. Senseless death. Insatiable violence.

This wasn't the first time Nicholas had encountered such brutality. He'd seen many frontier families slaughtered these past six years—men, women, children, infants. They came to build lives for themselves, but found only death.

Of course Indians weren't the only ones capable of such mindless violence. Europeans committed their share of atrocities, too—Indian children butchered and scalped by French and British soldiers and settlers, babies on cradleboards dashed against rocks, women raped and mutilated, old men killed while on their knees begging for their lives.

Violence, it seemed, was not the province of one race but a human trait.

Nicholas knelt beside the woman, closed her eyes, which stared unseeing at the blue sky. She was pretty and young, just a year or two older than Bethie. But there was nothing he could do for her or her slain children and husband.

Bethie fought to ignore her discomfort. Her stomach grumbled, and her legs had long since grown cramped from sitting confined in this dark thicket. Insects buzzed around her. Spiders and millipedes skittered over the carpet of rotting leaves beneath her. The tail of a snake slithered through the underbrush. She began to imagine—or perhaps she was not imagining—the cobweb brush of many tiny legs crawling over her skin. And once she thought she heard the low, grunting snuffles of a bear.

Remembering how the stallion had given them away last time, she had chosen a hiding place well away from, but in sight of, the horses and was forcing herself to stay put, so as not to create a trail into and out of the thicket. It didn't matter how uncomfortable she felt. She would do nothing to give herself away. Her life—and Belle's—might depend on it.

An eternity had passed since Nicholas had left them. Where had he gone? What would she do if he did not come back? What if he were overcome, taken captive, killed?

Fear jolted through her at the thought.

He would come back. He had to come back.

But the afternoon lengthened, and still he did not return. She was beginning to imagine that the most horrible things had happened to him, when the stallion whinnied.

She froze, pressed Belle closer to her breast, held her breath.

It was Nicholas. He called for her softly. "Bethie?"

A warm rush of relief swept through her. She crawled out from the thicket, Isabelle in her arms.

He held three chickens by their feet, their wobbly heads proof their necks had been broken. Over his shoulder hung a new set of saddlebags. But what she noticed was the look in his eyes.

Bleak. Dark. Anguished.

He draped the chickens and saddlebags across the stallion's back. "We need to ride."

Bethie reached out, touched his arm. "What—"

"There's a burnt farmstead a couple of miles south of here. No survivors."

Horrified, Bethie realized what he was telling her. A family had been attacked nearby. Their home had been burned, and they had all been killed.

She asked the question, though she already knew the answer. "Indians?"

"A Delaware war party."

A shiver of terror passed through her, but she tried not to acknowledge it. "W-were there children?"

He met her gaze, and the shadows in his eyes answered her question.

Tears blurred her vision. "And the chickens?"

"I decided I could either let the wolves and wildcats have them, or I could catch an easy dinner. There's grain for the horses in the saddlebags. It will help them keep up their strength until we reach the fort. The mares aren't used to this kind of life."

Her gaze shifted from the chickens to the saddlebags. "Are you sure it's right to be takin' from the dead?"

His voice took a hard edge. "What's the first rule of the wilderness, Bethie?"

She whispered. "Survival."

His hands gripped her around the waist, and he lifted her easily into the saddle. "There's a sheltered campsite up ahead. It's not as secure as the place we camped last night, but it will do, provided no one has already claimed it."

Then it occurred to her. "The Indians—did you see where they went?"

"They've headed southeast, and they're moving fast."

She sighed with relief. If they were moving southeast, perhaps they wouldn't be coming back this way.

"I wouldn't feel too safe just yet. That war party is headed straight for Fort Pitt."

# Chapter 16

For five more days they traveled southeast, keeping to the cover and coolness of the forest. They rode for the most part in silence, Nicholas in the lead, his gaze on the forest floor. It quickly became clear to Bethie how well he knew this country—every stream, every spring, every meadow and outcropping of rock. He knew the best fishing sites and where the deer would come down to drink at night with their spotted fawns. He knew which roots to eat, which plants would cure illness, and which would kill.

He set what felt to Bethie like a punishing pace, stopped only when there were tracks he needed to examine more closely or when the baby needed to be changed. He had draped a soft lynx fur across the saddle to protect Bethie's chafed skin, enabling her to ride harder and longer than before. Yet she knew he wished they could move faster.

But caring for a baby in the wild wasn't easy. Gathering moss, milkweed silk, and thistledown to line Belle's diaper skins had become a constant task in the evenings. Changing her slowed them down. Carrying her in the sling and nursing while sitting on horseback made Bethie's shoulders ache. Still, Belle was a good baby, more prone to contentment than crying. The rocking movement of the horse seemed to lull her, the dappled light of the forest to enthrall her.

The hours of silence gave Bethie time to think, to worry. The ride to Fort Pitt was only the first part of their journey. If they made it to the fort alive, they would have but a brief respite before setting out for Paxton. Unless she refused to leave the fort or . . .

What was she thinking? That Nicholas would give up his life in the wild, take her to wife, and become a farmer and the father of her child?

She had only to put her unspoken wish into words to realize how foolish it was. She was a woman without a husband, without a home, and Nicholas had never promised her more than passing protection. Yet she knew he had at least some feelings for her.

Hadn't he called her beautiful? Hadn't he showed her with his kisses and the heat of his hands that he desired her? When his touch had frightened her, hadn't he kept his word and stopped? And didn't he still hold her at night, keep her warm and safe, kiss her hair when he thought she was asleep?

Nicholas. Nicholas. How he confused her! How could he be this kind to her and not care for her? How could he care for her and yet simply ride away and leave her? And why was she even thinking of him in that way? Had she not decided when Andrew died that she would prefer to live as a widow than any man's wife?

But Nicholas was not any man. Nicholas had opened the door to mysteries she hadn't known existed when she'd lain in Andrew's bed. He had taught her to write her name, was teaching her to read so that she could someday teach her daughter. And most of all—more than any of the kindnesses he had shown her—he had not forced himself on her.

She didn't know much about him, yet she knew for certain she'd never meet another man like him.

She watched him ride just ahead of her, his dark hair lifted by the breeze, his body so attuned to the animal beneath him, the forest around him. Regret, like the sharp edge of a blade, cut her heart. Why had she stopped him? Why had she become afraid? He hadn't hurt her. He had done nothing but bring her pleasure. And yet when he had touched her there, she had been unable to control her reaction. Fear had surged through her, fear so strong it seemed to choke the light from the sun.

Her shame. Her taint. Her terror. Would it follow her forever?

If someone had told Nicholas six months ago that he and Zeus would soon be traveling through the wilderness with a woman, a baby, and two pregnant mares, he'd have called that person a liar and a damned idiot. For six years he had wandered, seeking oblivion in the vastness of this continent. He'd kept to himself, refused to get caught up in other people's lives. Their foolishness, their lack of planning, their ignorance were not his problem, and those who were unprepared for survival died. It was the way of the wild.

He couldn't remember the last time he'd felt a sense of purpose, a reason for being. But somehow Bethie had crept beneath his guard, gotten past the wall he'd built around himself, and now nothing was more important to him than getting her—and her baby—to safety.

He glanced back over his shoulder, worried. She was all but asleep in the saddle. In his eagerness to reach the fort as quickly as possible, he had again pushed her too hard.

He had just decided to scout for a place to make camp, when he heard the sound of something crashing through the forest. It was coming toward them.

He leapt to the ground, grabbed the mare's reins to stop her, lifted Bethie out of the saddle. "Get behind those rocks!"

Bethie's eyes were wide with terror, but she kept silent, did exactly as he asked.

Quickly, he tied the horses' reins to a nearby tree and had just enough time to grab his rifle, drop to the ground, and aim when a bull charged toward him out of the trees, a spear protruding from its back.

Nicholas held his fire.

Crazed with fear and pain, the animal bellowed, veered to avoid the frightened horses, then disappeared into the forest behind them.

He heard Bethie's sigh of relief, whispered to her fiercely.

"Stay back there, Bethie. Don't make a sound, and don't come out until I tell you to!" Then he stood, took up position behind a gnarled oak near the place where the bull had broken through the underbrush.

And almost immediately he heard it—rapid footfalls, labored breathing. Someone was running toward them.

Every muscle in his body tensed, readied to make the most of a surprise attack. A vision of the slain mother flashed in his mind, her eyes staring sightless at the blue sky.

He would not let them hurt Bethie or little Belle.

Then shouting echoed through the trees. "It got away, you fool. Isn't one enough to fill your belly?"

The language was Delaware. The voice came from a distance.

"I'm hungry, and this is my kill!" The man stood not more than twenty feet away.

Nicholas held his breath, hoping the bull's crashing and bellowing had been enough to cover the whinnies of the startled horses and praying the baby would not make a sound.

"Forget it, and come back to the fire. They'll have cooked and eaten all the meat by the time you catch up to that old animal. Besides, I don't think you sank your spear very deep."

"Listen, friend. When I sink my spear, I bury it all the way. Ask my wife."

Both men laughed.

"Well, you chase it down if you want. Go chew on its old hide. I'm going back to the fire for juicier meat."

*Go back. Go back.* Nicholas willed the warrior to heed his friend's advice and give up the chase. The seconds ticked by, each as long as eternity, each weighing the difference between life and death. *Go back.*

"I'll come with you, but I want the liver." Then the Delaware warrior strode off, heading back through the trees, his voice growing distant as he argued with his friend over who would eat which organs.

Nicholas let out the breath he'd been holding, didn't move until he was certain both men were far out of earshot. Then he strode silently over to Bethie, who sat behind the rocks, clutching Isabelle to her breast, a rock gripped tightly in her free hand. He knelt before her, pulled her into his arms, whispered. "It's all right, Bethie. They've gone. But we need to hurry. Can you ride farther tonight?"

She nodded, looked at him questioningly. "Are they the same ones—"

"I think so. We need to get out of here." He helped her to her feet, took her arm.

But she didn't budge. "W-why didn't you kill them?"

"If I had, the rest of the Delaware war party would know we're here now, wouldn't they? And they would come after us. Trust me, Bethie. We must go!"

They rode until Nicholas was certain Bethie could ride no more, headed for a site he knew ensured them protection from the Delaware. An ancient burial site made up of several mounds and surrounded by a heavy growth of trees, it was a place of loathing for most Indians, who believed dark spirits stalked among the mounds. The war party would not follow them there.

"Come, love." Nicholas lifted Bethie from her saddle, steadied her until she found her footing. He laid out their bed of furs while she changed the baby. He had no sooner covered her with the bearskin than she was fast asleep.

Quickly, he tended the horses, rubbed them down, gave the mares each an extra ration of grain, picketed them at the edge of the glade where a little spring fed into a tiny stream. It had been a hard day's work for the animals, and tomorrow would only bring more of the same.

But it wasn't the horses that worried him. It was the Delaware. Though he had hinted at it, he hadn't spelled out for Bethie what he feared lay ahead of them or why it was so necessary for them to move swiftly. The war parties were slaughtering every settler they encountered. But they weren't taking any supplies. That meant only one thing—they were in a hurry. Why?

It was this question that filled Nicholas's mind each day, kept him awake at night.

Then there was the recklessness with which they seemed to be traveling. They left clear tracks plain enough for a child to follow. And just this evening, two Delaware warriors had shouted to each other in what ought to have been dangerous territory. What had given them such confidence?

There was one answer to both questions that made sense. They were on their way to an important gathering, and they believed themselves surrounded by allies. Was it possible that they were converging with other war parties for an attack on Fort Pitt? Were they so certain of victory that they felt the Ohio Valley was already won? Had they joined together in such overwhelming numbers that their boldness was driving them to carelessness?

Shingiss had warned him last winter that the nations of the northwestern wilderness were joining forces to drive whites out. Nicholas was now certain that if they didn't hurry, they would arrive at Fort Pitt only to find it already under siege—and their access to it blocked. But even if they reached the fort, they would not be safe. If Fort Pitt was not already under siege by the time they arrived, it soon would be.

Nicholas had wanted to lead Bethie and her baby to safety. As the days passed, he began to fear he was only leading them into greater danger.

"I hate to wake you, Bethie, but we need to keep moving."

She felt Nicholas kiss her cheek, struggled to wakefulness from a dreamless sleep.

By the time she'd finished her breakfast of roast chicken and corn cakes and fed Belle, Nicholas had the fire out, the saddlebags packed, and the horses ready.

They followed the river as it made a sudden sweep northward toward its joining with the Allegheny and Monongahela rivers, keeping as usual to the cover of the trees. But they hadn't ridden far when they came across the burnt ruins of another farm.

Nicholas dismounted. "Stay here, Bethie. I don't want you to see this."

But Bethie didn't need to get any closer to realize what she was seeing. Lying in the grass around the charred remains of a cabin were several human bodies, the air above them thick with flies. She turned Rosa's head away from the slaughter, drew air deep into her lungs, fought to keep her breakfast.

Nicholas was soon back, his face grim. He strode over to his stallion, mounted. "This happened a few days ago."

She fought her queasiness, tried to be strong. "D-do you think it's the same ones?"

He drew alongside her. "No. This band is much larger—I'd say perhaps as many as thirty warriors. But they're headed toward Fort Pitt just like the others."

"'Tis the uprisin' you spoke of, is it no'? These attacks cannae be mere chance."

He nodded. "It's time we forsook the river and rode across country straight for the fort. We can reach Fort Pitt by dawn if we ride hard. Can you manage it, Bethie? It will be long and rough, and there's likely to be trouble."

She looked at him through eyes filled with trust. "I will go where you lead and do my best no' to be a burden."

He reached across, cupped her cheek. "You're not a burden."

They turned their horses to the east and rode through hilly, forested country. Despite the need to cover ground quickly, Nicholas kept the horses at a walk, unwilling to risk riding headlong into an encampment of warriors or finding themselves in an ambush.

They passed two more burnt farmsteads before noon, though there were no bodies at the second. As the two farms were located fairly close together, Bethie suggested that perhaps the occupants of the second farm had heard what was happening to their neighbors and had fled.

They *had* fled, but they hadn't gotten far. Nicholas spotted their bodies a half mile from their home. He led Bethie in a wide arc around the carnage.

It was early afternoon when he motioned for Bethie to stop.

Something didn't feel right.

Zeus snorted, jerked at the reins. The stallion's ears twitched, faced back.

*Behind them.*

They were being tracked.

Quickly, Nicholas read the landscape. Unsure how many men were approaching, he needed a defensible position. Then he kicked in his heels, urged Zeus to a canter. "Hurry, Bethie!"

A half mile ahead of them two steep hills rose from the ground. He knew that a small brook ran between them down a narrow gully, a natural place for travelers to water their horses—and the perfect spot for an ambush.

It took only a few minutes for them to reach the brook. Nicholas reined the horses to low-hanging branches near the water, grabbed his rifle, shot, and powder, then helped Bethie dismount.

"Nicholas, what—" Her eyes were wide, her face pale.

"We're being followed. Quick. Up here."

Leaving the horses as bait, he took Bethie by the hand and led her up the steep hillside, showing her how to step only on stone so as to leave no trace. Quickly, he chose the best spot, a rock overhang that gave him a view of the entrance to the gully.

"You stay here. Keep the baby quiet and out of sight. Here's a loaded pistol. Don't use it unless I'm gone and they find you—"

"But where—"

"I'll head back down, lay a false trail for them, then hide. When they move toward the horses, I'll attack. Don't give yourself away. With one saddle to three horses, they might think I'm traveling alone. If they kill me, you stay hidden until they leave, then head due east toward the fort. Don't waste time burying me. Do you understand?"

"Aye, but leave me one of the rifles. I can shoot, Nicholas."

Nicholas had expected her to show fear, and there was fear in her eyes. But her face also showed grim resolve. An image of her standing before her cabin, alone, frightened, and very pregnant, leapt into his mind.

*I am no' wantin' for means to protect myself!*

He handed her the weapon. "Very well. It's primed and loaded. But you are not to use it except to save your own life, do you understand?"

"But what if you're—"

"No! Fire only to save your own life! Once you fire, they'll know where you are, and they'll come for you. They're experienced warriors, Bethie. You'll have two shots, maybe three if you reload quickly." He placed his extra powder horn and a leather pouch of lead balls, on the ground beside her.

Bethie settled a sleeping Belle under a nearby tree, lay down on the rock, took up the rifle, and watched as Nicholas made his way carefully down the hillside and back to the horses. He stomped clumsily about in the mud. Then, deliberately stepping on the underbrush, he strode down the creek and disappeared.

He'd been out of sight for only a moment when she saw them—five Delaware warriors crouched at the mouth of the gully.

# Chapter 17

Bethie lay flat against the rock, hardly daring to breathe. She watched as the Indian men walked silently into the gully. Two held rifles. The rest carried war clubs and knives. One had small tufts of hair hanging from his belt.

Her stomach lurched. *Human scalps.*

Five against one. She searched the hillside across from her, searched for some sign of Nicholas. Did he know he was outnumbered? Could he see they carried rifles?

She glanced over her shoulder, saw that Belle had awoken and was sucking her thumb. She would be hungry soon. If she began to cry . . .

Bethie closed her eyes, muttered a silent prayer.

When she opened her eyes again, the warriors were directly below her. They moved cautiously, their heads turning as they searched the hillsides.

Her heart stopped dead.

One seemed to look directly at her, his gaze sliding over her like a breeze.

She knew the moment they saw the horses. Their attention shifted to the animals, and, crouched and ready to fight, they moved forward with more confidence. One bent down, traced the footprints Nicholas had left for them to find, gestured to the others. Four moved forward toward the horses, while the fifth, the man with the scalps on his belt, backtracked, disappearing up the hill into the trees.

Two pistol shots split the silence.

A knife whistled through the air, sank into flesh.

A cry. A grunt.

Three of the Indians fell to the ground.

Nicholas sprang from nowhere, grabbed a rifle from one of the men he'd shot, swung it at the fourth, who leapt out of the way.

Bethie saw Nicholas flip the rifle, aim it, fire at his attacker's belly.

Nothing happened.

It hadn't been loaded.

In horror, Bethie watched as the Indian gave a hair-raising cry and rushed in on Nicholas, war club in one hand, knife in the other. He swung the club, aimed for Nicholas's head.

There was a crack of steel on wood as war club met rifle.

Nicholas deflected the blow, leapt neatly back to avoid the knife.

And then she saw.

The fifth man, the man she had forgotten, the man with the scalps, stalked Nicholas from behind.

He stepped out from behind a tree. Raised his rifle. Cocked it. Took aim.

*Nicholas!*

Another shot rang out.

Isabelle screamed.

Below her on the hillside, Bethie saw the man with the scalps crumple, fall to the ground, slide lifeless down the hillside in a flurry of leaves.

Nicholas stared up at her, surprise and fury on his face.

So did the remaining Indian.

Only then did Bethie realize the shot had been hers.

Nicholas wrenched his attention off Bethie, back to the surviving Delaware, took advantage of the man's distraction to deliver a skull-crushing blow with the rifle butt.

The man fell to the earth, as good as dead.

Nicholas retrieved his pistols, pulled his knife from its temporary sheath deep in one man's chest, wiped it clean on the man's breeches. As the rush of the fight began to fade, his anger fused to a sharp edge.

She had defied him. She had fired the rifle, given herself away, put herself and Isabelle in danger. Had he not been clear with her? She was only to fire to save her own life, not to protect him. He could protect himself.

He found her sitting beneath a tree, a crying Belle clutched tightly to her breast.

She met his gaze, her violet eyes bright with unshed tears. "She willna quit cryin'. I've tried nursin'—"

He reached down, took Bethie by the shoulders, pulled her to her feet. "What in the hell were you doing? You could have gotten yourself and Belle killed!"

She blinked the tears away, glared at him. "I had to stop him. You didna see—"

He felt the last thread of his temper snap. "I told you to fire only to save your own life! If you hadn't hit him, I'd have been dead anyway—and those two men would have known you were here! They'd have come for you, Bethie, and there's no way you'd have been able to reload fast enough to hit them both! Don't you understand?"

"L-let go of m-me!"

Whether it was the tremulous note in her voice or the strange look in her eyes, something broke the force of his anger. Then he noticed things he hadn't seen in his rage. She was trembling from head to foot, her legs so wobbly she'd have likely fallen if he had released her. Behind her tears, her eyes held a haunted, tormented look he'd never seen there before. But it was a look he recognized, a look he'd seen in countless young soldiers' eyes.

She was in shock.

She had killed a man, and her mind was struggling to cope.

Anger turned into a fierce protectiveness. Nicholas pulled her into his arms, careful of little Belle, who was still crying, and pressed his lips to her hair. "You foolish, brave woman. I know men who couldn't have made that shot. You're a lot stronger than you seem."

"I—I dinnae feel very strong." Her voice was thick with tears.

He stepped back, cupped her face in his hands, wiped her

tears away with his thumbs. "Strong isn't about how you feel, Bethie. It's about what you do. It's no small thing to take a man's life, no small thing to risk your own. You just did both."

"D-did you feel this way, too, the first time you . . ."

The first time he'd killed.

They'd been crossing the Monongahela. The French had been waiting in ambush, had opened fire. Nicholas had returned fire, hit the young French soldier in the chest—some mother's son. He'd had brown hair.

Nicholas hadn't slept that night. But as the years had passed, he'd almost grown accustomed to killing. He derived no pleasure from it, but he was long past feeling remorse. Killing was part of life on the frontier. A man killed, or he died. And Nicholas had killed so many.

But Bethie was a young woman. She hadn't chosen to live here, but had been brought to the frontier by her fool of a husband. Until now she'd never had to take a life. Nicholas had hoped to spare her this.

He met her shattered gaze. "It's never easy, love."

The throaty squawk of a raven brought him back to the present. They were not safe here.

"Come, Bethie. We must move on. The sound of gunfire might well draw the rest of the Delaware down on our heads."

They covered ground quickly, headed almost due east through unending hills and forest. Bethie tried to ignore the queasy feeling in her stomach, tried to banish the image of the Indian she'd slain from her mind. She couldn't think about it now, not when there might be thirty Delaware warriors on their trail.

Nicholas wanted to press on until they reached the fort, and she would do her best not to be a burden, though the road be long. She was tired of fear, tired of danger, tired of running. The sooner they reached the fort, the sooner she would be able to rest.

She adjusted Belle's weight in the sling, tried to shrug the ache out of her shoulders. The baby was asleep again, her tiny thumb in her mouth, the fresh air and the motion of the horse better than the sweetest lullaby.

"Take this." Nicholas slowed his stallion, leaned toward her, handed her a strip of dried venison. "You need to keep up your strength."

She took the meat, though she had no appetite.

But he was watching. "Eat, love. For Belle's sake as well as your own."

She bit off a piece, chewed, watched the trees open to a wide blue sky as they reached the top of a rocky ridge. The June sunshine was bright and hot, and she found herself overlooking a lush valley, the rounded crowns of beech, maple, and oak like puffy green clouds floating below her. This was how birds saw the world, she realized.

"You're smiling." His deep voice interrupted her daydream. "A penny for your thoughts?"

Feeling foolish, she turned her head away, avoided his probing gaze. "I've never had a pennyworth of thoughts. Save your coin."

"I know that's not true. You're an intelligent woman, Bethie."

The tone of his voice was not mocking, but sincere, and she could not help but stare at him in amazement. A thick lump formed in her throat. She swallowed. "You're a strange man, Nicholas."

"I'll take that as a compliment." His teeth flashed white as he grinned. "So what made you smile?"

"You'll laugh. 'Tis nothin'."

"I willna laugh, lass." He mimicked her brogue.

"You're a haggis-headed fool!" She shook her head, could not hold back her smile.

"A . . . a what?" His handsome face took on a look of exaggerated indignation.

She gestured to the valley below. "I was thinkin' this is how birds see the world."

To her surprise, he didn't laugh. Instead, he looked out over the valley, nodded, his lips curved in a gentle smile.

Then, abruptly, his expression grew grim.

She followed the direction of his gaze.

A farmstead. But it wasn't burnt down. Horses stood in the paddock. And tiny specks that were people went about their chores.

"We must warn them." She pointed Rosa downhill.

Nicholas grasped her reins, stopped her. "There isn't time."

"We cannae just ride off and leave them to die!"

His voice took on a hard edge. "They knew what they were getting into when they came here, Bethie. War and slaughter are nothing new on the frontier. Either they're prepared to defend themselves, or they're not."

"How can one family defend itself against so many warriors? Do you no' care if they die?"

Her question was like a fist to his gut. "I've seen more death than you can imagine, Bethie. I've looked it in the face, slept with it, broken bread with it. Hell, I've been dead! The only person a man can save is himself."

"You're no' so coldhearted as that, Nicholas. You saved Belle and me." She looked at him as if he were a knight in shining armor, her violet eyes imploring.

It was on the tip of his tongue to tell her that he'd never intended to get involved in her plight, that his feelings for her were an accident, that the last time he'd tried to save someone they had died in agony, cursing his name.

He released her. "That remains to be seen, doesn't it? There's still plenty of time between here and Fort Pitt to die."

Silent tears slipped from her eyes, ran down her cheeks. She drew in a shaky breath. "Then we leave them to be butchered?"

Bethie's words lingered in the air, made him feel like a cold-blooded bastard.

"Damn it!" He jerked Zeus's reins, headed down the hill toward the cabin, certain he was making a terrible mistake.

It took longer to reach the cabin than Bethie had expected. It hadn't seemed so far away from the hilltop. Only when they drew in sight of it did she remember how she was dressed. She'd gotten so used to wearing only her shift and Nicholas's shirt that she'd forgotten to feel half naked. But the people who lived in this house were strangers. Not only that, her shift was travel-stained, her braid unkempt, her feet bare as an urchin's.

Nicholas reined in the stallion. “Stay here. Let me speak with them first.”

She nodded.

He had just urged Zeus forward again, when a voice rang out.

“Stay where you are, you bloody heathen!” A wiry man with gray hair stepped out from behind the barn, a long rifle in his hands.

Nicholas stopped. “I mean you no harm. I just stopped by to warn you about an Indian—”

“To warn me about an Indian? You are an Indian!” The man peered from behind his rifle, squinted.

“No, I'm not.”

“Well, my son Johnny here says you are.”

“I'm no' so sure now, Da'. He looks like a white man.” A boy of about eleven, all blond hair and freckles, peered out from behind his father.

Despite the grimness of the situation, Bethie fought a smile.

“That's because I am a white man.” There was a strong note of irritation in Nicholas's voice. “I've come to warn you there's an Indian uprising under way. There are war parties attacking up and down the Ohio River Valley. We've passed a half-dozen massacred families in the past few days, didn't want to see you become the next.”

“I see only you, stranger. You said ‘we.’ Who's with you?” The voice came from the other side of the barn, and a young man stepped forward. Apart from darker hair, he was a bigger version of his brother.

Nicholas motioned Bethie to join him. “We were attacked about a week ago, burned out by a forest fire. We escaped to the river and are on our way to Fort Pitt.”

She urged her mount forward, stopped beside Nicholas, tried not to care that the two boys stared at her.

Their father squinted. “What is she wearin'?”

“She no' wearin' much, Da'. And she's got a wee bairn.”

Bethie felt herself flush to the roots of her hair, was about to stammer something, when Nicholas spoke. “The fire happened at night. We fled with no warning and no time to prepare.”

The father nodded in understanding. "Johnny, get indoors. Search the chest, see if your ma has somethin' this poor lass can wear."

The boy shuffled past, casting Bethie shy glances.

She didn't realize how much she had missed another woman's company until the man spoke of his wife. "You're very kind. Are you sure she willna mind?"

"Aye, lass, I'm sure. She died last spring." The man gestured for them to dismount. "The name's Magee—Donnie Magee. What's mine is yours. Stop a while. Callum will tend your horses, and Johnny will have supper on soon."

Nicholas shook his head. "That's very gracious of you, Master Magee, but I'm afraid we can't stay, and neither can you. There's a large party of Delaware headed this way."

# Chapter 18

The sun was just rising when they neared Fort Pitt. Nicholas found himself leading a ragged and weary band that included not only Magee and his boys—both of whom turned out to be capable backwoodsmen despite their youth—but two other families as well. They'd come across Ian Calhoun and his wife, Minna, in the wild, already fleeing with their three small children to the fort. The Wallace family had been asleep when Nicholas had sighted their cabin and roused them from their beds.

It was next to impossible for a party that included seven horses and fifteen people, seven of whom were children, to move soundlessly through the forest and leave no tracks. Their only hope rested in speed. With the Delaware war party so close he could almost taste them, Nicholas had moved his saddle back to the stallion, riding with Bethie and Belle, while the remaining horses, including Rona and Rosa, each bore one child and one adult. Stopping only when Nicholas needed to scout ahead, they had alternated between a canter and a walk all night.

Now the fort was visible upriver, its high earthen walls rising almost from the riverbank. He had already scouted the area and knew the cabins in the Upper Town and Lower Town around the fort had been burned to the ground, likely the work of soldiers determined not to give the enemy any place to take cover. The hilly forest on all sides was filled with encamped Delaware and Shawnee. Severe erosion showed that the river had run high against the ramparts during the spring freshet, but the Monongahela was now well within its banks.

Which was good, because they were about to cross it.

Nicholas had chosen a spot downriver from most of the Indian encampments but within sight of the walls. He wanted the soldiers to see them, to cover them with their long rifles as they crossed the deep water and rode for the gates. Shingiss, leader of the Delaware, was likely too smart a tactician to slaughter women and children within full view of British soldiers. But Nicholas didn't want to take a chance. They needed to get across the river quickly, come under the protection of the fort's artillery and marksmen before anyone could attack.

"We'll cross here and head for the sally port." Nicholas nudged Zeus down the muddy riverbank, dismounted. He turned to the others. "Quickly! Children stay on the horses. Adults swim alongside. Bethie, you'll ride and hold Belle. I'll be right beside you."

She nodded, her sweet face set with a look of determination. The journey had been hard on her, he knew. She had dark circles beneath her eyes from lack of sleep. Dressed in a borrowed linsey-woolsey gown, she looked thinner than when they'd set out. But she had not wavered. She had not complained. She had even saved his life.

Nicholas led the stallion to the river's edge and into the icy current, the others behind him. He heard Bethie's quick intake of breath as the water reached her thighs.

"Belle's no' goin' to like this much. I willna be able to keep her quiet."

As soon as she touched the cold water, the baby began to cry.

"It will be all right. We're almost there. When we get to the other side, ride straight for the sally port. Can you see it?" He pointed to an angular wall on the river's edge.

Her teeth chattered. "Aye."

"Pass through the opening in that wall, and there's a drawbridge. Ride across."

The current was strong, but not dangerous. Zeus, accustomed to crossing rivers, had no difficulty mastering the water, even with Bethie on his back.

Behind them, the youngest Calhoun child was crying.

Then Nicholas heard a frightened whinny. One of the horses remained on the riverbank. A high-strung stallion, it shied away from the water, threatened to rear. The Wallace woman kept a tight hand on its bridle, but the stallion refused to enter the river. On its back sat the Wallace's daughter, a girl of about seven. She clutched its mane, a look of terror on her face.

Bethie saw the woman's predicament, saw that Master Wallace was already deep in the river with their youngest child, a boy. "She needs your help, Nicholas. Belle and I will be fine."

"Are you sure?"

She tried to smile through chattering teeth, clutched Belle close to warm her. "Aye. We've done this b-before, you know."

Nicholas gave her one last look, his blue eyes dark with concern. "Head for the sally port. Stop for nothing and no one."

Then he was gone, swimming in strong strokes back toward the bank.

Bethie watched over her shoulder as he reached the shore, took Goody Wallace's shawl, wrapped it over the stallion's head, and led the terrified animal into the water. Then she turned her attention to the far side of the river, which slowly drew closer.

Something whistled past her from behind, hit the water beside her.

Her head spun around, just as another arrow landed harmlessly to her left.

Her heart lurched. Behind her, frightened women and children screamed.

A war party stood beneath the eaves of the forest behind them, dozens of warriors, their faces painted with vermilion.

*The Delaware war party.*

Bethie's heart gave a sickening lurch. Her mouth went dry.

A shout went up from the grassy walls.

The soldiers had spotted them.

Shots rang out.

Abruptly the arrows ceased.

Bethie hazarded a glance at the riverbank, saw the war party running for the cover of the trees. Then she felt the stallion's hooves strike ground. The horse labored through the chest-deep water and was soon fighting its way up the steep, muddy bank.

*Ride for the sally port.*

She glanced back over her shoulder, saw the Magee boys right behind her, followed by the Calhouns, with the Wallaces and Nicholas taking up the rear.

*Ride for the sally port.*

An arrow whistled through the air.

The Indians were firing from the cover of the trees!

More shots from the fort.

She turned the stallion's head toward the fort, kicked in her heels. The horse sprang forward at a full gallop.

From the earthen ramparts above, soldiers shouted encouragement, waved them on. "Ride! Hurry! Ride!"

She was close enough now that the walls of the fort blocked the light of the rising sun.

"Ride!"

The sally port was before her.

"Ride!"

Thirty yards. Twenty. Ten.

She guided the stallion through the portal, saw the drawbridge, which the soldiers had already opened for them.

Cheers went up around her as, one by one, the horses and their wet riders crossed the bridge, entered the safety of the fort. Last of all came Nicholas riding with Goody Wallace and her little girl.

The bridge rose behind them.

Weak with relief, Bethie bent over the stallion's neck, patted its wet shoulder, sent a silent prayer of thanksgiving winging skyward. In her arms, Belle wailed indignantly, a beautiful sound that made Bethie smile.

They were alive. They were all alive.

Strong hands reached up, lifted her from the saddle, lowered her to the ground.

And then Nicholas was before her, his wet hair clinging to his chest, his chin dark with stubble, his eyes full of concern for her.

Later she would not be able to say whether he'd kissed her first or she had kissed him. But as they claimed each other with lips and tongue, she knew she'd never tasted anything sweeter.

Captain Écuyer stood before his window in his spartan office, staring out over the fort. His hands were fisted tightly behind his back, his brown wig and rust-colored uniform clean and neat down to the square loops of his buttons. "It's worse than you think. Gladwin is besieged by Pontiac and his Ottawa. Forts and outposts across the northwest are falling or have already fallen—Sandusky, St. Joseph, Presque Isle. Gladwin's last dispatch said the Wyandot and Potawatomi had joined with Pontiac. Curse their barbaric race!"

Nicholas leaned against the closed door, crossed his arms, bit back his reply. He knew Indians weren't the only ones capable of barbarity, but now was not the time to argue. "I assume Governor Amherst has reinforcements on the way."

Écuyer gave a rather ungentlemanly snort, and in his frustration his slight French accent seeped through. Swiss by birth, he seemed to strive to be more English than Parliament. "Our esteemed commander believes we are exaggerating the strength of the enemy and giving up hard-fought ground too easily. He thinks the fighting is over and the war won. Still, Dalyell is on his way to Fort Detroit with Rogers' Ranging Company, and Colonel Bouquet is supposedly marching toward us with his regiment of Scottish Highlanders—all told about eight hundred men."

Against a few thousand Indians—Ottawas, Ojibwe, Wyandot, Potawatomi, Shawnee, Seneca, Chippewa, Sauk, Kikkapoo, and Miami—all fighting together to protect their homeland against invading whites. Rogers' Rangers and Highland Scots were good, but they weren't invincible.

"How many men do you have?"

Écuyer turned away from the window, faced Nicholas, his gaze traveling over Nicholas's trail-worn clothing. "We're built to hold one thousand, but I've got only three hundred, counting traders, farmers, and backwoodsmen—the riffraff of a colony spawned in hell. They bring women and children, useless people who consume our resources but cannot fight! In all, His Majesty is feeding nearly four hundred and twenty mouths each day. We're desperately short of wood and flour. If we're put to hard siege like Gladwin, we won't last long."

*A colony spawned in hell.* Écuyer's loathing for those beneath his social station wasn't unusual, but under these circumstances, Nicholas found it particularly distasteful. On the frontier, such biases were a luxury none of them could afford. Braddock's arrogance and subsequent defeat ought to have been proof enough of that.

"What of artillery? I saw a few six-pounders on the walls."

"We can mount as many as eighteen cannon, but I've half that—three six-pounders, twice as many three-pounders."

Better than Nicholas had hoped, but not terribly useful in a siege. Shingiss could simply cordon off the fort, keep his warriors out of range, and wait until starvation forced Écuyer to surrender. Then it would be an outright slaughter.

"Perhaps it's wise to begin rationing now."

Écuyer turned away from the window, met his gaze. "Aye, a sensible plan. I'd like to send parties out to gather spelt and what food they can from the king's garden. I'd appreciate it if you could oversee those operations, Nicholas. I've been told there's no Englishman alive who is stealthier or knows the way of the heathen better than you."

So this was why Écuyer had wanted to speak with him alone. The two of them had never really known each other, never been more than acquaintances. Nicholas had thought it odd to receive a summons to the commander's office the moment he'd arrived. "We'll see."

Écuyer took a step toward him, betrayed his eagerness. "I'm ready to restore your rank as a first lieutenant and put all of our resources at your disposal."

"I didn't come here to join your regiment."

Écuyer's nostrils flared ever so slightly, and he spoke in clipped syllables. "Surely you intend to fight!"

"If Shingiss cannot be persuaded to leave in peace, there will be no choice for any of us but to fight."

Écuyer seemed to relax at this. "Shingiss and Turtle's Heart have no intention of leaving. They've been encamped for nearly two weeks. They accosted eleven traders at the mouth of Bear

Creek two weeks ago, warned them to flee, then ambushed them when they sought safety. Damnable liars, all of them!"

Shingiss *and* Turtle's Heart. The situation was dire, indeed. Turtle's Heart was a great orator, a leader who carried tremendous weight with his people. His presence beside his king meant the full might of the united Delaware nation was pitted against them.

As he'd feared, Nicholas had led Bethie from mortal peril into terrible danger.

The weariness of the past week seemed abruptly to catch up with him. "Is there aught else, Captain?"

"Not for now. You've had a long and tiring journey. It was damned heroic of you to lead those settlers to safety, I must say."

"Heroism had nothing to do with it." He hadn't intended to rescue anyone.

Écuyer smiled indulgently. "I've set aside quarters for you and your . . . wife in the officers' barracks. My men will see you get whatever you need."

It was on the tip of Nicholas's tongue to tell him that Bethie was not his wife in any sense of the word, but he stopped himself. If she weren't housed with him, she'd find herself sleeping in barracks among ruthless backwoodsmen who hadn't tupped a woman in years. And after the way he had kissed her in full view of the entire fort, he'd best claim her in some fashion or she would likely find herself the focus of lustful advances from men who thought she was an easy mark. There were, after all, at least three randy men for each woman within these walls. Without a man's protection, she would be little more than fresh meat thrown to wolves.

"Thank you, Captain. Good day." Nicholas opened the door to go.

"Should I send word of you to your father?"

Nicholas jerked his head around, met Écuyer's gaze. "Don't even think about it."

"Yer as pretty as an apple blossom, lamb."

"Thank you, Annie. 'Tis lovely." Bethie ran her hands over the soft blue linen of her skirts. She'd never owned so fine a gown. Nicholas had bought it for her, along with the new, white shift she wore beneath it and the doeskin moccasins on her feet. It must have cost him a fortune in hides. Surely he knew she could never repay him.

*There are no debts between us, Bethie, no ledger to tally.*

"Tell me, Annie, how did you come by such a gown already sewn?"

Annie's cherry cheeks drooped as the smile left her face. "Settlers pass through here and realize too late that they need an extra rifle a sight more than pretty gowns or flowery teacups. We do what we can, but there's no' much call for frippery on the frontier. Why, yer man is the only officer here to have his lady with him."

Officer? His lady?

Nicholas was but a trapper and she no more than a widow he'd rescued in passing.

She started to shake her head, stopped herself. She knew so little about him. For all she knew, he *could* be an officer.

No sooner had they arrived at the fort than the fort commander had requested to meet with Nicholas. She'd thought at the time the captain was merely eager for whatever Nicholas could tell him of happenings in the surrounding countryside.

Certainly Nicholas hadn't behaved like a military man who'd just received an order from his superior. He had barely paid the lieutenant who'd summoned him any heed, had insisted on settling Bethie and Isabelle first. Much to her surprise, the lieutenant had immediately assigned one of his men—a young private named Patrick Fitchie, who blushed to the roots of his carrot-orange hair every time he glanced at Bethie—to see that she and Belle were given suitable quarters and a hot meal. Only then had Nicholas turned and followed after the lieutenant.

Bethie had expected to find herself forced to lodge in a horse stall or even in the open air. Instead, Private Fitchie had led her to a grand room with wooden floors, a deep hearth, and a large bedstead of carven oak. When she'd asked Private Fitchie if everyone at Fort Pitt was housed in such comfort, he'd merely turned a bright shade of red.

She'd barely had time to glance around her, when a plump older woman with a kindly face had entered, sent by Nicholas with a new gown for her, fresh diaper cloths for Belle, and instructions to prepare a hot bath for both of them. With many a "poor lamb!" Annie had heated water, helped bathe the baby, then held Belle so that Bethie could bathe in peace.

"She has the face of an angel, just like her mother!"

Annie had even combed the tangles from Bethie's hair and braided it, despite Bethie's insistence that she could do it herself.

"Nonsense, lamb!" she'd said when Bethie had tried to take the brush from her hand. "Ye've had a frightful journey, and yer man thinks ye deserve a bit o' lookin' after."

Bethie hadn't known what to say, but something about Annie's words had left her feeling strangely giddy. Nicholas had bought her a gown and felt she deserved looking after.

Annie, it turned out, was the wife of one Master Charlie Baskin, the man who ran the trading post at the fort. She'd wanted to know everything about Bethie's journey. So Bethie had recounted the nightmare of the fire, the horror of finding massacred families, the terrifying moment when the bull had come charging out of the forest, their encounter with other settlers. She'd even told Annie about the fight in the gully.

"And so ye shot him—dead?" Annie had gaped at her in amazement.

A vague, sick feeling had stirred in Bethie's belly at the memory. "Aye. I couldna let him kill Nicholas!"

Annie had stopped brushing her hair, given her a quick hug. "Of course not, lamb! 'Tis a fine man ye've got, one well worth savin'. I saw how he kissed you this mornin'. 'Twas enough to make my old knees go all coggly."

"Aye." Certainly Bethie's knees had gone coggly, along with the rest of her.

"Now then, we're all finished. Unless there's anythin' else ye need, I'll be off home. You know where to find me if you need me."

Despite her deep weariness, Bethie was sorry to see Annie leave. It had been four long years since she'd shared the company of another woman. "Thank you, Annie. You've been very kind to me. But, nay, I'm afraid I dinnae know where to find you."

"Ye just ask anyone here where to find old Annie Baskin,

and they'll point the way." Annie gave Belle one last tickle under her chin and was gone.

Suddenly unable to stay awake one moment longer, Bethie lay down on the soft bed, with Belle in her arms, and was instantly asleep.

Richard Sorley watched from across the courtyard as the old Baskin woman shut the door behind her and walked off toward the trading post.

So, little Elspeth Stewart was here.

He smiled, felt a familiar itch in his groin.

He'd seen her ride in this morning with the others, watched as she'd wantonly kissed the big dark-haired trapper in front of everyone. Whoever he was, he wasn't the man she had married. But then his dear stepsister had always been a whore.

She had changed since the last time he'd seen her. She was rounder, looked more like a woman and less like the frightened girl he remembered. Oh, what a pretty thing she'd been back then! With her big round eyes, her skinny body, her budding breasts, she'd been everything to him.

Bitch!

It was her fault his father had sent him away. She had seduced him, lured him in, tempted him. And he had been helpless.

First, he'd tried to stop the itch by touching her. He would go to her bed at night, clamp a hand over her mouth, let his other hand have its way with her. For a time, that had been enough. Then he'd had to go further. Night after night, he'd held her flat on the bed with his body, forced her legs apart, buried his fingers inside her, and rubbed against her until his seed spilled.

Finally, the itch had grown so strong, and his tadger so hard, he'd known he had no choice but to mowe her, and mowe her good. He'd waited until everyone was asleep, then crept into the loft to her bed. She'd struggled a bit, as she usually did, pretending not to want him, but he'd always been bigger and stronger. He was a man, after all, and ten years older.

But when she'd realized what he aimed to do, she'd fought like a madwoman, and her struggles had awoken them all.

His father had given them both a good thrashin', called her a harlot, and accused her of putting a spell on his only son. Then he'd married her off to that old fellow from the meeting-house. Within a week she'd been gone for good.

That would have been the end of it. Except that the fire she'd lit inside him hadn't gone out, and he'd needed desperately to put it out. When his father had caught him in the woods with a neighbor girl too young for him to marry, he'd sworn the girl to secrecy with many threats, then forced Richard to leave.

And here he was, a soldier in the British army. How his father would hate that, if he knew! His father hated everything having to do with the English.

Now fate had brought Bethie back to him.

He smiled.

He would bide his time, wait for his chance. Then he would pay a call on his long-lost stepsister.

# Chapter 19

By the next morning, Bethie felt rested—and strangely out of sorts. So much had happened in the past two weeks. The Indians at the cabin. Nicholas's confession. Their narrow escape from the fire. Their flight through the forest. The fight in the gully. Riding all night with the Delaware in pursuit. The last, desperate dash to the fort.

She had even killed a man.

She'd grown so accustomed to being afraid and on the run that she scarce knew how to feel now that she and Belle were safe and settled. Anything sudden, even laughter, startled her. She felt restless, wary. It was as if some part of her were still out there, still fleeing through the wild, death but a step behind her.

She gently moved Belle from one breast to the other, glanced across the room to the corner where Nicholas had stashed his gear and bedroll. Near exhaustion, he'd slept on the floor last night, just as he'd done at the cabin. He'd made no move to touch her. He hadn't even kissed her.

*Nicholas. Nicholas.*

She sifted through what she'd come to know about him. He had family in Virginia. He could read and write. He'd once been a lieutenant in the Royal Americans. He'd been captured and tortured by Indians. He'd then married an Indian woman, planted a baby in her belly, openly taken other women to bed. Then he had somehow killed both wife and child.

But that was only part of who he was.

He'd helped with Belle's birth, holding Bethie's hand, encouraging her, holding her world together through the frightful pain. He'd saved their lives more times than she could count. He'd taught her to write her name, to read a bit. He'd shown her many acts of thoughtfulness. He'd kissed her, made her feel things she'd never felt before. Most of all, when she'd asked him to stop, he had stopped.

And now when they had reached safety and he could easily have left her to find her own way, he'd allowed everyone to think she was his wife to spare her sleeping among the others who'd sought refuge here.

Each of these deeds was a piece of Nicholas. Yet no matter how many times she looked at the pieces, tried to put them together, she came no closer to knowing him. The pieces didn't fit.

But it wasn't only Nicholas who confused her. She was a stranger to herself these days. Ever since that first kiss—it seemed so long ago now, though it was really only a fortnight—she'd felt a need for him she could not explain. That need had only gotten worse with time. Like a gnawing hunger it ate at her, pursued her even in her sleep. She wanted him to kiss her, wanted him to hold her against his hard man's body, wanted him to touch her as he had that night beside the brook.

*You've the heart of a harlot, Bethie Stewart.*

Perhaps she did. But if her desire for Nicholas was a sin, why did all of heaven and earth seem to sing when he touched her?

She felt so lost.

Belle touched her chin with chubby fingers, and Bethie looked down to see her baby daughter smiling up at her. She took Belle's little hand, pressed it to her lips, kissed it, smiled. "Are you finished, little one?"

She had just fastened her gown when a light knock came at the door and Nicholas stepped inside. He had bathed, shaved, and donned a new shirt of deep blue linsey-woolsey that made his eyes seem even bluer. Just the sight of him made it hard for her to breathe.

She stood, Belle in her arms, feeling suddenly like a silly girl of ten.

He stopped only inches from her, stroked Belle's cheek, smiled when the baby wrapped her tiny hand around one of his fingers. Then a look of amazement lit up his face. "She smiled at me!"

Bethie laughed. "She likes you. Is that no' true, little one?"

Belle smiled again, a wide toothless grin, then gurgled.

Bethie looked up, met Nicholas's gaze. The look in his eyes—a mix of potent male hunger and tenderness—made her stomach flip.

"I came to ask if you'd like a tour of the fort."

Nicholas guided Bethie through the crowded fort, watched her face light up with excitement. They had left Belle in Annie's care, the older woman beaming with delight at the chance to hold the baby again. He wanted to make Bethie smile, to chase the lingering shadows from her eyes.

"'Tis like a city!" She smiled. "I've never seen so many people in one place. To think Philadelphia is even bigger than this!"

Charmed by her innocence, Nicholas couldn't help chuckling. "Aye, Philadelphia is much larger and boasts fifty times as many people."

She looked up at him, amazement on her face, then looked at her feet, bit her lip. "I must seem a bletherin' bumpkin to you."

He tucked a finger beneath her chin, lifted it. "Nay, Bethie, love. When I look at you, I think only how brave and beautiful you are."

She shrugged off his compliment, smiled mischievously. "You are more than a wee bit brave and dashy-lookin' yourself, Master Kenleigh."

"I speak the truth, Bethie." He brushed the pad of his thumb over the softness of her lips, told her in the only way he could that he hadn't spoken in jest.

She met his gaze, the playful look in her violet eyes gone, replaced by one of deep female vulnerability.

"Shall we continue?"

He *was* speaking the truth. Her loveliness enthralled him. Everything about her proclaimed her femininity. The faint lavender scent that lingered from her bath. The gentle sway of her hips as she walked. The spun gold of her hair in sunlight. The soft, thick braid that hung to her waist.

The new gown fitted her perfectly—a bit too perfectly if one considered the way her creamy breasts rose in soft mounds above the bodice. Why hadn't he thought to bring her shawl? He didn't care if it was hotter than Satan's arse. He didn't want men eyeing her.

"Over there is the hospital." He pointed.

She gestured to a small building that stood apart from the others. "What's that?"

"The smallpox hospital."

She looked up at him, eyes wide. "Are there—"

"Aye. Écuyer says there have been a few cases this spring. Fortunately, they were isolated quickly, so the disease did not spread. Would you like to go atop the walls?"

"Is it permitted?"

He'd never seen a woman up there and doubted Écuyer would like it. But he didn't give a tinker's damn about the rules, not when she looked at him with such anticipation. What could Écuyer do to him? He was a Kenleigh, after all, and Écuyer needed him.

He took Bethie's arm. "Why not?"

From atop the high walls, Bethie looked out over the surrounding countryside, felt both dizzy and excited. "I've never been so far off the ground."

A warm breeze brushed her skin, carried with it the mingled smells of forest and river. Sunlight warmed her through the linen of her gown.

"It's beautiful country." His arm encircled her waist, pulled her closer. He smelled of pine soap, leather, and man, a heady scent that made her pulse quicken.

She saw the three rivers—the Allegheny, the Ohio, the Monongahela—trailing off to the east, the west, and the south like flowing ribbons of silver. She saw the hoofprints their horses had left in mud in their frantic dash to the sally port. She saw blackened earth where cabins had once stood. She saw the king's garden, the fields beyond the fort's walls that supplied food for the fort. She saw the forest stretching into the distance, a turbulent sea of green. Behind her a drummer tapped out a rhythm, accompanied by the tune of a fife.

But she saw no sign of Indians.

"Where are they?"

"In the forest. Watching. They won't come in range of the cannon or long rifles."

"Will they attack?"

"I don't know." Nicholas turned her, pointed to the tip of land that jutted out into the union of the three rivers. "There are the remains of the old French fort, Fort Duquesne."

"What are they doin'?" She pointed to a group of five soldiers who seemed to be wrestling with a cannon. From the looks they shot her way, she knew they weren't used to seeing a woman on the walls.

"They're adjusting the artillery to make certain they've got the curtain walls covered."

"Curtain walls?"

He smiled. "You're standing on the flag bastion. The walls that stretch between bastions are called curtains or scarps—the main walls of the fort. The bastions make it possible for soldiers to fire on anyone attacking the walls or other bastions. There are no blind spots, no place for an enemy to take cover."

"So that's why the fort is shaped like a star."

"Aye." He smiled, nodded, then pointed. "The defensive wall over there is the glacis. It gives retreating soldiers some measure of cover. The arrow-shaped walls just inside it are called ravelins. They offer additional cover. Whoever designed it was thinking of an organized attack by the French. That's why most of the defensive works are to the east."

Below in the parade grounds, people busied themselves with their morning chores. Mothers and fathers chased their children, cooked over open fires, hung laundry in the wind to dry. Soldiers marched in formation, worked to repair the flood damage, did their best to chase chickens off the ramparts. One rooster perched haughtily on the back of a grazing goat, keeping a careful watch on his hens.

Suddenly the fort seemed terribly exposed, a fragile haven

upon which all this life depended. "'Tis its own world, a little island surrounded by peril."

"Aye. You asked me earlier if the Delaware would attack. Bethie, they don't have to."

Immediately she understood. Inside they fort, the settlers and soldiers were isolated, cut off from their fields, with no way to hunt game. Time was on the side of the Indians. When the food ran out . . . "You think they'll put us under siege."

"Aye." He pulled her closer. "But perhaps reinforcements are already on their way. Would you like to visit the trading post?"

She brushed aside the sense of foreboding that had overtaken her. "Aye."

They had just reached the bottom of the stairs when the lieutenant who had summoned Nicholas the day before appeared and asked to have a word with him.

"Stay right here." Nicholas released her and joined the lieutenant a few feet away.

A ball made of an animal bladder rolled to a stop at Bethie's feet, followed closely by a very muddy boy of three or four. She smiled, bent down, picked up the ball, threw it gently to him.

The little boy caught it, smiled, rolled it back.

She bent down again, felt a man's hand close intimately over her bottom.

She gasped, lurched upright, spun about, a flush of fear and anger hot on her face.

But Nicholas already had the man by his uniform jacket. In one motion, he slammed the young soldier up against the curtain wall, pressed the blade of his hunting knife against the soldier's throat.

A hushed silence fell around them.

"Give me a good reason why I shouldn't geld you here and now!" Nicholas's voice was a rough growl, the look on his face one of primal male rage.

The man, a barmy-faced lad not much older than she, trembled, his eyes wide with terror. "I—I—I'm sorry. I—"

"Sorry is just the beginning!"

The lieutenant stepped forward. "I'm afraid Lieutenant Kenleigh is right, Private Huntley. Corporal, put this man in irons. Take him to the guardhouse to await a court-martial."

"Aye, sir!"

But Nicholas wasn't finished. "Do you know what the Cherokee do to a man who violates women? No? Touch her or any other woman again, and you'll find out!" Then Nicholas released the soldier, sheathed his knife.

Immediately, the corporal, together with several others, led the private away. The onlookers slowly drifted back to their conversations.

Bethie released a long, trembling breath, searched Nicholas's face, saw his gaze soften as he looked down at her. "It's all right, Nicholas."

"Like bloody hell it is!"

"I—I'm just a wee bit startled."

"I must apologize, madam." The lieutenant bowed his head with such respect that Bethie was taken aback. "I would never have imagined one of our soldiers would make such a bold assault on an officer's wife, or any woman for that matter."

"I'm no longer an officer, Lieutenant Trent."

Lieutenant Trent gave an impatient flick of his lace-adorned wrist. "As you wish. Rest assured the miscreant shall be punished. Good day to you both." With a quick nod of the head, he turned and walked away.

Nicholas took her arm. "Let's get you back to the barracks."

She gave him a little tug. "No' yet. I want to see Annie's tradin' post first."

"You've got to help me, Richard! They're goin' to flog me! Thirty-nine lashes!"

Richard glared at Silas, glanced nervously around. "Keep your voice down! I'm no' supposed to be here!"

"Can you get me out?"

"Are you daft? You shouldna have gotten yourself caught! I told you to be careful, did I no'?"

Silas nodded. "I didna think he'd see. Why, oh, why did I let you put me up to this?"

Richard reached between the bars, grabbed Silas by the throat. "Hold your whist, or I'll duff you one! 'Twas your own foolish idea!"

Silas coughed, pulled away. "I willna tell. I wouldna do such a thing, Richard! But you must help me. You're my friend!"

"I brought you this." Richard held out the lead ball.

"What is that for?"

"Tuck it in your mouth on the mornin' when they come to get you. Bite it while they're floggin' you. 'Tis to keep you from wailin'." Richard watched in disgust as a tear rolled down Silas's cheek, felt an urge to hit the spineless bastard.

Silas grabbed the ball with a sweaty hand. "I'm so frightened!"

"Pull your wits together! I've seen girls take a beating with less fuss than you!" Richard didn't tell him that one of those girls was the woman whose arse he'd grabbed today.

Richard had wanted to test the waters, to see exactly how much of a guard dog Bethie's man was. He had egged Silas on, then watched from the shadows as her man had threatened to cut Silas's cods off. He had no doubt the man—a bleedin' officer, no less—had meant every word he'd said.

Richard would have to be very careful.

Silas was still weeping. "I shouldna ha' done it."

"Christ, Silas! Dinnae be such a cutcher!" Richard gave a snort of contempt, turned, and walked past the sleeping guard out into the night.

Bethie poured cold water from the bucket Private Fitchie had filled into the glass bowl, then removed her clothes until she stood naked. Isabelle had finally fallen asleep, giving her a few precious moments alone. She dipped a linen cloth into the cool water, squeezed it out, pressed it against her throat and breasts, biting back a moan. It had been a hot and sticky day.

If only the water would cool her temper as well.

She didn't know when she'd ever felt more cankersome. She'd tried to make herself useful in the cookhouse this afternoon only to find herself hauled back to the barracks by a very angry Nicholas.

"You're not to leave this room without me!" He'd thrust her roughly through the door and slammed it behind them.

She'd stepped away, resisted the urge to pummel him. "I'm just tryin' to make myself useful!"

"And I'm trying to keep you safe! After what happened this morning, I would think you'd understand the danger!" A muscle in his jaw ticked, and she knew he was genuinely angry with her. "This place is filled with men who haven't touched a woman in years and are not above rape if it means getting their hands on you!"

She'd felt the blood drain from her face, felt some of her anger fade. "But I cannae stay in here all day every day! There must be somethin' I can do. I could work in the laundry or help cook—"

He shook his head. "Écuyer brought his own personal chef, and most of the officers have enlisted men or servants to see to their laundry and mending. They don't need your help, Bethie."

"Everyone else is preparin' for war. Minna is mendin' soldiers' uniforms. Goody Wallace is teachin' Bible lessons. But my hands are idle! I dinnae even cook our meals!"

He'd reached out to her, cupped her shoulders in his big hands. "'Tis admirable of you to want to help, Bethie, but I will not let you do anything that puts you in harm's way."

His words had only made her angrier. "Who are you to decide what I do and what I dinnae do? I am no' yours to command, Nicholas Kenleigh!"

He'd pulled her hard against him. "I wouldn't say that too loudly, or you're likely to find yourself sleeping with the other settlers!"

Then his mouth had closed over hers in a rough kiss.

Before she'd drawn a breath, he'd gone.

She hadn't seen him all evening. He was having brandy with the captain and had warned her he'd likely not return until very late. Which was just as well.

Part of her wanted to slap him. Part of her wanted to apologize. Part of her just wanted him to kiss her like that again. And again. And again.

She dipped the cloth in the water once more, squeezed it, ran it over her bare breasts, felt her nipples tighten against the pleasing chill.

The door opened.

"You're still awake . . ." Nicholas closed the door behind him. His gaze, as intimate as a caress, slid slowly down her naked body. His jaw clenched. His eyes darkened to midnight.

Burned as she was by the heat of his perusal, her first instinct was to hide herself. But she forced herself to face him, to stand her ground.

Wasn't this what she wanted?

# Chapter 20

A rush of air left Nicholas's lungs, caught in his throat, as seemingly all the blood in his body surged to his cock. His mind stumbled in search of words. "You should be sleeping."

Bethie stood before him, completely naked, her hair twisted atop her head, her skin glistening wet in the candle-light, her nipples tight and ripe. Shimmering strands of water trickled down her belly to her thighs or disappeared in the thatch of golden curls that hid her sex.

"'Twas such a sweltrie day . . ."

He took a step toward her, expected her to turn away, to cover herself, to ask him to leave. But she didn't. Instead, she dipped the cloth in the water, squeezed it out, pressed its dampness against the side of her throat, as if . . .

As if she had intended him to find her. As if she were trying to seduce him.

He took another step and another. Only when he stood before her could he see that she was trembling. He reached out, took the cloth from her, dipped it in the bowl, squeezed it. "Let me."

She closed her eyes, hid a gaze that held both fear and

desire, and he could tell she was pushing herself, forcing herself to confront whatever demons still lived inside her.

He'd be damned if he was going to let her face them alone.

Touched that she was giving him something so precious as trust, he pressed the cold cloth to her cheek, her throat, her nape. "Do you know what it does to me to touch you like this?"

Her eyes fluttered open, and she met his gaze for a moment, then looked away. Her voice was a whisper. "You feel . . . lust?"

"I feel much more than lust, Bethie. Lust is a need quickly satisfied. What I want takes time." He dipped the cloth in the water again, squeezed it. "I want to bring you pleasure—to touch every part of you, kiss every part of you, taste every part of you. I want to make you come again and again, until you're weak and sleepy and there's nothing in your world but the scent of me, the taste of me, the feel of me."

He heard her little intake of breath, watched a blush rise from her breasts to her cheeks. She lifted her gaze to his again, a look of confusion on her face, and shook her head. "But 'tis no' like that for women."

He touched the cold, wet cloth to the valley between her breasts, allowed his knuckles to graze one of her nipples, felt her heart skip beneath his palm. "It can be."

She shivered. But fear lingered in her eyes. Her hands were fisted at her sides, her body tense, proof she was still forcing herself, still fighting, still afraid.

He didn't want her to be afraid of him. She'd been terrified of him since the first moment she'd seen him, and that was his own damned fault. Only when she'd drugged him and tied him to her bed—

The memory stopped him, gave him pause.

What would she do now if he gave up control, if he put that same power in her hands?

He dropped the cloth in the water. Guided by instinct, he brushed aside any unease about his scars, his lingering memories of Lyda. He slowly loosed the ties of his shirt, pulled it over his head, and dropped it on the floor. Then he took up the cloth, pressed it dripping wet to his chest, gently placed her hand atop it.

She gaped at him, her eyes wide with surprise, and he saw her pupils dilate.

"I'm burning up, Bethie. Put out the fire."

Bethie could not breathe, could barely think, not with him watching her through those dark eyes, not with his skin so hot beneath the cloth. She slid the linen slowly over the hard planes of his chest, over his scars, over the wine-colored silk of his nipples. Then she moved lower, explored the ridges of his belly, felt his muscles jerk against her touch, saw the demanding bulge straining against his buckskin breeches.

Tendrils of panic snaked into her throat.

She swallowed them.

For as nervous as it made her to see such clear evidence of his physical need, she wanted him more than she ever had, and some part of her thrilled to know her touch affected him just as much as his did her. Before she realized what she was doing, she let the cloth fall to the floor at their feet and caressed him with her bare hands, hungry for the feel of him.

But rather than sating her need, each moment she touched him only made her want him more. His body was so different from hers, so hard, so strong. She fanned her fingers across the mat of dark curls on his chest, let her fingertips trace the curls where they trickled in a line down his belly and disappeared beneath his breeches.

"Untie them." His voice was tight, restrained, and she could tell he was holding back. "I want you to see me, to see what you do to me, to know that, no matter what I feel, I won't hurt you."

Even as he spoke the words, she knew some part of her wanted to do this. She remembered that day by the river when she had watched him bathe, remembered the shock she'd felt seeing that part of him—her fear, her fascination, her body's reaction.

She reached for the ties of his breeches with trembling hands, felt his strong hands close reassuringly over hers to help her. And then it was done. He guided her hands beneath the skin-warmed leather, over his hips, over the muscled roundness of his buttocks, over his corded thighs, as he peeled the leather away from his skin and let it slip to the floor.

His sex sprang free, stood rigid against his belly, rising

thick and hard from a nest of dark curls. Beneath, his stones hung, full and heavy.

Something clenched deep in her belly. Heat seemed to spread from her womb, turned to liquid between her thighs. She felt herself falter.

"The sight of me frightens you."

She said the first thing that came into her mind. "Now I know why it hurts."

He cupped her bare shoulders, ran his hands down the length of her arms, took her hands in his. "It should never hurt, Bethie. When a man enters a woman's body, it should bring her as much pleasure as it brings him."

His words made her light-headed. She wanted to believe him. She *needed* to believe him. But she'd lived with Andrew for four years, had lain beneath him, and had hated every moment of it. And before that . . .

But this was Nicholas, not Andrew. *Not* Richard.

Nicholas made her feel things she'd never felt before.

"Nicholas, I . . ." How could she explain this jumble of feelings inside her? How could she make him understand?

Before she found the words, he bent down and brushed his lips lightly over hers.

That simple touch, light as the sweep of a butterfly's wings, made the heat inside her explode.

With a whimper, she wrapped her arms around his neck, pressed herself against him as his mouth claimed hers in a melting kiss. Sensation overwhelmed her. The sweet rasp of his damp chest hair against her nipples. The thrust of his tongue deep in her mouth. The caress of his hands as they moved over her hot skin.

And then he stopped, releasing her. He turned and strode with a panther's grace to the bed.

Bethie's heart almost stopped. Had it gone this far? Were they really going to—

But then he did something she could never have imagined. He lay down on his back in the center of the bed, stretched his arms above his head, and closed his fists around the bedposts.

"My body is yours, Bethie. Touch me anywhere you want, any way you want. I won't let go of these bedposts until you say I can. I put myself in your hands. Whatever happens now is up to you."

For a moment she could do nothing but stare at him, her heart a hammer behind her breast. Even lying submissively on his back, he glowed with male strength and virility. No matter what he might pretend, he was not the submissive sort. And she realized he was doing this for her sake, trying to make her feel safe.

*Whatever happens now is up to you.*

Drawn to him despite her fears, Bethie crossed the room, sat on the bed beside him, let her gaze run the length of him. And then, with only her need for him to guide her, she rose to her knees, bent over him, kissed him.

True to his word, he did not release the bedposts, but met her kiss full-on, lifting his head from the pillow, invading her mouth with his tongue, teasing her swollen lips with his.

But suddenly she wanted to taste more of him, just as he had tasted her that night by the brook. She traced kisses across his beard-roughened jaw, down his throat, over the crest of his Adam's apple to his chest, licking his nipples as he had licked hers.

"Bethie!" His body jerked, and breath hissed from his lungs. But he did not release the bedposts.

She had never touched a man like this, had never felt attracted to a man's body before Nicholas, hadn't realized how much pleasure there was to be found in touching and kissing a man. It was as if some deep-seated hunger had awoken within her. She wanted more.

Emboldened by his response, she kissed her way across his chest, down the line of dark curls to his belly, letting her fingers find their eager way over the ridges and valleys of his muscles. She could feel the male power of him, feel the shifting of his muscles, the tension in his body as he deliberately restrained himself. He could overpower her in a heartbeat if he so chose. And yet he kept his word.

She dipped her tongue into his navel.

His grip tightened around the bedposts, and he groaned, a sound of pure male need.

Bethie knew where the heat of his need resided, knew which part of him burned hottest. She lifted her lips from his skin, gazed on the rigid length of his shaft. But the fear she had expected to feel was no longer there. Instead she felt insatiably curious.

*Touch me anywhere you want, any way you want.*

She reached out with one hand, fondled his stones, cupped their surprising weight in her hands, and felt the sac that held them draw tight. Then she ran her fingers tentatively over the swollen head of his shaft, explored its smallest features one by one—the slit in the center, the thick ridge at its edges, the tiny line of pinched flesh on the underside.

Breath hissed from his clenched teeth, and she looked up to find him watching her through eyes that had turned to smoke.

She closed her hand around him, slid her hand down his pulsing length, amazed by the feel of him. He was steel in silk, both hard and soft.

"Bethie . . ." His eyes closed, and the muscles of his arms bulged as he strained against his grip on the bedposts.

*Any way you want.*

Driven by that same deep-seated hunger, she hesitated for only a moment, then leaned down and kissed this part of him as she had kissed the rest of him.

Nicholas felt her hot mouth close over him, thought he would come undone. "Good God, woman!"

He fought to hold his hips still, to remain passive, as she ran her tongue lightly over the head of his cock, tasting him. He knew she had never done this before, and yet her tentative touch, her exploring kisses, were more arousing than the expert actions of the most skilled whore. And when she gripped him in her hand and guided him deep into her mouth, he knew it wouldn't be long until he came.

Was she ready for that? Was she ready to take his seed in her mouth? He doubted it.

"Bethie, let me . . . touch you. Let me show you how good it is! If you don't stop . . ."

But she did stop, left him hanging on the edge, hard and aching.

He opened his eyes, saw her watching him through eyes filled with doubt. "Let me give you the same pleasure, Bethie. Let me show you just how good it can be for a woman."

Her hair was a tangle of yellow silk, her lips swollen from

kissing him. But her eyes still held a shadow of fear. "Must you be . . . inside me?"

*Inside her.* That was where he wanted to be, where he needed to be. He wanted to plunge inside her, to feel her muscles clench around him as his thrusts brought them both release. But the last man entrusted with loving her sweet body had hurt her, abused her. He realized she wasn't ready for a man, not like that, not yet. He fought to subdue his own longing, looked into her eyes.

"No, love." He could scarce believe what he was saying. He must be insane! "I don't have to be inside you."

Bethie sat for a moment, shaken by his smile, stunned to her core by her own passion, by his words. "Aye, Nicholas. Show me."

And then she was in his arms as he pulled her against him, pressed his lips to hers in a kiss that seared her to her soul. He rolled her onto her back, and his lips followed the same path she had blazed on his flesh—over her lips, across her cheek, down her throat, to her breasts, where he laved her nipples with his tongue.

Delicious frissons of heat shot from her breasts to someplace deep in her belly with each flick of his tongue, each tug of his lips. She heard herself moan, heard herself whisper his name. *"Nicholas!"*

"I want you hungry and aching, Bethie. I want you to know what it's like."

Hands rough from years of living in the wild caressed her breasts, teased her nipples, while his lips traced fire across her belly. Just as she had done, he dipped his tongue into her navel. A dart of flame shot through her.

"I'm going to touch you now, Bethie, just as you touched me."

Then his hand cupped her sex.

Tremors of pleasure twined with alarm shuddered through her. Instinctively, she drew her thighs together. "N-nay!"

"Trust me, love. Pleasure, not pain." He moved the heel of his hand in slow, maddening circles on her woman's mound.

And there *was* pleasure—shocking, deep, aching pleasure. She could not think. She could not doubt. She could do nothing but feel. Ragged sensation tore through her, made her insides quiver. The cleft between her thighs ached. She was wet, weeping, molten. "Oh, Nicholas, please . . . don't . . . stop!"

She heard him chuckle, a deep erotic sound. "Now I'm going to taste you, Bethie, just as you tasted me. Spread your legs for me."

Bethie's eyes flew open and the breath caught in her throat as he parted her thighs, bent down, took her with his mouth. She cried out, unable to believe what he was doing, what she was feeling. His lips closed over the most sensitive part of her, and he began to suckle.

Unbearable, desperate, searing pleasure.

She heard him moan, the deep rumble vibrating against her tortured flesh.

"Mmm, you taste like heaven, love. So sweet."

Then his tongue teased her entrance, sent deep shudders through her, and for the first time in her life, Bethie felt empty. She wanted his kiss inside her. She wanted *him* inside her. But she couldn't say it. She couldn't tell him.

"Please, Nicholas!" Her hands fisted in his long hair, pushed him closer.

Something was building inside her, stalking her. Something wild. Something primal.

He tugged on her swollen flesh with his lips, sucked her into his mouth again, teased her with flicks of his tongue.

Helpless, frantic cries escaped her as the flames inside her grew higher and higher.

And then all at once, the fire within her drew itself together deep in her belly—and exploded. White-hot bliss surged through her, a pounding tide of molten delight, waves of pleasure so strong she feared she would come apart. "Nicholas!"

Her body trembled with the force of her climax, her inner muscles clenching hard again and again, until the fire faded to embers.

But Nicholas wasn't finished. He lapped her still-swollen sex with lazy strokes until the heat began to build again. Then he drew upon her sensitive bud with his lips, sucked it, teased it. And in a matter of minutes she was lost in another climax and another, until she was exhausted and floating, Nicholas by her side, a smile on his lips.

She curled against him, mumbled. “I never knew. I never knew, Nicholas.”

He pulled her into his arms, stroked her hair, his shaft still rigid. “Sleep, love.”

Bethie slept deeply that night.

His body yearning for release, Nicholas didn’t sleep at all.

But for the first time in six years, he felt content.

# Chapter 21

Bethie placed the bandage in the basket with the others she had rolled, then reached for another strip of linen. Isabelle lay beside her on a thick lynx fur, gazing about with bright blue eyes and sucking on her hand.

Nicholas had arranged for Bethie to spend a few hours each morning working in the hospital, provided Private Fitchie stayed with her—and provided she agreed to return straightaway to their quarters should the alarm sound. Bethie had agreed to his conditions, though she felt he was still making too great a fuss over one soldier's rudeness. Besides, what was the good of her helping in the hospital if she were to abandon it when her help was most needed? But Nicholas had insisted.

"There are some things a woman shouldn't see, Bethie," he'd said.

And so she rolled strips of linen into bandages she hoped would never be needed, made beds she hoped would remain empty, helped prepare salves she hoped would never be used, all the while listening to the surgeon, Dr. Aimes, talk about everything from treatments for different fevers to today's topic—the many causes for the fall of the Roman Empire.

He poured out a measure of laudanum for a soldier who

had broken his ankle. "For civilization to triumph, man must conquer his inner beast. The failure of Rome, madam, was its acceptance of the barbarian."

Bethie scarce heard him, her mind on Nicholas. For three nights now she had lain in his arms, felt the magic of his hands and mouth upon her. Never had she thought she would ache for a man's touch, his kisses, his embrace. Never had she thought a man could make her writhe with pleasure or plead for release. But Nicholas had shown her a new world, one she had not known existed. Now she could hardly wait each evening until the sun had set and Isabelle had fallen asleep. She wanted him, was greedy for him.

She was learning to please him in the same way he pleased her, with her hands, with her mouth. She had watched in awe the first time he'd reached his peak in her hands and spilled his seed across his belly. Like ribbons of melted, white silk it had shot from inside him, as his body shuddered with the power of his release, a look of intense pleasure, or pain, on his face.

He had never pressured her for more, never tried to enter her body. And for that she was grateful. And yet . . . Every time she drew near to her climax, she felt a deep need for him inside her, an empty yearning, as if that part of her truly longed to be filled by him. But she said nothing, hindered by the memory of Andrew's painful thrusts and Richard's rough probing.

*Nicholas. Nicholas.*

He had made these past three days the happiest of her life. And yet there were shadows.

Everyone believed she was his wife and Isabelle his daughter. It would be so easy to get lost in the daydream, to let herself believe it. But it was a lie, a misunderstanding that Nicholas had not challenged—in order, he said, to keep her safe. It pained her to deceive people who had been so kind to her—Annie, Minna, Goody Wallace, even Private Fitchie. They thought her the wife of an officer, a woman worthy of respect. In truth, she was naught but a widow, the daughter of a poor Scots-Irish farmer who'd tried to hack a living out of this unforgiving land—and had failed.

They weren't the only ones she was deceiving. Just as Nicholas had allowed everyone to believe she was his wife, she had allowed him to believe that it was Andrew, not Richard, who had taught her to fear a man's touch. She and Nicholas had never spoken of it, but she could tell that was what he thought. The thinly veiled contempt in his voice every time he mentioned her husband told her that.

What would he do if he knew the truth about her? What would he do if he learned it was her stepbrother who had come to her bed night after night? The tenderness in his eyes would disappear, and he would look at her with disgust and loathing. She would be tainted in his eyes, ruined.

Whatever else happened, she couldn't bear that.

Voices at the door broke through her thoughts, brought her back to the moment.

Private Fitchie pushed the door open, and two men entered supporting a third between them.

Bethie gasped.

'Twas the man who had touched her.

He wore no shirt, and blood was spattered on his arms and shoulders.

"So there's the soldier they flogged this morning. I was expecting to see him sooner or later." Dr. Aimes stood, pointed to a bed. "Lay him on his abdomen over there. Water and bandages if you please, madam."

"He fainted, Doctor. They had to wait until he came round again to finish it. Thirty-nine lashes and not a peep. He can be right proud of that, so he can."

"Thank you, Private. That will be all."

The two soldiers turned and left, casting Bethie furtive looks.

*Thirty-nine lashes.*

Bethie felt dizzy. It was not so much the sight of his torn and bloodied back that sickened her, as it was the knowledge that this was how he'd been punished for dishonoring her. Looking at him, she wondered if the punishment fit the crime. After all, he hadn't hurt her.

"Madam? Water and bandages?"

She grabbed several bandage rolls, placed them on the bed

beside the unconscious soldier, then poured fresh water in the copper bowl the doctor used for such things.

"Does the sight of blood upset you?" He began to wash the blood and bits of torn flesh from the soldier's back.

"Nay. 'Tis no' the sight of his wounds that startled me, Doctor, but knowin' that this happened because of me."

"Nonsense! Private Huntley was punished because he behaved in a manner unbecoming a British soldier. As it is, he got off lightly. I've seen men receive as many as a thousand lashes."

Her stomach rolled. "A thousand?"

"Aye. Most often the blows are delivered over a period of days, allowing the prisoner some respite but greatly increasing his dread of the pain. Of course, such a beating can prove fatal. The trick in meting out punishment is to remember that a hardened scoundrel cannot be reformed no matter how hard you beat him. But a young soldier, such as this one, can still be turned to good if his spirit is not crushed."

Something fell out of the man's mouth. The doctor picked it up, held it up for her to see. "A lead ball. He's bitten it flat, his attempt to preserve his pride and keep from crying out, I expect."

Then the man moaned, and his eyes fluttered open. His gaze lighted on Bethie, and his eyes grew wide. He lifted his head, tears in his brown eyes. "I never meant to frighten you, mistress. Forgi'e me! I'm so sorry! I'll no' put my hands upon you or any other man's wife again, and I'll curse any man who does!"

Unsure what to say or feel, Bethie fought back her emotions, dipped a cloth into clean water, pressed it to his sweaty brow. "Rest. 'Tis over now. Dr. Aimes will see you well tended."

Nicholas sank his spade deeply into the damaged earth wall, tossed another shovelful of dirt down into the rift that floodwaters had made in the Lower Town curtain wall. The wall would be a few feet lower here, but at least they could close the gap.

Sweat ran down his bare chest as he dug. It was only about

nine in the morning, and already the sun was blazing. He pitied the soldiers in their heavy, woolen uniforms. It was hard to believe that he'd ever worn one. How far away that life seemed now.

He should have felt more ill at ease here amid the trappings of his former life. There were too many echoes, too many memories. He hadn't spent this much time in a fort or taken orders from anyone in six years. Yet here he was among people who had known him, however briefly, as Lieutenant Nicholas Kenleigh. Such circumstances ordinarily would have driven him deeper into the wilderness, as he much preferred being nameless.

What had changed?

Nothing. Nothing had changed. He was simply repaying his debt to Bethie, making certain she and her baby reached home safely. That meant staying in the fort until the road east was again safe. His presence here was an unfortunate matter of obligation, nothing more.

Even as the words formed in his mind he knew them for a lie. Nothing would have kept him within these walls if he hadn't wanted to be here, if he hadn't wanted to be with her. There were others he owed far more than he owed Bethie, and he had turned his back on them and ridden away.

*I regret to inform you, madam, that your son is dead.*

The memory of cold words spoken long ago cut through him like a rapier. The pain surprised him. He'd become so good at not feeling, so good at locking the darkness away inside himself. But Bethie had changed that. Somehow she had broken through his defenses, opened a fissure into that sea of darkness.

Lord, he wanted her. No matter how many times he touched her, tasted her, he could not get enough of her. She was like a fever in his blood, an obsession. He enjoyed just watching her come, enjoyed watching her lovely face as the sweet shock of climax surged through her, enjoyed knowing he could bring her pleasure.

And though he'd not taken her in the usual way, she was a fast learner and becoming quite clever with her tongue and hands. The first time she'd brought him to orgasm, he'd feared the force of it would wake the entire garrison. He could not deny that he dreamt of burying himself inside her, feeling her hot and slick around him, but it was better this way. This way he could not get her with child.

For he knew this could not last. One day, reinforcements would arrive and disperse the Delaware. Then he and Bethie would resume their journey to Paxton, where Nicholas would leave her and her baby in her family's care. He'd left home to protect his family from the man he'd become. He would leave Bethie for the same reason.

"I want the accursed pet wolf and the bear turned out of the fort or put down immediately! And if the settlers can't keep their dogs tied up and quiet at night, I want the dogs shot! They're ruining my sleep. Offer half a crown in bounty to any man who kills a loose or barking dog." Écuyer's voice preceded him as he walked along the ramparts.

"Aye, Captain." The quartermaster ran after him.

Écuyer stopped at the bottom of the wall below Nicholas. "And make certain that those who are selling Indian corn are not making too much of a profit. I can't have the king's subjects slaughtering one another over grain. I should think that six shillings a bushel is sufficient in time of war."

"Aye, as you wish, Captain. Will that be all, sir?"

"Aye. You are dismissed."

The quartermaster—Clark was his name—hurried away.

"Master Kenleigh, I should like a word with you."

Nicholas handed his spade to Ian Calhoun, climbed down the rough embankment to the ground.

Écuyer looked him over with a frown. "You are not properly attired, Master Kenleigh."

Nicholas accepted a ladle of well water from one of the farmer's wives, slaked his thirst, cold water spilling down his throat and over his chest. He wasn't the only one working without a shirt. "It's a hot day."

Around him, men laughed.

Écuyer's cheeks turned a blotchy shade of red. He lowered his voice. "Do not show insubordination before the men. As a gentleman, Master Kenleigh, and as a former officer, you ought to understand the need for maintaining discipline."

Nicholas reached for his shirt, slipped it over his head,

ignored the ties. "You came over here to ask me to put my shirt on?"

"Of course not! I came to get your assessment of these colonials. Will they be ready to fight when the time comes?"

"Aye. As we discussed, I've checked their rifles and firelocks, seen to it every man among them has powder, fresh flints, and shot as is fit for his weapons. Most are solid marksmen and will have no trouble—"

"Fire!"

The shout came from the music bastion.

Nicholas climbed the embankment, saw a column of thick, black smoke rising from the forested hill to the east.

Écuyer labored up behind him, stood beside him, fought to catch his breath. "They've attacked another farmstead."

Nicholas shook his head. "They're just trying to get your attention. I suspect they're hoping you'll order a detachment to repulse them."

"An ambuscade?"

"Aye."

Lieutenant Trent shouted from below. "Should I sound the alarm, Captain?"

"No, Lieutenant. This is of no concern to us. Back to work!" Écuyer faced Nicholas again, the fire apparently forgotten. "I want you to assemble a force of twenty men to serve as escort to the farmwomen, who are to turn out to cut spelt and gather what vegetables—"

"Women, Captain?" Nicholas couldn't believe what he was hearing. "You would send women outside these walls?"

Écuyer glared at him. "Under armed escort, Master Kenleigh. Is it not their job to do such chores at home on their farms? Let them prove their worth by offering some service to their sovereign."

Nicholas crossed his arms over his chest, looked down at the older man. "I doubt there's a man here who would willingly send his wife—"

"Any woman who refuses is to be locked in the guardhouse! Be ready by noon. Is that understood?"

"No, sir. If I do this, I do it my way—colonial volunteers, men of my choosing, and no bloody drum and fife. There's no reason to warn Shingiss we're on our way out."

"You try my patience, Kenleigh."

"I'm certain I do. But you don't know these 'colonials,' as you call them. I do. Lock their wives up, and you'll have a riot. Send women up against seasoned Delaware warriors, and you'll lose the respect of every frontiersman here."

Écuyer's jaw clenched, and he lowered his voice. "Very well, Kenleigh. Noon."

Nicholas entered the darkness of the underground passage that led through the east ravelin, nodded to the fifty-odd men who stood crowded together, sacks, scythes, and weapons in hand. Most were German farmers, stout men and strong.

"We'll need a picket at the wood redoubt and two or three men to join me in keeping watch on the forest to the east. The rest will move quickly row by row, first cutting the spelt, then, if we have time, harvesting whatever is ripe. If we fall under attack, make an orderly retreat to this spot. No one is to pursue the Delaware into the forest, is that clear?"

The men nodded gravely.

"Two hours. No more."

Bethie closed the front of her gown, handed a well-fed and contented Belle across the table into Annie's arms. 'Twas Annie's custom to visit with her after the midday meal if she could spare the time. "The truth is, Annie, I dinnae know that much about him. He willna speak of his travail with the Indians, willna tell me what happened."

Annie cuddled Belle against her shoulder, patted the baby's back. Her face grew grave. "All I know is what I've heard others say. 'Tis said he was taken captive by the Wyandot while tryin' to save the lives of two young soldiers." Then she lowered her voice, leaned toward Bethie. "The two young soldiers were burnt alive, they say, while he was tortured and made to watch. They say he's lived alone in the wild since, mad from pain and grief."

Bethie felt her temper quicken. Who dared say such a thing about Nicholas! "He's no' mad!"

"'Twas not I who said it, lamb. He's a good man, to be sure, and a brave one. Why, when I heard he was leadin' the men out into the fields today, I—"

"What?" Bethie's stomach dropped to the floor.

"Didn't ye know, lamb? He's leadin' a force of men out to cut the spelts and harvest what food they can. They left at midday."

"He didna see fit to tell me." Bethie stood, torn between fury and fear. "Can you watch Belle for me, Annie? She won't be hungry again for a while."

"Aye, but there's nothin' ye can do for him until he returns. He likely kept it to himself so as no' to worry ye."

Bethie scarce heard her as she hurried to the door. "Thank you, Annie."

She opened the door and froze.

*Richard!*

Icy terror shot through her, froze the breath in her lungs.

She'd caught only a glimpse of her stepbrother. At least she'd thought it was him. One moment he was there, standing not thirty feet away from her door, an oily look upon his face. The next he was gone, vanished in the crowd.

Had she imagined him? The man she'd seen had the same reddish-blond hair, the same square face, the same freckles, the same filthy smirk. But he'd worn a redcoat uniform, and Richard had always hated the English. Perhaps she had merely seen a soldier who looked like him.

Why, then, had he looked directly at her?

"Ma'am, are you well?" Private Fitchie's face swam into view.

Bethie clutched the door frame, drew in a deep breath, tried to quiet her pounding heart.

Annie's hand settled reassuringly on her shoulder. "Bethie, lamb, what is it? Ye've gone as pale as a ghost!"

"I—I'm fine." But she shook from head to toe.

"Fitchie, help me get her inside." Annie, with Belle still in her arms, took one of Bethie's arms, while Private Fitchie took the other.

Bethie sat in the chair Private Fitchie pulled out for her. "I'm fine, truly I am. I—I thought . . . for a moment, I . . ."

"Be a peach, Private, and fetch her some fresh water. Be

off wi' ye." Annie settled her girth in a chair beside Bethie. "Now, lamb, tell me—"

From outside came the sound of rapid gunfire, the blare of a trumpet.

Private Fitchie stopped still in the doorway, turned to face them. "The alarm! We're under attack!"

For the second time in as many minutes, Bethie's heart seemed to stop. "Nicholas!"

# Chapter 22

"Fall back! Quickly!" Nicholas reloaded, aimed for a Delaware wearing a British officer's coat and gorget, fired. "Go!"

The warrior fell back amid rows of waist-high Indian corn, his death scream lost amid the war whoops and gunfire. There were probably fifty more just like him hiding out there, some in the corn, some in the trees on the edge of the forest.

Nicholas ducked behind the shelter of an apple tree, reloaded.

Men dashed past him, bags of radishes, summer squash, fresh greens, beans, peas, sheaves of spelt clutched to their chests. Most were already well behind him on their way back to the ravelin, but a few had dropped their burdens to fight. He needed to get them out of here.

"The rest of you—fall in behind me! Make for the glacis!"

An arrow sang past his shoulder, landed harmlessly in the dirt.

He found the warrior who had fired it, put a ball through his throat, then reloaded.

Men scrambled low to the ground, ran backward, reloading and firing as they went.

The blast of a howitzer. The whine as the ball arced through the air. The explosion of impact.

Stunned silence.

The Delaware apparently hadn't planned on facing down artillery.

"Go! Now!"

Behind him came the sound of retreating feet as the remaining men turned and ran straight for the cover of the glacis. Once inside, they'd be only footsteps away from the safety of the ravelin, bearing a sizable harvest.

But Nicholas stood his ground.

Ahead of him, on the main path that bisected the garden stood Shingiss. The upper half of his face was painted with vermilion, a scar clearly visible where a hunter's bullet had grazed his forehead long ago. A single eagle feather stood up from his scalp lock. Turkey feathers hung from his pierced ears. A copper ring hung from his nose, and many strands of wampum decorated his throat. His breechcloth, belt, and the deerskin mantle that hung over his right shoulder were embroidered with quills, wampum, and moose hair. His hands were empty and turned palms up in a stance of peace.

Nicholas lowered his pistol. *"Hé, Shingiss, Sakima Lenape." Greetings, Shingiss, Great Chief of the Delaware.*

Shingiss acknowledged his greeting, spoke to him in Delaware. "Ken-lee. You fight with these Long Knives?"

Nicholas searched for the right words. The man Shingiss had met years ago would not have been here. "I stand beside men who want only to feed their wives and children and to live in peace. Why do you make war upon them?"

"We make war upon those who take our lands, kill our game, treat us like animals, bring sickness, deny us weapons and trade. My people go hungry on their own land."

It was true, every word of it. Governor Amherst had placed strict limits on the goods being traded to Indian people of all nations, forced them into a state of poverty and hunger, denied them rifles for hunting, as well as powder and lead. He meant to weaken them, drive them away. But clearly it was a policy that had blown up in Amherst's face.

"You speak the truth, Shingiss. I have seen this. And yet you will not bend the ears of the English or turn their hearts toward your words by slaughtering their women and babies still at the breast."

"They cannot remain. Is not the land east of the mountains enough for them?"

"The men whose families you have killed came here from lands even farther away than the English. They came because they had no food."

Shingiss's face grew taut with anger. "They kill all the game in their own hunting grounds and come over the sea to take from ours! They are a savage, sickly people who do not know how to live. They cannot stay!"

"They have no place else to go."

"Will you die with them?"

"If I must." Nicholas met the chief's gaze head-on. "My woman and her baby are here. I would not risk them falling to a Lenape warrior's arrow or coming under a Shawnee knife."

"So Ken-lee has taken a woman." A faint smile played on Shingiss's otherwise grim visage. "If you wish to leave this place and lead her over the mountains, none of my men will stop you. No one of them will raise a hand to you or your woman. I give you my word."

"Thank you, great Sakima. I will think upon what you have said. I ask you to hear me as well. It is better to make a new treaty with the English than to fight them."

"No, Ken-lee. The time for words and treaties is past. We will fight. Go, Ken-lee. Return to your woman. Lie with her. When the fort is taken, I will do what I can to see that you are both spared."

*"Làpìch knewël, Shingiss." I will see you again.* Nicholas turned and walked down the path toward the fort.

He'd gone but a few steps when he heard someone running toward him through the corn. A catch of breath as muscles tensed. The whoosh of a tomahawk as it swung toward his skull.

Nicholas dropped to his knees, the tomahawk missing him by inches. Then in one move, he pivoted, slit the belly of his attacker wide open with his knife.

The warrior, a young man of perhaps eighteen, stared at

Nicholas in surprise, fell to the ground with a groan, clutching his intestines.

Shingiss gave an outraged shout, and Nicholas knew it was not directed at him. The young warrior had shamed his chief by attacking Nicholas. Now the boy would die unmourned.

Nicholas wiped his blade off in the dirt, stood, walked back to the fort without once looking over his shoulder.

Bethie stood on the ramparts, a scream caught in her throat. She'd seen Nicholas take his leave of the chief, watched in silent horror as a painted warrior, war club raised, had run stealthily up behind him. She'd seen Nicholas drop, turn, and kill the man with one cut of his blade.

Barely able to breathe, she watched him approach the fort until he disappeared in the shadow of the glacis. Then she hurried to the front gate to meet him. But she wasn't the only one.

By the time she reached the gate, a small crowd had gathered, mostly made up of men who'd been part of the foraging party. The quartermaster barked orders at the men, tried to direct the flow of vegetables and grain to the various kitchens and storehouses, but few people seemed to pay him any heed. When Nicholas crossed the drawbridge and walked through the gate, a cheer arose, not only from those gathered at the gate, but from the men on the ramparts.

"Bloody well done, Kenleigh!"

"You showed that bastard!"

"Good show, Lieutenant!"

She took in the sight of him all at once—the blood on his shirt, the wind playing in his hair, the sweat on his brow, the power of his stride, the dark rage in his eyes—and she wanted nothing more than to slap him soundly across the face. She might have done exactly that, had he not taken her by the arm and pulled her callously through the throng and across the parade grounds back toward the officers' barracks.

Private Fitchie hurried after them, a look of terror on his face. "I tried to keep her in the barracks, like you said, sir, but she wouldna listen!"

"What in the hell were you doing up on the ramparts? You shouldn't be out of our quarters during an alarm!" Nicholas walked so quickly she had to run to keep up.

"Dinnae talk to me like that!" She jerked on her arm, but he held fast. "You didna see fit to tell me you were goin' into danger. I had to learn it from Annie!"

"I didn't realize, madam, that your approval was required."

"Oooh! My approval? You haggis-headed bawheid!"

Annie stood in the doorway, a smile tugging at her lips, Isabelle in her arms.

Bethie felt a surge of waspish temper. What did Annie find so amusing?

"If you want to call me names, love, I suggest you try calling me something I can understand." Nicholas pressed Bethie up against the wall, kissed her roughly. "Otherwise, I'm likely to miss the insult."

How dare he kiss her! She pushed him away. "Fine! You're a foolish arse! You do understand those words, do you no'?"

Nicholas glared at her. "Annie, do you mind? I need to talk to my wife."

He wanted to talk? Fine! She had a few more things to say. "How about 'bastard'? Is that clear enough?"

Annie smiled. "Belle and I will pay a visit to the tradin' post. Ye take as long as ye need. Come fetch her when ye're . . . um, done."

Bethie barely heard her. "Or 'whoreson'? Do you understand that one?"

"Thank you, Annie." Nicholas reached out, grabbed Private Fitchie by his collar. "Don't let anyone disturb us. Do you understand? The first person to open this door dies!"

"Aye, sir. But . . ."

Bethie didn't know when she'd felt so angry. "Maybe 'bloody idiot'?"

Nicholas held a hand over her mouth, stifled her curses. "But what? Speak up, Private!"

"You will no' hurt her, sir . . . will you?"

"She'll be lucky if she escapes with her life!" With that, Nicholas pulled Bethie none too gently through the doorway, slammed the door behind them, and dropped the bar in place.

He turned to face her, a look of raw masculine fury on his face, his eyes blue fire. With a growl, he jerked her against him, captured her lips with his, forced his tongue deep into her mouth.

This was no gentle kiss, no attempt at seduction. It was raw, savage, brutish.

It was wonderful.

Bethie found herself kissing him back, her passion every bit as rough as his. Tongues invaded, twined, stroked. Teeth nipped, bit, ravished. Hands tore at clothing, thrust it aside, sought tender skin. And then they stood naked, fevered flesh against fevered flesh, panting their desire.

Almost beyond reason, Nicholas pulled her with him onto the bed, rolled onto his back so that she was astride him. Then he settled her so that her woman's mound pressed against his aching erection. "Let my cock do for you what my tongue does."

For a moment she looked confused, even afraid. But then he rocked against her, flexed her hips, showed her exactly what he meant. Her eyes closed, and she gave a long, throaty moan.

Slowly, she moved over him, her hands resting on his chest, her warm, wet folds sliding over his shaft as her most sensitive flesh rubbed against the length of him. He knew the exact moment she found the most pleasurable angle, because her breath broke and her thighs drew taut against his hips.

"Oh, God, Nicholas!" Her pace increased, and so did the pressure.

He was close, so close to where he wanted to be, so close to being inside her. He could feel her core pulse against him, knew she was more than ready for him, knew he could bury himself inside her with one clean thrust. He heard breath hiss from between his teeth, focused on the sweet glide of her wet woman's lips over his cock, the weight of her breasts in his hands, the pebbled hardness of her nipples against his palms. It was enough. It would be enough.

It was never enough. He could never get enough, not enough of Bethie.

He could tell she was desperate now. Small whimpering noises escaped her throat. Her head was thrown back in sensual abandonment as she ground herself against him. Then her breath caught in her throat, and every muscle in her body seemed to tense.

She came with a cry. "Nicholas!"

The sight of the rapture on her face pushed him over the brink. He heard himself groan, a deep, guttural sound, as the bliss of orgasm slammed through him.

Later that afternoon, Shingiss's men came out of the forest a second time, tried to shoot or drive off horses and cattle grazing in the fields around the fort.

"They're trying to draw our forces outside the walls, trying to provoke a battle," Nicholas warned Écuyer. "The animals will return on their own."

But the captain, outraged over the substance of Shingiss's remarks to Nicholas, didn't listen. Instead, Écuyer waited until the Indians had seemingly gone back into the forest, then sent a small party of men out to round up the animals under military escort.

The results were predictable. The Delaware poured out of the forest, and though a few were killed, shot by retreating soldiers, they managed to capture one of the militia, James Thompson, whom they killed and scalped within sight of the walls.

This provoked outrage from the entire garrison. Soldiers and militia gathered on the ramparts to curse the Delaware. Only when the air sang with arrows was it clear that Thompson's killing had been a distraction, one that enabled warriors to creep in the shadows of the riverbanks and surround the fort.

Écuyer told his men not to fire, afraid they would not be able to hit the Indians, who still lurked in the shelter of the steep riverbanks. Instead, he ordered several rounds to be fired from the howitzers and the cannon. Within two hours, the attack was over.

But no one celebrated. Looking out over the landscape, it was now perfectly clear.

Fort Pitt was under siege.

* * *

For two days, nothing happened. Indians were spotted prowling around the fort, checking the walls for weaknesses, reconnoitering. On the third day, just after midnight, two Delaware leaders approached the fort, pleaded to speak with Ken-lee. A guard was sent to wake Nicholas, who quickly dressed and hurried to meet the Indians outside the gates.

As Nicholas left the safety of the fort again, Bethie knelt beside her bed and prayed.

"They want to meet to discuss our situation," Nicholas explained to Écuyer, who sat at his desk drinking tea as the sun peeked over the horizon. Nicholas had misgivings about helping the arrogant bastard and trusted Shingiss far more than he trusted Écuyer. But Bethie's survival and that of every other man, woman, and child inside the fort depended upon a British victory.

"Are they sincere, or is this just another ruse, another attempt to provoke us?"

"I would guess the latter. They are desperate. They will use any means at their disposal to win."

Écuyer took another sip of tea. "So must we. Tell them they may approach the fort safely. You and I will meet with them and hear what they have to say. We will give them gifts, of course, some small token of our regard. And we shall see."

"Why does it have to be you, Nicholas? Why? Is there no one else in this bloody garrison who can speak their tongue?" She felt his strong arms surround her, turned to face him, resting her hands on his shoulders.

"They have asked that I be present, and the captain has commanded it. I have no choice, Bethie."

Bethie laid her head against his chest, listened to the strong rhythm of his heart. He was so alive, so strong. "Promise me you'll no' take foolish risks! I couldna bear it if you should be hurt, Nicholas."

She heard his deep chuckle, felt his fingers in her hair. The sun was barely up, and she'd not had time to braid it.

"There is still time before I must go, and Belle is still asleep." The husky tone of his voice told her just how he thought they ought to spend that time.

Richard watched from the shadows of the soldiers' barracks as his dear stepsister's man left their quarters and strode off toward the main gate. The big trapper would be tied up for at least an hour, talking with the heathen, interpreting their words for the captain. Richard needed less than half that time.

But first he had to get past Private Fitchie. The boy had become Bethie's lapdog. Richard had seen the shy, adoring glances he'd tossed her way. She had seduced him, too, had probably taken him to her bed when that husband of hers was out acting the hero.

Richard watched, smiled when Fitchie clutched his belly. So the doctor's cures *did* work. Richard had gone to him, complaining that his belly had turned to stone. The doctor had given him a tincture to make his bowels move—and Richard had poured all of it into Fitchie's coffee this morning.

Within minutes, Fitchie had doubled over, and soon he seemed to be dancing.

"You'll have to choose, lad. Is it to be duty or a trip to the privy house?"

Even as Richard spoke the words, Private Fitchie grabbed his breeches and ran.

Bethie sat down in the chair, opened her shift, lifted a fussy Belle to her breast, tried to reassure herself that Nicholas would be fine. This was not to be a battle, after all, but an exchange of words and gifts. There would be no gunfire, no warriors with war clubs, no arrows flying through the air. And if anything went wrong, he'd be well within reach of the marksmen on the ramparts.

But that wasn't the only thing troubling her.

Nicholas had told her this morning that if this parlay led to peace, they would be free to leave the fort and continue on their way to Paxton. "You might even be home before the first leaves turn," he'd said. "Don't worry."

But how could she not worry? She knew what awaited her in Paxton.

An image of the face she'd seen the other day leapt into her mind. She shuddered. Whoever it was had looked so much like Richard. But it couldn't be him. It couldn't be. Not here. Not so far from Paxton. Not in a British uniform.

She had not told Nicholas yet, but she wasn't going to Paxton. She would stay here with Annie, if Annie and Charlie would take her in. She could work as hard as any other woman, help them run the trading post. Just the other day Annie had said she was getting too old to handle it all herself. And if Annie and Charlie turned her away, she would plead with Nicholas to take her to Ligonier or farther on to Lancaster, where she could surely find a position as a seamstress or day maid. Now that she could read some and write her name, it would surely be easier to find work.

But just as terrible as the fear of facing her stepfather and his vile son again was the knowledge that Nicholas still intended to leave her. She'd thought perhaps that their time together would change his mind, that his desire for her might turn to affection. Living here in the fort, where everyone believed she was his wife, had made anything seem possible.

She knew he cared for her, or at least she hoped he did. Why else would he get so angry with her? Why protect her, provide for her, risk his life for her? Why make such tender love to her? Never once had he pushed her further than she'd been willing to go. Never once had he taken her as a man takes a woman. Did that not show he truly cared for her?

And yet he spoke of leaving her in Paxton as if it were a trifle, merely the next stop on his journey. His voice sounded in her imagination. "Farewell, Bethie. It's been good to know you. Take care of Belle."

Could it truly be that easy for him? Did she mean so little to him?

She didn't realize she was crying until her vision blurred. And then she knew the terrible truth: She had fallen in love with him. She had fallen in love with Nicholas.

"Nay, Bethie." She stood abruptly, carried Belle to her cradle, began to dress. "Dinnae be silly! He doesna love you."

She had her back to the door when she heard it open.

"Little Bethie Stewart."

She whirled about at the sound of his voice. Terror exploded in her breast. "Richard!"

"Good morning, sister." He stroked the bulge in his breeches. "'Tis time you and I got to know each other again."

# Chapter 23

Even as he rendered the words into English, Nicholas knew Turtle's Heart was lying.

"He says Ligonier has been destroyed and that the Ottawa and Ojibwa are advancing many hundreds strong toward us from the north. He says that, out of caring for us, they have persuaded the Six Nations to hold back their attack so that we might evacuate the fort and take our women and children east over the mountains. If we do not leave now, the Six Nations will come and destroy us."

Écuyer smiled, seemed almost to be enjoying himself. "Tell Turtle's Heart that I thank him for his kind warning, but the garrison at Fort Pitt is well equipped to defend itself. Tell him that three great armies are on their way here to punish those who have taken up arms against the Crown. Six thousand are on their way to Fort Pitt as we speak. Three thousand more have been sent north to punish the Ottawa and Ojibwa. A third is coming up from the south to destroy the Delaware and Shawnee. Tell him they should protect their women and children, for I fear for their safety."

Nicholas translated those lies, as well, wondered if Turtle's Heart understood the concept of a thousand. Wars among Indian nations rarely measured in hundreds.

Turtle's Heart watched Écuyer through inscrutable brown eyes as the silence stretched. Finally, he spoke. "Tell him we will take his words to Shingiss and will consider all that has been spoken."

Nicholas repeated Turtle's Heart's words in English.

Écuyer nodded, motioned two young soldiers forward. "Tell them we appreciate their warning and concern for our safety. Out of our regard for them, we offer these blankets and handkerchiefs as tokens."

As Nicholas interpreted, the soldiers placed a neatly folded woolen blanket and small, linen handkerchief into each of the two Delaware warrior's arms, looks of terror on their young faces as if they expected to be killed at any moment.

Turtle's Heart nodded. "Thank him for these gifts and tell him that Turtle's Heart holds fast the chain of friendship with the English."

Then Turtle's Heart and his companion turned and walked down the Monongahela bank toward the forest, where Shingiss was no doubt waiting.

As a drummer began a retreating beat and Écuyer's escort disappeared behind the glacis and back toward the drawbridge, Nicholas watched the warriors walk away, feeling vaguely uneasy, then turned and followed Écuyer.

Ahead of him, Trent and Écuyer were talking in low tones.

Écuyer chuckled. "Within a month we could be rid of them all without having fired a shot."

"Let us hope the blankets have the desired effect. What of the two privates?"

"Both have already survived smallpox, and the doctor assures me they cannot contract the disease again. Still, we're taking no chances. Their uniforms will be burned, and they shall be quarantined for a fortnight."

Nicholas stopped in his tracks, stared at the two officers' backs, almost unable to believe what he'd heard. "You gave them blankets infected with smallpox?"

Écuyer turned to face him, a smile on his arrogant face. "Aye. Rather ingenious, don't you think, Master Kenleigh? My idea, you know. Given that the savages cannot withstand the disease, this simple act could mean the saving of Fort Pitt."

"And it could mean the horrible deaths of countless innocent Delaware and Shawnee!" A spectacle of horror unfolded in Nicholas's mind—women, children, elders convulsing with fever, dying by the hundreds, their bodies covered with pustules.

Écuyer fussed with the lace at his wrists. "Really, Master Kenleigh. Is there such a thing as an 'innocent' Indian? I should think you more than most understand their savagery."

Nicholas turned, started after the Indians, was immediately restrained by two soldiers, who dragged him back inside the fort at gunpoint. He glared at Écuyer. "Who's the savage now?"

Écuyer's face reddened. "You forget yourself, Master Kenleigh."

"And you've just made me an unwitting accomplice to murder!"

"Step outside the gate without authorization, and I'll have you shot for treason."

"Go to hell!" Fists clenched, Nicholas shoved away the soldiers who restrained him and pushed past Écuyer, ignoring Trent's shocked gasp.

With no way to warn Shingiss, Nicholas strode off in a rage toward the ramparts, determined to pick up a shovel and slam it into dirt before he slammed his fists into Écuyer's arrogant face.

"It *was* you!" Bethie's legs turned to water, her heartbeat a roar in her ears, panic like ice in her veins.

*This could not be happening!*

"Aye. I thought you saw me. I've had my eyes on you since the mornin' you arrived, watchin', waitin'. Now lie down on the bed and spread your thighs for me like a good little whore." He strode toward her with the confidence of a predator, that familiar lewd smile on his freckled face.

Terror choked her, blurred her vision. The years melted away, and she suddenly found herself back in her stepfather's cabin, in her bed in the loft—afraid and alone. She could feel Richard's hands groping her, feel his fingers thrusting inside her, hurting her.

He'd come to her almost every night, touched her, hurt her, rubbed himself against her. He was ten years older and so much stronger. She had tried long ago to fight him, knowing she could not win, knowing he would only hurt her worse if she tried. If she'd cried out, Malcolm would have come with his leather strap and beat her again, and her mother would have known her shame. She'd bitten back her screams, tried not to feel it, waited until he was done to let the tears come.

"P-please, Richard! P-please dinnae do this!"

"You're afraid. Good. I always liked that. Lie down, little one, unless you want me to tup you on the floor."

A baby cried.

*Belle!*

Bethie blinked, woke from her living nightmare. She was not in her bed. She was not in the loft. She was in Fort Pitt in the quarters she shared with Nicholas. Nicholas, who had taught her to read. Nicholas, who had saved her life. Nicholas, who had made love to her, who'd brought her bliss.

She hardened her heart against Belle's weeping, hoped Richard wouldn't notice her daughter, and walked forward on trembling legs until she stood between him and the cradle. "N-nay, Richard! I—I am n-no' a frightened little girl, but a woman. Get out!"

His step faltered. His smile became a look of mild disgust. "Aye, 'tis true. You are no' the bonny wee lass you once were—all yellow hair, big eyes, and long legs, thin and wary like a wild rabbit. I remember when you started to grow paps. Small and sweet they were, but no' now. Still, a woman or no', I want to finish what we started."

At his words, tendrils of nausea snaked through her belly, and bile rose in her throat. She swallowed hard, her mind racing for some way out of this. "H-he'll kill you! If you touch me, he'll kill you!"

He reached out as if in defiance, grabbed her arms, his fingers digging painfully into her flesh as he dragged her against him. He looked down at her through flat brown eyes. "And how is he goin' to hear of it? Do you want him to share in our family secrets?"

And in one terrifying instant, she saw the awful choice before her. She could submit, suffer Richard's touch, and keep her taint hidden. Or she could fight him, knowing full well he would hurt her, knowing that her bruises would betray her disgrace to Nicholas, to the whole world.

The breath left her lungs in a single sob, and she closed her eyes against her fear, her dread, her grief.

*Nicholas!*

Chuckling to himself, Richard forced her step-by-step backward toward the bed, his fingers biting into her arms, his voice slick with lust. “Go ahead and weep, lass. I like it.”

Her reaction came so swiftly, it surprised even her. Fueled by white-hot rage, Bethie drove her knee into his groin with all the force in her body.

Richard grunted, crumpled, lay writhing on the floor.

She dashed past him, grabbed the poker from the cold hearth, ran back, placed herself between her baby and the man who had all but ruined her life. “Get out, Richard! Crawl out like the animal you are! So help me God, you will no’ touch me again!”

Ashen-faced and trembling, Richard slowly got to his feet. Still bent double, he turned as if to go. Then he spun about, lunged for her.

Bethie swung the poker, aimed for his head.

But he caught it, wrenched it from her grasp, threw it to the floor.

Before she could take a single step, he grabbed her by the hair, hauled her up against him, forced her to meet his gaze. “Bitch! If you’ve unmanned me, I’ll kill you!”

She ignored the pain in her scalp, glared at him. “You were never a man, Richard!”

Pain exploded in her skull as his fist connected with her cheek, sent her sprawling across the bed. A flash of lights. Swirling gray. The taste of blood.

Driven by equal parts of fear and fury, she fought her way back to consciousness, saw him unbuttoning his breeches, tried to roll away, to reach the other side of the bed.

Rough hands clawed at her, pulled her back. “You’re no’ goin’ anywhere until I’ve finished wi’ you, Bethie Stewart—Englishman’s whore!”

“You will no’ touch me! No’ again!” Desperate, she screamed, kicked, scratched, struggled with all her strength.

Her nails tore skin from his face, left four bright streaks of red.

He howled in outrage, hit her again and again, left her spinning on the edge of pain and forgetfulness.

From far away, she could hear Belle crying.

And then he was upon her, his legs forcing hers apart, his body holding hers helpless against the bed.

She heard herself whimper, felt the wet slide of tears down her cheeks, struggled to speak. "Nay!"

Richard laughed. "This is goin' to be good!"

The creak of the door on its hinges. Richard's surprised gasp.

"Get the hell away from her!"

*Nicholas!*

Bethie's last thought as darkness pulled her under was that he knew.

Now Nicholas knew.

Nicholas took it all in at once—Bethie lying beaten and unconscious on the bed, the soldier holding her down, his breeches unbuttoned, Belle's terrified wailing.

Primal rage surged from his gut. He looked into the soldier's shocked eyes, saw a dead man. "Get the hell away from her!"

Before the soldier could button his breeches, Nicholas rounded the bed, drove his fist into the soldier's face, knocked him to the floor. "You like to beat women? You like to hurt them? Try me instead."

The soldier cowered, tried to scoot away. "I-it's no' like that! Please, sir! You cannae kill me!"

Nicholas grabbed him by his collar, jerked him to his feet. "No? And why not?"

"I—I'm Bethie's brother!"

Stunned, Nicholas stared into the soldier's eyes, saw there the unspeakable truth.

Suddenly all the pieces fell into place. Her fear of men. Her unwillingness to discuss her family. Her reluctance to return to Paxton.

Her husband hadn't been the only man to mistreat her.

*Oh, God, Bethie!*

"If you tell, everyone will know your wife is a whore! Bethie will be shamed for life! You have to let me go!"

"That's what you think!" In a black rage, Nicholas slammed his fist into the bastard's jaw again and again and again, until the soldier's head lolled stupidly on his shoulders. Nicholas wanted to kill him, spill his blood, watch the light fade from his eyes as life left his body. He might have killed him then and there, had not the sound of Belle's frantic crying pierced his fury.

He dragged the unconscious man around the bed to the still-open door, tossed him roughly into the dirt.

Men stopped working, stared.

Nicholas barked out a string of orders, certain they would be obeyed. "Get the quartermaster! This man attacked my wife! See to it he is locked in the guardhouse! Send for the doctor! And get Annie from the trading post! Quickly!"

Bethie struggled to wake from the depths of a nightmare. Richard had come for her. He had beaten her. He had tried to rape her.

If only her head didn't hurt so badly. If only the nightmare would leave her in peace.

"Bethie, love, can you hear me?" It was Nicholas.

A hand stroked her cheek.

"She's suffered quite a severe beating. I've left laudanum for her pain, but I shouldn't be surprised if she remains unconscious for some time." That was Dr. Aimes. "You might well need a wet nurse for the baby, at least for a day or two. If you'll excuse me, I need to see to the man who did this."

Beating? Unconscious? Wet nurse?

*It hadn't been a dream!*

A spark of panic ignited in her belly, moved sluggishly to her mind, became confused. What had happened? Why couldn't she open her eyes? Where was Belle? But before the answers could form, she was adrift, conversation flowing over her like water.

"Rest assured, he will pay for his crime," Captain Écuyer said.

"I should have killed him when I had the chance!"

"It's better that you didn't, Kenleigh. A British fort is no place for frontier-style justice. He will be tried in a court-martial, and, after he is convicted, he will be shot."

"It must be handled discreetly, Captain. I would not have her suffer more than she already has."

"Of course. All shall be sworn to secrecy. Tell me, Master Kenleigh, does your father know of your marriage?"

"I've had no contact with him for six years. Why do you ask?"

"I should think my question obvious. You are heir to your father's estates. I'm certain he would have preferred you to make a dynastic match and marry a woman of your own class, not the daughter of Scottish rustics, no matter how lovely or pleasant she might be."

"You go too far, Écuyer."

"Perhaps. But bad blood will out, as they say. Now I must be going. We are at war, and I've many duties."

Bethie heard the sound of a door shutting, felt a cold cloth against her aching forehead. Warm lips brushed over hers. Nicholas.

She tried to speak his name, but it came out a moan.

"Bethie? Bethie, can you hear me?"

She tried to dig her way out of the darkness, put all of her strength into saying one word. "Belle . . ."

"Belle is fine, love. She's safe, and so are you. I won't leave you, Bethie."

She felt him warm beside her, smelled his scent, sensed his strength.

Then she surrendered and slept.

Nicholas gazed down at Bethie's sleeping face. Dark bruises and lacerations marred both of her cheeks. There were bruises on her throat, arms, and inner thighs as well, the marks of a predator.

*Damn it!*

He ought to have been here. He ought to have prevented this.

Instead, he'd been unwittingly helping Écuyer murder the

Delaware, who were intent on killing the English. And while he'd been caught up in the drama outside the gates, a man—no, an animal masquerading as a man—had beaten and tried to rape his own sister, or stepsister, as it now seemed.

So much violence. So much brutality. He thought he'd seen everything both the wilderness and the so-called civilized world had to offer. And then he'd seen this.

Why hadn't she told him?

As soon as he asked the question, he knew the answer. He had secrets, too—memories so terrible that even the act of recounting them was unbearable.

He shuddered to think what would have happened to Bethie had he not arrived just then. He'd been on his way to work on the ramparts, ready to spend his rage in the dirt, when he'd noticed that Private Fitchie was not on duty outside their door. Still haunted by a vague sense of uneasiness, he'd come to investigate. If only he had come sooner.

"Nicholas?"

She was awake.

"I'm right here, love. How do you feel?"

Her violet eyes were clouded by pain. "My head . . . hurts."

He reached for the laudanum, poured a small amount into a cup, lifted her head, held the cup to her lips. "Drink this, love. It will take the pain away."

Her nose wrinkled as she swallowed the bitter liquid.

Nicholas lowered her head gently back to the pillow. "Just rest, Bethie."

For a moment she lay silent, then tears spilled from the corners of her eyes. "I'm sorry, Nicholas. Please forgi'e me."

He wiped the tears away with his thumb. "Forgive you for what, Bethie? None of this was your fault."

"I'll no' blame you if you tell people the truth about us and set me aside."

He pulled her against him, kissed her hair, torn between fury and tenderness. "Why would I do that, love?"

Her voice, already weak, quavered with emotion. "I've brought shame on you."

Nicholas tilted his head, looked straight into her eyes. "That is not true. You've done nothing wrong."

"B-but he is my . . . *brother*." The last word was an anguished whisper.

"Your stepbrother. Aye, I know."

Whatever Bethie had expected from Nicholas, it was not this. She'd been so certain he would turn away from her the moment he knew the truth. But here he was, beside her, comforting her.

Perhaps it was his kindness, or perhaps it was the lulling effects of the laudanum, but she found herself telling him everything.

How her father had been killed while helping neighbors build their cabin when she was only ten. How her mother, burdened with a daughter and no living sons, had sought a husband at the meetinghouse and found Malcolm Sorley. How her gospel-greedy stepfather had taken them to his home farther west, where he lived with his already-grown son, Richard. How Malcolm had found her lacking in piety and overblessed with beauty and had made it his duty to beat the fear of his vengeful God into her. How Richard had watched the beatings with a strange look in his eyes that made Bethie afraid.

"The first time he came to my bed, I was twelve. I didna know what men did with women, didna understand what he was tryin' to do. When I started to protest, he told me Malcolm would punish me if he found out."

"And then he raped you."

"Nay. At first, all he did was t-touch me, run his hands over me." She shuddered, a feeling of deep horror mingling with utter revulsion in her belly.

Nicholas held her closer. "I'm right here, Bethie."

"But then he began to . . ." 'Twas almost impossible to say it. She took a deep breath. "Then he began to put his fingers . . . inside me."

"I'm so sorry, love."

"It hurt, but he didn't care. I tried to fight him. I tried! But he was so much stronger."

"A little girl can hardly be expected to fight off a grown man, Bethie. It was not your fault. You did everything you could."

She pushed on, desperate to get the words out. "He laughed. He laughed at me, laughed when . . . when he saw my maiden's blood on his hands."

"Dear God! Bethie, I—"

"Every night I went to bed, hoping and praying he would stay away. And every night I would hear him creep up the ladder to the loft. He hurt me. He rubbed himself against me." A wave of nausea assailed her.

"You should sleep. Tell me the rest later. It's too soon."

"Nay! I must finish! You must know!"

"I know everything I need to know about you, Bethie. There's nothing you can tell me that will change the way I feel about you."

But Bethie scarcely heard him. She had started the story. Now she must finish it.

She told him how one night when she was fifteen, Richard had come to her and told her it was time for her to become a woman. Afraid of the pain and unable to bear it any longer, she had fought him, and her struggles had awakened Malcolm, who had beaten her almost senseless, accused her of seducing his only son and leading him down the path of eternal damnation.

Bethie was trembling now, her body shaking uncontrollably. Tears slid, unheeded, down her cheeks. "Three days later, he married me off to Andrew, a man my father's age, and sent me away. Andrew knew what had happened, said he forgave me, but I could always see it in his eyes—the pity, the shame."

The helpless rage that had been brewing inside Nicholas all day began to boil. "And what of your mother? Did she do nothing to help you? Did your stepfather beat her, too?"

"Aye, he beat her. But she hated me. She said I had cursed her womb because I had been born alive and her sons had all been stillborn. When Malcolm told her I had bewitched his son, I think she believed him." Her voice broke into quiet weeping at this deepest betrayal.

Her grief was almost more than he could bear. Rage, fueled by anguish, burned hot inside him. Richard Sorley would die. It would be Nicholas's great pleasure to kill him.

But not tonight.

Gently he scooped Bethie's bruised and trembling body

into his arms, laid her head against his chest, let her tears soak through the cloth of his shirt. "It's over now, Bethie. None of them will ever harm you again."

"I—I am no' deservin' of such kindness. I am tainted, do you no' see that?"

"All I see, Bethie, is the woman I—"

*Love.*

"—care deeply about and wish to protect."

The word had come to him so naturally, had slipped onto his tongue as if he'd meant it.

And to his astonishment, Nicholas realized he did.

He loved her.

He was in love with Bethie Stewart.

# Chapter 24

Bethie awoke in Nicholas's arms the next morning, aching with milk and longing to hold her baby again. Though her head throbbed and her entire body ached, she felt a strange sense of lightness inside, as if something dark and heavy had been lifted from her. And it didn't take her long to realize why.

Last night she had told Nicholas everything, every horrible detail, and he had not pushed her away. Instead, he'd held her, comforted her, assured her no one would hurt her again. And as the laudanum had taken hold and she'd drifted off to an untroubled sleep, the last thing she remembered him saying was that he still cared for her.

*All I see, Bethie, is the woman I care deeply about and wish to protect.*

'Twas not a declaration of love, to be sure, but it was far beyond anything she'd dared hope for. And when he'd looked at her, it was not pity or shame she saw in his eyes, but tenderness, concern. Nicholas knew, and still he stayed by her side.

Nicholas. Nicholas. She loved him. With everything she was, she loved him. Uncertain though their future might be, she felt some peace in knowing that much.

He stayed with her, refused to let her get out of bed for three days, except when absolutely necessary. Private Fitchie, much embarrassed by the cruel trick that had been played upon him and blaming himself for her suffering, was back on duty outside her door, ferocious in his devotion. Annie paid several calls each day, bringing what gossip she had—which was considerable, given that she was the hub of the fort's gossip mill.

But no one ever spoke to Bethie about Richard. When she finally asked Nicholas, all he told her was that Richard would never trouble her again.

The court-martial of Richard Sorley convened three days after the attack. Nicholas watched in disgust as Sorley accused Bethie of seducing and bewitching him, described how she'd seduced him when she was but a child. His words were so revolting that Nicholas spied the officers giving Sorley blatant looks of contempt. Nicholas was the only other person to testify. The officers reached a verdict within minutes: guilty.

Écuyer rendered his sentence immediately. "Private Richard Sorley, you are hereby sentenced to be executed by firing squad at dawn tomorrow for the reprehensible and capital crimes of assault and attempted rape. And only God will have mercy on your soul."

There was no shortage of volunteers for the firing squad among either the soldiers, who seemed to have despised Sorley, or the militia, who had apparently grown to respect Nicholas for his woodcraft and bravery. But when Sorley was led, weeping, from the guardhouse the next morning, taken across the drawbridge and bound to a stake, only one of the dozen rifles aimed at him was loaded.

"Ready!"

Nicholas lifted his weapon, thought of a young girl who had lain, terrified and alone, in the darkness.

"Aim!"

He aligned the front sight with Sorley's black heart, heard the sound of that young girl's desperate pleas, her weeping.

"Fire!"

He pulled the trigger, killed the bastard who had hurt her.

And later, those who were there told how Nicholas Kenleigh,

after firing the single, fatal shot, strode angrily over to the man who had tried to dishonor his wife, ripped the blindfold off the man's face, glared into his dying eyes—and cursed him to eternal hell.

After four days of lying abed, Bethie was restless and wanted nothing more than to scrub their quarters from one end to the other. Her head no longer ached, and her bruises were beginning to fade. Between the sticky July heat, Nicholas's healing salves, and the lingering feel of Richard's hands upon her, she also longed to take a bath.

Nicholas had left before she'd awoken, and when she'd asked Private Fitchie where he'd gone, the boy had claimed not to know. Worried about Nicholas and feeling more than a wee bit cankersome, she'd asked Private Fitchie to bring water, soap, and a brush so that she could clean the floor, only to have Minna and Goody Wallace enter, arms full, to do the job for her. When she'd tried to help, they told her to sit and have some tea, saying that Nicholas would be upset with them if they allowed her to do anything strenuous.

Minna had stood firm. "We owe you both our families' lives, so please dinnae argie wi' us."

In short order, the room had been swept and scrubbed from one end to the other, and the bed linens had been stripped and replaced with new, sweet-smelling linens Annie had sent over from the trading post.

"A gift from yer husband, a thoughtful man and a brave one," Goody Wallace had said as she'd made the bed. "I've ne'er seen a man so in love wi' his wife as your Master Kenleigh."

Her words had made Bethie smile, though it still bothered her that she and Nicholas were allowing these good people to believe a lie.

By the late afternoon, she and Belle were all that remained in need of cleaning. 'Twas then she learned she would have to bathe her daughter in cold water, as Captain Écuyer had recently ordered the rationing of firewood. Though Bethie thought the water felt heavenly when pressed against her throat with a cloth, Belle, who'd been fussy all day, had shrieked in protest when Bethie had dipped her in the bucket. By the time Nicholas walked through the door, Bethie was close to tears herself.

"I can see I've arrived just in time." He strode through the door, a smile on his face, his shirt stained with sweat.

Annie came through the door behind him, a bundle beneath her arm, followed by two soldiers carrying what looked like a horse trough with legs, a third carrying firewood and a fourth carrying dinner from the officers' mess.

"What is all this about?" Bethie stared in amazement.

Nicholas grinned. "I heard you wanted to take a bath."

"She should eat her supper before it grows cold!" Annie dropped her bundle on the bed, scooped Belle from Bethie's arms. "How is Auntie Annie's little Isabelle?"

As abruptly as they'd arrived, the soldiers left, Annie behind them with Belle in her arms.

Nicholas gestured to the table. "Sit and eat, love. It's not much, I'm afraid."

Bethie sat, lifted the cloth from her plate. Boiled beef and some dearly won greens. "Will you join me?"

"Aye, after I get this fire started. Young Fitchie should be back with water at any moment."

"Fire? But I thought—"

"That it's against general orders to burn wood in the barracks? Aye, it is. But Écuyer is letting me break the rules tonight. It seems he owes me."

Soon their plates were empty, and the bathtub—for that's what it surely was, a proper bathtub—was filled with steaming water and floating sprigs of lavender, which Nicholas admitted to have stolen from the king's garden and which filled the room with their heady scent.

"Fit for a princess." Nicholas set a bar of soap on a chair beside the tub.

Bethie felt almost giddy with excitement. "I've never had a bath so grand!"

Then Nicholas reached out, cupped her cheek, drew her near. "I want this to be a new start for you, love. It's over. Sorley is dead. He was executed early this morning."

It took a moment for his words to sink in. "Richard is . . . dead?"

'Twas such momentous news she barely knew what to feel. Grief? He'd been her stepbrother. Happiness? He'd all but ruined her life. But then one emotion stood clear from the rest: relief.

"There's more." Nicholas looked gravely into her eyes. "I was on the firing squad. I fired the shot that killed him."

"You? You killed him?"

Nicholas nodded, his lips a grim line. "I wish I could say I felt some compassion for him in the end, but I didn't. I was happy to pull that trigger."

Unsure what to say, Bethie laid her head against his chest, stunned by what he had done for her. 'Twas no small thing to take another man's life.

He kissed her hair. "Your bathwater is getting cold. I'll be right outside the door if you need me."

As he released her and turned to leave, it dawned on Bethie that somehow Nicholas had known. Somehow he'd understood her need to wash all traces of Richard from her bed, her home, her body.

"Nicholas, stop! Dinnae go. Bathe with me."

He turned to face her, a lopsided grin on his face, held his arms out to his sides, looked down the front of his sweat-stained shirt. "It's a tempting invitation, love, but I'm covered with a day's worth of sweat and dirt. I'll foul your water."

She stepped forward, rested her hands on his chest. "You can wash me first, and then I'll wash you."

He brushed a finger over her cheek. "Bethie, I'm not sure that's a good idea. I don't want to rush you. I don't want—"

"I want you, Nicholas. Do you no' understand? You make me feel clean."

Nicholas looked into her eyes, saw her need, a need for something far beyond mere sexual gratification. "Very well, then. It would be my pleasure."

He helped her to undress, threw her gown and shift in a heap on the floor. She didn't know it yet, but he was never going to let her wear either of them again. He intended to burn them. The bundle on the bed held new ones stitched by Annie and Minna.

Then he steadied her as she stepped into the bathtub, felt

his gut clench when he saw the bruises that marred her soft skin, marks of another man's cruelty.

After tonight, there would be no other man.

"Oh, this feels heavenly! And it smells heavenly, too!" She gave a gratifying sigh of pleasure.

Only the first of many, if Nicholas had anything to say about it.

First, Nicholas washed her hair, felt her go limp in his hands as he massaged the lavender-scented soap into her scalp, rinsed it away. "Does that feel good?"

Her answer was a soft "mmmm."

Next he washed her arms, amazed for a moment at how slender they were, how soft, how fragile they seemed compared to his own. He rinsed the soap away, bent down, kissed the yellowing bruises, so clearly left by a man's big hand.

Then he washed her feet, her slender calves, her thighs, coming within inches of her golden curls before withdrawing his hand.

She moaned in frustration. "Nicholas!"

He chuckled. "Patience, love."

She splashed him, gave him a smile that turned his blood to flames. "I find I am no' a patient woman tonight."

"Is that so?" He slicked his hands with soap, moved around the tub until he sat behind her, slid his hands over her breasts. "Then I'll have to teach you how good it can be when you wait, when you savor it."

She moaned, pushed the weight of her breasts deeper into his palms.

He molded them, shaped them, ran his thumbs over their taut peaks, and knew from her rapid breathing that she was as aroused as he was. He bent down, nipped the sensitive skin just beneath her ear, felt her shiver, let his soap-slick hands slide down her breasts to her belly.

"Oh, aye, Nicholas!" She arched, lifted her hips off the bottom of the tub, in anticipation of his intimate touch.

Then he slid his hands back up to her breasts, rinsed the soap away, unable to suppress a chuckle at her disappointed moan. "Were you expecting something, love?"

But his need was building, too, and a man—or a woman—could wait only so long.

This time when his hands slid down her body, one stopped to tease her nipples, while the other slid down into her curls, delved into her soft folds, sought her most sensitive flesh.

As her head fell back and a whimper left her throat, he bent down, took her in a deep, openmouthed kiss.

Bethie welcomed the invasion of his tongue, relished the heat of his kiss, as sensations almost too good to be true flowed over her. The caress of warm water on her tingling skin. His fingers flicking and teasing her aching nipples. The pressure of his hand against her throbbing sex.

Liquid heat gathered in her belly, became a molten blaze. But she wanted more. She wanted him inside her. She tried to speak, to tell him what she wanted. The words came out in ragged pants. "Nicholas . . . please . . . inside me!"

"Are you certain, Bethie?"

"Oh, aye!" If tonight was to be a new beginning, then she would have it all, and she would fear nothing.

He growled, and she felt his finger make slow, erotic circles over her entrance once, twice, three times.

"There is no man but me, Bethie. There never was."

Then slowly, so slowly that it made her whimper in anguish, he slid his finger deep inside her slick and aching core.

The sweet shock of it sent her spiraling over the edge. Pleasure buffeted her, wave upon fiery wave, tore a cry from her throat, as he prolonged her climax with deft, penetrating strokes.

For a moment she lay still in the water, floating, stunned that an act that had once brought her so much pain and suffering could be so pleasurable. And a tremor of anticipation shot through her as she wondered what it would be like to have his thick, hard shaft inside her.

Then she opened her eyes, looked up into a gaze that burned with need. She couldn't help but smile, thinking of all the ways she would torment him. "Time for *your* bath."

Bethie lingered over him, knowing it would drive both of them to a frenzy of desire. She washed his long hair, rinsed the day's dirt and sweat from his shoulders, arms, and chest, secretly savoring the feel of him beneath her hands—the roughness of his body hair, the hardness of his muscles, the softness of his skin.

He smiled, a sensual twist of his lips that made her heart beat faster. "Dinnae be thinkin' you can fool me, lass. I know what you're doin'. You're tryin' to tease me, to drive me mad."

His attempt at Scottish brogue made her laugh. She did her best to mock his English. "You, sir, are mine to do with as I please."

Then she reached beneath the water, took his erection in her hand, and began to stroke its length, taking extra time to tease the satiny tip.

His laughter became a quick intake of breath, and his hands slowly clenched around the sides of the tub, as she built the rhythm, stroke upon slow stroke. But just as she felt him nearing his peak, she stopped, went to wash his feet.

"Wench!" He groaned, kicked water at her.

She shrieked, chided him. "It serves you right for makin' a lady wait."

He grabbed the soap from her hands and in a blink had scrubbed and rinsed his legs. Then he dropped the soap, stood, stepped out of the tub. "The lady need wait no longer."

Water ran in glistening rivulets over his sun-browned skin to the floorboards. His hair clung in dark, wet ropes to his chest and shoulders. His shaft stood, thick and heavy, against his belly.

There was no more teasing, no more games.

He pulled her against him, his fingers buried in her wet hair, his lips hot on her mouth.

Then he carried her two short steps to the bed, laid her on the soft linen, stretched out above her. They rolled and twisted in a tangle of limbs, locked in a heated kiss, desperate for the taste of each other, the feel of each other.

Bethie broke the kiss, reached down, took his length in her hand, stroked him. "I want you inside me."

Nicholas thought his heart might actually break through his chest. He took a deep breath, fought to rein himself in. Those were words he'd never expected to hear. "Bethie, I don't think—"

"Please."

The look of innocent trust in her eyes made something twist in his stomach. After all she'd been through, that she should trust *him* . . . "As you wish—but not like this."

He rolled onto his back, settled her astride him, reached down, held himself so that the head of his cock met her heated core. "It's up to you now."

She looked surprised at first, then she smiled, bit her lower lip—and lowered herself so that the head of his shaft nudged inside her. She gasped, a soft, sweet sound, then lifted her hips, withdrew from him, before lowering herself upon him, taking a bit more of him this time.

Months of suppressed need, of wanting her, of wanting to be inside her, had left him on the brink, and Nicholas began to wonder if he would survive the night. As she gradually took more and more of him into her slick heat, he fought the urge to thrust, forced himself to hold his hips still, to let her determine the pace.

He reached up, stroked the beaded velvet of her nipples with his thumbs, tried to make his muscles relax as inch by torturous inch she took him inside her. When he thought he could take no more, she lifted her hips once more, then slid down the length of him, taking all of him.

"Oh, Nicholas, it feels . . . so . . . good!" Her eyes were closed, a look of bliss on her sweet face, her hair a damp, tangled mass that hung to her hips. She was the most beautiful sight he'd ever seen.

"I've wanted you for so long!" He clasped her hips, moved in slow circles beneath her, fighting to hold on as her tight sheath caressed him, carried him toward the edge. "No man but me, Bethie!"

Bethie heard the strain in his voice, heard her own whimpered reply. Never had she felt anything like this. It was erotic beyond imagination, being joined to this big man, his body inside hers, a part of hers. He stretched her, filled every inch of her, made her complete. Each thrust felt better than the one before, made her desperate for the next, as she moved with him, rode the fire.

How had she lived without this? How had she lived without him?

She heard her own keening cries, called his name as the pleasure built inside her. "Oh, oh, Nicholas!"

"My God, Bethie! I can't hold back, not anymore! You're

too sweet, too tight!" His jaw was clenched, his brow furrowed as if in pain.

"Then don't hold back!" She bent down, kissed his sweat-slick chest. "Love me, Nicholas!"

With a feral growl, he rolled her onto her back, wrapped her legs around his waist, looked into her eyes. "No man but me!"

Then he was thrusting into her, deep and hard, his shaft driving against some secret spot inside her, drawing frantic cries from her throat. His lips were on her mouth, her eyelids, her cheeks, her throat. His voice was a ragged whisper. "No man but me!"

Her body trembled at the power of his words, the potency of his loving, as he carried her up and up and up to a place she'd never been before. Tears slipped from the corners of her eyes, tears that cleansed, tears that purified, tears that washed the past away.

Precious torment. Sweet surrender. Shattering bliss.

"Nicholas!" She cried out as the force of it hit her, drew the life from her body, and gave it back again, pleasure showering her like tears, like rain, like starlight.

"No man but me!" His body shuddered, and she heard his deep groan, as he, too, succumbed, spilling himself inside her.

Then, in the stillness, he kissed her tears away.

# Chapter 25

The siege lengthened through July, and with it came heat, hunger, deprivation. The people of Fort Pitt were woefully low on everything but water. Of firewood for cooking and washing there was precious little. Food was just as scarce, as the Delaware and Shawnee, having already killed or driven off most of the wild game, also fed off the king's garden—and kept it under near-constant watch.

Nicholas led almost daily forays, some into Lower and Upper Town to gather whatever wood they could from the burnt cabins, and some into the garden and fields after spelt, vegetables, cattle, even the occasional startled rabbit. Though they left the fort at different times of day and from different ports and sometimes managed to take the Indians by surprise, they came under attack each time, risking their lives and sometimes gaining little for it. So far they'd lost only one man, a militiaman who'd taken a ball to the belly while tending the cattle. Two others had been injured.

There could be little doubt as to who was faring better thus far. As hungry soldiers watched from the ramparts, Indian canoes traveled up the rivers loaded with corn harvested from the surrounding farmsteads. And although the Indians had not yet launched another direct attack, they were always present around the fort, coming right up to the walls in the dark of night, hiding in the ditch, penetrating the glacis, frightening people with their death whoops. And just so the English could see their strength, they openly crossed the rivers out of range of the cannon, many hundreds of them. Although Captain Écuyer had told messengers sent by the chiefs that Fort Pitt had supplies and ammunition to outlast a siege of three years, Nicholas knew that unless reinforcements arrived, they would not survive three months.

"You take my portion." Bethie slid her slice of salted pork onto Nicholas's plate, ignored her growling stomach. "I am no' hungry just now."

"Bethie, eat." Nicholas frowned at her, tossed the precious slice back onto her plate.

"But you work much harder than I. You need a man's portion." She started to toss it back, but the scowl on his face stopped her.

"You're feeding a baby. Eat!"

She ate her meager breakfast, watched as he cleaned his pistols and long rifle, realized what he was doing. "You're going out again today."

He looked down the barrel of the rifle, slid the cleaning rod down its length. "Aye. The corn is ripe, and Écuyer doesn't want it falling into Indian hands."

"Why must it always be you? Can no one else lead them this time?" She stood, paced the length of the room, a knot of fear in her belly.

"We've been through this before. The men trust me to lead them and—"

"And you know every beanpole and row of that garden now. Aye, I know. But surely the men who planted and tended the bloody garden know it just as well."

"Aye, but how many of them are good marksmen? How many of them have faced down a charge of painted warriors?" Nicholas stood, set his rifle on the table, pulled her into his arms. "Most of them are privates, like young Fitchie. They've seen little of real battle. If we're not able to harvest the spelt and the corn, we'll starve before help arrives." He paused, smiled. "Of course, we can always eat the dogs."

Bethie laughed despite her fear. The captain's loathing for barking dogs—and the settlers' resulting hatred for him—had become fort legend. "How can you jest about something so grave?"

He nuzzled her ear. "It made you laugh, didn't it?"

Then he kissed her, a gentle, languorous kiss, and she tasted the salt on his lips.

These past three weeks with him had been wondrous, the most precious of her life. Yet it seemed that love came at a price. Never had she felt more keenly the fear of loss, for never had she stood to lose so much. If aught were to happen to Nicholas . . .

Right now, in this moment, he was alive and strong. How she wished she knew some words of enchantment, a bewitchment to keep him safe until help could arrive.

"What will we do if reinforcements dinnae come?"

It was the question Nicholas asked himself every day. A part of him thought he might have been wiser to take Shingiss's offer of safe passage and lead Bethie away from all of this. But with so many warriors from so many nations traveling through the forest, they would have been running a gauntlet all the way over the mountains and beyond. As it was, they'd barely made it to Fort Pitt alive.

And though Nicholas had some store of pemmican, cornmeal, and salt pork in his gear, it wasn't enough to feed the two of them for more than a few weeks. Besides, Écuyer would surely search the barracks once food ran out and press all personal stores into service. He'd already done as much with livestock. Those who had cattle or chickens had been forced to sell them to the Crown for coin they might not live to spend.

"I suppose Écuyer would be forced to abandon the fort and ask Shingiss and the other chiefs to let us pass in peace back over the mountains."

"Would the chiefs allow this?"

He remembered Shingiss's words in the garden. "I'm not sure. I doubt it. Still, Écuyer will have no choice but to trust them and risk the journey or to wait until we are so weakened by hunger that Shingiss and his allies are able to take the fort."

"What would the Indians do to us?"

She felt so sweet, so fragile in his arms. He inhaled the lavender scent of her hair, pressed his lips to her brow. "If we abandon the fort and journey east, I suspect they will try to ambush us somewhere along the way. If they take the fort, it will follow days of bloody battle."

"Nay, I mean what will they *do* to us, to you, to the soldiers, to the women and children."

He could feel her fear, but he had no honeyed words to assuage it. He would not lie to her. "This is war, Bethie. It's a war such as I've never seen. I imagine they would kill most of the adult men and torture the rest. They would kill the smallest children and babies—those they deemed young enough to be a burden on the trail home. The women and older children they would either kill outright or take captive."

She seemed to consider this for a moment, her gaze seeking out Isabelle, fear for her baby written on her face. "Annie says you were taken while trying to save the lives of two young soldiers and that you were forced to watch as they were burned to death. Is that true?"

Whatever he had expected her to say, it was not this. Her words felt like a fist to his stomach. It took a moment before he could answer. "Aye."

"And they tortured you." Her voice was almost a whisper.

"Aye."

Screams. Burning pain. The stench of scorched flesh.

*"Nicholas! For God's sake, help us!"*

Nicholas stepped back, tucked a finger beneath her chin, forced her to meet his gaze. "I won't let them take you, Bethie. I won't let them take either of you."

He would kill Bethie and Belle himself before he let that happen. The last bit of powder, his last bit of lead, he would save for them.

"And that is why I need to lead the men out to the garden today."

"When are you goin' out?"

"Now."

* * *

Bethie was in the hospital changing the bandages on a soldier who'd accidentally shot himself in the foot when the alarm sounded.

*Nicholas!*

He'd left for the garden little more than an hour ago and had not yet returned.

Dr. Aimes took the bandages from her hands. "Thank you for your help, madam. You'd best be off to your quarters."

Heart pounding, Bethie removed her apron, hurried outdoors.

What she heard turned her blood to ice—hundreds of voices raised in war cries.

The fort was under attack.

Gunfire from the ramparts. The blast of a cannon. The bitter tang of gunpowder.

She'd truly intended to fetch Belle from the trading post and return to her quarters, as she had promised Nicholas she would, but he was out there, fighting for his life. Her feet turned instead to the east, and she ran toward the east ravelin, where men were rushing through with sacks and baskets loaded with Indian corn and vegetables.

Private Fitchie ran after her. "The lieutenant will have my hide if you dinnae do as he says! You're to go to your quarters!"

"I cannae, no' so long as he's out there!" She ran through the throng toward the drawbridge, searched through the crowd, praying to see his face.

She heard a soldier talking to the quartermaster.

"Are they all in?"

"All except Kenleigh and McKee."

Barely able to breathe, she pushed through the throng, tried to get closer to the bridge.

And then she saw him. He strode over the drawbridge, his shirt torn and bloodied, a man draped over his shoulder. He did not see her, but shouted to one of the sergeants, lowering the man he carried carefully to the ground.

"He needs the surgeon. He took a ball to the knee."

"Aye, sir!"

Then he turned to the quartermaster. "Is everyone in and accounted for?"

"Aye, Kenleigh, but that was damned close."

"Too close."

She knew the exact moment he saw her, knew he was beyond furious.

He closed the distance between them. "What are you doing out here! Get Belle, and get back to our quarters now!"

"But you were out there, and I—"

"This is the second time you've defied me, and I won't tolerate it!"

Tears pricked her eyes. "You're hurt! At least let me—"

"It's nothing! This is war, Bethie. You'll likely see far worse before it's over. There are God knows how many warriors on the other side of these walls. Now go!" He turned to Private Fitchie. "You have my permission to drag her, carry her, do whatever you need to do to see that she is safely indoors. Get her out of here, and then report to your commanding officer."

Private Fitchie nodded sharply. "Aye, sir!"

Bethie started to object, but Private Fitchie was already pulling her in one direction, and Nicholas had disappeared in another.

The attack lasted all day and into the night, showed no sign of letting up. Before the sun had set, Captain Écuyer had taken an arrow in the leg, and a corporal and one of the frontiersmen had been killed. The Delaware and Shawnee had taken cover wherever they could around the fort—in the shelter of the steep riverbanks, in the garden, in the burned-out ruins of Upper and Lower Town—and fired both arrows and lead balls on anything that moved.

Although Écuyer's marksmen were highly trained, they could not bring down targets they could not see. And Nicholas, who had positioned himself on the Monongahela curtain directly above the officers' barracks with a team of militia marksmen, quickly realized they had a problem.

"The fort is positioned so much nearer the Monongahela that they are able to fire arrows over the walls while using the riverbank for cover," he told Écuyer. "Your marksmen cannot reach them. Cannon are of no use. They simply hide or shift from one position to another."

The captain grimaced as the surgeon finished bandaging his leg. "What do you suggest, Kenleigh?"

"A direct assault on the riverbank from the cover of the west ravelin. A team of grenadiers could toss grenades directly into their stronghold, forcing them into the open."

Écuyer gaped at him. "You would send men outside the walls in the midst of battle?"

"It's the only way we're going to dislodge them from the riverbank."

Écuyer shook his head. "That's suicide! I won't risk it."

Nicholas left Écuyer's quarters sure the captain was making a grave mistake.

Bethie heard the blast of another cannon being fired, wished for the thousandth time she knew what was happening. The battle had raged all night—artillery blasts, gunfire, drums, and shouting punctuated by silence. Somehow Isabelle had slept through it, unaware in her innocence that their lives were in danger. But Bethie had paced the room all night, praying that Nicholas would be safe, that no lives would be lost, that the Indians would give up and leave them in peace.

But it was well past noon, and judging from the gun and cannon fire, the fighting was growing fiercer. She'd opened the door twice, hoping to be able to see Nicholas on the ramparts, to know for certain he was unhurt, but the sight of spent arrows, their darts buried in the soil only footsteps away, had convinced her not to step outside. So she had stood in the open doorway, breathed air heavy with the smell of sulfur and smoke, watched British regulars hurrying across the parade ground on some unknown errand.

Her only word of the battle had come from Private Fitchie, who had come by once just before noon to check on her, his young face covered with sweat and lined with fatigue. "Sergeant Harmon got shot through the lungs, and one of the grenadiers was shot through the leg, but none of ours have been killed today, mistress. One of theirs got blown in two by a cannon ball."

"Have you seen Nicholas?"

"Aye, mistress. He's up there in the thick of it." Private Fitchie had pointed over the rooftop to the ramparts directly behind her.

*In the thick of it?* Bethie hadn't liked the sound of that at all. "How goes the battle?"

"The enemy are hidin' along the riverbank, close enough to get their arrows over the wall. But Master Kenleigh and Paddy are flushin' them out."

"Paddy?"

"Aye, Paddy. He's our man of straw. The soldiers pass him up and down the curtain wall, hold him up on a pole where the Indians can see him. When the Indians break cover to shoot at poor Paddy, Nicholas and the other marksmen pick them off. It's my job to keep the men supplied with powder and balls."

He'd looked so young in that moment, both afraid and proud. Bethie had leaned out of the doorway, given him a kiss on the cheek. "Be safe, Private Fitchie."

He'd flushed scarlet, but she'd seen a smile on his face as he'd hurried away.

Afternoon stretched into evening, and still the fighting did not lessen. Bethie sang to Belle, paced the floor with her, played with her on the bed, and had just finished nursing her to sleep when she smelled it: smoke. At first, she'd thought it was just the scent of the battle carried on a breeze. But then it grew stronger. She was about to open the door to see what was burning, when the door flew open and Nicholas stepped inside.

His face was wet with sweat and streaked with the black of gunpowder. She could tell he hadn't slept.

"Nicholas!" She ran to him, threw her arms around him.

He kissed the top of her head, gave her a squeeze. "There isn't time, Bethie. Be ready to flee the building."

"Wh-what?"

Outside the door, several flaming arrows landed with a hiss and a thud in the dirt.

"They're firing lit arrows over the wall, and both this barracks and the captain's house have been hit several times. So far we've been able to douse the fires from the ramparts, but I want you to be ready to flee should the need arise. We've evacuated the upper floor, but I think you're safer for the moment where you are."

Outside the door, Bethie saw women hurrying to the wells with buckets. "I could help to carry water."

Nicholas understood her need to help, used the best argument he had to dissuade her. "No, love. Isabelle needs you. What would happen to her if you were hurt or killed?"

*What would happen to me?*

He thought the words, but he didn't say them.

"If I can help in no other way, then let me at least give you something to eat and drink." She pulled away from him, hurried to the table, where she saw one of his leather pouches near the water bucket. Quickly she dipped his cup into the water and pulled a chunk of pemmican from the pouch. "Drink, and take this with you."

Suddenly the hours of fighting began to tell. Nicholas stood beside the table, drank his fill, took several bites of pemmican, gave a groan of pleasure when Bethie touched a cold, wet cloth to his face and throat. "You know how to make a man feel almost grateful to have been in battle, Bethie, love."

She smiled, a fragile smile that did not hide her worry. "If you can stay awhile, I have ways of makin' you feel even more grateful."

He could tell from the purple shadows beneath her eyes that she hadn't slept well, if at all. He bent down, tilted her chin up toward him, kissed her. "I bet you do, and I can't tell you how much I'd love to see what you have in mind. But I need to get back. I just came to warn you in case you need to flee. Be ready."

In truth, anyone could have warned her of the fire danger. But he'd wanted to see her, needed to see her. Now that they'd had to put out fires on the rooftops several times, Écuyer understood the danger of allowing the Indians to remain in the cover of the Monongahela bank. At the captain's request, a dozen militiamen had volunteered to make one quick grenade strike from the west ravelin. As soon as it was dark, Nicholas would lead them out.

"I'd best return to my post." He kissed her nose, forced himself to let her go.

As he turned away, she called after him. "Nicholas, please be safe!"

# Chapter 26

The plan was simple. Nicholas would lead the men out over the drawbridge to the west ravelin while the marksmen covered them from the ramparts and distracted the Indians with Paddy. Once in position, they would each throw a hand grenade along the riverbank, some to the north, some to the south, forcing the Indians to break cover so that marksmen, already prepared, could finish them off. Then Nicholas and his men would quickly make their way back through the ravelin to the drawbridge and into the fort.

Nicholas looked into each man's eyes. "Tomahawks and knives only until we reach the sally port. And, boys, don't light those fuses too early. I don't want to bring anyone back in pieces."

The men chuckled.

"Ready?"

A dozen heads nodded.

Nicholas signaled the sergeant on the ramparts, heard a volley of grenades land in the ditch just outside the walls, clearing away any Indians who might lie in ambush.

Slowly the heavy drawbridge began to lower.

Tomahawk in hand, grenades in a leather pouch on his shoulder, Nicholas waited.

War whoops. A volley of rifle fire from the walls.

Then the drawbridge was open.

On the other side stood the ravelin and, beyond that, the moonlit water of the Monongahela, gliding smooth and silent.

He led the men across, spied Indians hiding in the shelter of the ravelin, charged.

Surprised, and perhaps afraid the rest of the garrison was on its way out, most of the Indians fled out through the sally port and down to the river. Those who remained were quickly dispatched.

"Form two lines—one north, one south. Go!"

The men did as Nicholas ordered while he covered them, firing upon two Indians who'd recovered from their surprise and turned to fight.

"They know we're here, boys. Let's do what we came to do!"

Quickly the men in front of the two lines lit their fuses, stepped out of the sally port, threw their grenades, retreated.

Small explosions. Frightened shouts. Cries of pain. The whine of a passing arrow.

Almost immediately, gunfire from the ramparts increased as marksmen took down those who'd fled their cover. The plan was working.

By the time the sound of the first explosions had died, the next men in line had already lit their fuses and hurled their grenades. Frightened shouts turned to outright cries of retreat as the second, third, and fourth waves of grenades hit.

It seemed the mission would go off without a hitch, when one of the militiamen slipped and fell to the sandy riverbank. Three Indians, crouching at the river's edge, saw the fallen man and made straight for him.

They were Wyandot.

And then Nicholas saw him.

*Atsan.*

Even through the darkness, the war chief's gaze bored into Nicholas. The man who had ordered Eben and Josiah's death. The man who had spared Nicholas's life, embraced him as a son. The man whose daughter, grandchild, and son Nicholas had killed.

A wave of conflicting emotion slammed into Nicholas, hot

and thick. Shock. Rage. Gnawing regret. But there was no time. He could not settle this here.

"Cover me!" Nicholas leapt down, reached for the fallen militiaman, jerked him to his feet. "Time to get out of here! Go!"

As Nicholas turned to follow the militiaman, he heard the end-over-end rush of a tomahawk hurtling through the air and Atsan's shout of warning. He had just enough time to push the militiaman through the sally port when something exploded against the back of his skull, sent him plummeting into darkness.

Bethie lay in the big, empty bed, fully clothed, listening. The shooting seemed to have died down. Awhile ago it had grown so fierce she was afraid the walls were about to be breached. But now the fort was almost quiet. Perhaps that meant Nicholas would be returning soon.

Maybe it would be over by morning, and maybe . . .

She hadn't realized she'd fallen asleep until a knock on the door woke her. She hurried from bed to answer it, expected someone to tell her the building was on fire. Instead she found several battle-weary men bearing Nicholas between them.

Her heart stopped. "Oh my God! Nicholas!"

He hung limply between them, his eyes closed. But he was breathing. He was alive.

"Lay him on the bed." She stepped aside to let them enter, hurried around to the other side of the bed. "What happened?"

"He took a tomahawk to the back of the head," said one of the men as they laid him back on the mattress. "It was the handle that got him, no' the blade. If it had been the blade, his brains would be—"

"Hold your whist, Bill! This is his lady here!"

Filled with dread, Bethie leaned over him, touched her hand to his cheek. "Nicholas, can you hear me? Nicholas?"

He didn't move, didn't answer, lay still as death against the pillow. But he wasn't feverish, and his breathing was deep and even.

"The surgeon says all we can do is wait and see if he wakes up."

Bethie nodded, fought back her tears. "Thank you, gentlemen, for bringin' him home. Can one of you fetch water for me—and bandages? I want to clean the wound on his arm."

"Aye, ma'am. I'll see to it." The one who'd first spoken picked up the water bucket from the table, started out the door, turned back. "If it makes you feel any better, he saved a good man's life out there. If it hadn't been for him, I dinnae know how many of us would have made it back inside the walls alive."

"H-he went outside the walls?"

"Aye. He led us out to the west ravelin so we could fight back those Indians who were shootin' fire over the walls. Nicholas Kenleigh is a man among men, the bravest of the lot. We're all prayin' for him tonight."

As the men shut the door behind them, Bethie didn't know which emotion burned hottest inside her—fear or fury.

Bethie kept vigil at Nicholas's side all night and through the next day. She removed his sweat-stained clothes, bathed his body with cool cloths. She cleaned the wound on his arm, where it seemed a ball had grazed him. She trickled water into his throat, urged him to drink. She spoke to him, and she prayed.

Dr. Aimes came to check on him around noon, told Bethie there was nothing to be done. "I've seen men wake after being unconscious for weeks and be in complete command of their faculties, but I've also seen men drift away and die or wake to be helpless as newborn babies. Keep talking to him."

And so she did. She spoke to him of her childhood before her father's death. She told him how hard her life had been before he'd arrived on her doorstep. She told him she loved him, could not imagine a single sunrise without him. But if he heard, he showed no sign of it.

Annie brought her meals and fresh water, shared with her news of the battle. "Some of the fight has left them. They're gatherin' under the bank again, but no' so close this time. Yer man put a lick of fear in them, he did. No one has been killed or injured all day, thank heavens! But look at you, lamb! Ye've no' slept a wink! Let old Annie take the little one, and you get some rest."

Beyond exhaustion, Bethie nursed Belle, kissed her, handed her over to her auntie Annie, then lay down beside Nicholas, her head on his shoulder, and slept. When she awoke, she found him still unconscious, but his arm was wrapped around her, holding her close.

Nicholas heard the blast of a cannon, was certain it had been fired inside his skull.

"Open your eyes, love. Please open your eyes!" It was Bethie. She sounded upset.

He tried to answer, heard himself groan instead. His head hurt like hell. What had happened? He tried to remember, fought to clear his mind. The Indians had surrounded the fort, fired lit arrows over the wall. Had he been shot? Aye, a ball had grazed his right shoulder. But that was yesterday, and the wound had been minor. Why did he feel so weak?

"Nicholas? Can you hear me?"

He fought the blinding pain in his head, willed himself to speak. "Bethie."

"Oh, thank God! Oh, Nicholas!" Her lips brushed his cheek. Something cold was held to his lips. "Drink."

He didn't realize until the cool water slid down his throat how thirsty he was. But before he could ask for more, he was drifting again.

Later—how much later he couldn't say—he opened his eyes, found himself in bed, Bethie bathing his brow. His head throbbed, almost sickeningly so.

"How do you feel?"

His throat was dry. "I've been better."

She held out a cup, gently lifted his head. "Drink."

Three times she refilled the cup, held it to his lips before his thirst was slaked.

He struggled to remember how he'd been injured, could not. "What happened?"

"You went outside the bloody walls and got hit by a tomahawk. Luckily, it struck your thick skull. Otherwise you might have been hurt."

She was angry. He could see from the dark circles beneath

her eyes that she hadn't slept well for some time. "I'm sorry . . . I frightened you."

"You did more than frighten me, Nicholas!" Her voice broke. Tears spilled onto her cheeks. "You almost got yourself killed!"

"I'm fine, love." He reached up, cupped her cheek, wiped the tears away with his thumb. "How goes the battle?"

"The battle is all but over. Annie tells me the Indians have pulled back."

After five relentless days and nights of fighting, the silence left everyone inside the fort feeling uneasy. No one could understand why the Indians had seemed to withdraw back into the forest. The entire garrison held its breath.

Nicholas recovered quickly, but Bethie wouldn't let him out of her sight. Never had she been so desperately afraid as when he'd lain still, silent and sleeping.

"If you so much as think of leaving these walls, I'll take your pistol and shoot you in the bloody foot!" she'd shouted at him.

"Bethie, I know this has been hard on you, but I need to do my part—"

"You've done your part! You've taken on more than your share of the risk!"

But what began as an argument soon turned to the sweetest lovemaking she'd ever experienced, Nicholas deep inside her, whispering to her all the ways he wanted to love her, as he brought her to one shattering peak after another and found his release inside her.

Still, Bethie was so determined to keep him from danger that when Captain Écuyer knocked on their door one morning, she had half a mind to shut it in his face. Only the knowledge that insubordination could get them thrown out of the fort kept her from doing just that. She didn't like Écuyer one bit. Any man who could shoot a dog . . . well, there weren't words.

"I want to thank you for your bravery and diligence, Kenleigh. I assure you I shall acquaint the commander in chief with your services to His Majesty these past months. I know you harbor no affection for me, but you are a man of courage and honor. You have done your duty with spirit, in the finest British tradition, and I respect that."

Bethie watched as Nicholas took in the captain's words, answered with silence.

Écuyer shifted uncomfortably. "Damn it, Kenleigh! What are they up to? Why have they withdrawn? We're still surrounded, and yet we've watched hundreds cross the river, head east."

"They're taking the battle elsewhere. That's the only explanation. They have us by the throat, and they know it. They have not truly withdrawn. There were Ottawa out there—and Wyandot."

Écuyer's gaze met his. "You think they mean to attack Colonel Bouquet."

"That's my guess. They hope to maintain the siege and at the same time destroy your reinforcements. They remember Braddock's defeat and hope to accomplish the same thing with Bouquet."

"If they do, it will be the end of us."

"Aye."

"For once I hope you're wrong, Kenleigh."

Two days later, three expresses arrived, carrying word from Colonel Bouquet. Reinforcements had reached Ligonier and were on their way. But scouts had reported a massive gathering of Delaware, Shawnee, Ottawa, and Wyandot just west of a place called Bushy Run. Colonel Bouquet was walking into a trap. But unlike Braddock before him, Bouquet and his regiment of Scottish Highlanders knew it.

Four more days passed, days of tense silence, days of hunger. The wood was almost gone. There was no flour, no cornmeal. Only salt pork and a bit of beef remained. In every heart lurked one shared fear—that Colonel Bouquet and his troops had been ambushed and defeated.

Bethie began to suspect she was losing her milk, as Belle seemed always to be hungry. Nicholas had opened his stores of salt pork and pemmican and shared them in secret with her, giving her the larger portion despite her protests.

"I'm used to going hungry. You've a baby to feed."

And although some short forays were made to the king's garden, they were repulsed by the Delaware, who, though reduced in numbers, now considered the garden and its bounty theirs and kept it under close watch.

And so the weary occupants of Fort Pitt sat hungry in the heat—and waited.

August 10, 1763

Bethie was having the most delicious dream. Nicholas was making love to her, entering her from behind as she slept on her side, his lips on her nape, his fingers teasing her most sensitive spot, flicking it, rubbing it, caressing it.

She awakened to hear herself cry out as the bliss of climax washed through her, sweet as the sunrise.

He nuzzled her ear, his voice deep and husky. "Good morning."

As the last ripples of pleasure faded into languor, he began to move again, thick and hard inside her. He wasn't finished with her yet.

He drew her onto her knees, spread her thighs farther apart, thrust into her hard, his hands grasping her hips as he built the rhythm, stroke upon stroke. "Oh, God, woman, you feel good!"

She felt his stones slap against her, felt his power as he drove into her, filled her, his cock striking just there, where she needed it most. And then it hit her, harder than before—not sweet, but wrenching, overpowering. She cried out, called his name as her inner muscles quaked in fierce ecstasy, bringing him to a shuddering climax inside her.

For a while they lay in each other's arms, hovering on the edge of sleep.

Then they heard the sound of rifle fire, shouts, drums.

Nicholas kissed her, leapt from the bed, his face grave. "Stay here."

But as he drew on his breeches, there came a knocking at the door.

Nicholas opened it to find Private Fitchie, an enormous smile on his young face. "They've made it, sir! They're just outside the gates! They won a great battle at Bushy Run, and they're here! It's over, Master Kenleigh!"

Nicholas felt a warm rush of relief, saw tears well up in Bethie's sweet eyes. She didn't know it, but he'd been planning to leave the fort with her tonight, to sneak out under cover of darkness, to take his chances with her and little Belle in the wild.

Now he wouldn't have to.

He shucked his breeches, crawled back into bed beside her, pulled her against him, stroked the tangled silk of her hair.

She sniffed back her tears. "It's over, Nicholas! It's really over!"

He nudged her with his revived erection. "Is it now, lass? Or maybe it's just beginnin'."

Life at Fort Pitt changed overnight. The king's garden and surrounding fields were harvested, their bounty added to the fresh provisions brought by Bouquet's troops. Four hundred additional regulars meant more labor for rebuilding the damaged walls, preparing for another onslaught should one come. And Bouquet, hearing how the Indians had hidden along the riverbank and had only been dislodged with great daring, ordered the building of several redoubts at key points outside the fort overlooking the river.

Bouquet was effusive in his praise of all who had fought in the battle—British regulars, militiamen, farmers. He thanked Nicholas personally. But Nicholas was appalled to hear him likewise praise Écuyer for giving infected blankets to the Indians.

"Governor Amherst and I had discussed doing just that in our letters these past months, and you were bold enough to enact it on your own. Well done, Écuyer."

Écuyer bowed his head. "I am your very humble and obedient servant, sir. But I fear it had no effect."

Nicholas turned his back and walked away.

The day after his arrival, Bouquet gave the orders that all women, children, and other "useless" people should prepare to leave two days hence for Ligonier under heavy military escort. It was on that day Bouquet summoned Nicholas to his office for a private meeting with him and Écuyer.

"In light of your courage, knowledge, and skill, I am prepared to advance you to the rank of captain and charge you with creating your own company of rangers." Bouquet spoke the words as if he were offering Nicholas all the kingdoms of the world. "It is a great honor, one I do not offer lightly. Your wife and daughter will, of course, be escorted safely to Ligonier and housed as comfortably as possible until this rebellion has been quashed. What say you?"

Nicholas looked both men in the eyes, allowed his contempt to show. "I'm afraid I must decline. I've seen enough death and brutality—on both sides, gentlemen—to last until the world's ending. What I cherish travels east, and I go with her. Good day to you both. I leave you to yourselves."

The night before they left Fort Pitt, there was a commotion on the walls, and the colonel sent for Nicholas.

"One of the faithless savages is standing across the river. We've fired at him, but he won't budge. He has asked to speak with you."

Nicholas climbed to the top of the ramparts, looked across the Monongahela.

Atsan.

"I must go across and speak with him."

Taking only his knife, Nicholas paddled a canoe left by the retreating Delaware. Across the river, Atsan stood alone, his war paint washed away.

Atsan spoke first, using the Wyandot tongue. "You live. I feared that tomahawk had split your head."

"You tried to warn me. Why?"

"I do not wish you dead, Sa-ray-u-migh. Had you stayed with my people, I would have treated you as an honored son."

"I know." Nicholas had to tell him. "Mattootuk is dead."

"You killed him." It was a statement, not a question.

"Aye. He tried to kill my wife and daughter. He left me no choice."

The old man's body tensed, but no sign of emotion played

on his face. “Mattootuk was angry with you over Lyda’s death. They were both prideful—a failing they received through their mother’s blood. Mattootuk refused to see what was clear to everyone else—that his sister brought her end upon herself.”

Regret as sharp as a knife sliced through Nicholas, forced the breath from his lungs. “I did not seek her death.”

“There was a time when you would gladly have killed her.”

“Not while she carried my child.”

“No, not while she carried your child.” Atsan lifted the talisman that hung around his neck, the sign of his house, draped it over Nicholas’s head. “Mattootuk was my last surviving son. It is right that you take this. Go in peace, Long Knife. Father many children.”

“Go in peace, Atsan.”

Atsan looked at him through eyes that seemed older than the forest. “There will be no peace for us now. Only war. It is over.”

Then the old man turned, disappearing into the trees and leaving Nicholas to sort out the tempest inside him.

# Chapter 27

Bethie's stomach pitched and rolled. The cabin where she'd lived the worst years of her life came into view around the bend, grew larger with every passing second. She took a deep breath, reminded herself that she wasn't here to stay, that Nicholas was with her, that nothing could happen to her.

Nicholas reined the wagon to a halt, took her hand in his, his eyes dark with concern and misgiving. "You don't have to do this, Bethie."

"But I must. I must tell them about Richard. And I . . . I want to see my mother."

"Then let's get it over with." Nicholas gave her hand a reassuring squeeze, released it, took the reins, snapped them over Zeus's rump.

They had left Fort Pitt with everyone else deemed a burden by Colonel Bouquet and traveled to Ligonier, where Nicholas somehow managed to buy a wagon. Then Bethie had bade her new friends a sad farewell. Most would remain in Ligonier until the frontier was safe once again. They had poured too much blood and sweat into their farms to leave them—and they had no place else to go.

Hardest of all had been saying good-bye to Annie.

"I'll never forget you, Annie. You've been so kind to me."

"Nor I you, lamb. But yer in good hands. That strappin' man of yers will take good care of both of ye. Come next summer, ye'll have another babe, as sweet as this one. Oh, let Auntie Annie hold you one last time!"

Talk of another baby had startled Bethie, but she'd smiled, handed Belle into Annie's arms, her vision blurred with tears as Annie kissed Belle's chubby cheeks.

Reluctantly, Annie had handed Isabelle back. "Be off wi' ye now. And may God bless and protect ye."

"You, too, Annie."

They had traveled from Ligonier east toward Philadelphia, stopping in Harrisburg, where they'd stayed at an inn. Never had Bethie enjoyed so lavish a roof over her head or so soft a bed. When she'd protested to Nicholas that she'd never be able to repay him and that he was surely well on his way to becoming penniless or landing in a debtor's gaol, he'd only kissed her and told her not to worry.

She had asked Nicholas only to take her as far as Ligonier, but he'd shaken his head, told her it wasn't safe, insisted that he go with her all the way to Philadelphia. When she'd asked him if he thought she'd be better able to find work there, he'd frowned, mumbled something about leaving the future to take care of itself.

Although that future was fast approaching and so much lay unspoken and unfinished between them, Bethie hadn't pushed for an answer. She hadn't even had the courage to ask Nicholas what he intended to do once they reached Philadelphia. She feared his answer. Did he care about her enough to stay with her? Or would he turn his horse's head west and return to the wild that was so much a part of him?

She told herself that either way she would be fine. She was not the girl Richard had violated, nor was she the frightened young woman Andrew had taken to wife. She was stronger now, braver. Whether Nicholas was with her or not, she would do her best to build a good life for herself and Isabelle. But she knew in her heart that, although she could survive without him, the only place she was truly alive was at his side.

Stopping in Paxton had been her idea. She told herself it was her duty to let Malcolm know what had become of Richard. But a part of her wanted to see her mother, to show her

Isabelle, to ask her to come with her to Philadelphia to start a new life free from Malcolm and his fists.

As they rolled to a stop before the cabin, Bethie found it hard to breathe, found herself wishing she'd let Nicholas talk her out of doing this. She clung to him as he lifted her and Belle to the ground.

"I'm right here, Bethie. I won't let him hurt you."

She met his encouraging gaze, felt some of her fear melt away.

The cabin and barn looked more worn down than she remembered. Weathered clapboard shingles hung loosely from the roof. The parchment window was torn. Flies buzzed around a pile of manure on the side of the barn, the stench of which was overwhelming. Chickens pecked listlessly in the dirt.

She'd taken one step toward the door, when it was thrown open and Malcolm Sorely stepped outside. The years had been cruel to him. His coppery hair was dulled with gray, his face haggard and covered with gray stubble, his skin ruddy and mottled by the sun. He seemed a man bent and old, as if bowed under the weight of his own dourness and cruelty.

The look of shock and loathing on his face might have made Bethie laugh had her fear of him not run so deep. His gaze traveled from her to Isabelle to Nicholas and back again.

"What are you doin' here?"

Bethie's heart hammered in her breast. For a moment she was ten years old and terrified. Then she felt Nicholas behind her. She was not a little girl. She was not helpless. She was a woman, a mother, and she would not let Malcolm frighten her.

She met her stepfather's hate-filled gaze, lifted her chin. "I've brought news, and I've come to see my mother."

Bethie heard her mother's reedy voice call from within. "Who is it, Malcolm?"

"It's that bedeviled daughter of yours come back to stir up trouble, Greer. She's brought a strange man wi' her. Who is this?"

"He is Nicholas Kenleigh, my . . ." She hesitated.

"Her husband." Nicholas's voice, so strong, helped steady her.

"She's already got a husband." Malcolm's gaze shifted

between them. "So it's an adulteress you've become, Bethie Stewart?"

Nicholas stepped out from behind her, one aggressive stride, and for the first time in her life, Bethie saw fear in her stepfather's eyes as he measured Nicholas's strength and found himself outmatched.

Nicholas's voice was soft as silk—and deadly. "The old man you married her off to died and left her alone and unprotected in the middle of a war."

"Nicholas saved my life and Isabelle's."

Malcolm looked at the baby. "Whose get is she?"

"She is Andrew's child." Bethie held Belle closer.

"She doesna look like him." Malcolm sneered, lifted his gaze to Nicholas. "She doesna look like either of them."

Bethie ignored the insinuation. "Doesna Christian charity demand you invite us in, Malcolm?"

Malcolm looked at her, then at Nicholas, seemed to bite back whatever words he'd been about to speak. "Come in if you must, but dinnae be expectin' to stay for supper."

"We wouldn't dream of it." Nicholas offered Bethie his arm, and she took it, grateful to feel him beside her.

They followed Malcolm through the door.

Bethie stared about in shock and dismay. The cabin was filthy, the floor covered with dirt, dried leaves, crumbs, dead flies, mouse droppings. A rancid smell that could only be rotten straw from bedding gone sour permeated the air, together with the stench of unwashed bodies. Grease, melted wax, and bits of food stuck to the surface of the rickety wooden table that in her childhood had been bright and newly hewn.

Most shocking of all was her mother. She sat at the table, paring potatoes, fear in her eyes, an old and weary woman who was not yet forty. It hurt Bethie to see her like this, careworn and aged and afraid.

"What's wrong, Bethie? Do you no' like what you see?" Malcolm went to stand on the opposite side of the table beside her mother. "Your daughter's lookin' down her nose at us, Greer."

Her mother looked up at her, fear and despair in her eyes. "Why have you come here, lass? Why?"

Bethie tried to ignore her mother's rejection. "We're on our way to Philadelphia, Mother. I—I wanted to see you again, to show you your granddaughter. This is Isabelle. She was born at the end of March."

Her mother's gaze rested on Isabelle for the briefest of moments before it dropped to her potatoes. "Pray she didnae curse your womb as you did mine."

The words hurt like a blow, cut much deeper. "W-would you like to hold her?"

"I've supper to prepare. Can you no' see that?"

Bethie swallowed the tears that welled up inside her. She chided herself for ever thinking things could be different. Her mother had never loved her.

"I've come with news of Richard." She saw and felt Malcolm go rigid, and her stomach knotted.

"How come you by news of him? He went back east to find work as a seaman."

Bethie steeled herself against the rage she knew would come. "I saw him at Fort Pitt. He was wearin' a British uniform, servin' under—"

His fist would have hit her squarely on the cheek if Nicholas had not caught Malcolm's wrist in midair.

Nicholas wrenched Malcolm's arm behind his back, forced him up against the far wall, knife at his throat. "Men who hurt women are my favorite men to kill. Touch her, and I'll send you straight to hell—with a smile on my face!"

Malcolm struggled, but Bethie could see he was no match for Nicholas's greater strength. "My son would never join the English!"

Bethie started to answer, but it was Nicholas who spoke first.

"Your son was serving at Fort Pitt under the command of Captain Simeon Écuyer. Écuyer tried him in a court-martial and sentenced him to death by firing squad after he beat my wife and tried to rape her in our quarters. Your son, Master Sorley, is dead."

"'Tis her fault! She bewitched him, seduced him, led him to a path of sin!"

Bethie squeezed her eyes shut against Malcolm's vile words. It seemed like only yesterday she'd stood here, bleeding and beaten, as he shouted similar words at her, then sent her away.

"Leave Bethie out of this! He found that path on his own,

and he paid the price." Nicholas sounded enraged, and Bethie feared for a moment he might truly kill her stepfather.

"I dinnae believe you, English! He cannae be dead! 'Tis lies meant to torment me!"

"It's the truth, old man. I fired the shot that killed him. I watched him die. Live with it." Nicholas released Malcolm, and Bethie watched as her stepfather crumpled to the floor, a broken man.

Then her mother stepped forward from the shadows, met Bethie's gaze, pointed a bony finger at her. "Get out! Go! Is it no' enough that you shame me before my husband! Will you now destroy our hopes, bring grief into our home?"

Bethie blinked back her tears, even as the pain caused by those words hit home in her breast. She tried one last time. "Come with me, Mother! Come away from here! Come away from him! You dinnae need to live with him any longer! I'm goin' to find work in Philadelphia and—"

"He is my husband! I'll no' go wi' you! Get out! You are no' welcome here!"

Bethie felt Nicholas slip his arm round her waist. "Let's go, love. You've done all you can. Leave them to the life they've chosen."

With one last look at her mother, Bethie allowed him to guide her out the door and back to the wagon. Numb, she said nothing as he lifted her into the seat, nothing as they rolled down the rutted road back toward Harrisburg. But when they rounded the bend and were out of sight of the cabin, Nicholas reined the horses to a stop and took her into his arms.

Then Bethie let the tears come.

They arrived in Philadelphia late one afternoon in September when the first hint of autumn was in the air. Bethie gaped in amazement as Nicholas drew the carriage to a stop before an inn under the sign of The Three Crowns.

"You cannae mean to stay here!"

He lifted her and Isabelle to the ground. "Aye, I do."

He led her up the stone steps and through the door. Inside, stylishly attired gentlemen sat around polished tables eating, drinking, talking, smoking. A few looked over their shoulders toward the door at her and Nicholas. She felt out of place in her gown of plain blue linen—no matter that it was the finest gown she'd ever worn.

A tall, older woman walked toward them, dressed in a gown that shimmered and dripped with lace. "Master Kenleigh! It's been . . ."

"At least seven years, madam." He strode forward, took the woman's hand, bent to kiss it. "I see those years have in no way withered your beauty."

"It's a good thing you look like your father, or I'd not have recognized you." She look him up and down, a frown on her face.

"Are you criticizing my tailor, madam?" Nicholas gestured toward his linsey-woolsey shirt, leather breeches, and beaded moccasins with a look of feigned insult on his handsome face.

Bethie thought him ruggedly handsome, the most handsome man she'd ever seen. But clearly this woman did not. "I suspect, Master Kenleigh, that you've not seen a tailor in seven years either."

Nicholas smiled, chuckled. "How right you are, Matilda, dear."

Bethie watched them speak amicably, realized she was seeing yet another side of Nicholas she'd not known existed. Who was this man who spoke so easily with a woman who ought to have been far above his station? Who was he that he could afford to stay here? Surely the innkeeper didn't take payment in pelts!

"Matilda, I'd like to introduce my wife, Elspeth."

"Your wife?" Matilda's eyebrows rose in surprise, but she took Bethie's work-roughened hand between her silky-smooth ones, smiled. "Felicitations are in order, Master Kenleigh. Welcome to The Three Crowns, my dear. We shall do all we can to keep you comfortable."

"Thank you, madam." Bethie didn't know whether she should curtsy or what she should do. And how long was Nicholas going to keep up this lie about her being his wife? They were no longer in the wilderness among strangers. They were in Philadelphia among people who knew him, who knew his family.

Nicholas seemed to realize she felt uncomfortable. "Matilda, we've traveled a long way, and I would see my wife and daughter quickly settled. If you would be so kind, I'll take your best room with a cradle for Isabelle. Please send up some supper and a bottle of good wine when you can. After supper, I think my wife would like a hot bath."

"I can't give you my best room, as it's already taken. But I've another that will do nicely." The woman turned, gave instructions to an eager lad of about fourteen. "I'll show you upstairs."

Nicholas offered Bethie his arm, and the two of them followed Matilda up the stairs and down a hallway to a corner room.

Matilda unlocked the door, handed Nicholas a large, brass key. "Supper will be up soon. A cradle is already on its way. Ring the bell if you need anything."

"Thank you, Matilda. I can see we're in good hands, as always."

Bethie stepped through the doorway, felt as if she'd stepped into a dream. The room was much larger than her cabin. The bedstead itself was enormous, with a coverlet so lacy it might have been a lady's gown. There was a polished table, chairs covered with rich, embroidered cloth, and in the corner a tall mirror.

She felt dizzy, almost sick. All these months she'd known there were things about him that didn't make sense, but now it all came together. His fine speech. His reading. His bottomless purse. He was no trapper. He was no soldier, nor even an officer.

Feeling she'd been deceived, she turned to face him. "Who *are* you?"

Nicholas sat below in the public rooms, his third—or was it his fourth?—brandy almost gone, feeling like an ass. He ought to have realized that bringing Bethie here would make her feel uncomfortable—and lead her to demand an explanation. But he had stupidly assumed that a short answer would be enough and that, in the end, she might be pleased to learn that the man who wanted to marry her—the man who had already claimed her as his wife before the entire world—was wealthy beyond her imagining.

She had listened while he'd listed the properties he would inherit in England and Virginia and told her of Kenleigh Shipyards, where for three generations his family had built ships for the Royal Navy and merchant marine. Then she'd flown into a rage, tears streaming down her face.

"You misled me, Nicholas Kenleigh! You let me believe you were a trapper, then perhaps a soldier who'd been kidnapped by Indians and then fled the war. But none of it was the truth!"

"Every bit of it was the truth!"

"How can it all be true? How? And what of your Indian wife and her baby? I've never demanded an explanation, never asked you to tell me what happened to them. I've trusted you all this time. But now I find you're no' the man I thought you were! And I'm wantin' the truth—all of it!"

But he'd never spoken to anyone of what had happened that summer. Oh, aye, he'd told them Eben and Josiah had been tortured and burned to death. His own scars were plain enough that anyone who saw them knew that he, too, had been tormented. But he'd never said more than that. And never had he told anyone about Lyda.

When he'd faltered, Bethie had picked up Belle and made for the door.

"Where are you going?"

"I dinnae belong here. I'm goin' to find a place to stay among my own kind. Maybe your Matilda will hire me to work downstairs in her kitchens."

He'd blocked her path. "You're going nowhere!"

"You cannae tell me what to do! We both know you're no' really my husband!"

"In every way but one I am your husband, Bethie, and you will not leave this room!"

"Fine, Master Kenleigh. If I cannae leave, then you must, for I cannae stand to be near you!"

Most of his life he'd had to watch out for scheming parents who wanted to entrap him in marriage to their daughters because of his wealth. To think that he should now lose the woman he loved because he was propertied—well, there was some kind of perverse irony in that, but he'd had a bit too much brandy to work it out.

Damn her!

An annoying voice inside his head reminded him that it wasn't just about the money. It was about truth. Bethie had asked for the truth, and he had refused to give it to her.

The darkness inside him yawned deep and wide, a chasm he'd kept blocked off through sheer will for six long years. She'd already rent a fissure through that weakest spot in his defences, already come terribly close to letting that darkness escape.

So she wanted the truth. All of it. Well, then, he would give her the truth.

He tossed back the last of his brandy and, ignoring the curious glances of those around him, strode toward the stairs.

"He's here!"

Alec Kenleigh dropped the knight he'd been about to move against Jamie Blakewell's queen, stood, stared at the innkeeper. "My son is here? In Philadelphia?"

Matilda leaned toward him as if about to impart a great secret, whispered. "He's here—in The Three Crowns, sir!"

Jamie stood. "It's about bloody time! I was beginning to think Écuyer had made the whole thing up."

Alec could scarcely believe what he'd just heard. "Are you certain it's him?"

"Aye, sir. I spoke with him, settled him in his room. He's here with his wife, a lovely young woman, and their baby—a girl, I believe. He asked for the best room, but I could not give it to him, as you've already taken it."

Alec started for the door. He'd waited six long years for this moment, six years of watching his wife, Cassie, suffer the anguish of not knowing whether her son was alive or dead, of watching his daughter, Elizabeth, blame herself for her brother's abrupt departure, of watching every member of his family suffer for the love of a young man who'd turned his back on them. Six terrible years of wondering what he might have done different, of feeling helpless, of fearing he would never see his eldest son alive again.

"Alec, wait!" Jamie blocked his path. "Do you think it's wise to go charging into his room at this late hour? He's got a wife and a baby. They might well be sleeping."

"Damn it!" Alec met Jamie's gaze, realized his brother-by-marriage was right. Jamie knew Nicholas better than anyone. The two were only four years apart in age. Although Nicholas was Jamie's nephew, they were more like brothers.

"We've waited six years, Alec. What's one more night? We came to bring him home. The last thing we want to do is barge through his door and provoke an argument."

Alec closed his eyes, took a deep breath, every fiber of his being desperate to see his son and heir. "Aye, you're right. But I won't leave here without him."

"No. We won't leave here without him."

Alec turned back to Matilda, took her hand in his. "Thank you, madam, for informing me. Please let me know immediately if Nicholas makes to depart. Wake me, if you must."

"Of course, sir, as you wish. 'Tis always my pleasure to be of service to your family." She turned and left, closing the door behind her.

Jamie settled himself before the chessboard. "Were you about to take my queen, or did I imagine that gleam in your eye?"

Alec strode to the sideboard, poured himself a brandy, his emotions in turmoil. "I'm afraid I've lost interest in the game. My God, he's here!"

Jamie chuckled. "Lovely. You forfeit. I win."

# Chapter 28

Bethie lay on the bed and wept, feeling as if her heart were being trampled. The pain of it astonished her.

Nicholas. Nicholas. It wasn't only that he had deceived her. He had refused to tell her the whole truth when she had asked him for it. She had all but begged him to explain, and he had walked away rather than trust her with his secrets. And what truth he had shared meant they could never be together, not as husband and wife.

Voices drifted into her memory as if out of a mist.

*"You are heir to your father's estate. I'm certain he would have preferred you to make a dynastic match and marry a woman of your own class, not the daughter of Scottish rustics, no matter how lovely and pleasant she might be."*

*"You go too far, Écuyer."*

*"Perhaps. But bad blood will out, as they say."*

As much as she hated to agree with Captain Écuyer about anything, he was right. Nicholas's father was English gentry, a man of property. He would want his heir to marry a woman of good family, a woman who could advance his family's connections and fortune, not the daughter of Ulster redemptioners, a woman whose parents lived in filth, a woman with shameful secrets in her past.

*Bad blood will out.*

If only she didn't love him, it would make things so much easier. She would be able to nurse her anger, turn her back on him, start a new life here in Philadelphia without sparing a thought for him. But she *did* love him. With all that she was and ever would be, she loved him. And she knew she would spend every day of the rest of her life missing him, wanting him, longing for him.

Already she longed for him. Where had he gone? Had he taken a room for himself down the hall? Had he left the inn, gone to walk the city streets? Was he downstairs conversing with those well-dressed gentleman she'd seen earlier today?

She tried to imagine him dressed like that—all lace, powdered wigs, and velvet—and could not. The Nicholas she knew wore buckskin and linsey-woolsey. He bathed in icy rivers, rode bareback, moved through the trees like a ghost. He could kill without hesitation, but he was also gentler than any man she'd ever known.

Aye, she loved him. But she might as well have fallen in love with the moon. He was beyond her, and if he lacked the sense to see it, she did not. As a trapper, he would have found a good and devoted wife in her. As the son of gentry, he could only find regret and shame.

She sat, wiped the tears from her face, removed her gown, feeling oddly detached from her own actions, as if some other force were making her body move, for certainly she lacked the will. She crossed the room in her shift, checked on Isabelle, ran her hand over her daughter's downy head. She had just turned back toward the bed, when someone jiggled the door handle.

Nicholas's angry voice came from the other side. "Bethie, open the door."

Fury warring with relief, Bethie walked to the door, hesitated. It would only make things harder on her if she shared her bed with him again. But she could almost feel him through the door, and she wanted nothing more than to touch him again, to kiss him, to feel him beside her, even if it was for just one night.

"Either open the door, or I'll break it down!"

"You wouldna do that."

"Try me!"

Bethie quickly turned the key, stepped back as the door opened.

Nicholas strode in, locked the door behind him. His eyes glittered with rage and some dark emotion she did not understand. She could feel the tension in him, the anger. She could smell the drink on his breath. Her pulse quickened. Instinctively, she moved away from him.

"For God's sake, Bethie! I'm not going to hurt you! Surely you know that by now!" He glared at her, walked right past her to the window, stared out into the darkness. "You asked me to tell you the truth, so I'm going to tell you. But you're going to have to listen to it, and it won't be easy."

Bethie sat on the bed, waited, chilled by his warning, the coldness of his voice.

For a long while he said nothing. When at last he spoke, his voice was flat, almost empty of emotion. "We were attacked at night—a Wyandot war party. We repulsed them quickly. Two young soldiers, boys I'd taken under my wing, gave chase as the warriors fled. Their names were . . . Eben and Josiah."

She saw him shut his eyes, as if it hurt to speak their names.

"I knew they were about to be ambushed, taken captive. I shouted for them to stop, but they either couldn't hear me or didn't listen. Before I could reach them, they'd been overcome. I thought I could free them . . . but I was taken, too."

Nicholas felt the brandy in his stomach churn as he told Bethie how they'd been brought north to the Wyandot village, how he'd known they would be sacrificed, how he'd warned Eben and Josiah, but they'd chosen not to believe him. He told her how the Wyandot had promised to adopt them, had feasted with them as honored guests, had offered them sexual delights. And for the first time in six years, he spoke Lyda's name aloud.

"The woman who came to me was named Lyda, the daughter of their war chief, Atsan. Her mother's line was likewise powerful. I knew none of this at the time. I knew only that I would not risk getting her with child. I refused to leave any part of myself with the Wyandot, nor could I betray my fiancée, Penelope. So I sent Lyda away untouched, even though I knew it would be my last chance to enjoy a woman."

He told Bethie how he'd sought for a way to escape and had failed, how the next evening they'd been tied to stakes in the war chief's longhouse, how the entire village had gathered to watch as the women cut them like cattle, shoved burning embers one at a time beneath their skin.

His body began to shake as the memories he'd tried so hard to forget were unleashed. "Lyda took the lead in my torment. She was angry that I had rejected her. I tried not to cry out, knew it would be worse for me if I did. But Eben and Josiah—they were just boys! I couldn't bear their suffering, felt I ought to have been able to prevent it. I shouted something at Atsan—I can't remember exactly what. My mind was . . . the pain . . . I couldn't think clearly."

He told her how confused he'd been when Lyda and her grandmother had stopped burning him and instead had begun the horrendous process of treating his wounds, every bit as painful as the torture itself. But even as they'd given him cool drinks of water and rubbed salve into his blistered and charred flesh, it had soon become clear that what he'd endured was only the merest hint of what still lay in store for Eben and Josiah.

Nicholas turned from the window, sick to his stomach, sat in a chair before the hearth, buried his face in his hands. Though he could hear Bethie's quiet weeping, the sound of it was all but drowned out by the echoes of screams and curses, of cheering bystanders, of roaring flames.

*"Nicholas, you bastard! What did you say to them? Help me! Oh, God, help me!"*

He fought to put the horror of it into words, willed himself to speak. "They smeared their bodies with pitch . . . forced them into the fire pits . . . burned them alive, but slowly, so slowly. Whenever they would pass out, the Wyandot women would douse the flames, spread salve on their burns, weep with them over their pain. Then, when they were revived, they would cover them with pitch and start again."

Raw emotion surged from his gut—rage, grief, deepest remorse.

"My God, Bethie! They begged me again and again to help them! They begged me to kill them, begged me to end their agony, but I was still bound and could do nothing! Nothing!

I shouted to Atsan to take me in their place, to set them free, but he didn't listen."

He took a deep breath. "At dawn, they dragged the boys, horribly burned but still alive, outside, tied them to racks, and burned them to death as a sacrifice to their god of war. I did not see it, but I heard it. Eben and Josiah died believing I had betrayed them, that I'd persuaded the Wyandot to spare me, but had abandoned them to torment. They died cursing my name."

Bethie knelt before him, tears wet on her cheeks, her violet eyes soft with sympathy. "It was no' your fault, Nicholas. There was nothin' you could have done."

He took her face between his hands, all but shouted at her. "Are you sure of that?"

She did not pull away or shrink from his anger. "Aye, Nicholas. You almost died tryin' to save them. You did more for them than most men would have done. Can you no' see that?"

He stood, afraid her compassion would shatter him, and stalked back toward the window. "There's more. You wanted the truth."

She whispered. "Aye."

He stared unseeing into the darkness. "I later learned Lyda had arranged for me to be spared for one reason—she wanted me to play the stud, to give her my get." He heard Bethie's gasp, forced himself to continue. "But, of course, I was badly burned, and the wounds quickly festered. Lyda and the women of her clan fought to heal me, kept me bound hand and foot to a berth in their longhouse. For the rest of the summer, I lay there, more dead than alive and out of my mind with fever, while they forced me to drink, forced me to eat, cleaned my burns."

Bethie waited for him to continue, tried to comprehend what he'd already told her. She'd known he'd been tortured. But to hear him describe it, to imagine how much he had suffered, how much those two boys had suffered—it nearly made her sick. She wanted desperately to comfort him, to wrap her arms around him, but she sensed he did not want to be touched.

"The first time it happened was only days after my fever broke. I'd grown so accustomed to pain that it seemed a reprieve sent from heaven. I awoke to find myself already hard, already inside her. I was still tied to the berth, but even had I been cut free, I doubt I could have stopped her. I was very weak, and it had been so long since I'd felt anything but agony. It was over quickly. She walked away with a smile on her face while her mother's family watched and laughed. There is no privacy in a longhouse."

Bethie listened, stunned and horrified, as he described how again and again Lyda had taken advantage of his bonds and his physical weakness to arouse him and use his body for her own ends. Bethie hadn't thought such a thing could happen to a man.

"I tried to refuse, tried to keep my body from responding, but I couldn't. Not until I was strong enough to stand and they cut me free was I able to keep her from taking what she wanted from me. But it was too late. She was already carrying my child. That fact kept her alive—for a while."

Bethie could feel the tension inside him, his hatred for himself. She understood that hatred, that deep shame. "So you stayed with her."

He nodded. "I hated her as I've hated no one, and I would not leave my child to be raised by her. I had planned to stay until the child was weaned, then escape with it back to Virginia. So I began to live as one of them. I ate with them, hunted with them, joined the fellowship of their warriors. Atsan accepted me as his son, honored me as a warrior. I smoked, and drank, and joked with him—the man who had ordered Eben and Josiah's deaths.

"But I rejected Lyda utterly. I brought meat to her fire for the child's sake, but I refused the other duties of a husband. Yet, the more I turned from her, the more desperate she became to have my attention. Purely for hatred's sake, I began to dote openly upon other Wyandot women, to bed them, to give them everything I would not give her."

Nicholas laughed, but it was not a pleasant sound. "Her own people began to reject her, even the men who'd once followed her like lovesick hounds. They felt she had become unnaturally attached to me and that if she were unhappy with me as a husband, she should divorce me in the Wyandot way by putting me out of her mother's longhouse."

"But she didn't because she wanted you."

"Aye. No man had ever rejected her, and she simply wanted what she could not have. She didn't love me, if that's what you're thinking. I don't know if she was capable of love."

"If she had loved you, she wouldna have hurt you. She wouldna have stolen from you."

"At first I'd thought she'd merely stolen a baby. By the end, she'd stolen my soul."

Nicholas steeled himself for what he knew was coming, described how one afternoon in late winter, Lyda, her belly swelling, had come inside to find him buried between her youngest sister's thighs. Aware she was watching, he'd taken that moment to plunge her sister into an intense orgasm. Lyda had turned and run out of the longhouse in tears.

"It gave me pleasure to see the hurt upon her face. I was happy to cause her grief." He could feel it as if it were yesterday—the rage, the hate, the urge for vengeance. "When she wasn't back by sundown, I searched for her. I expected to find her pouting somewhere, or perhaps rutting with some young warrior still fool enough to fall for her pretty face."

Suddenly he found it all but impossible to speak. He'd known where telling this story would lead him, and still the lancing pain surprised him. "I found her in a ravine. She had slipped on the ice, fallen, broken her neck. She was dead. I touched my hand to her belly, but it was still. The night before, the women of her clan had been feeling the baby move, and then . . ."

He squeezed his eyes shut against the memory, felt Bethie walk up behind him.

Her small hand rested on his back. "You didna mean for either of them to die."

He turned to face her, overwhelmed with hatred for himself. "Didn't I? I took delight in humiliating her, in hurting her! If I had shown her the smallest kindness that day, if I had forsworn my lust for vengeance, she would not be dead, and the baby . . ."

Bethie pressed herself against him, wrapped her slender arms around him. "You didna kill her, Nicholas. 'Twas an accident. How were you to know she would slip and fall?"

He cupped Bethie's face in his hands, forced her to meet

his gaze, spoke between gritted teeth. "You don't understand. I was an animal! I didn't care about her! I didn't care about any of the women I used! I gave no thought to the other children I might have sired! I didn't care about anything!"

"Except for the baby. And your friends, Eben and Josiah. You cared about them."

Her words were a fist to his gut. He sat on the bed. "Aye, I cared about them."

Bethie sat beside him, took his hand. "You did the best you could, Nicholas. You cannae punish yourself forever for wrongs you did not intend."

Her words hung in the air for a moment, and Nicholas wondered what he had done to deserve her, this loving, giving woman. "I left the Wyandot village the next morning. It took me two months to reach Virginia again. My parents had thought me dead, so my arrival quite surprised them. Amid the celebration, I learnt that Penelope, my fiancée, had married another. And then the nightmares began."

He told her how Eben's and Josiah's screams and curses had followed him into his sleep, how his sister Elizabeth had come to comfort him in the night, and how in his rage and confusion he'd almost killed her.

"I took only what I needed and rode west." His voice betrayed him, caught in his throat as he struggled to choke out the rest of it. "I left my mother weeping . . . in her nightgown. She begged me not to leave, and still I rode away. I wanted to protect them from the man I had become."

"You've a family that loves you, Nicholas. That's somethin' to be cherished, for certain, somethin' I've never known. Why did you no' go home?"

"Sweet Bethie, always so forgiving." He sought for the right words. "I didn't go home because I believed the man they loved no longer existed."

She knelt before him, her eyes filled with tears. "'Tis no' your fault that you survived and the others didna. You cannae give them back their lives by refusin' to live your own, Nicholas."

He pulled her against him, buried his face in the sweet-smelling silk of her hair. "Is it really that simple, Bethie? And what of the animal I became? That creature is still inside me."

"I know no animal, Nicholas. I know only the man who held my hand when I gave birth, the man who risked his life time and again to protect mine, the man who forgave my shame, the man who holds me in his arms and makes the world disappear. I know only the man I love, Nicholas. Only you."

He started to tell her she bore no shame and never had, when her last words struck him. His heart seemed to stop.

*Only the man I love.*

"Do you mean that, Bethie?"

She stood before him, silent tears streaming down her face, took off her shift. Then she slowly removed his shirt and breeches, kissed his scars one by one, bathed him with her tears. And when at last he joined his body with hers, the fissure inside him cracked wide open, but rather than darkness spilling forth, there was white light, only light.

Bethie lay with her head on Nicholas's chest, listened to his heartbeat as he slept. Between the brandy he'd drunk, the torrent of emotions that had poured through him, and the passionate release of their lovemaking, he was surely exhausted.

She knew it had taken all his strength to tell her what he'd told her, and she tried to grasp it all. She'd known that he'd been tortured. She'd been able to see that for herself. But the horror of it . . .

She ran a finger over one puckered scar. Now that she knew what they'd done to him, she was able to read the strange pattern on his skin as she might the words in a book. The lines were what remained of knife cuts, the puckered burns the scars left by glowing embers. There were so many of them.

*So many.*

Her eyes, already sore from crying, pricked with fresh tears. She could not imagine how much he had suffered, nor how horrible it must have been to watch, helpless, as his two young friends were burned slowly to death. How desperate must he have felt to witness their torment! How it must have crushed him when, after he'd offered his life for theirs, they died cursing him! How alone he must have felt, tied up, in pain and sick with fever—as if even God had abandoned him.

And that woman—Lyda—what she had done to him! Lyda

had forced herself on him, as surely as Richard had forced himself on Bethie. But hadn't Nicholas's humiliation been much worse? Aye, it had. The entire clan had watched as Lyda had forced his body to oblige her, had taken her pleasure of him, had stolen his seed.

'Twas clear now why he'd understood her need to be clean after Richard had tried to rape her. He must have felt the same urge when they'd at last cut away his bonds and—

Then Bethie remembered, and regret sliced through her. *She* had tied him to her bed. She had drugged him, then bound him by wrist and ankle. He had fought like a wild animal to free himself—and had failed. She'd thought at the time he was simply angry at being bested by a woman, but it had been so much more than that. What terrible memories it must have stirred in him!

And when he'd first made love to her—hadn't he forced himself to lie on his back, his fists around the bedposts, his submissive position an echo of that which Lyda had forced upon him? Aye, he had—for her sake. Somehow he had understood her fear, had felt her hidden pain, and though he'd known nothing about Richard at the time, he'd found a way to soothe her, to show her that she could trust him.

Tears blurred her vision as she realized the sacrifice he'd made for her.

His hands stroked her hair. "What's wrong, love?"

Startled, she looked up to find him watching her. "I thought you were sleepin'."

"Just dozing." He shifted his weight, held her closer. "Tell me what's troubling you."

She sat, looked into his blue eyes. "I'm sorry, Nicholas. I'm sorry for tyin' you to my bed. I didna know—"

There was such anguish in her voice that Nicholas set aside the jest that had come to mind, wiped her tears away with his thumbs. "How could you have known? You did what you had to do to feel safe. So did I. I held a pistol to your head, remember?"

Her lips curved in a sad smile. "You've done so much for me. If no' for you, Belle and I would have died a dozen times over. If no' for you, I wouldna be able to read. If no' for you, I would never have known how precious a man's touch can be."

"I assure you, love, there was no suffering involved, either in teaching you to read or in showing you the pleasures of lovemaking. Besides, you've saved my life, too—once when I would have bled to death and again when I would have been shot in the back."

She had saved him in other ways, too, but Nicholas did not yet know the words to tell her exactly what she'd done for him.

God, she was beautiful. She sat, looking at him with doubt in her tear-bright eyes, her hair in glorious disarray around her shoulders, the pink crests of her breasts peeking through the golden strands, tempting him. "Of course, there is a way you can repay me . . ."

She ran her fingers through the hair on his chest, stopped to tease one flat nipple, her lips curved in a seductive smile. "And what would that be?"

"Marry me."

Her smile vanished, and she shook her head. "You would come to regret it one day. And your family—"

"—has no say in this decision."

Her answer was not what Nicholas hoped to hear. "I'll think on it."

# Chapter 29

Bethie awoke early the next morning to Nicholas's kisses.

"I'm going out for a while, but you keep sleeping, love. I'll ask Matilda to send up breakfast in an hour. Would you like a bath?" His hand crept playfully beneath the covers, cupped the part of her that was still damp with his essence.

She opened her eyes, pushed herself against the delicious pressure of his hand. "Aye, I'd like a bath—if it's no' a burden for her. Mmmm. Dinnae stop."

"It's no' a burden, love. And perhaps I willna be leavin' just yet." With deft strokes of his fingers, he brought her quickly to the edge, then unlaced his breeches and slid into her with one slow thrust.

It was a fast coupling, hard and hot, and left Bethie feeling warm and languid long after Nicholas had gone. She rose slowly, nursed Belle, her mind drifting through everything that had happened the night before.

She hadn't meant to tell him she loved him, had meant to keep her feelings for him secret. But in her anguish over his pain, the words had slipped from her tongue. Yet she would not take them back. She had no idea what she would do.

Nicholas, though he had spoken no words of love to her, was bent on marrying her. Though Bethie's heart wanted nothing more than to spend the rest of her life with Nicholas as his proper wife, she feared the differences between them would bring them both a lifetime of regret. What if one day her mother or Malcolm should wander up to their door? What if the story of what Richard had done at Fort Pitt became widespread? What if, in her ignorance and poverty, she shamed him before society? How would Nicholas and his family feel then?

A knock came at the door, and with it a breakfast of eggs, bacon, bread, butter, and hot tea. Breakfast was followed by a bath. Trying to keep her mind off her troubles, Bethie brought Belle into the tub with her, laughed as her baby daughter splashed, giggled, and cooed in the warm water. She had just dressed and put Belle down for her morning nap, when another knock came at the door.

The innkeeper entered, followed by three other women bearing all manner of brightly colored cloth and lace. "Your husband sent Madame Moreau and her daughters to take your measurements and prepare a wardrobe for you, madam."

"A w-wardrobe?"

Madame Moreau swept into the room, directed her daughters to lay their burdens across the bed. "Let's get a look at you."

Bethie didn't know what to do or say. "B-but my baby is sleepin'."

"We shall be quiet as mice, *n'est-ce pas*?"

*"Oui, maman,"* the dressmaker's daughters whispered.

"Oh, you are a pretty little thing—flawless skin, lovely hair, and your eyes—what an unusual color! And your figure, madame, *c'est parfait*. I can see why your husband is so smitten. With my talent and his coin, you shall look like a princess!"

Bethie wasn't certain she wanted to look like a princess, but in short order, she found herself in her shift being measured in every conceivable way while Madame Moreau and her daughters whispered away in French, held swatches of cloth, samples of lace, bits of ribbon up to her skin or beside her eyes. Bethie had never seen so many beautiful colors—lavenders, delicate shades of blue, soft ivories, sweet pinks, buttery yellows—nor had she ever touched anything so soft as the silks, so rich as the velvets, or so ornate as the embroidered damasks.

'Twas like being in a fairy tale. And that's what frightened Bethie. For she knew that, sooner or later, all fairy tales end.

Jamie watched as Alec spoke with the innkeeper, felt his brother-in-law's frustration mount. It was a frustration Jamie shared.

For six long years, he had wondered every day what had become of Nicholas, his nephew, childhood companion, closest friend. And Jamie was more than a little curious to see what sort of forest sprite had captured Nicholas's heart, for he had no doubt it was due to his love for her that Nicholas had finally emerged from his self-imposed exile.

"What do you mean Nicholas left?"

"He rose early, sir, and went into the city."

"Did you ask him where he was going?"

The innkeeper gaped at Alec in indignation. "Certainly not, sir! How my guests spend their time is none of my affair."

"Of course, Matilda. Forgive me."

"But, sir, his wife is still here, as are his horses. I'm certain he will return shortly, and when he does I shall notify you at once."

"I would be most grateful, madam. But while he is away, I think I should like to meet my daughter-in-law."

"Regrettably, she is indisposed at the moment, sir."

"Is something wrong?"

"No, sir. Her husband, your son, sent Madame Moreau to fit her for a new wardrobe."

Jamie chuckled. "Poor thing. We ought to rescue her, Alec. It would be the chivalrous thing to do."

Alec met his gaze, smiled. "Indeed."

Nicholas looked into the mirror, saw himself as he'd never expected to see himself again—dressed as a gentleman. He'd purchased one complete set of garments, ordered the rest of his wardrobe, complete with drawers and handkerchiefs, to be made and delivered by week's end. But six years of living in the wild had done more than broaden his shoulders and slim his waist. It had changed his tastes, as well. "On second thought, no lace."

"As you wish, sir. Might I suggest a good wig maker, sir?" The old man cast a disapproving glance at Nicholas's hair, which still hung unbound to his waist.

"No, thank you. I never could abide wearing one."

The man's gaze remained fixed on Nicholas's hair. "Very well, sir."

As the tailor finished mending the hems of his breeches, Nicholas mulled over the news he'd heard on the street. A group of Scots-Irish frontiersmen from Paxton had attacked a village of peaceful Conestoga Indians and slaughtered everyone they could get their hands on—men, women, children. A handful of Conestogas had escaped to Lancaster, where Quakers, outraged by the carnage, had given them refuge in the local gaol. But the frontiersmen, eager to avenge the deaths of their loved ones after a spring and summer of bloodshed, had followed them, had broken into the gaol and hacked them down, even the babies, leaving their bodies scattered on the cold ground.

The thought of it made Nicholas's gorge rise. Hadn't there been enough killing? What good could the frontiersmen possibly gain by butchering innocent Indians? Or perhaps they, like Écuyer, didn't believe there was such a thing as an innocent Indian. But the Conestoga were not only peaceful, making their living by selling baskets and brooms, they were Christian, as well.

All of Philadelphia was in a state of outrage about the murders. Every public house and square was abuzz with the news—and the rumor that more than a thousand frontiersmen were now on their way toward Philadelphia, armed and ready to fight unless the British garrison turned over the Moravian Indians it was sheltering.

Nicholas had no doubt the garrison's commander would refuse such a demand. But would the frontiersman actually attack Philadelphia? That they had no love for Englishmen or Quakers went without saying. Too many of them had brought old hatreds with them from Scotland and Ireland and looked down upon the peace-loving Quakers as cowardly and effeminate. But to attack Philadelphia would be foolhardy, an act of suicide.

Suddenly Nicholas felt weary. He'd seen so much killing over the past six years, so much mindless barbarism. When would it end?

"Very well, sir. That should do nicely." The tailor stepped away.

"Thank you, sir." Nicholas slipped out of his waistcoat, removed his shirt, unbuttoned his new breeches. "Would you be so kind as to wrap these?"

The old man gaped at him from beneath his powdered wig. "You're not going to wear them, sir?"

Nicholas chuckled. The tailor was clearly astonished that Nicholas was willing to show himself again clad in leather breeches and linsey-woolsey. "Oh, certainly, I'm going to wear them. But not just yet."

He didn't want to give Bethie a shock. She'd already endured enough. When he took off his trapper attire and again clad himself as a gentlemen, he would do it before her eyes, so that she would know him and not think him a stranger.

By the time Madame Moreau had finished with her and packed her things, and gone, Bethie felt that she, too, needed a nap. But Belle had awoken, and Bethie had just finished nursing her, when yet another knock came at the door.

Bethie laid Belle in the center of the big bed, hurried to answer it.

It was the innkeeper again. "You have guests, madam."

"Guests?"

"Matilda, we're not guests. We're family." A tall, handsome gentleman with blond hair and green eyes pushed past the startled innkeeper, bowed, lifted Bethie's hand to his lips. "I am Jamie Blakewell, Nicholas's uncle. And you, my dear, are a picture of loveliness. You have no idea how happy I am to make your acquaintance."

Another man stepped forward. "As am I."

Bethie felt the breath leave her lungs, felt her knees go coggly.

There before her stood an older version of Nicholas. Tall,

with bright blue eyes, his raven-dark hair shot through with silver, he could be no one but Nicholas's father.

"You're . . . you're . . ." But it was hard to breathe, and she felt dizzy.

Two sets of strong arms shot out to steady her, help her into a chair.

"See now! In your impatience you've frightened the poor girl!" The innkeeper sounded vexed. "If you had waited until your son returned—"

"I—I'm fine—just a wee bit surprised." Bethie didn't want to cause a scene.

The man who'd called himself Jamie smiled at her. "See, Matilda? She's just a wee bit surprised."

Nicholas's father gazed at her through eyes so like his son's that Bethie could not help feeling affection for him. He touched a hand to her cheek. "Matilda, would you be so kind as to bring us some tea?"

"As you wish, sir." The innkeeper turned and left them alone.

"I'm sorry we startled you, my dear. My name is Alec Kenleigh. As you've no doubt guessed, I'm your husband's father." He sat in a chair beside her.

Bethie swallowed, prepared to tell them the truth, prayed they wouldn't be too angry with her. "I—I'm Elspeth—Elspeth Stewart. But I am no' your son's wife, and this is no' his baby."

Alec's brow knitted in puzzlement, and he exchanged glances with Jamie, who looked likewise confused. "When you feel up to it, Elspeth, why don't you tell us how you came to know my son, and why, if you're not his wife, he has claimed you as such."

Bethie snuggled Belle on her lap, told them how Nicholas, gravely wounded, had come upon her cabin in the forest, held a pistol to her head, forced her to help him. She told them how he'd helped her through Belle's birth and how she'd come to trust him. She told them of Mattootuk and the fire and their flight to Fort Pitt. She told them of Nicholas's heroism during the siege and of their journey to Philadelphia.

Of Richard and Malcolm Sorley and events in Paxton, she

said nothing. Nor did she reveal that she and Nicholas had shared a bed.

They listened, asked the occasional question, treating her with nothing but kindness.

"I didna know who your son really was until yesterday when we arrived here. I thought he was a trapper and a soldier. If I had known . . ."

Alec watched a dark shadow pass over the sweet face of the young woman his son loved, felt a surge of fierce protectiveness. He knew from Captain Écuyer's letter some of what she had suffered during her young life, much more than she had revealed, and he was glad that Nicholas had put a bullet through her bastard stepbrother's heart. "If you had known—what then?"

She looked at him through pleading eyes. "I wouldna have let him pretend to be my husband. 'Tis no' fair to him. I know you dinnae want him to marry a woman like me, a woman of no family. You dinnae need to hide your thoughts for my sake."

And in that moment Alec knew without a doubt that she loved Nicholas, too. "My dear, I want Nicholas to marry the woman he loves, a woman who loves him. From where I'm sitting, that appears to be you."

Her face turned an adorable shade of pink at his words, and her big eyes, so blue that they seemed to be violet, gazed sadly into his. "He has no' spoken such words to me."

"No, but his actions show that you mean the world to him. Did you know that after he arrived at Fort Pitt, my son wrote out his will and testament, claiming you and Isabelle as his wife and daughter and naming Isabelle his heir?"

The genuine astonishment on her face proved she had not known. "Wh-what? Why would he do so haggis-headed a thing as that?"

Jamie chuckled, and Alec could tell his brother-by-marriage was likewise charmed by this beautiful young woman. "It seems pretty clear, doesn't it? He wanted to make certain you were well cared for if he should die in battle."

"But Isabelle is no' of his blood!"

Alec valued her honesty. Another woman might not hesitate

to lie about her child's parentage when a fortune was at stake. "I suspect that when you provide him with a son, Nicholas will rewrite his will, taking care to make certain Isabelle is well supported."

The color rose in her cheeks again. "But we're no' really married!"

"You will be. Soon." Alec shared a smile with Jamie, could almost read his brother-in-law's thoughts.

The Kenleigh-Blakewell clan was going to cherish Elspeth and her baby girl.

Nicholas took the stairs two at a time, packages tucked beneath his arm, eager to see Bethie again, to set things straight. She was his wife in all ways but one. She might well be carrying his child. It was time they married in the church—till death do us part and all that.

He'd been to the goldsmith's, purchased a ring for her, a simple gold band. It would do until he had time to find something worthy of her—a polished sapphire surrounded by diamonds or perhaps a ruby. He'd persuaded the nearest Anglican priest to marry them on Saturday—a mere three days hence. Now all he had to do was persuade the bride that wedding a well-to-do Englishman would not be a mistake.

He understood her concern. Having grown up among the landed *élite*, he knew how people gossiped, particularly jealous women. Some would look down their noses at Bethie because of her humble birth. Still others would disregard her because of her Scottish blood and manner of speech. Others would despise her for her youth and beauty. But Jamie and Bríghid had faced down even more formidable obstacles and were happy together. Why could he and Bethie not do the same?

He strode down the hallway, knocked lightly on the door so as not to startle her, opened it—and felt as if he'd been kicked in the stomach.

In chairs on either side of Bethie sat his father and Jamie. Both looked almost as he remembered them, though his father had more silver in his hair, and his eyes held more worry.

Nicholas stared at them in disbelief, found he could not

speak. A part of him cried out that he was not ready for this, that he needed more time.

But then his father stood, strode toward him, embraced him in a crushing bear hug, and Nicholas knew he had waited far, far too long.

"Nicholas!" His father's voice was rough with emotion. "My God, Nicholas!"

Nicholas dropped his packages, answered his father's embrace with his own fierce hug, held the man he'd never thought he'd see again, the man he'd thought had surely disowned him by now. There were no words, no room for anything but feelings.

After a moment—Nicholas had lost all sense of time—his father held him out at arm's length, looked him up and down. "Apart from your desperate need for a barber, you don't look bad for six years in the wilderness. My God, I'm glad to see you alive, son!"

"I say he looks like hell!" Jamie muscled his way in, embraced Nicholas, slapped him hard on the back.

"Is that so, Jamie, old boy? Bethie finds me 'dashy-lookin'. She said so herself." He met Bethie's gaze, saw the sweet smile on her face, the glitter of tears in her eyes.

Jamie cuffed him lightly on the chin, grinned. "Love is blind, as they say."

Nicholas looked from the man he thought of as a brother to his father. "There is so much I would ask you, so much I would know."

His father nodded, turned to Jamie. "Would you mind keeping my beautiful daughter-in-law company while I speak privately with my son?"

Jamie met Nicholas's gaze, and a slow smile spread across his face. Then he turned to Bethie, lifted her hand to his lips. "It would be my great pleasure."

Nicholas didn't like that one bit. "Watch yourself!"

Jamie gazed at him, a feigned look of innocence on his face. "I'm a happily married man, the father of five." Then his expression sobered. "I've got five children, Nicholas. Five. Three of them you've never even met."

Nicholas nodded, felt the first edge of what he'd done to himself—what he'd done to his family—press in against him.

He shifted his gaze to Bethie. "I'll be back soon, love. Jamie, do try to be charming—but not too charming."

For the second time in as many days, Nicholas told someone the full story of what had happened to him that terrible summer of 1756. Surprisingly, it was more difficult to tell his father what Lyda had done to him than it had been to tell Bethie. Perhaps it took a man to understand exactly how Lyda had humiliated him. She had forced his body to respond, controlled him, used him.

After he finished, neither of them spoke for some time.

Then finally his father broke the silence, his voice strained. "I don't know what to say. We knew you had been brutalized. We knew from your scars that it had been terrible, beyond imagination. But the rest of it . . . what she did to you . . . the baby . . . we had no idea. My God!"

"How could you have known? I was unable to speak of it."

"I am so sorry, Nicholas. So sorry." Then the tone of his father's voice changed. "But I need to know why you left. I need to understand why you turned your back on your mother and left her weeping. Do you have any idea how much she has suffered these past six years?"

Nicholas felt his own temper rise. "I left because I no longer felt fit to live among you."

"That's absurd! No matter what you were going through, we would have faced it with you, as a family, but you chose to leave."

"I nearly killed Elizabeth! I nearly killed my own sister!"

"And for six long years, she has blamed herself for your decision to leave!"

Nicholas turned away, strode across the room, his guilt pressing heavier upon him. "I never intended that."

"I'm sure you didn't, but that's what she's had to live with since she was sixteen. She's a married woman now, you know—a mother with a child of her own."

Nicholas tried to picture his sister as an adult woman, a mother, and realized how much had changed these past years. Emma Rose had been little more than a baby. She'd be nine now. And William, Alec, and Matthew . . .

But his father wasn't finished. "We have lived every day these six years wondering if we'd ever see you again, wondering if you were alive or if perhaps you'd been killed by illness or accident or violence and lay unburied and unmourned, a nameless pile of bones in some forest bog. My God, Nicholas, can you imagine wondering that about your child? Your mother doesn't even know that I came here looking for you. She believes I'm here on business. She's already lost you twice. I was afraid the heartbreak would kill her if we failed to find you."

Nicholas turned, faced his father's wrath. "I'm sorry. There's nothing I can do to take back the pain these past years have caused you all. At the time, I truly believed that leaving was the best course of action for everyone. I don't expect you to understand. Hell, I'd still be out there, headed back west, if it hadn't been for Bethie. I meant what I said that morning. I *was* dead."

His father took a deep breath. "She loves you very much."

"I know."

"She loves you so much that she thinks you'd be better off with a woman of your own class and believes I should intervene to prevent this marriage."

Nicholas felt his temper build again. "And will you?"

His father shook his head. "You have my blessing, Nicholas. She is a wonderful girl with a pure heart. Your mother will cherish her and little Isabelle."

"Bethie's had a rough life. It will be good for her to have family. I hope in time you and Mother can be for her what her own parents were not."

"We will, I'm certain, if she'll let us. When I think of what that bastard did to her—"

"How do you know about that?" Then it dawned on him. "And how in God's name did you know I was on my way to Philadelphia?"

His father retrieved a letter and a document signed by Nicholas's own hand from a nearby sideboard. His will and testament. He'd entrusted it in confidence to the captain.

Nicholas looked at the signature on the letter, gave a snort of disgust. "Écuyer! The bastard!"

"We can talk about that later. In the meantime, for what it's worth, Nicholas, I'm proud of the man you've become. I know what you did for Bethie. I know what you did at Fort Pitt. No father has ever been more proud of his son and heir than I." His father's voice was strained at these last words, and his eyes seemed oddly bright.

Nicholas might have said something in response—if the strange lump in his throat hadn't stopped him.

"Now fetch your bride. I'd say a celebration is in order. And I must get a letter off to your mother with the next post."

# Chapter 30

Bethie held Belle securely in her lap, adjusted the baby's lace collar. She scarce recognized the two of them, dressed as they were in the first of their new gowns. Bethie's was a soft blue silk with ivory lace flowing from the bodice and elbows. Belle's was of simple white linen and lace. A tiny white bow had been fastened to her downy hair, while Bethie's hair had been coiled regally atop her head. They looked like princesses, for certain, but would they fool anyone?

Outside the carriage window, the streets of Philadelphia rolled by. Inside the carriage, Jamie and Nicholas continued to jest with each other, while Nicholas's father looked on, clearly amused. The affection the two younger men felt for each other—and Alec's fatherly love for them both—touched her deeply, perhaps because she'd never seen such closeness in a family before.

Jamie winked at her. "So help me to understand, Nicholas—you held a pistol to her head?"

Nicholas's rich baritone voice sounded in her ear. "Aye, I did."

"You held a pistol to the head of a woman ripe with child?"

"Aye, and clearly she found it charming."

Bethie gaped at him in disbelief. "You're daft!"

"Is that normally how you seduce women, Nicholas—with cold steel?"

"Of course not. To seduce them, I use hot steel."

Bethie gasped, shocked by the lewdness of his comment, felt her face flush.

"I'm sorry, love. Did I say something wrong?"

"My apologies, Bethie, dear. Clearly my son has spent far too long in his own company."

The carriage rounded a corner, drew to a halt.

Alec glanced out the window. "Ah, here we are. Are we agreed, gentlemen? One of us is to be at Bethie's side at all times, and under no circumstances is she to be abandoned to the vicious company of women."

Jamie and Nicholas responded with a single, "Aye."

Feeling more cosseted and protected than she'd ever felt before, but nonetheless terrified, she accepted Nicholas's help alighting from the carriage and stared up at the large, three-storied brick house before them. A friend of his father's—a man named Benjamin Franklin—had agreed to host a dinner party to welcome Nicholas home and to introduce Bethie into society.

"When they see my affection for you, it will curb their tongues," Alec had explained the night before.

After dinner last night, Nicholas and Jamie had taken turns teaching Bethie what manners and etiquette she would likely need. Though she'd been horrified at the thought of a party, the two of them had made her laugh until she'd quite forgotten to worry. But now, as she stared up at the grand house and its many glass windows, her fears returned.

They had agreed to tell a simple version of the truth: Nicholas had encountered Bethie, a widow living alone, far west on the frontier and had fallen in love with her, claimed her as his wife, and helped her and little Isabelle to escape to Fort Pitt, where they had survived the siege. That they had not been married in a church was a fact they had saved for the ears of the priest, who was set to marry them in a private ceremony on Saturday—only two days hence.

Of course, Bethie had not yet agreed to marry Nicholas, but it didn't seem to matter to him. Everyone, including Nicholas's father, seemed to believe the question of their marriage was settled. Whenever she pointed out yet another reason why Nicholas should take a more fitting bride, the men cast aside her concerns and reassured her that everything would be fine. But Bethie wasn't convinced. Nicholas had done so much for her. She did not want to repay his kindness by becoming a source of shame or embarrassment for him and his family.

"Shall we?" Nicholas slipped his arm around her waist, gave her a reassuring smile.

Her heart swelled with love for him. Though she fancied him in leather breeches—or none at all—the sight of him dressed as a gentleman made her belly flutter. He wore a matching coat and breeches of dark green velvet with brass buttons. His waistcoat was of ivory satin and matched his ivory silk stockings. But he looked more manly than the other gentlemen she'd seen on the street—broader in the shoulder, more muscular in the thigh with no need to wear pads on his well-defined calves. And his hair, although tied back with a black ribbon, still hung to his waist.

She adjusted Belle's weight in her arms, let Nicholas guide her up the steps and through the doors, Alec and Jamie before them.

"Good to see you as always, Ben." As Bethie watched, Alec shook the hand of a heavyset older man with a balding head, large, kind eyes, and a firm mouth. "Thank you for hosting this tonight. I am in your debt."

"Nonsense, Alec. Come in, and make yourself at home. Welcome, Jamie. You're looking well. Now where is Nicholas? I've a mind to take a switch to his backside for worrying us so these past years."

Nicholas chuckled. "You can try, old man, but I doubt it will reform me."

Bethie saw surprise and a touch of sadness in Master Franklin's eyes as he measured Nicholas against the younger man he remembered.

"My God, a boy rode to war, and a man has returned." He shook Nicholas's hand fiercely. "I cannot tell you how relieved I am to see you alive and whole."

"Thank you, sir. Allow me to introduce my wife, Elspeth Stewart Kenleigh, and our daughter, Isabelle."

At the sound of her name, Isabelle buried her little face

shyly against Bethie's breast, but Bethie forced herself to meet the kindly man's gaze. "'Tis a pleasure to meet you, sir."

"The pleasure is entirely mine." Master Franklin took her free hand, kissed it. "You make me wish I were a young man again, my dear."

Bethie heard Nicholas click his tongue in disapproval. "What would your wife say, sir?"

Master Franklin tossed back his head, laughed. "Deborah would probably say she also wishes I were a young man again!"

Nicholas retrieved Bethie's hand from Master Franklin's gentle grasp. "Be warned, Bethie, love. Ben has quite a way with the ladies."

Bethie looked up into Nicholas's teasing eyes. "I'll remember that."

The evening passed in a whirlwind of introductions until Bethie was quite confused and could remember no one's name. She'd never met so many people at once in her entire life. Almost everyone was very gracious to her, more so than she would have imagined.

Almost everyone.

The evening seemed to be passing smoothly when Nicholas cursed under his breath.

Bethie followed his gaze to a beautiful young woman dressed in a gown of yellow silk embroidered with bright red flowers. Upon her head was an elegant powdered wig. Her skin was unnaturally white, and Bethie realized it was powdered, even the swell of her breasts, which rose rather bountifully above her bodice. A dark beauty mark had been affixed to her cheek. She moved with the regal grace of a swan. And her gaze was fixed upon Nicholas.

"Nicholas, my dear, I am so relieved to see you safely home again. You've no idea how I worried and prayed for you. But that's not the first time I've lost sleep because of you." She held out her hand to him, gazed seductively at him from beneath her darkened lashes.

Nicholas smiled, took her hand, kissed it. "Sylvia. Thank you for your prayers, though that is not usually what gets you on your knees, is it? May I introduce my wife?"

But Sylvia ignored Bethie, tickled Belle under the chin and

smiled. In contrast to her painted face, her teeth appeared almost as yellow as her gown. "What a lovely child. She doesn't look like you, Nicholas. I would think so vigorous a man would make his mark in his offspring."

Nicholas's voice held a hint of warning. "She is my daughter by adoption, Sylvia. Elspeth was widowed."

Then the woman's cold, brown eyes fixed on Bethie. "A child—and a child bride. How pleased I am to meet you, dear."

Bethie could tell Sylvia was anything but pleased to meet her, felt her own temper stir, bit back her words for the sake of Nicholas and his family. "'Tis a pleasure to meet you, miss."

"She's lovely, Nicholas. I can see why you fell for her. Her eyes are such a unique shade of blue, and her skin—baked brown in the sun like that of a wild Indian. Perhaps she shall start a new fashion and we shall all bake our faces, though I think few of us would choose to do so by working in our own fields."

Bethie's heart raced as her temper swelled.

But Nicholas laughed. "Am I right in remembering that your thirtieth birthday has just passed, Sylvia, my dear? Forgive me for not congratulating you sooner. You don't look as if you've aged quite that much these past years, though it is hard to see beneath all that paint."

Sylvia gaped at him, then stomped off in an angry swirl of skirts.

Jamie came up behind them, a devious grin on his face. "Well done, Nicholas. That was brilliant! But I believe they are calling us to dinner."

"I'd like just a moment with Bethie, if you don't mind, Jamie."

"Not at all. I'll eat your share."

When they were alone, Nicholas took both her and Belle into his embrace. "I know her words hurt you, but you've no reason to feel shame for who you are, Bethie."

"But she's right. My skin is brown, no' white like hers. And my hands are rough from workin'. These people only speak to me because of you."

He ran a finger down her cheek. "Her skin is covered with layer after layer of paint and powder, and her hands are flawlessly smooth because she's never done a useful thing in her life. She is pampered and spoiled and—"

"You were lovers." Bethie voiced what most troubled her.

"That was a long time ago, Bethie, and there was no love involved. There is only one woman for me now, and that is you. I adore every inch of your sun-kissed skin, from the tip of your nose to that tasty little beauty mark on your left nether lip."

Bethie gasped. "I dinnae have a beauty mark on my—"

He grinned devilishly. "I'll show it to you—in the mirror tonight. Now let's join the others."

Nicholas watched proudly as Bethie made her way through her first formal dinner. She was an intelligent woman, and what they had forgotten to teach her, she quickly learned through observation. She seemed to be enjoying the conversation, and Jamie, Ben, and his father were making a special effort to include her. Nicholas would make a point of thanking them in private later.

The fare was outstanding, the wine superb. It had been so long since Nicholas had eaten any of these dishes that he had to fight to keep from moaning with each bite. He knew without asking that his father had hired additional cooks and provided much of the food for the meal. Ben was a prominent and powerful man, but he was not wealthy, at least not by Kenleigh standards.

They had just started upon the second course, when there was a ruckus in the hallway and a well-dressed older man strode into the dining room.

Every man at the table stood. Nicholas followed their lead.

Ben bowed slightly, gestured toward a vacant chair. "Governor Penn. What an honor. Won't you join us?"

"I'm afraid I'm here on dire business, Ben."

From outside came the sound of tolling church bells.

"So it would seem."

The governor looked around the table, acknowledged the other men by name, then turned to Nicholas. "Nicholas Kenleigh. I hear we have you to thank for the survival of many at Fort Pitt. Captain Écuyer speaks quite highly of you."

"Governor Penn." Nicholas gave a respectful bow, then took his seat along with the others.

"It seems the troubles on our frontier have followed you to Philadelphia. Ladies and gentlemen, an army is upon our doorstep. Some fifteen hundred Scots-Irish frontiersmen from the area of Paxton are marching on our town. They've sent messengers demanding the garrison turn over the Moravian Indians to them for slaughter or face an attack. They're expected to be here by morning."

For a moment there was silence, then shouting.

"Bloody Scots-Irish! They're no better than barbarians!"

"What are we going to do?"

"We must arm ourselves, protect our wives and daughters!"

"Bloodthirsty Presbyterians!"

"Will the garrison stop them?"

Nicholas saw Bethie blanch, felt the hurtful barbs as if they had struck him. This was what she had feared—that her class, her Scottish blood, or her past would cause him and his family embarrassment. This was precisely why she was hesitant to marry him.

Down the table from them, Sylvia smirked, gazed malevolently toward Bethie.

Determined to show Bethie where his loyalties lay and prove to her that they could not be shaken, he raised his voice above the din, stood, rested a hand upon her shoulder. "Excuse me, gentlemen! Might I remind you that my bride is Scots-Irish? I am surprised that any of you would condemn an entire people based on the actions of a few—or a thousand. Is that not exactly what these Paxton men are doing regarding the Indians?"

His father stood also and, beside him, Jamie. "Quite right you are, Nicholas. On behalf of my daughter-in-law, who has my affection, I demand an apology, sirs."

Ben stood. "I apologize, sirs, for the ill-chosen words of my guests. Your lovely and gentle Elspeth is a guest in my home and quite welcome here. Madam, I am deeply sorry."

People cast one another sheepish glances, voiced their own apologies.

Nicholas, Jamie, and his father resumed their seats, but

Nicholas pulled his chair a bit closer to Bethie's, grasped her hand beneath the table. She was trembling.

But the smile had left Sylvia's face.

It was Governor Penn who next spoke. "I want your advice, Ben. Already we've rolled cannon into the town squares, and some of the men are ready to organize into military-style units. The garrison, of course, is under arms and ready for battle."

Nicholas listened while the Quakers, who were renowned pacifists, discussed their plans for war, and felt suddenly overwhelmed by the absurdity of it all. He didn't realize he was laughing out loud until Governor Penn turned to face him.

"You find this amusing?"

"Aye, sir, I must say I do. When it was the frontiersmen's wives and children who were being slaughtered, you spoke of peace, refused to aid them, refused to send them troops, refused even to send them lead, flints, or powder. And they died by the hundreds—men, women, children. But now, when you perceive that your own wives and children are in danger, you forget all talk of peace and rush for cannon and muskets."

Shouts of outrage filled the room, but Ben held up his hand for silence.

"You've lived out there for six years, Nicholas. You've seen things we cannot imagine. I would hear more from you."

"It's quite simple, sir. The Scots-Irish settlers have suffered horribly in this war. When the government of Pennsylvania chooses to spend coin sheltering Indians rather than helping to defend their fellow British citizens against Indians who are slaughtering their families, the settlers get the impression no one in Philadelphia cares whether they live or die."

The governor stared at him in horrified disbelief. "Are you suggesting, sir, that we turn peaceful, Christian Indians over to them to be slaughtered?"

"No, sir. Nor am I defending their murder of the Conestogas—a reprehensible act. But I'm suggesting you take a moment to see this from their point of view. Men rarely act without reason, and barbarians are just as often English as Scottish or Indian. The killing must stop."

Ben nodded thoughtfully. "Governor, we must proceed cautiously. We must think this through and not rush to fire those rifles, which until now have lain in happy neglect in our homes. Otherwise we shall make hypocrites of ourselves for all time."

"And now if you'll excuse me gentlemen, this topic of conversation is distressing to my wife." Nicholas rose, helped Bethie to her feet. "Father, Jamie, if you wish to stay, I can have the carriage sent back for you."

His father and Jamie nodded, and Nicholas could see they were both worried about Bethie and furious on her behalf. He had no doubt that franker, more heated words would be exchanged the moment she was out of earshot. He slipped his arm around her waist, thanked Ben for his hospitality, and led Bethie out to their waiting carriage.

Bethie laid a sleeping Belle in her cradle, felt Nicholas's hands encircle her waist. They'd spoken little on the way home. Nicholas had been too angry and Bethie too near tears.

He turned her to face him, pressed her head against his bare chest. "I'm sorry, Bethie. No one meant to hurt you."

She rested against his strength, felt tears sting her eyes, dreaded what she must say. "Whether they meant to hurt me or no', they said what they feel to be true. And whether I love you or no', I cannae be your wife."

"You are my wife, Bethie, in every way that matters. I'll not let you go."

She looked up into his eyes. "And what of future parties, where people will tittle of the poor barbarian Scots-Irish girl Nicholas found on the frontier? What of your family if word of my . . . past reaches Virginia? What of our children, who will grow up in wealth and comfort to one day look upon their baseborn mother with shame and loathing? I couldna bear that!"

Tears poured freely down her cheeks now, and she fell across the bed.

She felt him stretch out beside her, did not resist when he pulled her into his arms and kissed her tears away. "That's not going to happen. No child of my body could possibly feel anything but love for you."

"'Tis sweet of you to say so, but you cannae know that for certain."

"Aye, I can." He pressed his hand against her belly above her womb. "I love you, Bethie Stewart. Any child you conceive of me will be born of that love. You'll be a light to our children, as you are a light to Belle—as you are a light to me."

She looked into his eyes, saw the full force of his feelings revealed there, felt as if her heart were singing. *He loved her.* Oh, how she had longed to hear those precious words! And yet . . . "I dinnae know if our love will be enough."

"It will be more than enough." Then he covered her mouth with his, and she forgot everything but him.

Nicholas held Bethie in his arms, watched her sleep, the air still warm with the musky scent of sex. If he lived a thousand years, he would never grow tired of her.

How he wished they were already well on their way to Virginia. But they weren't. They were here in Philadelphia in the middle of what promised to be a bloodbath unless the frontiersmen from Paxton could be persuaded to leave in peace.

God, he was sick of the violence! He was sick of killing. He was sick of watching other people kill and be killed. For six long years, he'd been surrounded by death, immersed in it, coupled with it. No matter how many men he'd killed, there was always another. And another. And another. In this war, killing seemed always to lead not to peace, but to more killing. And as men struggled to survive, the innocent inevitably paid the highest price.

The peaceful citizens of Philadelphia didn't stand a chance against seasoned Scots-Irish frontiersmen who'd spent the past ten years fighting for their lives. But the Scots-Irish would certainly find defeat at the hands of the disciplined British garrison. Either way, once the shooting started, innocent people would die. And although Nicholas felt reasonably certain he'd be able to keep Bethie and Belle safe should fighting erupt in the city, he did not want to see it come to that. Not again.

It had to end. Somehow the killing had to end.

And then it came to him. He knew what he had to do.

Whether it would work he had no idea. But he knew he had to try.

Nicholas pulled Bethie closer, looked out the window, and waited for dawn.

# Chapter 31

Bethie watched sleepily, felt the stirrings of arousal as Nicholas got out of bed and strode naked to the wardrobe. His dark hair hung down almost to the muscular curves of his buttocks, which tightened and shifted as he slipped into his leather breeches. He pulled his linsey-woolsey shirt over his head, tucked it into the waist of his breeches, turning as the cloth slid down his chest to give her one last glimpse of his muscular belly.

It wasn't until he reached for his pistols that she awoke fully. Then the events of the night before came flooding back to her, and she remembered.

She sat up, not aroused now, but afraid. "Nicholas? Where are you goin'?"

His gaze met hers, and she saw there hard resolve. "I'm going to ride out, try to talk with them."

"But you're English! You heard what Malcolm said at the cabin. They hate the English!"

He checked the pistols, ran the cleaning rod down their barrels. "I have lived on the frontier among them. I fought beside them at Fort Pitt. I think they'll listen to me."

She stepped from the bed, went to him, heedless of her nakedness. "And if they put a ball through your skull instead?"

He tucked the pistols in the waistband of his breeches, turned toward her, rested his hands on her shoulders. "They won't."

"And how can you be sure?"

He pulled her against him, held her. "I can't, love. But neither can I sit here and do nothing—not when innocent people will surely die."

Her fear grew and became anger. "You once told me that war and slaughter are nothing new, that the only person a man can save is himself, that survival is the only rule that matters!"

He stepped back from her, tilted her chin upward. There was an almost sad smile on his face. "You're the one who showed me how foolish that philosophy was, Bethie. Don't ask me to forget that lesson."

Then she knew she could not stop him. Tears pricked her eyes. "Why must it always be you? Why must you be the one to ride out and speak with them?"

"This time is different. At Fort Pitt, I went out because I was the best at killing, at surviving. But this time I have a chance to do something far better. I have the chance to *save* lives, to stop the killing before it starts. I can't let that chance pass by." He kissed her, one gentle, slow kiss, then stepped away from her. "I need to go, love."

"Then let me come with you! These are my people, my neighbors! Surely they will listen to me, to both of us!"

"Absolutely not! These men are armed and angry. I don't want you anywhere near them."

"But I can help! I know I can! If it's safe enough for you—"

"No!" He seemed genuinely angry now. "Do not defy me on this! Stay here with Belle. My father and Jamie will look after you."

Tears of fear and fury spilled over, ran down her cheeks. "Damn you, Nicholas Kenleigh! You'd best come back to me alive!"

He gave her a lopsided grin. "Of course, love. I don't want to miss my own wedding."

Then he seemed to hesitate. He took his pistols, considered them for a moment, laid them down on the table. He spoke as if to himself. "No more killing."

And then he turned, walked out the door, and was gone.

For a moment Bethie stared after him, too shocked to move. He was unarmed. He was on his way to confront an armed mob, and he was unarmed.

"That haggis-headed—" She threw on her shift and dressing gown, dashed down the hallway, knocked frantically on the door. After a moment Jamie answered, wearing nothing but a bedsheet, which he'd tied haphazardly around his hips.

"Bethie? What's the matter?" He let her inside, shut the door behind her.

"Jamie, who is it?" Alec emerged from an adjacent room, clad in a black velvet dressing gown.

Fighting panic, she told them of Nicholas's plan, of her fear that he would be hurt, perhaps even killed. "He is unarmed! We must do somethin' to help him!"

Jamie and Alec exchanged glances, then Alec opened the door, wrapped an arm around her shoulder. "Thank you for warning us, Bethie. Go back to your room. You'll be safe there until we return. We'll take care of Nicholas. I promise."

She looked up into Alec's eyes, so like his son's. "I couldna bear it if aught were to happen to him!"

"Nor could we."

Nicholas had almost finished saddling Zeus when footsteps and familiar voices interrupted him.

"Cold. Damp. Dreary. The perfect morning for a ride, wouldn't you say, Alec?"

"I've seen better, but this will do."

Nicholas snorted in disgust, turned on them. "Where do you two think you're going?"

Jamie entered a stall farther down and began to saddle his stallion. "We were about to ask you the same question."

And then Nicholas understood. "Bethie. She woke you."

His father pulled his saddle from the wall, walked to his mount. "And it's a damned good thing she did."

Nicholas led Zeus to the stable door, mounted. "You're not coming with me. Stay here, and watch over her for me. Let me do this alone."

Then he kicked in his heels, urging Zeus forward at a canter.

Behind him, Jamie led his horse from its stall, waited for Alec. "Not this time, Nicholas. Not this time."

By the time Bethie had nursed Belle, dressed, and left her baby in the innkeeper's caring arms, the men were far ahead of her. Clad in her plain linen gown and wearing her new winter cloak, she rode Rosa as fast as she dared. The ferryman reluctantly took her across the river—after she had assured him that she was not a bondswoman fleeing service or a runaway daughter, but a wife following her husband. He even pointed out which way the men had gone, after she pressed a coin into his dirty palm.

The air was cold with the crisp bite of autumn, the sky overcast and gray, the trees arrayed in shades of red and orange. She kept just off the road, using the skills Nicholas had taught her when they'd fled to Fort Pitt. She didn't want him to spot her, didn't want him to send her back. She was so tired of standing helplessly by while he risked his life, so tired of waiting to know whether he was dead or alive, so tired of doing nothing. These were her countrymen, her people. If he could not convince them to lay down their weapons, perhaps she could.

Nicholas had given up arguing with Jamie and his father by the time they'd reached the opposite side of the river and had turned to planning their strategy.

Jamie sounded insulted by his plan. "So you want us to stand there and say nothing."

"Why is that?" His father frowned.

"The moment you open your mouth, Father, our cause is lost. These people are not fond of Englishmen."

"Oh, that again," Jamie muttered.

"You might not realize it, but your Oxford accents make you sound more English than bloody King George."

Jamie chuckled. "We *are* more English than bloody King George."

"Now that you mention it, son, I will say that your speech has become, shall we say, more colorful?"

"That's one way to phrase it." Jamie grinned. "It's all those endless years of conversing with his horse."

Nicholas was about to offer a witty retort, when he heard—or perhaps felt—many hooves beating the ground. "They're just ahead."

Jamie nodded, all jesting aside. "I feel it, too."

They rode in silence until the front line of riders came into view.

Nicholas dismounted, stood in the middle of the road, one hand on Zeus's reins, the other at his side. "Don't draw your weapons unless you absolutely must."

His father and Jamie dismounted and stood behind him, their pistols primed and loaded.

The horsemen drew near, riding at a gallop. Already Nicholas could see individual faces. A man toward the center of the mob motioned for them to clear the road. Zeus jerked on the reins, his animal instincts apparently telling him to make way for the horde that was bearing down upon them, but Nicholas stood firm.

On the road ahead of them, the riders slowed their mounts, then reined them to a walk.

Nicholas held up a hand in greeting.

"You're blockin' the road, friend."

"I've come to talk, to stop you from throwing your lives away."

There were snorts and chuckles, and some of the men drew their pistols. But a man in the center of the front line raised his hand, held them back. "There's no need for anyone to die today, providin' no one gets in our way."

"That's the problem. The garrison is already under arms, and the good citizens of Philadelphia have dusted off their muskets." Nicholas smiled at the irony of Quakers rushing to arm themselves and heard men laugh as word of what he'd said was passed through their ranks.

The man dismounted. He wore a buckskin coat and breeches, and his face was as weathered and brown as the leather on his back. "Who the bleedin' hell are you?"

"The name is Nicholas Kenleigh. I came to Philadelphia from the siege of Fort Pitt, where I fought against the Delaware and Shawnee, and I've come out here of my own accord to ask you not to do this."

A whisper passed like a breeze through the throng.

"My name's Matthew Smith. I was there at Fort Pitt, too. I remember you. You've got balls of granite, Kenleigh. But we've come for the Indians, no' for the wee Quakers and their pretty wives."

The crowd of frontiersmen burst into laughter, their horses shifting restlessly beneath them.

"The garrison will not release them to you. You know that. If you try to take them, there will be a battle."

"Those savages are allies of the ones who killed our families, our women and children! The Quakers would not protect us from slaughter, but when the Indians ask for protection from us, our blood still on their hands, the good people of Philadelphia take them to their bosom! 'Tis an outrage!"

The horde erupted into angry shouting.

When it died down, a man began to chant a verse. "Go on, good Christians, never spare, to give your Indians clothes to wear. Send them good beef and pork and bread, guns, powder, flints and lead, to shoot your neighbor in the head!"

Cheers.

More angry shouts.

Nicholas understood their fury. He would not try to explain the Indian point of view, for he knew for certain none of these men wanted to hear that they were considered invaders in someone else's homeland. From the frontiersman's point of view, the west was open for the taking. Scratch your mark in the tree bark, and the land was yours. That the war had left thousands of Indian families without land and sustenance mattered little to settlers.

"The Indians at the fort are Christianized and were nowhere near the frontier this summer."

"If they are truly Christian, why did they no' warn us of this uprisin' before it happened? Why did they share information and supplies wi' those who butchered us? And why now do they hide here, disguised as allies? I'll tell you—they come here to be given stores of food through the winter so they can come back and scalp us in the spring!"

Bellows of outrage. Calls for bloodshed.

"On to Philadelphia!"

"We want justice!"

Nicholas felt the mood of the frontiersmen shift against him, felt their anger and hatred build. The line of horsemen pushed forward, driven by restless fury. More pistols and rifles were drawn. The stench of bloodlust permeated the air.

But almost as quickly as they arose, the shouts faded to silence, and Nicholas realized the men were staring past him.

He looked over his shoulder, thought he would explode.

*Bethie*. She rode one of the mares, her hair unbound and hanging freely over her new cloak. She had disobeyed him again, had followed them—alone.

From between gritted teeth, he spoke to his father and Jamie. "Take her back to the inn—now!"

Jamie looked at him, doubt in his eyes. "She may be of help, Nicholas. She's one of them."

Nicholas understood what Jamie was trying to say, knew he might well be right. But this crowd was on the brink of violence, and it infuriated him that she would defy him again, put herself in danger. Against his better judgment, he forced himself to stand still and let her speak.

Bethie met Nicholas's gaze, looked into eyes as cold as slate. He was angry with her, as she had known he would be. But she'd overheard the men's shouts and knew it was not going well for him. That's why she had come.

"Listen to him! Please! He is my husband. He has lived among you, fought beside you. He knows what you have suffered!"

The man who was apparently their leader glared up at her. "What does he know of our sufferin', lass?"

There was a murmur of agreement in the crowd, and she heard more than one man curse Nicholas and call him a *Sassenach*. More than a few had drawn their weapons, looked eager to spill his blood.

Then Nicholas took the linsey-woolsey of his shirt in his hands, tore it down the middle, exposing his scarred body.

The crowd fell into hushed whispers.

"I burned in the fires of the Wyandot. I know about living and dying and surviving. And I know about killing. If I've killed one man, I've killed a hundred. And what you want isn't justice—it's vengeance!"

From deep in the crowd came a shout. "What's wrong with vengeance?"

Shouts of agreement, curses.

Bethie waited until it was silent again, raised her voice. "I know you are angry. But more killin' cannae bring back those you have lost. Is this what your loved ones would want—for you to endanger the lives of innocent people?"

For a moment there was silence as the men seemed to ponder this.

Their leader, the man who stood before Nicholas, spoke up. "Only those who oppose us need fear harm. We've not come to fight the people of Philadelphia, though they showed no mercy for us when we were being cut down!"

More shouts of agreement.

"You are brave men and strong, and I see you're no' afraid to fight. But you cannae overcome the entire city. If you march into Philadelphia today, you're goin' to die. Your blood will be spilled for nothin'! Is that what your wives and children would want?"

Silence stretched, heavy and pregnant, beneath the weight of the gray sky.

Bethie looked into Nicholas's eyes, saw that his anger had softened.

Their leader's gaze shifted from Bethie back to Nicholas. "What would you have us do, Kenleigh?"

"Choose men to represent you and present your grievances to the city fathers for redress. The rest of the men should go home to their families."

"That might work for a man like you, an Englishman wi' powerful friends." The man nodded toward Jamie and Alec. "But who are we to trust?"

Nicholas's father answered, his voice strong, unwavering. "Benjamin Franklin. I assure you he will listen to you, treat fairly with you."

The men in the crowd seemed to consider this.

Bethie felt the tide begin to turn. "I have met him! He's a good man, and an honest one."

"And how do we know he'll be willin' to meet wi' us?"

Alec answered. "I give you my word. I am Alec Kenleigh, Nicholas's father. I am a member of the Virginia House of Burgesses and have the honor of calling Franklin my friend."

Someone snorted. "Why should we believe an Englishman?"

Jamie raised his voice. "England is far from here, friend, and we are all colonists. What you suffer, if left unchecked, will come to our doorsteps soon enough. Besides, there will be plenty of time for killing later—if we're lying."

Bethie added her word to theirs. "If you cannae trust them, then trust me! I am a daughter of this frontier, and I promise you—"

"Believe nothin' my stepdaughter says! She's an Englishman's whore!"

Bethie felt as if she'd been struck.

*Malcolm!*

He pushed through the throng on his horse toward the front of the line. "And dinnae believe him, either! Nicholas Kenleigh killed my son!"

It happened so quickly.

Malcolm raised his pistol, pointed it at Nicholas's bare chest.

"Nay!" Bethie heard herself scream, heard what sounded like several shots being fired.

She didn't realize Malcolm had changed targets until the ball struck her in the shoulder.

Searing pain.

Her own startled gasp.

The swirl of gray sky as she fell from Rosa's back.

Darkness.

The first thing Bethie became aware of was pain. Her left arm seemed to be on fire.

The second was the deep baritone of Nicholas's voice, the feel of his strong arms around her. "Bethie?" He sounded anxious.

Then she heard his father speak. "We must get her back. I've bound it as best I can. The ball passed cleanly through, and the bleeding is not bad, but she needs a surgeon."

A surgeon? What had happened?

"I'll ride ahead, fetch the best I can find to the inn." That was Jamie.

Then she remembered.

*Malcolm!* He'd shot her!

She struggled to open her eyes, saw Nicholas's worried face looking down at her. "Malcolm . . ."

"Easy, Bethie. He won't bother you again."

"How's the lass? Poor thing!" This voice she didn't recognize. Then she saw his face, remembered. He was one of the frontiersmen from Paxton. He'd been standing in front of Nicholas, talking with him. Their leader. "I never did like that man, but I cannae believe he would try to kill his own daughter. It's a good thing your father and uncle are fast with a gun and aim true, Kenleigh. We'll bury the bastard off the side of the road here and be done wi' him."

Malcolm was dead? But then what would happen to . . .

"My mother . . . we must . . . help her."

"Shh, love. Don't worry about anything. We'll take care of it." Then Nicholas spoke to the leader of the frontiersmen. "I'll send Franklin a message as soon as I'm able and ask him to meet with you this afternoon."

"Very well, Kenleigh. We'll send the men home and await Franklin here. But tell me—did the Quakers truly roll cannon into the town squares for fear of us?"

"Aye, they did. If you wanted to lay bare their hypocrisy, you've done it. It's a lesson they won't soon forget. Now I must tend to my wife."

"May God go wi' you both."

"I'm sorry, Bethie. I know this is going to hurt." Then Nicholas scooped her into his arms and stood.

She gritted her teeth against the pain as he lifted her onto the stallion's back and mounted behind her.

The next thing she knew she was lying in their bed in the inn. Nicholas sat beside her, his face lined with fatigue and worry. "Nicholas."

He smiled at her, his gaze tender. "I'm here, love. How do you feel?"

"Thirsty. And my arm hurts."

He lifted her head, held a cup of cool water to her lips. "The ball passed through the flesh of your shoulder. The surgeon says it should heal cleanly if we can keep it from festering."

She drank, sank back against her pillow. "Wh-what happened? Did they listen?"

He brushed a lock of hair from her cheek. "Aye. Most are on their way back home. Ben met with their leaders this afternoon."

"I'm sorry. I wanted to help. I wanted—"

"You did help, Bethie. I don't know if we could have stopped them without you. What you did was incredibly brave. But it doesn't change the fact that you defied me again, and this time you were almost killed." The tone of his voice told her he was still angry with her.

"Do you forgi' me?"

"It's not a matter of forgiving you, love. Do you know the dread I felt when I realized he had fired at you instead of me? Do you know how afraid I was when I saw you fall? My God, Bethie, in that moment I thought I'd lost what matters most to me! I don't ever want to feel that way again!"

She saw the anguish in his eyes, raised her right hand to touch the whisker-rough skin of his face. Then she remembered. "I've ruined the wedding, have I no'?"

He chuckled. "You're not getting out of it that easily."

The wedding was delayed for two weeks to allow Bethie to heal. They sought to bring Nicholas's mother northward from Virginia, but she had fallen ill with a fever and could not attend. When the grand day arrived, Bethie was scarcely ready for it. As the carriage turned onto Second Street and Christ Church loomed into view, she felt close to tears.

So much had happened these past few days. As her shoulder had healed, Jamie had journeyed to Paxton to fetch her mother from the wretched cabin—or, if she proved unwilling to leave, to at least tell her of Malcolm's death. But when Jamie had arrived, he'd found her already dead and buried.

When Jamie looked into the matter, no one seemed to know how or when she had died.

Bethie knew Malcolm had killed her mother in a rage over Richard's death. The guilt of having carried that news weighed heavily upon her, though Nicholas tried hard to persuade her that any guilt belonged solely to her stepfather.

"You did all you could, Bethie." He'd held her as she'd wept. "You asked her to come away with you, and she chose to stay with him instead."

*Bad blood will out.*

'Twas another mark against her family, another source of shame. But it hadn't deterred Nicholas or his father from bringing her into their family.

She fingered the lace of her bodice, barely able to believe this was real. Any moment now she expected Nicholas to tell her that it was all a mistake. Or perhaps his father would think it through, change his mind, and demand that his son marry a woman of breeding.

She felt Alec take her hand, give it a reassuring squeeze. "Everything will be fine, Bethie."

Across from her, Jamie dandled Belle on his knee. Dressed in a gown of white satin, the baby looked like a tiny angel, her short, golden hair a halo.

Nicholas had ridden ahead of them to the church with Master Franklin, who had agreed to act as a witness. They were there, inside the church, waiting for her now.

The last time she'd been married, Bethie had been dragged to the church, bruised and battered and in deepest shame. This time she'd been treated like a princess. She nervously smoothed the expanse of ivory silk brocade that was her wedding gown. Embroidered with tiny golden roses and shot through with threads of real gold, it was a gown fit for a queen. It had been Alec's wedding gift to her. Around her throat hung a cross of real gold, a gift from Jamie and the symbol of Saint Bride, or Saint Bríghid as she was known in Ireland—the homeland of both Jamie's wife and of Bethie's transplanted Scottish ancestors.

"'Tis identical to the cross my wife wears," Jamie had explained when she'd looked at him in surprise. "Wear it as a reminder that you need never be ashamed of who you are or where you come from."

Bethie had been so deeply touched she'd scarce been able to speak.

The carriage drew to a halt, and a hired footman opened the door.

Alec lifted her to the ground. "Watch your skirts."

Jamie alighted behind them, a giggling baby in his arms, strode up the walk ahead of them and through the church's doors.

Her pulse tripping, Bethie let Alec guide her up the walkway, through the doors, then froze. Ahead of her before the altar, with Master Franklin and Jamie beside him, stood Nicholas. He wore a velvet jacket and breeches of deepest midnight blue. His waistcoat and stockings were of ivory silk, and the brass buckles on his shoes gleamed gold. He was clean-shaven, his long hair brushed back and bound at his nape. But what she noticed was the look on his face—a combination of intoxicating male desire and unbridled love that left her breathless.

Her knees nearly gave way.

"He's waiting for you, Bethie."

She nodded, forced herself to speak. "W-would you walk with me down the aisle? I have no father to give me away, and I fear my legs will no' carry me."

Alec smiled gently down at her, his blue eyes warm. "Why do you think I'm standing here with you, my sweet? From now on, I'm your father. You have a family, Bethie. You'll never be alone again."

And in that moment Bethie's misgivings melted away. With Alec to steady her, she walked down the aisle to join her life to that of the man she loved.

# Chapter 32

Nicholas looked out the carriage window onto Kenleigh land, felt his blood sing. After all this time, after all these years, he was almost home.

How strange it all seemed—and how familiar. The broad, blue sky. The scent of river, pine forest, tilled earth. The fields lying empty, their bounty harvested and stored away for winter. He'd been born here, raised here. He'd learned to swim, ride, shoot here. Someday he would die and be buried here.

It wasn't the end he had expected for himself. He had expected to die alone on the frontier, the screams in his mind finally silenced by a chance arrow to the back, the teeth and claws of a cougar, the biting cold of a bitter winter. But Bethie had lifted that fate from him, had broken him open with her violet eyes, soft lips, and generous heart, had brought him staggering from the darkness into daylight.

He turned away from the window, took her hand in his, felt the warm gold of his wedding band heavy upon her finger. She looked up at him, and he could see beyond the smile on her face to the worry that hid behind her eyes.

Nicholas couldn't blame Bethie for feeling nervous. She'd gone from having no real family to being part of an enormous extended family that bridged two continents. Being loved and cared for by so many people would be a new experience for her, one Nicholas desperately wanted for her.

He leaned down, whispered for her ears alone. "It will be fine, love. You'll see. My mother will adore you—and Belle."

She squeezed his hand, and for a moment anxiety showed on her face. "I dinnae want to disappoint you, Nicholas."

He kissed her forehead. "You won't."

Then Belle giggled, drawing her mother's gaze. Across from them, his father and Jamie entertained the baby, making ridiculous faces, tickling her tummy, nibbling her tiny toes. Almost seven months old, she looked more and more like her mother each day, the same golden hair, the same sweet face, the same violet eyes. Nicholas had already prepared the paperwork necessary to adopt her. Isabelle would be a Kenleigh before the new year.

Bethie laughed. "You're spoilin' her. She'll be the most coddled lass in the county."

Jamie bounced the baby on his lap. "No, that honor goes to Emma Rose."

"I'm afraid it's true." His father looked so contrite that Nicholas almost laughed. "I find I can deny her nothing. She reminds me so very much of her mother."

Jamie chuckled. "And that doesn't terrify you?"

"Indeed, it does. In a few years, I'll have to keep her under lock and key."

"How many offers of marriage have you received for her? I've lost count." Jamie helped Belle stand and bounce on her chubby, little legs.

"Seven."

Bethie gaped at them. "How old is she?"

His father and Jamie answered together. "Nine."

"Oh, my!" Bethie laughed.

At their words, regret suddenly pressed down on Nicholas. Emma Rose was nine. Alec, William, Matthew, Sarah, and Elizabeth were all married to people he'd never met. They had children of their own, nieces and nephews he'd never seen. They lived in homes he'd never visited.

Jamie and Bríghid had five children, one of whom they'd named in memory of him, never expecting to see him again. Fionn and Muirín, Bríghid's brother and his wife, had three children and were expecting another soon. Only Ruaidhrí, Bríghid's restless younger brother, was still unmarried. Now captain of his own ship, he was more often at sea than at home.

So much had changed, and he'd missed all of it.

His father seemed to read his mind. "They're all here—everyone except Ruaidhrí, of course. They've waited so long. They've all come to welcome you home, Nicholas."

And suddenly, as the full weight of what he'd done to all of them hit him, Nicholas wanted to stop the carriage. He needed to breathe, to think, to rein in his emotions.

He felt Bethie squeeze his hand. "Nicholas?"

His father leaned forward, rested a hand on Nicholas's knee. "It's going to be fine, son."

"My God, I've been so selfish! I never—"

"None of that matters, son. What matters is that you're finally home."

Jamie handed Belle back to Bethie. "You don't owe anyone an explanation, Nicholas. Hell, after all you've been through, it's a miracle you're sane."

But he heard another voice, his mother's voice, pleading with him, begging.

*Please, Nicholas, don't go!*

Then his own voice, cold and lifeless.

*I regret to inform you, madam, that your son is dead.*

He met his father's gaze, let the words come, for it was the truth. "Of all the wrongs I have done in my life, the most terrible has been to hurt those I most love."

His father's eyes held only compassion. "So it is for all of us."

He felt the carriage turn the last bend in the road, knew Kenleigh Manor had come into view. He took a deep breath, steeled himself.

Bethie could sense Nicholas's anguish, taste his deep regret. She wanted to comfort him somehow, but knew there was little she could do.

"There's your new home, Bethie." Jamie pointed out the window.

She leaned forward, thought she might faint. The house was made of red brick and stood three stories high, with wide steps out front and a porch with four white columns. There were glass windows everywhere. It seemed unbelievably grand, hardly a fitting home for the daughter of Scots-Irish redemptioners.

"I'm afraid I shall get lost inside so big a house!" She stared in amazement at Jamie and her father-in-law, both of whom smiled kindly back at her.

Nicholas caressed her hand with his thumb. "One day it will belong to our children, Bethie—all of this."

The estate included the miles and miles of land they had traveled from the river—how many hundreds of acres she could not guess.

She looked into his eyes, still stunned. "'Tis more lovely than I could ever have imagined."

Somewhere a bell clanged in welcome, and she saw children rush out onto the steps, followed by well-dressed men and women—Nicholas's family.

*Her family.*

The butterflies in her stomach fluttered and swirled, and before she could catch her breath, the carriage had rolled to a stop.

Nicholas took her hand, kissed it, and it touched her that he should feel concern for her, when she knew that he was consumed inside by his own feelings.

She smiled up at him. "Go to them, Nicholas. Go to them."

He nodded, opened the door, stepped to the ground, and was swept into a throng of men and women who looked so much like him they could only be his brothers and sisters.

"Nicholas!"

"Welcome home, brother!"

"Bloody hell, but you need a barber!"

A young woman with her father's dark hair stepped forward, remorse in her eyes, tears streaming down her face. Her hands were fisted in her skirts. "Nicholas, I . . . I'm so sorry."

Nicholas drew her into his arms, held her for a moment, then stepped back, taking her hands in his. "No, Elizabeth. 'Tis I who am sorry. You are and always have been blameless. You did nothing wrong. You came to comfort me, and I repaid your love and kindness with selfishness. I hurt you terribly. Can you find it in your heart to forgive me?"

Elizabeth nodded, her lips curving in a smile, even as she wept. "Oh, yes!"

He embraced her again, held her tight.

And suddenly Bethie felt close to tears. She blinked quickly, swallowed hard, fidgeted with the ribbons on Belle's dress.

"Shall we?" Her father-by-marriage stepped from the carriage, turned back for her, lifted her and Belle safely to the ground.

She accepted his arm, walked with him to stand beside her husband.

"This is your new sister-in-law, Elspeth Stewart Kenleigh. Bethie, if I might, this is Sarah and Matthew and Alec and Elizabeth and William."

Each of them greeted her in turn, the men with a polite kiss on the back of her hand, the women with an embrace and kiss on the cheek, as she repeated their names.

"Father, what about me?"

A little girl appeared from behind the others, dressed regally in silk, ribbons, and lace, her red-gold curls spilling over her shoulders. She looked expectantly at Nicholas and Bethie through bright blue eyes.

Bethie glanced at Nicholas, saw on his face that his heart had just melted.

He stepped forward, took the little girl's hand, kissed it, gave a courtly bow. "Emma Rose. I've heard tales of your beauty, and I see that every word is true."

An adorable pink flush stole into Emma Rose's cheeks. "You're my brother, aren't you?"

"Aye. I am Nicholas, your eldest brother. And this is my wife, Bethie, and our daughter, Isabelle."

Bethie bent down, smiled. "I am so happy to meet you, Emma Rose. What a bonny lass you are! Isabelle is lucky to have you as her aunt."

Emma Rose blushed again, then looked straight at Nicholas, suddenly solemn. "Is it true you were hurt by Indians and then ran away?"

Nicholas nodded. "Aye, 'tis true."

"Are you going to run away again?"

Nicholas touched a finger to her nose. "This time I'm home to stay."

Emma Rose smiled at him, only to be swept off her feet by her father.

"How is my little princess?"

Emma Rose giggled, wrapped her arms around her father's neck. "Papa!"

"Most coddled lass in the county," Jamie whispered from behind Bethie, then strode off to embrace a beautiful dark-haired woman Bethie knew must be his wife, Bríghid. A flock of small children gathered around them.

Then abruptly Nicholas's brothers and sisters stepped back, and on the stairs before them stood a tall woman, her red-gold curls frosted with white, her lovely face lined with years of worry, her green eyes shimmering with tears. "Nicholas!"

Nicholas stepped forward. But instead of embracing his mother as Bethie had expected, he knelt before her, his head bowed, his hands bunched into fists at his sides. As he spoke, his voice shook. "Forgive me, madam, for I have done you a most grievous wrong."

His mother reached out, touched his head, then knelt with him, framing his face with trembling hands. "There was never anything to forgive. Thank God you're home! Oh, Nicholas!"

Tears poured down Bethie's cheeks as she watched the two of them embrace, listened to his mother sob for joy against her son's shoulder. Then Nicholas lifted his mother up and swung her around.

She laughed, her cheeks wet with tears, her smile bright. "Put me down, son, and introduce me to my new daughter-in-law and granddaughter."

Nicholas placed his mother gently on her feet. "Mother, may I present Elspeth Stewart Kenleigh and our daughter, Isabelle. If it weren't for Bethie, I wouldn't be here. She brought me back to life. She brought me home." He met Bethie's gaze, and she saw in his eyes a peace that had never been there before. "Bethie, your mother-by-marriage, my mother, Cassie Blakewell Kenleigh."

"Mistress. 'Tis a joy to meet you at last."

Cassie kissed Bethie's cheek, stroked Isabelle's downy head. "My husband and son have written and told me all that you've done, Bethie. I could not love you more if you were my own daughter. I hope that in time you shall come to think of me as a mother. Welcome home."

The shaft of joy that pierced Bethie's heart was as bright and pure as sunlight.

Nicholas brushed Bethie's hair as she read.

"'There is a . . . con-cat-en-ation of all events in the best of possible worlds; for, in short, had you no' been kicked out of a fine castle for the love of Miss Cunegonde; had you no' been put into the Inquisition; had you no' traveled over America on foot; had you no' run the Baron through the body; and had you no' lost all your sheep, which you brought from the good country of El Dorado, you wouldna have been here to eat preserved citrons and pistachio nuts.'

"'Excellently observed,' answered Candide, 'but let us cultivate our garden.'"

"And that, my love, is the end." Nicholas set the brush and the book aside, pressed a kiss to the sensitive skin of her nape, drank in the scent of her skin.

But Bethie seemed lost in thought. "I love your mother and father, Nicholas. I love Jamie and Bríghid. I love your brothers and sisters. I even love Takotah, though at first she frightened me."

Nicholas kissed his way along the column of her throat. "They love you, too."

"They are truly kind people, though I dinnae think I shall ever learn everyone's name."

He nipped her earlobe. "You will—with time."

"Do you think this is the best of all possible worlds?"

Nicholas chuckled, slid her shift from her shoulders, kissed the scar on her left shoulder. "Without a doubt, love. Mmmm, you taste good."

She giggled. "I'm no' jestin', Nicholas!"

He slid his hands beneath the cloth to cup her breasts, flicked his thumbs over her tightening nipples. "Neither am I."

She shivered, pressed her breasts deeper into his hands. "And all you went through—was it worth this? Just like Candide, if you hadna been taken captive, if you hadna run from home, if you hadna been livin' in the wild, if the Frenchmen hadna cut your—"

"Then I would have found you some other way." His cock was raging hard, his blood hot. "Come to bed, wife."

"Are you certain?"

"That you should come to bed?" He took her hand, pressed his erection into her palm. "Oh, aye."

"Nay, you daftie! Are you certain we'd have met some other way?"

Perhaps it was the tone of her voice, but something stilled him. He turned her to face him, knelt before her. "Aye, Bethie. It must be so, for I could not face this life without you."

She looked into his eyes, brushed a strand of hair from his face. "You have so many who love you. You'd have found your way home without me."

He cupped her face gently between his hands. "No, Bethie. I was a dead man, blind to their love. I cared about nothing, not even my mother's tears. I lived without joy, took life without remorse. You made me feel again, forced me to face my past. You saved my life, but more than that, you saved *me*. No matter what I may have done for you, there is no gift greater than the one you have given me."

"Oh, Nicholas! I need no gifts! Just love me, and I shall count myself the happiest of women."

He brushed his lips over hers. "I do, Bethie. With all my heart, I do."

# Epilogue

October 30, 1774

Nicholas stood against the wall of his father's study, sipping his evening cognac and doing his best to stay out of the fray while his father, his uncle, his brother William, and his sister Emma Rose argued about the burning of the HMS *Peggy Stewart*. It was in all the papers. People had spoken of little else for a fortnight, emotions in the colonies running high, talk of rebellion against the Crown growing.

"Mob justice is no justice at all!" Even at age seventy-six, his hair almost entirely turned to silver, Alec Kenleigh was a daunting figure when he was angry. "Poor Stewart was forced to burn his own ship or risk being hanged, and yet the crime was not his. That crowd would have burned that ship heedless of its human cargo. The Crown has made some grievous errors in its governance of these colonies, but you cannot tell me it is enough to merit breaking bonds with Britain and turning this land over to such . . . *rabble*!"

"Father, I am not alone in believing it is time to sever bonds with Britain." William had traveled from his nearby estate to bring news of unrest in Annapolis. "Benjamin Franklin is not a man of poor judgment, nor is he given to immoderate anger, and yet even *he* believes reconciliation may be impossible."

"George Washington as well," Jamie added. "He's a Virginian, Alec, and a man whose judgment I trust."

Nicholas had his own thoughts on the subject. The split from Britain was inevitable. He'd seen the cracks begin to form and the rift widen during the war against the French and Indians. Parliament and the British commanders had seemingly done all they could to alienate the colonists, disregarding their superior knowledge of the land, treating them as lesser men. Only William Pitt had seemed to understand the colonists' perspective. But it was too late. The colonists had already come to see themselves not as Englishmen, but as Americans.

The seeds for this strife had been sown long ago.

Nicholas didn't want a war, but he feared it was unavoidable. He had never discussed this with his father. Alec Kenleigh would never turn against the Crown, not with estates in England and his beloved sister and her family living outside London. And Nicholas had sons—three so far. He did not want to see them lose their youth and vigor in bitter fighting or spend their blood in battle.

William pressed on. "We cannot remain silent when other good men speak out."

"Well said, William!" Emma Rose's cheeks were flushed with temper. Still unmarried at twenty, she had taken what their father deemed to be an excessive interest in politics. "Hester and Amity—"

Father cut across her. "The Harris sisters are filling your head with dangerous notions and nonsense! I would do well to forbid any further association with them."

Emma Rose gaped at him in surprise, her astonishment quickly turning to fury. "Hester and Amity are loyal Virginians, father."

"Loyal Virginians? If they and their ilk should get their way, the blood of Virginians will soon stain the ground."

"'Tis better to die on our feet fighting than to live on our knees!"

Nicholas took a slow step forward, struggling to keep his voice calm. "What do you know about fighting, Emma Rose? Have you been in battle? Have you witnessed true slaughter or cared for wounded men or watched them die? I've seen war enough to sicken my soul. You'd best pray this conflict does not turn to bloodshed, or you may find yourself burying your brothers and nephews."

For a moment there was silence.

Emma Rose's gaze dropped to the floor, her bluster gone. "Aye, Nicholas. You are right. It must not come to bloodshed. Forgive me."

Father stood. "Whatever occurs, know this: I will *not* allow this conflict to divide our family and turn us against one another."

The door to the study opened and Nicholas's mother appeared.

"This talk of war sickens me." She glared at them, one at a time, then met Nicholas's gaze. "If you're quite finished arguing, Bethie's labor has begun."

Nicholas set his glass aside, left the study, and took the stairs two at a time.

Bethie gazed down at her newborn son and stroked his dark, downy hair, too lost in the wonder of him to notice her exhaustion and lingering pain. "He looks so like his brothers—peas in a pod, the four of them."

"Aye, he does." Nicholas took one of the baby's clenched hands, opened the little fist, touched each tiny finger, the joy on his face making Bethie's heart swell.

He'd been beside her throughout her travail, as he had been each time she'd given birth. It had lasted nine hours, much longer than her last birth. They'd been nine arduous hours, too, her pangs coming fast and hard. Somehow, though she'd given birth six times before, she seemed to have forgotten how very much it hurt. Nicholas's strength, the sound of his voice, his soothing touch had held her together.

Outside the bedroom curtains, it was not yet daylight.

The baby looked up at her through eyes that would soon turn blue, as all of their children's eyes had done. Given his first bath by his grandmother and wrapped in a soft blanket, he seemed to study them, a slight frown on his little face. He opened his mouth, gave a little cry.

Nicholas pressed a kiss to Bethie's temple. "He's hungry."

With Nicholas's help, Bethie bared her left breast, wincing as the baby latched on and began to nurse, his suckling causing her womb to clench painfully. She closed her eyes, fought not to moan, the after-pains as fierce as true birthing pangs. Nicholas rubbed the hard curve of her womb as Takotah had taught him when Alexander was born, the pressure seeming to ease some of her discomfort.

She tried to take her mind off her pain, her words halting. "What do you think . . . of namin' him Benjamin after dear Mr. Franklin? He has ever been . . . so kind to us."

Nicholas smiled. "The old man will strut about Philadelphia as proud as a tom turkey when he hears the news. Benjamin it is, then. Benjamin James?"

"Aye, I like that." She stroked the baby's cheek. "Benjamin James."

Out of nowhere, her mother's words came back to her.

*Pray she didnae curse your womb as you did mine.*

How long ago that day now seemed, how distant the grief and loss. Far from having a womb that was cursed, Bethie had been blessed beyond measure.

"Why are you laughing?"

"I was just recollectin' what my mother said the last time I saw her—about Isabelle cursin' my womb as I had cursed hers."

"That makes you laugh?" Nicholas frowned.

He never liked discussing her mother or stepfather.

Bethie tried to explain. "I am now the mother of *seven.* There was a time when I feared that perhaps . . ."

His frown faded, gentle understanding dawning on his face. "Her bitter words hold no power over you. They never did. But even had you never borne another child, I would have loved you and Isabelle just the same."

It was sweet to hear him say such a thing, sweeter still to know he meant it.

"How different our children's lives are from the one I knew. They'll never suffer poverty or hunger. They'll never be beaten or abused. They'll never be left alone to fend for themselves. If aught should happen to us, they have aunts, uncles, and cousins who love them and would provide for them and keep them safe. I cannae tell you how much peace this brings me."

Nicholas stroked her hair. "I am glad to hear it."

The baby pulled away from her nipple, apparently done feeding. She closed her shift, adjusted the baby's blanket, and lay back against her pillow.

A light knock came at the door.

Nicholas answered. "Come."

Alec and Cassie, whom Bethie now called Father and Mother, peeked in. Mother had dark circles beneath her eyes from a sleepless night, a smile on her face. "The children are most eager to meet their new little brother."

Bethie shared a smile with Nicholas. "Aye, send them in."

Emma Rose ushered in six children still dressed in their nightclothes. Belle, very much her mother's helper at age eleven, carried little Mary, only two, on her hip. Behind her came her brothers—Alexander, nine; Nicholas, six; and Matthew, almost four. All of the boys were dark of hair and tall for their age, very much resembling their father. Catherine, on the other hand, was fair of hair and resembled Bethie. She entered last, a smile on her sweet face.

The children tiptoed across the room, noisily shushing one another, their faces alive with anticipation.

Bethie turned the baby, holding him so they could see his tiny face.

"Oh, Mama, he is beautiful—and so little!" Belle smiled brightly. "He looks just like you did, Matthew! Do you see the new baby, Mary?"

"Baby?" Mary peered sleepily at her newborn brother, but was clearly unimpressed. She popped her little thumb in her mouth and laid her head on Belle's shoulder.

The boys drew closer, smiles on their faces.

Little Nicholas reached out and gently touched the top of the baby's head. "He can ride my pony if he wants, Papa."

Nicholas chuckled softly. "That's most kind of you, son."

Alexander nudged his little brother. "He's too little to ride a pony! I shall help Belle read him stories, Mama."

"I'm certain he will like that, Alex."

Little Matthew looked up at Bethie. "Do you think he likes me?"

Bethie gave Matthew's head a few reassuring strokes. He was no longer the youngest son in the family. "Aye, for certain, he does."

Emma Rose drew closer. "Oh, Bethie, he is so sweet! I cannot wait to hold him!"

Nicholas's father leaned forward, his wife beside him, and looked down at the baby. "He is a handsome boy. Can you fathom it, Cassie? Thirty-one grandchildren."

Nicholas chuckled. "Your love has borne fruit, as it were."

Then little Catherine reached out, took one of Benjamin's little hands in hers, her smile broadening. "I do not know him well, Mama, but already I love him."

And Bethie found herself blinking back tears.

Nicholas allowed the children to visit with their mother for a few more minutes, then nodded to Emma Rose and his parents, who shepherded them from the room.

"Come, children. It's time for breakfast, and your mother must rest."

The door shut, and he and Bethie were alone again.

He stroked her hair, grateful for her safe delivery and so relieved that her travail was over. It had not been the easy birth he'd prayed for. Each time a pain had gripped her, he'd felt beset by guilt and so bloody *helpless*. So it had been when each of their children had been born.

"You have made me a father seven times now. I've no words fit to thank you for your sacrifice or the gift you've given me, but I *do* have this."

He took her right hand and slipped the ring on her third finger.

She glanced down at her finger, and her eyes went wide, her breath leaving her lungs in a rush. "Oh, Nicholas! This is so . . . *beautiful*!"

"'Tis a blue diamond from India." He'd had his man in London searching for years to find a stone the color of her eyes. The center stone was surrounded by glittering white diamonds, the gold band decorated with filigree in the shape of roses.

She looked up at him, clearly astonished, her eyes brimming with tears. "I never imagined such a gift."

He knew that was true, for she had never once asked him to

uy her jewels or gowns or frippery of any kind. "I am glad it leases you."

"I shall treasure it always. Thank you."

"'Tis but a trifle, a symbol of my love." He looked down nto her eyes, struggling to find the right words. "If I could, I vould gather the stars from the sky and lay them at your feet. 'our love has been my salvation."

She gave him a quavering smile, a tear spilling down her heek. "You have cared for me, protected me, given me a ome, children, a family. Never once in these ten years have ou hurt me, shamed me, been unfaithful, or given me reason doubt you. You have the keepin' of my heart, Nicholas, and ou always will."

Outside the window, the sun began to rise.

# Author's Note

he idea for this novel came to me long before I started writing ovels. I was sitting in a college history class and read in my text-ook a short paragraph about the Paxton Boys, who had marched n Philadelphia in February 1764. They were enraged over the pparent indifference of the Pennsylvania government toward e brutality they had endured during the French and Indian War nd the subsequent Indian revolt known as Pontiac's Rebellion. ly textbook called this event "the first American civil war" and ave a few lines of information about it. I had never heard of it efore and began to gather research on it, thinking that one day I ight write a novel and want to include it.

The results of that research appear in this book. While this is work of fiction, I have tried very hard to remain true to the spirit the terrible year of 1763, when the frontier, already soaked in ood from the French and Indian War, exploded into further vio-nce. The events occurred generally as described, with one nportant exception. In this novel, the Paxton Boys' march on niladelphia occurs in late September 1763, five months earlier an it truly happened. This is the result of my need to condense story so that I could fit both the siege at Fort Pitt and the Paxton oys' Rebellion into one story.

Although I did take some small liberties with the siege at Fort tt—notably the grenade attack outside the West Ravelin—I ave Douglas McGregor, educator at the Fort Pitt Museum, to ank for the fact that I was able to use actual soldiers' diaries reconstruct many day-by-day events of the siege and place icholas at the heart of them. I have used the names of real ople in many instances—those of wounded and slain soldiers, for example—and have drawn from old census records for name common in Western Pennsylvania at that time. Captain Simeo Écuyer and Colonel Henry Bouquet are both historical figures and Captain Écuyer did, indeed, order barking dogs to be shot This alone qualifies him for infamy.

But far worse and unforgivably, he gave blankets from th smallpox hospital at the fort to Turtle's Heart and Mamaltee, tw Delaware chiefs, as gifts—the first documented instance of bio logical warfare on the North American continent. While histori ans generally believe the blankets had no effect, there was a outbreak of smallpox among Indian people in the Ohio Valle later that year. American Indians have not forgotten this.

The history of our nation is complicated and multifacetec and the violence of 1763 has had an impact on our culture today It helped to define annihilation as the means European settler would use to deal with indigenous people. Further, it drove wedge between the American colonists and Great Britain. Whe the Scots-Irish frontiersmen of Paxton next took up arms an marched together, it was to fight beside the citizens of Philadel phia against the British in the war for American independence.

Those who've read the "author's cut" of *Carnal Gift* wi notice discrepancies between *Carnal Gift* and *Ride the Fire*. Th version of *Carnal Gift* that was first published had a hundre pages cut in order to meet the original publisher's maximur page length. The entire Nicholas plotline was removed from th book. In the midst of writing *Ride the Fire* at the time, I adjuste *Ride the Fire* accordingly.

When I got the rights back to *Carnal Gift*, I decided to sel publish the story as I had written it—a much better version of th story, in my opinion. Only when I sat down to work on edits the manuscript to *Ride the Fire* for this reissue did I realize th the version of *Carnal Gift* that is currently available is now ou of sync with *Ride the Fire*. In *Carnal Gift*, Nicholas is take captive after the battle at Fort Necessity in 1754, and Jami Blakewell, the hero from *Carnal Gift*, is also present. In *Ride th Fire*, Jamie isn't present, and Nicholas is taken in 1756. In bot stories, Nicholas is captured in the same way and suffers th same torment. Only the time line and the issue of Jamie's pre ence is different.

I considered revising *Ride the Fire* to bring it into alignment with *Carnal Gift*, but when I considered what that would entail, I realized the best thing I could do is to leave the story intact. I believe readers now have the best versions of both novels. And isn't that what readers truly deserve?

**She came to him when he needed her the most . . .**
**Now he rushes to save her before it's too late . . .**

FROM *NEW YORK TIMES* BESTSELLING AUTHOR

MAYA BANKS

# WHISPERS IN THE DARK

**A KGI Novel**

She comes to him at his lowest point, and is the only thing that gets Nathan Kelly through his captivity, the endless days of torture and the fear that he'll never return to his family. With her help, he's able to escape. But he isn't truly free, because now she's disappeared, and he's left with an all-consuming emptiness as he struggles to pick up the pieces of his life.

Shea has been on the run from people who will stop at nothing to exploit her unique telepathic abilities. She never wanted to drag Nathan into peril, but she doesn't have a choice, so she reaches out to him for help. Finally face-to-face, Nathan refuses to let her go again—but the danger that follows her may prove to be more than he can handle.



M1051T0212

FROM *NEW YORK TIMES* BESTSELLING AUTHOR

# MAYA BANKS

## THE KGI SERIES

**THE KELLY GROUP INTERNATIONAL (KGI):** A super-elite, top secret, family-run business.

**QUALIFICATIONS:** High intelligence, rock-hard body, military background.

**MISSION:** Hostage/kidnap victim recovery. Intelligence gathering. Handling jobs the U.S. government can't . . .

THE DARKEST HOUR

NO PLACE TO RUN

HIDDEN AWAY

WHISPERS IN THE DARK

ECHOES AT DAWN

SHADES OF GRAY